WILD
STORM

RICHARD CASTLE

WILD STORM

A Derrick Storm Thriller

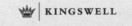 KINGSWELL

LOS ANGELES · NEW YORK

Published by Kingswell, an imprint of Disney Book Group. No part of this book may be reproduced or transmitted in any form or by any means, electronic or mechanical, including photocopying, recording, or by any information storage and retrieval system, without written permission from the publisher.

For information address Kingswell,
1101 Flower Street, Glendale, California 91201.

For publicity address Kingswell,
125 West End Avenue, New York, New York 10023.

Editorial Director: Wendy Lefkon
Executive Editor: Laura Hopper
Designed by Alfred Sole

Mass Market ISBN 978-1-4847-1638-0
V567-9638-5-15058

Printed in the United States of America
First Paperback Edition, April 2015
10 9 8 7 6 5 4 3 2 1

CHAPTER 1

**NINETEEN THOUSAND FEET ABOVE YORK,
Pennsylvania**

At the very moment Flight 937 was targeted—the moment when the three-hundred-plus souls aboard were brought into a peril whose magnitude they did not understand—the man in seat 2B was thinking about a nap.

Seat 2B was partially reclined, and he was breathing deeply. A rakish sort, tall, dark, and broad-chested, he had his thick hair swept fashionably to the side. Beyond his apparent physical allure, there was also an ineffable quality to him—call it charm, charisma, or just natural magnetism—that made the flight attendants pay him more attention than was strictly necessary.

His face was tanned, albeit in something of a windburned way. He had just spent several weeks climbing in the Swiss Alps, finishing his trek by solo-climbing the sheer north face of the Eiger in a shade under four hours. Not record territory. But also not bad for a man who didn't make his living as a climber.

He still wore his hiking books. Some of his gear was stowed above him in a weathered rucksack. The rest was packed below, in the belly of the Boeing 767-300 that had been plowing dutifully through the sky since Zurich.

They had been making a long, slow descent toward Dulles International Airport and the man in seat 2B was looking forward to the evening, when he planned to take his father to an Orioles game. It had been two months since they had seen each other, which was too long. They had bonding to catch up on.

The 767 banked slightly to the right, then straightened. It was a sturdy aircraft and the flight had been smooth, with only the barest hint of turbulence as the plane had passed under a high ceiling of clouds a few minutes earlier. The man in seat 2B had his eyes closed, though he was not quite asleep. He was in that transitional period, when the conscious part of his brain was slowly ceding control to the subconscious.

Then came the loud *chunk*.

His eyes opened. It was definitely not among the sounds one wants or expects to hear on an airplane. It was followed by voices, plaintive and panicked, coming from behind him on the left side of the aircraft. From above him, the seat belt sign chimed. The plane was no longer flying smooth or straight. It had entered a shallow, wobbly dive to the left, pitched at roughly ten degrees.

Physiologists have identified the two possible reactions to a threatening stimulus as being fight or flight. But those are, in fact, merely the instinctive responses, the ones gifted to humans by their simian ancestors. Fancying themselves members of a more evolved species, *H. sapiens* have learned to overcome those base, brutish urges. They are polite, civilized, especially when surrounded by many other *H. sapiens*. They value decorum—even over survival, at times.

As a result, most people's response to an emergency is to do nothing.

The man in seat 2B was not most people.

As the other first-class passengers exchanged nervous glances, the man in seat 2B unfastened his seat belt and walked back toward the midsection of the plane. His fight-or-flight juices were flowing—heart rate increased, pupils dilated, muscles bathed in red blood cells and ready for action—but he had long trained himself how to harness that chemistry in a productive manner.

Passing through business class into coach, he reached the emergency exit rows. Without speaking to the passengers, all of whom had their necks craned to see outside, he bent low and took his own gander out the window. It took perhaps a second and a half for him to assess what he saw, perhaps another two seconds to decide what to do about it. He walked back toward the first-class cabin. There he found a flight attendant, a pretty ash blonde whose name tag identified her as PEGGY. She was clutching the side of the fuselage.

The man's voice did not rise as he said, "I need to speak to the pilot."

"Sir, please return to your seat and fasten your seat belt."

"I need to speak to the pilot now."

"I'm sorry, sir, that's not—"

His tone remained calm as he interrupted her again: "Respectfully, Peggy, I don't have time to argue with you. Whether you want to recognize it or not, we have entered into what pilots call a death spiral. It's just a slight pull now, but there's nothing your pilot is going to be able to do to stop it from getting worse. Unless you let me help him, the spiral is going to get tighter and tighter until we hit the ground at what will likely be a steep bank and a very high rate of speed. Trust me when I tell you it won't end well for either of us, whether we're wearing our seat belts or not."

He finally had Peggy's attention—and cooperation. She walked unsteadily toward a phone, lifted it, and spoke into the receiver.

"Go ahead," she said, nodding toward the door to the cockpit. "It's unlocked."

The pilot had the gray hair and crow's-feet of a veteran flier. But in his many thousands of hours of flight time, he had never faced anything quite like this. He was leaning his weight against the flight stick, the muscles in his arms straining. The plane was responding, but not nearly enough.

The man from seat 2B did not bother with introductions.

"One of your ailerons on the left side is gone and another is just barely attached," he said.

"I've added power to the port engines and applied the rudder, but I can't keep us straight," the pilot replied.

"And you won't be able to," the man from 2B said. "I don't think I'll be able to get your aileron functioning. But I think I can at least get it back in place."

"And how are you going to do that?" the pilot asked.

The man from seat 2B ignored the question and said, "Do you have any speed tape in your flight kit?"

"Yeah, it's in the compartment behind me."

"Good," the man said, already heading in that direction.

"We're not the only ones," the pilot said.

"What do you mean?"

"Three planes have already crashed. No one knows what the hell is going on. Air traffic control is calling it another nine-eleven. Planes just keep dropping out of the sky."

The man from seat 2B paused over this news for a moment, then drove it from his mind. It was not pertinent to his present circumstances, which would require all of his concentration. "What's our altitude?" he asked.

"One-eight-six-two-five and falling."

"Okay. I'm going to need you to reduce airspeed to a hundred and forty knots, lower to fourteen thousand feet, and depressurize the plane. Can you do that for me?"

"I think so."

"What's your name, Captain?"

"Estes. Ben Estes."

"Captain Estes, I'm going to get you back some control of this aircraft. Hopefully enough to get us down safely. Just keep it as steady as you can for me for the next five minutes. No sudden moves."

"Roger that. What's your name, son?"

But the man from seat 2B had already departed the cockpit. He stopped briefly at his seat, opening the overhead bin and bringing down his rucksack. He pulled out a Petzl Hirundos climbing harness, several carabiners, and a seventy-meter length of Mammut Supersafe climbing rope. The plane had slowed. It was now tilted roughly fifteen degrees to the left. The man in seat 2B felt his ears pop.

The woman in seat 1B was peppering him with questions: "What's going on? Are we going to crash? What are you doing?"

"Just trying to avoid deep vein thrombosis," the

man in seat 2B said finally. "It's a silent killer, you know."

With that, he was on the move again, back to the coach section, toward the emergency exit rows. In this part of the plane, real terror had set in among the passengers. They had seen the wing. They felt the plane's bank. Some were sobbing. Some had grabbed on to loved ones. Others were praying.

"I'm going to need you folks to clear out of here," he said to the people seated in the exit rows. "There's much less chance of your being sucked out of the airplane if you do."

Those words—*sucked out of the airplane*—and the image they produced—had an immediate effect. The four seats, two in each row, emptied as the man from seat 2B stepped into his harness and attached one of his ropes to the front of it. He took the other end, looped it several times around seat 20B, and tied the sturdiest knot he knew.

He yanked hard to test it. The man from seat 2B could bench press 330 pounds and squat at least twice as much. He knew those numbers were nothing compared to the forces that might soon be exerted on this rope. He just had to hope it would hold.

Clamping the roll of speed tape in his teeth, he removed the seal from the emergency door, grasped it in both hands, and threw it out of the plane. He ignored the screams from several nearby passengers and concentrated on his next task.

As a kid, the man from seat 2B had enjoyed rolling down the window of his father's Buick—always a Buick—and cupping his hand against the wind that rushed at him, pushing at it in a test of his young strength. At sixty miles an hour, it was a struggle. The plane was moving more than twice as fast—140 knots is equal to 160 miles an hour. But he wasn't a kid anymore. He flattened himself against the floor, took one deep breath.

And then he began to crawl onto the surface of the wing.

He was pointed forward, toward the plane's nose, keeping one foot braced against the side of the porthole. The wind tore at him, doing its best to pry him loose. Only by keeping his profile flat could he keep himself from being swept away. The rope that tethered him to the plane might or might not hold his weight if called upon. The man from seat 2B was not especially keen to find out.

His objective, as he continued creeping ahead, was to reach the leading edge of the wing. He worked his way there slowly, with hands made strong and calloused by weeks in the mountains.

When he reached the edge he grasped it, then began inching away from the body of the plane, toward the tip of the wing. He slid one hand, then the other, not daring to move too quickly, until he reached the section of the wing where he could hear the aileron flapping behind him.

Now came the first hard part: getting himself turned around.

As if he was doing a pull-up, he yanked himself toward the leading edge of the wing. Then he hooked his right arm around it, followed by his right leg. The force of the wind was now keeping at least part of him pinned to the plane. Trying not to think about how much of his body was dangling fourteen thousand feet above southern Pennsylvania farmland, he reached his left hand out behind him. He followed it with his right hand until he was facing behind the plane. He wriggled toward the back edge of the wing.

Now the second hard part: grabbing the aileron.

The sheet of metal was a moving target, and there was no way he could reach it anyway—not without losing what little purchase he had on the wing. He grasped, instead, for the narrow strip of metal that had kept the aileron from flying away. Once he had it in his right hand, he began pulling it toward himself—right hand, left hand, right hand, left—until he had it.

He was thankful for the rubberized toes of his hiking boots. He doubted loafers would have had enough grip to keep him on the wing, especially as it continued its inexorable downward tilt. The death spiral was setting in. If the wing got much more pitch to it, his job was going to become impossible.

With the aileron finally in his hands, he moved on to the third hard part: securing it back in place.

Trapping the aileron under his body, he peeled a length of speed tape. While it looked like duct tape, speed tape was made from aluminum. It first came into heavy use during the Vietnam War, when it was used in the field to temporarily fix helicopters that had been damaged by small arms fire. In air force slang, it was called Thousand-MPH tape.

The man from seat 2B hoped the name wasn't overselling the tape's abilities as he attached the first strip of it to the sheet metal of the aileron. Then another strip. Then another. It was heavy tape, and it had a heavy job to do. When he felt he had used enough, he moved the aileron into what he judged was close to its original position. Or at least close enough. He pressed it down, keeping it there with his wrists as he unspooled more tape with his hands. He added several more pieces until he had something like confidence in his jury-rigging.

Then came the critical moment, the one when he needed to take his hands off the aileron. If it didn't stay in place, he might as well just jump off the plane. There wouldn't be time to repeat what he had just done before the death spiral took them down. This was the moment of truth for him and every other man, woman, and child aboard.

He let go.

The aileron held.

AS THEY MADE THEIR FINAL APPROACH TO DULLES airport, a phalanx of fire trucks and ambulances were lining the runway. Battling valiantly, with at least some control returned to him, Captain Estes had willed the plane to limp through the final hundred miles of its journey. It was later opined that only one of America's finest pilots could have pulled off what he had done. He was destined for a *Time* magazine cover, a book deal, even a guest appearance on a highly rated ABC television crime drama.

The man who made it possible had returned to seat 2B, as if nothing at all had happened, as if he were just another passenger. Even when his fellow travelers tried to thank him, he just shook his head, gestured toward the cockpit, and said, "I'm not the one who landed this thing." The plane touched down to the sound of boisterous cheering. When Peggy the flight attendant—who was already planning her own special thank you to Captain Estes—came on the public-address system and said, "Welcome to Dulles airport," the passengers burst into applause again.

The man in seat 2B felt hands pounding his back. He experienced no special euphoria, no thrill of being alive, only dread. The other passengers did not know about the larger tragedy that was unfolding outside the plane's doors. They were unaware that whereas they had escaped certain death, hundreds of other passengers on this day had not been so lucky.

Peggy announced that they could turn on their approved portable electronic devices, though most had already done so. They were already sending a feverish onslaught of *you'll-never-believe-what-happened-to-me* texts and *I'm-okay-yes-I'm-okay* e-mails.

The man in seat 2B did not share in their joy. He could have easily guessed what was waiting for him when he powered up his phone.

It was a text from a restricted number. It said only: *Cubby. Now.*

Being summoned to the cubby meant only one thing: a job awaited.

There would be no Orioles game for him.

The man in seat 2B did not even bother retrieving his carry-on luggage, which would only slow him down; nor did he wait for the main cabin door in the middle of the plane to be opened. He opened it himself before the Jetway extended, dropped from the plane, then commandeered a passing baggage trolley. He was soon off airport property, heading to his destination.

Captain Estes was accepting tearful hugs and grateful handshakes from all the passengers who exited in the usual manner. He would hear many of their stories in the upcoming weeks and months and get a deeper understanding of all the lives he had helped save: a woman who was pregnant with twins, a seven-year-old on the way to visit her grandmother, a medical research scientist who was helping to cure cancer, a nun who had given her life to the poor, a father with six adopted children—remarkable people, all of them.

But in that moment, Captain Estes was only thinking of one man, a man who had already slipped away.

"I never even got his name," he said to the flight attendant when all the passengers were gone.

"He was seated in 2B," Peggy told him. "Why don't you check the manifest?"

The captain returned to his cockpit and scanned down the list of the passengers.

The man from seat 2B was named Derrick Storm.

CHAPTER 2

WEST OF LUXOR, Egypt

Flat and featureless, hot and barren, the expanse of the Sahara Desert that stretched for some three thousand miles west of the Nile River was a great place to hide. But only if you were a grain of sand.

Everything else stuck out. And so Katie Comely had no problem distinguishing the dust cloud rising several miles in the distance.

She trained the viewfinder of her Zeiss Conquest HD binoculars on the front of the plume and saw the glinting of windshields. There were vehicles, at least four of them, traveling along in a lopsided V formation, closing in at between forty and fifty miles an hour.

It was not, in any way, a covert approach. But the men that Katie worried about were not the type to bother with subtlety.

Bandits. Again. They were always a problem in the desert, but even more so since the revolution of 2011 and the April 6 uprising. It was all the authorities could do to keep order in the towns and cities. The outlying areas had become as lawless as they had been in the days that followed the fall of the Roman Empire. In the two months since Katie had been on the dig, the expedition had been raided three times by outlaws who had helped themselves to everything they could carry. One or two of the items were later recovered by Egyptian authorities. The rest disappeared, sold on the black market for a fraction of what they were actually worth.

The expedition had hired a security force—really, just two aging locals with even older weapons and without the heart to use them—but it had been outnumbered and outgunned all three times. The force had since been doubled in number to four. She hoped that would be enough.

Katie adjusted the binoculars, trying to get a better view. She was twenty-nine, only a few months removed from defending her dissertation. Her PhD sheepskin still had a new-car smell to it. The University of Kansas had instructed her on how to pry open the secrets of antiquity. It had not taught her how to deal with armed thieves.

She adjusted the hijab on her head. The garment served at least two purposes. It shielded her fair face from the sun. But it also made her at least slightly less conspicuous. In her native Kansas, her yellow hair and blue eyes made her just another corn-fed local girl on the cheerleading squad. Out here, amid all these swarthy, dark-haired Arabs, they made her something of a freak.

If only she could have found a way to hide her gender. While Egypt was more progressive than many other Muslim nations when it came to its attitudes toward women, Katie still felt men leering at her everywhere she went.

She lowered the glasses, feeling her brow crease. "Do you want to take a look?" she asked the man next to her.

Professor Stanford Raynes—"Stan" to the guys back at the Faculty Club at Princeton—was tall and lean, with a pointy chin and a few too many years on him to harbor the crush on Katie that he did.

"I'm sure it's fine," he said.

Katie tolerated the crush, even encouraged it, partly because it was so benign—he never laid a finger on her, never acted inappropriately around her—and partly because he could make or break her career. A world-famous Egyptologist, he had doctorates in both archaeology and geology. He had revolutionized the field by using seismograms to locate many heretofore hidden sites, finding lost pyramids that generations of Indiana Jones wannabes had only heard rumors about. He was also the source of her funding for this, her first dig as a true professional in one of the most hypercompetitive fields in all of academia.

"I'm worried," she said. "Aren't you worried?"

"Just some youngsters racing cars in the desert, I'm sure. And if not, that's why we've got those gentlemen," he said, gesturing toward the four men with guns.

The vehicles were still closing in, now roughly a mile away, driving in a straight line toward the dig site with a determination that, to Katie, seemed to signify malignant intent.

"They're probably just merchants trying to sell us something," the professor suggested. "Fruit or vegetables or trinkets. Anyhow, I'm going into the tent to get some water, and I suggest you do the same. I keep telling you, it's very easy to get dehydrated out here."

"I'm fine," she said. "I just . . . I can't lose Khufu."

The professor disappeared. Katie, however, continued walking in the direction of the dust cloud, toward the tented staging area where the valuables they brought up from under the sand were being carefully wrapped and readied for transport. There were crates of varying sizes, some small enough for a few tiny figurines, others carrying huge slabs of carved granite that weighed a thousand pounds or more.

Among the artifacts she had personally discovered was a life-sized bust of Khufu. One of the early pharaohs of the Fourth Dynasty, a god-man who ruled Egypt some 4,500 years ago, he was generally accepted as being the pharaoh who built the Great Pyramid of Giza. Little else was known about him. If verified, the pink granite statue would be just the second known depiction of the ancient king.

It would also be the kind of find that would propel Dr. Comely into the first rank of young archaeologists. Perhaps it would even lead to a rare tenure-track professorship at a leading research university. But only if she could get it back to the lab.

The dust cloud now appeared to be at least three stories high, and the vehicles—they were pickup trucks, with men riding in their flatbeds—were just a few hundred yards away.

Close enough that Katie could see their guns without the aid of her binoculars.

"Professor!" she shouted. "It's them. They're back."

Raynes reappeared from his tent.

"Are you sure?" he asked.

"Just look!"

He grabbed the binoculars from her outstretched hand, focused them, then swore.

"Okay, okay. Let's . . . let's not panic here," he said.

Then—in a voice that sounded a lot like panic—he began shouting in excited Arabic at the sleepy-eyed guards. Katie only spoke a few words of the language, enough to be polite on the street and ask where the restroom was. She had been meaning to improve her skills. She was lost as soon as a conversation started.

The moment the professor's instructions to the guards were issued, one of the young assailants rapidly closing in pointed his AK-47 in the air and gleefully squeezed the trigger. A rapid burst of ten or twenty rounds flew into the atmosphere. Katie counted at least six other men with guns in the raiding party.

To Katie's dismay, the four guards did not return fire. They took one look at what was coming and, as if in practiced unison, reached the simultaneous conclusion that they were not being paid enough to do anything about it. They turned and ran.

Katie felt a shout escaping from her lungs. The professor was also berating them in Arabic. His admonishment bounced off the guards' backs as they fled.

The bandits were now on them. They were mostly young, barely out of their teens, their dark beards still scraggly. The leader—or the man who appeared to be the leader—was older, perhaps in his late thirties or early forties, with strands of white in his beard.

They pulled to a stop near the staging area and hopped off the pickup trucks with the apparent intention of helping themselves to whatever was there. The professor rushed at them—courageously, foolishly, and completely unarmed—and did not stop even as several gun muzzles were trained on him. Katie rushed behind him, yelling at him to stop. He was unbowed.

The leader unleashed a stream of words at the professor. Katie tried to pick them up, but to her unschooled ear it sounded like, "Badaladaladagabaha."

The professor responded while trying to wrestle a crate away from two bandits, an effort made all the more pathetic by the fact that he lacked the strength to rip it from them. The charade ended when the leader walked up behind Raynes and bludgeoned his head with the butt of his rifle. The professor crumpled to the ground.

Katie screamed and rushed to his side. The young men were actually laughing.

"Cowards. You're all a bunch of thieving cowards!" she yelled. As if they could understand what she was saying, the men laughed harder.

The leader circled around so he was facing Katie. He pointed his gun at her.

"Get him out of here," he snarled, in heavily accented English. "Get him ice for his head. I need him healthy so he can dig up more treasure for me."

The leader translated what he said for the benefit of the men, who roared in approval. Katie glared at him defiantly, weighing her options, which she had to admit were few.

"Take him away," the leader said, again in English. "Or maybe I take you, his pretty young girlfriend, as hostage, huh? Maybe we have some fun, huh?"

Again, the leader repeated his words in Arabic. The response was lustier this time. Katie could feel several pairs of lascivious eyes undressing her.

Beaten and scared, she lifted the half-conscious professor under the arms and began dragging him toward his tent.

"I'm sorry, Katie," he murmured. "I tried. I tried."

CHAPTER 3

LANGLEY, Virginia

I n that strange way that only a spy grows accustomed to, Derrick Storm did not know precisely where he was going. Only that he was in a hurry to get there.

From the moment he retrieved his Ford Taurus from a private garage just off the premises of Dulles airport, he kept the tread of his right hiking boot mashed into the car's floorboard. He braked only when it was the last means of avoiding collision.

Storm occasionally took grief from D.C.-area acquaintances over his choice of the vehicle while he was there. To them, it seemed staid for a man of Storm's panache. Storm just smiled and accepted their ribbing. Much like Storm himself, the car preferred to hide its true capabilities. It had a twin-turbocharged 3.5-liter engine with 365 horsepower worth of unruliness under its hood, and a heavy-duty police suspension system that could handle the extreme demands Storm occasionally had to place on it.

The radio was off. The information reported in the early hours of a mass tragedy was usually wrong. In its haste to be first with the news, the media sometimes seemed to prefer guessing over reporting. Storm didn't want to muddy his mind with it. He concentrated, instead, on keeping the Taurus's tires on the pavement. He did not always succeed. At least one Nissan Sentra driver was thankful for that fact.

And yet, for all his haste, his final destination was a mystery to him.

Any half-wit troglodyte with Google Earth can get a pretty good gander at the Central Intelligence Agency's headquarters, which rests on a leafy campus just across from Washington, D.C., alongside a sweeping bend in the Potomac River. A slightly more sophisticated operator can figure out which buildings house the National Clandestine Service, one of the CIA's more shadowy branches.

But no one—no matter how good a hacker he is, no matter what he thinks he knows—will ever lay eyes on the cubby, the home to an elite spy unit created by a man named Jedediah Jones.

Not even Storm, who had given the cubby its tongue-in-cheek sobriquet, knew its precise location. He knew of only one way to get there, which he began executing as soon as his Taurus and its smoldering tires came to a rest in the visitors' parking lot at CIA headquarters.

It involved presenting himself at the main entrance to an agent who responded to Storm with all the excitement of a man receiving patients at a dentist's office. Normally, this portion of Storm's journey involved some waiting as another agent was summoned from the cubby. Storm was mildly surprised to see the well-muscled, dark-complexioned shape of Agent Javier Rodriguez already coming down the hallway toward him.

But only mildly. Rodriguez was one of Jones's most trusted subordinates. He was usually involved when Jones called for Storm.

Rodriguez was grinning as he walked up. Storm was not in a joking mood, in light of the seriousness of what was happening in the world around them. And yet, even in the midst of a crisis—or, perhaps, especially in the midst of a crisis—there were rituals to uphold. Gallows humor helped men like Storm and Rodriguez survive their jobs with their sanity intact. A certain bravado, even if it was false, needed to be maintained.

"Why, Agent Rodriguez, it's almost like you were watching me drive here and knew exactly when I was going to arrive," Storm said.

"You owe that Nissan Sentra driver an apology, bro."

"Send me her address. I'll write a note."

Rodriguez's only response was to hold up a black hood between his thumb and forefinger and give it a brief shake.

"I don't suppose you'd let me promise to just close my eyes this time?" Storm asked.

"Sure. If I drug you with pentobarbital first."

"The hood it is," Storm said, and dipped his head. At six foot two, Storm was a head taller than Rodriguez.

"The cubby it is," Rodriguez replied, slipping the hood into place.

The unit that called the cubby its command post did not exist—at least not as far as anyone connected to it would admit, even under the most creatively cruel torture. It was a detachment within the National Clandestine Service that had no name, no printed organizational chart, no staff assigned to it, and no budget. The CIA bought a whole lot of $852 toilet seats and $6,318 hammers to hide its expenditures.

Its leader, Jedediah Jones, was a veteran bureau-crat who used his considerable executive talents and cunning to build this agency-within-an-agency-within-an-agency, the CIA's version of Russian *matryoshka* dolls. Its missions and achievements were as secretive as everything else associated with it. It had occasionally been credited with saving the world. It had also been accused of trying to destroy it. Either way, it did so quietly.

Storm had long ago given up trying to guess where he was being led when he was taken to the cubby. He assumed it was underground somewhere, though for all he knew it could have been under-water or even in the clouds. The trip there involved the seemingly random application of g-forces from all directions: up, down, left, and right.

Technically, Storm did not work for Jones or for the CIA. He was a former private investigator turned independent contractor. While his adven-tures had taken him across the world, he was often called on to inquire into matters that had domestic ties, which was—again, technically—illegal. The CIA's jurisdiction was strictly international. As a result, Storm's missions did not exist. In the same way the cubby did not exist. He might as well have had DERRICK STORM PLAUSIBLE DENIABILITY on his business card, because that's what he provided the powerful men who required his unique skill set. He was paid handsomely for his services, one of which involved accepting the fact that he would be treated as expendable if it became convenient.

He knew he had reached his destination when he heard the clacking of keyboards. When his hood was finally removed, he was greeted by the usual sight. A cadre of men and women sat in front of a bank of computers, their eyes reflecting the contents of the walls of LCD screens in front of them. Jones called them techs. Storm called them nerds—a term he used with both respect and love, because their digital wizardry had been an invaluable aid to him so many times.

Several of the nerds' monitors contained satellite images of the crash sites of what were once airplanes, their broken pieces now spread over whatever field or forest where they had come to rest. One of the nerds was zooming in on a piece of what might have once been an engine. Another nerd was comparing a piece of shredded landing equipment to a picture of what it looked like when it came out of the box.

Storm, who had yet to see the repeated loops of television footage that were transfixing the rest of America, stopped to gawk at them. While he didn't doubt Captain Estes, who had called it another 9/11, seeing the detritus that littered the screens made the disaster more real.

"So it's that bad," he said.

"No, bro," Rodriguez said. "It's worse."

THE BRIEFING ROOM WAS JUST OFF THE MAIN COR-ridor. It had a wall-sized, flat-screen monitor on one end, but its central feature was a polished conference table surrounded by high-backed leather executive chairs.

Seated in one of the chairs was Agent Kevin Bryan, a small-statured man who appeared to be every bit as Irish as his name. He was also one of Jones's top lieutenants. He and Rodriguez were often teamed together. If Jones was the bread, Bryan and Rodriguez were the peanut butter and the jelly.

"All right, talk to me like I don't know anything," Storm said. "Because right now I don't know anything other than the fact that I owe my life to the versatility of speed tape."

"Told you that story was true," Rodriguez spat at Bryan. "That's what you get for doubting my boy. Twenty bucks."

Bryan extracted a twenty-dollar bill from his wallet and handed it to Rodriguez as he began talking. "Okay, we're looking at four planes, all of which were heading toward Dulles airport and came into difficulty when they were at approximately twenty thousand feet in altitude. The National Transportation Safety Board has yet to recover any of the black boxes, so we don't have detailed information for any of these yet. But we were able to, ahh, appropriate some initial information from the Federal Aviation Administration."

"Go," Storm said.

"I won't tell you about Flight 937, because you already know about that one firsthand. So I'll start with the initial plane to go down. It was Flight 312, coming in from Amsterdam Schiphol."

An image of an Airbus A300 appeared in hologram as if it were floating above the table.

"It was coming in on the same approach path as 937. As a matter of fact, all four planes were coming in on a northeast approach toward Dulles runway twelve-thirty," Bryan said. "Four-fourteen was using an Airbus A300 that had reported no recent maintenance problems. It was a perfectly routine flight. Then, at 1:55 P.M., its pilot was reporting he had lost his left engine. Pilots spend hours in simulators training for such things, so he began putting engine failure procedures into place, except they didn't work. The plane began rapidly losing altitude and the pilot said it was responding as if it hadn't just lost its left engine, but its entire left wing. That was his last communication before he crashed at a steep angle into a wooded area near Interstate 83."

Bryan clicked a button and the hologram changed to a McDonnell Douglas MD-11.

He continued: "Next we have Flight 76, coming in from Stockholm Arlanda. It was a cargo plane registered to a company called Karlsson Logistics. Again, it had been a routine flight. Again, it was a plane with a spotless maintenance record. Three minutes after 312 distress call, at 1:58 P.M., Flight 76 had its last communications with the tower. Then nothing. It was like it simply ceased to exist. It was found in a farm field near Glen Rock, Pennsylvania, a few miles away from the other ones. The theory is that the pilot had no control when the plane hit the ground, because it hit hard and fast. Residents in the area reported thinking it was everything from a bomb to an earthquake."

Storm only shook his head. Whatever had happened to Flight 76 had obviously been too catastrophic to be fixed with speed tape. He was thankful there were no passengers, but that would be little comfort to the families of the crew members.

Agent Bryan had changed the plane floating above the table to a Boeing 747.

"Finally, we have Flight 494, inbound from Paris Charles de Gaulle," he said. "Again, there was nothing about this aircraft that would have indicated trouble. At 2:07 P.M.—nine minutes later—it reported a loss of hydraulic pressure in its rear rudder. As I said earlier, pilots are trained for such things, though by this point, flight control was apparently freaking out. They knew what had happened to the first two planes. They were determined to get this one down safely and really thought they could. Then the pilot came back on and said it was far more catastrophic. A pilot can't see behind himself, of course. But as near as the man could figure, the entire tail section of the airplane was just gone."

"Gone?"

"Gone. What was left of the plane crashed into a forested area of Spring Valley Park. Your flight was the final one to report difficulty, about five minutes later, and the only one to survive."

"Have any groups claimed responsibility?"

"Several are trying to, but none that we think have the capability to pull off something like this," Bryan said. "Whoever is really behind it isn't bragging about it yet. We don't know what they want or why they did this."

Storm concentrated on the desk in front of him for a moment before speaking. "So we have four different aircraft that seemed to suddenly lose valuable parts at approximately 2 P.M."

"That's right," Bryan said.

"And we can be pretty sure it wasn't some kind of nine-eleven–style hijacking," Storm said. "There were no hijackers aboard my flight, and none of the other three reported anything. As far as we know, their pilots were still at the controls when the planes went down."

"That's right," Bryan said again.

There was more staring at the desk.

"You think maybe it was sabotage?" Rodriguez asked.

"Talk it out for me."

"Somebody on the ground was able to plant a small explosive at different points on each plane—the wing, the tail, whatever," Rodriguez said. "The passengers on your flight said they heard a sound when the aileron came apart. Maybe the explosives were all set to go off within a few minutes of each other."

Storm shook his head. "I don't like it. These planes were coming from four different airports in four different countries—four sophisticated countries that have long experience taking terrorism and airport security pretty seriously. It's hard to imagine what kind of organization could breach all four. And if you did go through all that trouble, why stop at one plane in each place? And why would they fixate on four airplanes that were not only traveling to the same airport but heading there via the exact same location? That's far too big a coincidence."

Rodriguez was nodding as Storm continued: "We need to think about that location. The geography has to be the common link here. Bryan, can you compare the four flight plans and find the places where they overlap within a mile or two?"

Bryan began typing furiously. On the flat screen on the far wall, Storm watched as Bryan manipulated the four flight plans on top of each other and began searching for points of intersection. Closer to Dulles, there were many of them—all four planes were on the same approach. Farther from Dulles, they were scattered.

The point of first convergence was slightly south of York, Pennsylvania.

"What's there?" Storm asked, pointing.

Bryan zoomed in on the spot where Storm had gestured. When he got in close enough, they saw a chunk of green that was labeled, "Richard M. Nixon County Park."

"Maybe they were enemies of the thirty-seventh president?" Rodriguez said.

"That wouldn't narrow it down much," Storm said. "No, this is our key. This spot. Everyone is talking about what happened in the air. But my bet is it was something on the ground that is responsible for this."

"What could do that to an airplane from the ground? Some kind of surface-to-air missile?" Rodriguez asked.

"Something like that. If it was, you would think someone would have seen it. A rocket is not exactly invisible. It's loud and bright and leaves a contrail. Can we dispatch some folks to make some gentle inquiries?"

"Got it," Bryan said.

"Okay, so that's getting us closer to figuring out what happened," Storm said. "Where are we on the why?"

Bryan nodded at Rodriguez, who walked over to the large flat screen. Bryan's jumble of flight plans disappeared with one touch from Rodriguez.

"Until someone credible claims responsibility, we're mostly just fumbling in the dark," Rodriguez said. "The current theory is that this is just random violence by some sick dude or dudes. No one has any clue what they want."

"That's not a very satisfying theory," Storm said. "Are you sure there's not anything the victims had in common? Maybe this was more targeted than we realize."

"Not that we've been able to sort out so far," Rodriguez said. "There were definitely some heavy hitters on board all the planes."

"Like who?"

"We've had the nerds at work, searching for patterns among them. Nothing has popped so far. Not sure I have anything to tell you."

"Humor me. Give me the biggest name on each flight."

Rodriguez shrugged. "Okay, let's see here. Flight 312 had Pi aboard."

A photo of an unshaven, unkempt young man with a mop for a head of hair appeared on the screen. He vaguely resembled a grown Muppet.

Rodriguez continued: "Pi is the leader of the International Order of Fruitarians, a quasi-religious group that tries to convince people that fruit is the original diet of mankind—nutrition as God intended. Really, it's a cult. It slowly lures innocent college kids, especially unsuspecting young women, into its clutches and then eventually brainwashes them into doing things like selling flowers at the airport."

"Maybe the father of one of these kids who lost his daughter to this nonsense decided to seek ultimate revenge and fire a rocket at the airplane the guy was on," Storm said. "A father would go to any length to protect his daughter from a monster like that."

Rodriguez let that pass. "Flight 76 was the cargo flight. Beyond the crew, the only passenger was a Karlsson executive named Brigitte Bildt, who had some business in the States and decided to hop aboard. She was not the company's CEO, but she apparently ran the day-to-day operations and was also involved in a lot of its strategic decision-making."

A photo of a middle-aged woman with blue eyes and kinky brown hair was now being projected. It appeared to be a corporate head shot—no frills, no glamming up. She had been looking at the camera with a certain gravity, almost as if she was aware of the seriousness of the way the photo would someday be used.

"Is it possible Karlsson Logistics had business enemies?" Storm asked. "Maybe it was involved in some kind of leveraged takeover that Bildt was pressing for?"

"We're looking into all possibilities," Rodriguez said. "Moving on, Flight 494 had a couple of bigwigs, a professional athlete, some business types. But the biggest name was Congressman Erik Vaughn."

A new image appeared. It was the beady-eyed, puffy-faced visage of the congressman, topped with helmet hair that never seemed to move.

"Eww . . . am I allowed to say I hate that guy?" Storm asked.

"You wouldn't be alone. He chaired the Ways and Means committee and he's one of those small-government zealots. He has used his position as leverage, refusing to bring any matter involving taxation before Ways and Means unless he gets a guarantee of reduced spending somewhere. I don't think there's a group whose funding he hasn't cut. The young, the old, highway funding, the whole concept of foreign aid. . . . You can go on and on with him."

"We'd have a long list of people who'd love to see him die in a plane crash," Storm acknowledged.

"There were others, too. Some more famous than others. And I guess it depends on your definition of famous. One of the people on the first plane down was Rachel McCord."

"The porn star?" Storm burst.

Rodriguez arched an eyebrow. "Gee, Storm, how did you know about her?"

"I . . . I . . . read about her in a magazine once," Storm said. "Anyhow, what's my job in all this? Why does Jones want me here?"

As if he had the room bugged—and, really, he probably did—a trim man of about sixty with buzz-cut, iron-gray hair and steely blue eyes walked through the door.

JEDEDIAH JONES'S TITLE WAS HEAD OF INTERNAL Division Enforcement. Its acronym was no accident, given that it neatly described his prevailing modus operandi.

Storm owed his existence to Jones in more ways than one. While it was Clara Strike who first discovered Derrick Storm—then a struggling private investigator who was considering changing his name to Derrick Aarons just to move it up a few notches in the Yellow Pages—it was Jones who took Storm's raw abilities and honed them into polished proficiencies, turning Storm into a rare asset.

Their long association had been mutually beneficial in other ways as well. It had made Storm a rich man, one with a contact list of friends and sources that was even more invaluable than all the money he had amassed. And the missions that Storm had been able to complete—often against impossible odds— had been an invaluable boost to Jones's career.

And yet there was always tension between the

men. Jones knew he could never fully command Storm, who prioritized many things—his own moral code, his sense of patriotism, the welfare of his friends and family—over his orders from Jones.

And Storm, likewise, knew where Jones's loyalties lay. And it wasn't in their tenuous relationship. For all Storm had helped him achieve, for all the times Jones had deployed substantial resources to save Storm, Jones lacked sentimentality toward him. After a botched mission in Tangier, Morocco, Jones had faked Storm's death, leading the world to think he had perished for four long years, not caring about the impact it had on Storm's loved ones. What's more, Storm knew that if it ever became expedient to have his death become real, Jones wouldn't hesitate. He would leave Storm bleeding in a river full of piranhas if it benefited CIA goals or Jones's sometimes-warped ideas about what was best for the country.

"Is he up to speed?" Jones asked, not bothering to immediately acknowledge Storm.

"As up to speed as any of us are at this point, sir," Bryan said.

"Excellent," Jones said, finally turning to his protégé. "Do you have a vehicle here?"

"Yes."

"Great. We're going to ask you to ditch it for the time being. Where you're going, you're not going to be Derrick Storm, and I don't want you driving some souped-up hot rod, even if it is wrapped in a bland coating."

"All right. Who am I and where am I going?"

"Not far. To Glen Rock, Pennsylvania."

"That's the Flight 76 crash site."

"Correct. And it's also where the National Transportation Safety Board has set up its investigation into what took that plane down. The NTSB will take its sweet time figuring it out, following all their policies and procedures and then coming out with a report in a couple of months outlining what they think might have happened. We don't have a couple of months. I want to know what they know before they know it."

"Why Flight 76?"

"One, because it's as good a place to start as any figuring out what happened up there," Jones said. "Those flatfoots from the FBI allowed this to happen on their turf and we're going to stick it up their ass by cleaning up the mess for them.

"And, two, because the woman who owns the plane, Ingrid Karlsson, is a friend of mine. She's been an aide to me and this agency on numerous occasions. She's asked me for a favor and I don't want to disappoint her."

Storm looked for telltale signs of artifice from Jones, even though the man was too cagey to give them with any frequency. Still, Storm knew Jones didn't do favors without the promise of a significant return. Storm wondered what it was this time—or if he'd ever find out.

There was never just one layer with the head of Internal Division Enforcement.

"Okay," Storm said. "And I'm guessing you have a plan for me beyond waltzing into an NTSB-secured crash site and asking them to show me their underwear?"

"Of course," Jones said. "Follow me."

CHAPTER 4

THE MEDITERRANEAN SEA, South of France

The rug was from the sixteenth-century Ottoman Empire, a perfect and near-priceless specimen restored to a glory not seen since Suleiman I himself last walked on it. Resting on top of it was a desk made from rare, Cuban mahogany, harvested from an old-growth rain forest and hand-carved by a master artisan who toiled for a year on its intricacies. Perched on that was a ringing phone, connected to a network of satellites that guaranteed users global coverage, from the peaks of Antarctica to the icy reaches of the North Pole.

The woman answering it was Ingrid Karlsson, who might have been fifty—only her birth certificate knew for sure—and who might have been the world's richest woman. Much as with her age, she would neither confirm nor deny speculation.

"Yes?" she said, and then listened to several minutes of excited jabbering on the other end of the line.

When the voice stopped, Karlsson said, "She's dead? Are . . . are you sure? There is no mistake?"

She waited for the reply, then said only "thank you" before ending the call.

She sat perfectly still for a moment. Her gray-blue eyes stared straight ahead. Her near-black hair, which was chopped in straight bangs across her forehead, fell in shimmering strands down to her shoulders. Swedish by birth, a resident of Monaco for tax reasons, she had written a book—half memoir, half polemic—entitled *Citizen of the World*. Nevertheless, she retained the trademark stoicism of her homeland in the face of tragic news.

She pressed a button on the desk. In Swedish, she said, "Tilda, come in here, please."

A statuesque redhead, dressed in brief shorts and a form-fitting knit top, appeared in the door.

"Yes, ma'am."

"One of our planes has crashed in the United States," she said. "Brigitte is dead."

"Yes, ma'am."

"We must make a video. We will share it with the press and on the Internet."

Tilda's head tilted as she hesitated. While once a common request, this was now unusual. But she recovered with, "Yes, ma'am. Right away."

Tilda disappeared. Karlsson bowed her head, thinking of Brigitte, thinking of all they had achieved together. Ingrid Karlsson was the only child of a man who bequeathed her a modestly successful Swedish shipping company when she was in her twenties. Over the ensuing three decades, Ingrid had taken it and—one ambitiously leveraged acquisition at a time—turned it into the world's largest privately held logistics company, an empire that included a massive fleet of container ships, planes, trucks, and railroad cars. All told, Karlsson Logistics had a presence in sixty-two countries and on four continents.

The press had taken to calling her "Xena: Warrior Princess," for her aggressive business style, Amazonian stature, and more-than-passing resemblance to the 1990s cult-television icon. She detested the nickname at first, then warmed to it when she realized it was meant as a sign of respect, a symbol of her strength and success.

And the success had been considerable. Her estimated wealth, which started in the many millions, burgeoned into the billions. She freely shared her riches with her employees, both her personal staff, to whom her loyalty was fierce, and her corporate workforce, which enjoyed salaries and benefits beyond what any publicly traded company could offer.

Brigitte had been her most trusted executive during the last decade and a half. More than just a right hand, she was treated like a partner, even though Ingrid retained sole ownership of the business. There was even talk—since neither was married—that the two may have been more than just colleagues. But that was only speculation.

What was known was that Brigitte Bildt had increasingly become the public face of Karlsson Logistics, the one who held the press conferences and opined in the media on matters of importance to the company.

It was a role ceded to her willingly by her boss. During her younger years, Ingrid had enjoyed her prominence. She reveled in the nightlife of Monaco. She flew stunt planes at air shows. She played polo better than most of the men at charity benefit matches. It was all to the delight of the paparazzi, who could always sell another photo of a real-life warrior princess to the tabloids.

But she also used her celebrity as a kind of pulpit to preach a message of free trade, international cooperation, and global thinking. She spoke for groups of policy makers and for academics, saying that governments that meddled in the markets or tried to enforce national boundaries—whether through force or through oppressive tariffs—were merely standing in the way of history. She envisioned a world map without lines on it. She had once funded a conference of geographers who presented papers speculating on the death of the nation-state as an organizing construct. "One day," she told them during her opening remarks, "we will all be citizens of the world."

But through the years, she had grown weary of the spotlight, of journalists who would rather gossip about her sexuality than tackle important issues, of being a target for the kind of criticism that came with such high visibility. Her social life became more private, centering on smaller gatherings with thoughtful friends or valued associates. She had lost her appetite for fame.

Her final gesture of withdrawal from public life was to commission a yacht, pouring a reported $1 billion of her fortune into its construction. She named it *Warrior Princess* and signed the shipbuilders to aggressively worded nondisclosure agreements.

Rumors of its grandeur were legion. Even the Russian oligarchs were said to ooze jealousy over its alleged specifications: a mix of gas turbine and diesel engines said to deliver more than one hundred thousand in total horsepower; a triple-reinforced hull that was both bulletproof and bombproof; luxuries that included a full-size cinema, a library, private gardens, a swimming pool, a full discotheque, and a 5,200-square-foot master suite; and a superstructure built to withstand the pounding of a Category 5 hurricane. Aerial photographs of the 565-foot-long vessel tended to be from a distance. No one had ever photographed the inside.

Nevertheless, Ingrid Karlsson was going to give the world a small glimpse of it now. Tilda had returned with a high-definition video camera attached to a tripod, which she set in front of the desk.

"Are you ready, ma'am?" she asked.

Ingrid nodded. Tilda zoomed in on her boss, then pushed a button. The small red light on the front of the camera illuminated.

"I lost a loved one today," she began. "And I am aware, on this most horrible of days in the world's history, that I am not alone. My heart shatters at the loss of Brigitte Bildt, my valued colleague, my best friend, my North Star. But my heart shatters also for the many thousands who share in my suffering."

She bowed her head for a moment, then continued: "Right now, we can only speculate as to who is responsible for this senseless act. We can only guess as to what ideology or religion compelled them to murder innocent hundreds and what goals they hoped to accomplish with this slaughter. Perhaps soon we will have more details, but already—in our shattered hearts—I am sure we all understand the root cause of this tragedy.

"It is us. It is our desire to live as petty, warring tribes rather than as citizens of the world. It is our tendency to focus on the tiny streams of our differences rather than on the great oceans of our similarities. It is our corrosive belief that one country or one God or one belief is greater than another. It is our governments, which focus on their narrow agendas rather than on peace and prosperity for all."

Her voice was rising now. "We cannot continue in this reckless manner. It remains my fervent hope that someday, the wrongheadedness of our twenty-first-century thinking will perplex schoolchildren in the same way we today are bewildered by ancient astronomers who believed the world was flat."

She paused, lowered her gaze to the desk in front of her, then looked back at the camera. "But I am not speaking to you today simply to offer meek words. The wolf has snatched our children, our husbands, our mothers. It is time to find the wolf and destroy it. Toward that end, I would like to offer a bounty of fifty million dollars to any individual or group who captures the person or persons responsible for this attack.

"To the perpetrators of this horrible act, I say: you will be found. You will be brought to justice. There is no hole you can hide in, no tree that is tall enough, no den my wealth cannot penetrate. I will personally spare no expense to see that you are found. And I will aid any corporation, government, group, or individual who requires my resources or assistance to achieve this goal.

"I do this for Brigitte. And for all the shattered hearts in the world."

She offered the camera one more steely glance.

And then it melted. The Amazonian warrior princess—the woman whose toughness and determination had built an empire—bowed her head and wept.

CHAPTER 5

HERCULES, California

The handkerchief in Alida McRae's left palm had started the day dry, clean, and crisply ironed, but it had since devolved into a rumpled, sweat-soaked wad.

Sitting in the now-familiar waiting room at the Hercules Police Department headquarters, she pulled the cloth slowly from her balled-up left hand until it was straight. Then she repacked it into her right hand and pulled with her left. She had been repeating this nervous gesture for several minutes as she waited for her fourth—no, fifth—appointment with the police chief.

White-haired and sixty-seven, Alida was always nicely dressed and perfectly coiffed. She was what people liked to call a "handsome woman," a phrase she quietly detested. Men were handsome. Dogs were handsome. Women were either beautiful or not beautiful, and if she had reached an age where she could no longer be described by that word, she could accept that. She just didn't want to be patronized when it came to her looks—or anything else for that matter.

And patronized was the perfect word to describe what she felt like every time she came to the Hercules Police Department.

It had now been twenty days. Twenty days since

her life had been turned upside down and shaken. Twenty days of worrying and wondering what had happened. Twenty days of dread.

Twenty days ago, her husband, William "Bill" McRae, a sixty-eight-year-old retired father of three grown sons and grandfather of seven, had gone for his daily jog. A creature of almost comically well-ingrained habits, he left either shortly before or shortly after seven o'clock each morning. He followed the same five-mile course each day, a long loop that began and ended at their house and typically took him anywhere from forty-five to forty-seven minutes, depending on how frisky he was feeling. Other than Sundays—and the occasional holiday—he had been doing it the same way for years.

Except for twenty days ago. He went out like usual, at 7:02 A.M. By eight, Alida had first noted his absence. By 8:15 A.M., she had decided to do something about it. Every now and then, when he hadn't hydrated properly or had eaten too much salt the night before, his calves cramped. She once found him a half mile from home, crawling home rather than accepting rides from passing motorists.

As she drove his route, she had expected to find him doing something similar. Maybe limping along with a sprained ankle, or perhaps something even more stubborn and silly. Instead, she did not see him.

She returned home. He still wasn't there. She called one or two folks she knew who lived along some of the roads he jogged. They were friends who had often joked about how the "Bill Train" was a minute early or two minutes late on any given day. But, no, they all said they hadn't seen him.

By nine o'clock she called the Hercules Police Department in a state of high anxiety. Something horrible had happened to her husband. If it wasn't a natural occurrence—he had suffered a heart attack or stroke somewhere and fallen into a ditch—it was an unnatural one. He had been beaten by wilding youths. He had been mugged. Something. She felt it deep in her bones.

How long has he been missing, ma'am? the dispatch asked.

He should have been back an hour ago, she heard herself say.

The young dispatch had been polite enough not to laugh, but just barely. *Nothing to worry about, ma'am, I'm sure he'll be back shortly.*

They had treated her like an old hen who was pecking after her husband. And even now that the disappearance had stretched to nearly three weeks, she felt like their attitudes had not improved much.

Yes, they had made an effort to find him. Perhaps even a lot of effort. But in some fundamental way, she still felt as though they viewed her as a batty old lady.

"Good afternoon, Mrs. McRae," the chief said, appearing in her line of vision just as she had the handkerchief balled up in her left hand again.

"Good afternoon, Chief," she said.

"Why don't you come with me? We can talk in my office."

Alida rose and followed the chief, determined to stand her ground and get some results this time. She had done her homework on him. He had been one year away from retirement for four years now, but his wife kept saying they couldn't afford it. He had moved to Hercules because it was near the wine country and he enjoyed trips up that way. He was, everyone kept telling her, a "good cop." She just wished she had seen more evidence of it.

When she reached his office, she sat in the same chair she had the previous three times. He closed the door. She did not wait for him to sit.

"Have you heard anything?" she asked, hating the desperate quality to her voice but knowing there was nothing she could do to make it go away.

The chief said nothing as he crossed the room, rounded his desk, and settled heavily in the chair behind it. He put his elbows on the desk, crossed his hands, and fixed her with a sincere gaze.

"Mrs. McRae," he said. "I hope you know by now that if I *had* heard anything about your husband, I would have called you immediately."

"So you've said, but I—"

"Mrs. McRae," he said again. And there it was: that patronizing tone. He continued, "I know you don't think we're doing anything, and I know you think we don't care. But the fact is, we've dedicated an incredible amount of resources to this case. We've done everything I know how to do. We filed a missing persons report with the feds. We did the canvass. The dogs. The media."

She nodded. "The canvass" had started the afternoon after he disappeared, after Alida had made her first foray down to the police station and managed to impress on them the strangeness of what had occurred. The chief had sent four officers out to cover Bill's entire jogging route, knocking on doors, showing his picture, and asking if anyone had seen him. They all had. A thousand times. Just not that morning.

"The dogs" came the next day. The chief had

his own K-9 unit, plus one that had come from nearby Richmond. They let four German shepherds sniff some of Bill's jogging clothes, then sent them running along his route, their hypersensitive noses leading the way. They left, barking and full of energy, did the entire circle, and came back an hour and a half later with their tongues dragging. Because he had done the route so many times, they never lost his scent. But they also never found any deviation from his course. As far as the dogs were concerned, they had done a bang-up job tracking the man along five miles of sidewalk and roadway. It was just their human partners who remained mystified.

"The media" was the final step. The chief had held a press conference, holding a blown-up picture of a smiling Bill McRae for all the local stations to put on the air. It was a story that played well: a genial grandfather who simply vanished one day. The *Hercules Express* had run two articles about it. Millions of people in the Bay Area had been told to alert authorities if they saw him. None did.

"I know we've done a lot already," Alida said. "I just feel like . . . there must be something else we can do. I heard about a kidnapping case in Oregon where they issued an Amber Alert. Maybe we could—"

"Mrs. McRae, Amber Alerts are for children. Your husband was a grown man."

Was. The last two or three visits, the chief had mistakenly slipped into past tense when talking about her husband.

"You don't understand, Bill is—"

"I know, I know. He is just not one to just disappear," the chief said, echoing the words Alida had apparently said too many times now.

The chief fiddled with something on his desk, keeping his head down for a moment.

"Mrs. McRae, this is difficult for me to say. But with everything happening on the East Coast today with those airplanes, we're going to be on terrorism watch for the next couple of days at the very least, and I don't have the resources to . . ."

He let his voice trail off. He was shaking his head. He finally looked up. "Mrs. McRae, we checked everything on that jogging route ten times and we never found the slightest hint that anything was out of place. We interviewed more people than I can count. We haven't heard a whiff of anything resembling a ransom demand. We haven't found any bloodstains or anything suggesting foul play. We've got those notifications on all his credit cards and bank accounts. There's been no activity. I think you're going to have to seriously consider the possibility that your husband has simply wandered off, for whatever reason, and he won't be found until he wants to be found."

Alida squeezed the handkerchief tightly. The chief had hinted around this several times. This was the most direct he had been about it.

"I know, I know, you think that's impossible," he continued. "And this is hard for me to even suggest. But there was a man down in Van Nuys a few years ago, same thing. Damon Hack was his name. A gentle family man who liked to play fantasy football with his buddies. He lived quietly, no enemies, no debts, never a hint of dissatisfaction with his life—just like your husband. And it turned out he had been squirreling away cash for years, twenty, forty bucks at a time until he had enough to flee. They found him in Las Vegas a few months later, living on the street, having blown through all his cash but still with no plans to go back. And there was nothing anyone could do. He was a grown man who had made a decision to live a different life, which was his choice."

"No," she said. "You don't understand. Bill was the most reliable man who ever lived. He was like sunrise in the east. He was a scientist. Life was logical and orderly with him. He was not just—"

She stopped. She realized she was repeating herself. She had slipped into past tense, too.

She had been relying on this police chief too much. A police chief who had clearly given up. And that was fine for him.

She would not give up. Not as long as her Bill was out there and in danger.

CHAPTER 6

GLEN ROCK, Pennsylvania

Derrick Storm had done disguises. He had been a Venetian gondolier. He had been a reporter for a soy-related trade publication. He had been a doctor, a lawyer, a barista, a math teacher, a race car driver, a Hollywood screenwriter, a ditchdigger, and so many more they blurred together.

Every time he assumed a new identity, he did as much research as possible so he could credibly carry off his cover. Sometimes, he studied his "role" for a week or more, to the point where he felt like he understood the person he was trying to become almost as well as someone who had actually lived that life.

This time he had no such luxury. As he made the ninety-minute drive from Langley up to the rural Pennsylvania town where Flight 76 had come to a tragic rest, he took a crash course in the Federal Aviation Administration, courtesy of "Professor" Kevin Bryan.

But, really, all Storm had to convince the world that he was George Faytok from the FAA's Office of Accident Investigation and Prevention was a flimsy white badge and his own chutzpah.

His orders from Jones were to figure out what

made the plane go down and figure it out fast. He was driving in a white Chevrolet with an FAA seal that one of the nerds had gotten by hacking into an FAA public relations guy's computer, downloading it, and turning it into a decal that another one of Jones's agents had hastily slapped on the side. On the back was a bumper sticker that instructed other motorists to call a 1-800 number if they saw the vehicle being driven unsafely.

Like that was even possible, given how underpowered the engine was compared to Storm's usual standards. Storm hated Chevys. He was a Ford man for a reason.

It was dusk, heading on full darkness, by the time Storm reached Interstate 83's exit 4. He turned off the highway on Forrest Avenue, which wasn't actually forested at all. He passed through a small town, then some typical modern housing subdivisions, and then made a turn on Kratz Road. In the way that this part of Pennsylvania did, it quickly transitioned from suburbia to farmland. He followed the winding road through a patchwork of woods and fields until he reached a police checkpoint.

This, Storm knew, was to keep out the riffraff—reporters, especially. Not that the fallen cargo plane had been as interesting to the media. The other crash sites of what were collectively being called the "Pennsylvania Three" were already becoming magnets for grieving family members; and, hence, for cameras. This site had no such hysteria. It was the quietest of the Pennsylvania Three.

Storm rolled down his window and presented his George Faytok badge. The local cop manning the roadblock had no idea that the FAA actually had little to no business at a crash investigation site being run by the National Transportation Safety Board. They were two completely separate federal agencies. The NTSB wasn't even part of the Department of Transportation.

Luckily for Storm, such administrative distinctions were lost on a young patrolman who was just trying to get to the end of his shift. The cop waved Storm through and told him to park the car along the side of Kratz Road.

Storm followed the instructions and was soon walking toward the crash site, which rose above the road on a small hill. He could already see the temporary light stanchions that had been erected over the field so investigators could continue working through the night. Their sodium halide glow cut through the advancing darkness.

Underneath, a small horde of humanity, moving in no discernible pattern, scurried about. Storm could already make out some of the larger pieces of the plane, strewn in a long line from the point of initial impact to their final resting places. The main fuselage had broken into several parts. He saw an engine here, a wing piece there, a tailpiece somewhere else. There were a lot of other plane parts that were even less identifiable. Confusing matters further was the plane's cargo, which was scattered over a wide area.

If Storm had an advantage going into this melee, it was simply that there were so many people—with so many different parts to play—and most of them didn't know what the others were supposed to be doing. It would allow him a certain amount of anonymity. All he had to do was act like he belonged there and had a job to do.

He bypassed the large tent that he could guess was serving as a temporary command center. Most of the people who would have known the FAA had no direct role in the initial phases of an investigation—and would have told him to get lost—were likely under that canvas awning.

Storm made a direct line toward the field. He moved from broken piece to shattered bit, not knowing exactly what he was looking for but, at the same time, not wanting to miss anything. He made brief eye contact with any number of NTSB employees, none of whom seemed to register that he wasn't one of them.

He stopped to eavesdrop on a few conversations without being obvious. He heard bits of the jargon that Agent Bryan had hastily tried to teach him. But nothing really popped out. Much of it was just loose talk about colleagues, accommodations, travel, or other things that did not interest Storm.

He had started at the back of the debris field and was working his way forward, if only because that was the opposite direction that most of the other people were going. That way, he wouldn't see the same person twice. Eventually, Storm knew he might have to risk making contact with one of the men or women scurrying around him. For now, he wanted to be a fly on the proverbial wall.

He had just reached a particularly interesting piece of metal and bent over to study it when someone decided to swat at the fly.

"Excuse me? Who are you?" someone asked.

"George Faytok," Storm said, without a moment's hesitation. "I'm with the FAA."

Storm stood. And then, because he had long

ago learned the best defense was a good offense, he added, "Who are you?"

"Tim Farrell. I'm with the Structures Working Group."

Storm nodded, knowingly. Bryan had explained this part to him. The NTSB's "Go Team" consisted of eight working groups, each responsible for investigating certain aspects of a crash—everything from the Systems Working Group (which studied the plane's hydraulics, pneumatics, and electronics) to the Human Performance Working Group (which studied the crew's drug, alcohol, and medical problems).

"Hell of a thing, isn't it?" Storm said.

Farrell wasn't distracted. "I'm sorry, Mr. Faytok, but what is the FAA doing out here?"

"Oh," Storm said. "We've had some changes to 8020.11C. I'm surprised you didn't hear about them."

"Excuse me?"

"Sorry, 8020.11C. That's the number for our Aircraft Accident and Incident Notification, Investigation, and Reporting Policy. There have been some changes to Chapter One, Section Nine, Part . . . oh, jeez, C or D? I can't even remember anymore. Don't ask me to quote line and verse. It's the part that governs our interactions with the NTSB. What it says is I actually have to lay eyeballs on what you guys are doing."

Farrell jammed his fists in his side. "I hadn't heard about that."

"It's still your crash site," Storm said, raising his hands as if to surrender. "That hasn't changed, obviously. It's just one of those typical cover-your-ass things. I guess there was a superlight that went down in Ohio or something and some wires got crossed between you guys and us. Some higher-up who felt the need to justify his job decided we had to tighten up on our monitoring. Hence, policy change."

Farrell fingered a cell phone clipped to his belt. "I think I have to call the IIC."

Bryan had taught Storm this, too. The IIC was the Investigator-in-Charge, the person responsible for coordinating all the working groups, the highest ranking official at the site. If the IIC got involved, Storm might as well slap handcuffs on himself. Impersonating a federal official to gain access to a secure crash investigation site broke at least four laws he could think of off the top of his head. It would certainly land him in the local jail for a spell. Jones would probably let him rot there as punishment for allowing himself to get caught.

"I already talked to him," Storm said, breezily. "But waste his time if you want to. I'm sure he's got nothing better to do."

Storm bent back over the piece of metal he had been studying. Farrell unclipped his cell phone. Storm readied himself to flee.

Farrell pushed the two-way talk button on the phone and said, "Hey, I'll be back in a second. I'm just looking at something with this guy from the FAA."

"The FAA?" the voice on the other end said.

"Yeah, I guess they've had some kind of policy change."

"All right. See you back here in a bit."

Storm felt his insides relax. He focused his attention—for real this time—on the piece of metal that had caught his eye previously.

"Pretty weird, huh?" Farrell said.

"I'll say," Storm replied.

"What do you think? It's a piece of the forward pressure bulkhead, right?"

"Sure looks that way to me," Storm said, as if he had personally studied hundreds, if not thousands, of forward pressure bulkheads.

"What do you think did *that*?" Farrell asked, pointing to a line that had been cut in the metal.

In a field full of things that had been twisted and sheared by the force of impact, this line was perfectly straight. Even Storm's untrained eye could tell the angle was wrong. And yet the cut was incredibly precise.

"I don't know," Storm said.

Except he did know. Among Storm's abiding interests were high-tech weaponry and gadgets, which he jokingly called "toys." He was constantly pressing Jones to give him an inside line on the latest toys—the classified stuff that no one else got to see. Not long ago, Jones had arranged for Storm to make a visit to a military contractor for the demonstration of a new high-energy laser beam.

You could take down an airplane with this thing, the engineer had told him.

The words came back to Storm now. The weapon he had seen was still in beta version. It needed to be shrunk down to a more usable size and then made sturdy enough for the battlefield. What it didn't need was more power. It was already a hundred kilowatts—the equivalent of one thousand 100-watt lightbulbs being focused in one tiny beam, only a few hundred nanometers wide.

The heat that resulted was incredibly intense.

Storm had watched a demonstration of the laser easily slicing through a thick sheet of metal.

The incision looked exactly like the one that had been cut in the piece of metal in front of him.

CHAPTER 7

PANAMA CITY, Panama

The most striking feature of Eusebio Rivera's seventieth-floor penthouse—something all visitors to it beheld with wonder—was a massive saltwater fish tank.

It occupied an entire wall's worth of space, and it separated his home office from his bedroom suite, meaning he could see it whether he was at work or at leisure. It was filled with fish in every color of the rainbow: clown fish and angelfish, hawk fish and lionfish, hamlets and grunts, all swimming happily above a plastic reef that had been made to look just like the real thing.

What they didn't see—unless they looked very carefully—was Rivera's favorite part of the fish tank, the reason he commissioned it for his home in the first place. Camouflaged in the craggy recesses of the imitation coral, just below all those oblivious fish, was the drawn, menacing, monstrous face of a moray eel, watching, waiting, needing only to decide which part of the smorgasbord he wanted for his lunch before he struck.

Some moray eel owners went out of their way to make sure they stocked fish that the creature wouldn't eat. Not Rivera. He often kept the eel in a small side section of the tank, separated from the other fish, so it would be plenty hungry when he unleashed it. He loved watching it hunt.

Rivera thought of himself as being just like that moray eel. He was not as pretty as the other inhabitants of the tank. He was, truth be told, overweight and somewhat homely. He certainly wasn't as beloved as, say, the clown fish. His flesh may well have been toxic, just like the eel.

But he never went hungry. The moray eel could lie in wait for hours or even days, never moving, until it became part of the scenery. And then it snatched what it wanted.

Patience. It was all about patience.

Take, for example, the bottle of Ardbeg whiskey he had pulled from his liquor cabinet on the wet bar that occupied the other side of his home office, the one opposite the fish tank. It was Scottish in origin, naturally, and was already aged more than twenty years when he bought it. Rivera was under the mistaken impression that whiskey continued to age even after it had been bottled, so he waited another ten years to open it. He had been biding his time for just the right occasion.

There just hadn't been many of them lately. Not until tonight, anyway.

He pressed a button on his desk, paging his personal secretary, who sat outside his office in a small sitting area. It was a space she shared with Hector and Cesar, Rivera's well-armed and well-paid bodyguards, who kept an eye on a bank of security cameras.

"Is he here yet?" Rivera asked in raspy-sounding Spanish.

"No, sir. But security just called to say his Cadillac

has pulled into the parking garage. So I expect him any moment."

"Excellent," Rivera said.

He needed a little celebration, given the events of the past year. Rivera was the founder and sole proprietor of the Grupa de 2000, an engineering and construction firm that specialized in dredging, marine construction, and commercial diving. He had been a young man when he founded it in 1977, the year the United States agreed to return the Canal Zone to Panamanian sovereignty by the year 2000.

Back then, in the seventies, Rivera liked to joke that there were three wheelbarrows and two shovels in the entire country. He exaggerated—but only slightly. Panama in 1977 was woefully unprepared for the responsibility of maintaining and operating the most economically and strategically important waterway in the world. Its capital city was an embarrassment, not even third rate.

Things had changed much in Panama since that time and it was because of men like Rivera. He was part of the new breed, one that learned at the knee of U.S. contractors until it had the technological know-how needed to be autonomous. The ascendance of these native-controlled companies brought both pride and prosperity across the tiny isthmus. It spurred a building boom that transformed Panama City into a first-rate metropolis with a skyline that rivaled that of Miami or Boston. The growth had only accelerated after authority for the canal was officially returned to Panama on December 31, 1999.

It was quite a moment for Panama, one that was euphoric but also bittersweet. The country had long fought for leadership of its most important resource.

And yet by the time it finally won it, the canal was already slowly starting to become obsolete. Larger container ships, ones that could not fit through the canal's narrow locks, were bypassing Panama and going around the tip of South America. The ships were called post-Panamax and super post–Panamax, and their very names spoke to the urgency of Panama's situation. The riches from the most lucrative trading relationship in the entire world, the one between China and the East Coast of the United States, were slowly slipping away.

The announcement, a few years later, of the Panama Canal expansion project—an ambitious widening of the locks that would allow larger ships (and more of them) to begin routing themselves through Panama—looked like it would solve all that. As long as the expansion happened, the boom would continue.

Then the construction delays hit. And the world credit crunch occurred. And the project surged wildly over budget.

The Autoridad del Canal de Panama, the authority that oversaw all aspects of the canal, continued to insist publicly that all was well. Meanwhile, it had begun a series of desperate appeals: first to the Panamanian government, which pleaded poverty, then to the United States, which had, so far, refused all entreaties.

Construction had ground to a virtual halt. Panama kept pretending all was well. But Rivera, who had leveraged himself under the belief the expansion project would continue unabated, knew better. The Autoridad del Canal de Panama had paid his company for two days of work in the last thirty. He had more than a thousand workers who depended on him for their livelihoods, leases that were past due, and loans that were in danger of slipping into default. He was on the brink of a crisis, of losing all that he had worked for over the last four decades.

The phone on Rivera's desk bleeped twice.

"Sir, Mr. Villante is here," he heard.

Rivera went to the fish tank and raised the partition that separated the eel from the other fish. The creature darted to the other side. The other fish gave it a broad swath, but it was no danger to them. Not then. The eel always preferred an ambush. Rivera would enjoy watching it later.

"Send him in, send him in," Rivera said.

Carlos Villante was a deputy director of the Autoridad del Canal de Panama, a dashing sort blessed with good looks and style. As the man who oversaw the expansion project and had a heavy hand in awarding the contracts for it, he was Rivera's most important contact within the authority—the moray eel's cash cow, as it were.

Rivera had opened the door to his office before Villante could even reach it to knock.

"Come in, Carlos, come in," he said.

"It is nice to see you, Eusebio."

Rivera shook with his right hand, while displaying his prized Scotch in his left. "This is the bottle I have been telling you about, the one I have been saving for happy news," Rivera said. "I am glad you will be able to enjoy this with me. Come, come."

Villante allowed himself to be escorted to a sectional couch that overlooked the canal and the skyscrapers that lined it, most of them built with the money made by the canal, either directly or indirectly. As a deputy director of the authority that ran the canal, Villante was considered important, influential. Rivera knew he was not the only man to court Villante's attention.

Yet Rivera did so cautiously. In a region of the world where graft flowed freely, Villante made it known to Rivera and others he would not accept a bribe.

However, he did drive a Cadillac, so it stood to reason he was accepting money from somewhere. Rivera and others had gone to great lengths to figure it out, with no success. To be sure, he was in *someone's* pocket. And once Rivera figured out who, he would have it as a bargaining chip to use with the deputy director. In the meantime, Rivera employed the lower level of inducement that was perfectly aged Scotch.

"What are we celebrating?" Villante asked, lowering himself into a suede-covered captain's chair.

Rivera handed him a glass of amber-colored liquid. "You have heard about the airplanes that crashed in the United States, have you not?"

Villante looked at him sharply, then set the glass down. "That is not something to celebrate. That is something to mourn."

"Ordinarily, I would agree with you. And when I am in church on Sunday, I will light a candle in the memory of all those who perished, then go to confessional to wash myself of the sin of feeling so much joy. But for now, we must drink: Erik Vaughn was among the lost."

"Vaughn?" Villante said. "I had not heard that. I was listening to the news on the way over and they said they had not released the names of any of the passengers yet. Are you sure?"

"Beyond a doubt," Rivera said without elaborating. "The only shame of it is that the U.S. has grounded all air travel for the time being, which means I will have to wait to travel to his grave to spit on it."

Villante did not need Rivera to explain his animosity for Congressman Erik Vaughn. The Autoridad del Canal de Panama had sent its director, Nico Serrano, to the United States to lobby for the three billion dollars needed to get the expansion project going again. It was a pittance to a government whose budget was nearing five trillion. And yet the congressman made it his personal mission to see that no aid was extended. A matter like that could be choked in committee, and Vaughn had squeezed the life out of it.

"With Vaughn out of the way, we'll get our money," Rivera continued. "I have already made phone calls to friends in the U.S. capital. The new Ways and Means committee chairman will be a man named Jared Stack. He bears us no animosity that I know of. The urgency of our situation must be impressed on him. You must tell Mr. Serrano to go back to the United States the moment the planes start flying again. My equipment has sat idle for too long."

"You seem very confident of the outcome."

"There is no doubt," Rivera assured him.

Villante tilted his head. "If I didn't know any better, I'd think you sabotaged that plane yourself."

"Now, now," Rivera said, smiling. "What would give you that idea?"

He raised his glass. "Let us drink: to the death of

Erik Vaughn, and the inherent reasonable nature of Jared Stack."

At the moment they tilted back their glasses, the moray eel darted out of the crevice where it had been hiding, snapped its jaws around an unsuspecting fish, and then retreated back to its den.

CHAPTER 8

FAIRFAX, Virginia

The image of a piece of a laser-incised sheet metal had chased Storm all the way back to Virginia.

Actually, it was two pieces of metal. There was the one he had seen on the ground in Pennsylvania. And there was the one he had seen in mid-flight as he clung to the wing of the airplane. He was, naturally, too busy to notice it at the time. But in his mind's eye, he could look back and see that the aileron also had a straight line singed into it.

Not for the first time in his life, Derrick Storm was only alive because someone's aim was just off. In the case of Flight 76, the laser had struck the underside of the cockpit, which had been catastrophic. On Flight 312, it had lopped off the wing. On Flight 494, it was the tail. All were parts that a plane could not fly without. Storm had been nothing more or less than lucky.

The idea of a weapon that powerful—in the hands of someone unafraid to use it to its ultimate and deadly capability—had Storm pushing the Chevy well past the speed limit. If he got a ticket, George Faytok would just have to deal with the points on his license.

He did not share his conclusions with the National Transportation Safety Board about what had happened to Flight 76. He did not feel like wasting the energy or, more importantly, the time. The NTSB would eventually put it together. Or not. A crash investigation like that was an exercise in closing the barn door after the horse has bolted, something that did not interest Storm. As long as flights remained grounded, the laser could not hurt anyone else. That was all that mattered for the moment.

Likewise, he had not yet briefed Jones, albeit for different reasons. With Jones, there was always the question of what he would do with the information he had been provided.

Storm wasn't sure if he wanted Jones knowing about the laser. Or, at the very least, he wanted the opportunity to think through the ramifications of giving him such knowledge. And Storm was going to the one place where he did his clearest thinking.

It was not, perhaps, the place people might have expected for a world traveler like Storm to find solace. Storm spoke eight languages. He owned a secret retreat in the Seychelles. He had once undergone rituals that signified his lifelong bond to an aboriginal tribe in the Australian outback. An orphanage in Bacău, Romania, bore his name. A man in Tangier, Morocco, considered him a brother and would welcome him to his Moorish castle at a moment's notice. The chief clerk at the International Court of Justice in The Hague owed him a thousand favors. A remote village above the Arctic Circle in Finland still thought of him as a conquering hero. There were those and dozens of other locations around the world where Derrick Storm could have gone and been welcomed, accepted, and treated like family.

Yet his preference was still a dowdy, split-level

ranch in Fairfax County, Virginia. And that was the front door he was pushing through shortly after ten o'clock.

"Hey, Dad, it's me," Storm called out.

"In here," Carl Storm responded from the living room.

Derrick walked in to see his father emerging from his Barcalounger. Carl had a full head of hair that had gone white. His eyebrows remained stubbornly black. His forehead was deeply lined, but it somehow made him look rugged instead of old. People often told Carl Storm he looked like the actor James Brolin. There was no question where Derrick had gotten his good looks.

The room was dark. The only light came from the television. The baseball game—the one the Storm boys were supposed to have attended—had been played under flags lowered to half-staff after Major League Baseball decided it was not going to be cowed by terrorists. The Orioles were putting the finishing touches on a 13–1 drubbing of the Yankees.

"Sorry we weren't there to see it in person," Derrick said, nodding at the game.

Carl Storm was on his feet. Derrick's mother had died when he was a young boy. Carl had never remarried. It had been just the two of them for a long time. Carl had been a single dad with a demanding job at the Federal Bureau of Investigation, but he had done everything he could to be twice the parent to his motherless son.

"You think I care about that after what you went through today?" Carl said. "Come here."

Derrick met him halfway across the room and Carl wrapped his arms around his son. Even if

Derrick had noticed a softening in Carl over the past few years, he remained a powerful man. His hugs still packed a wallop.

"Still, I'm going to make it up to you," Derrick said. "Rain check. Just as soon as I get the chance."

"Don't worry about it. I understand. To be honest, I'm a little surprised to see you here. What's up?"

"You got some time to talk?"

"You know you never even have to ask," Carl said. "You want a beer?"

"That would be great."

Carl returned with two Pabst Blue Ribbons—PBR being the only beer that Carl ever stocked. He muted the television and they sat, Carl in the Barcalounger and Derrick on a paisley patterned sofa. As with the rest of the house, the living room hadn't changed much since the lady of the house had passed. Whether this was a kind of tribute to her—or just a bachelor's reluctance to even attempt redecoration—was always a bit unclear to Derrick.

As they drained their drinks, Derrick told him about his experience aboard Flight 937, about what he had seen at the crash site and his certainty about what had caused the damage. Carl was retired now but hadn't lost any of the skills that had made him one of the FBI's best. He listened thoughtfully through the whole thing and was shaking his head when it was over.

"Sometimes I wonder when we'll learn," Carl said.

"What do you mean?"

He sighed. "Did I ever tell you about Ton Son Nhut?"

Derrick shook his head.

"Ton Son Nhut was an air force base just outside of Saigon," Carl said. "It was where most grunts arrived when they came in-country. And you have to remember, there were a half million guys in Vietnam at any point in time, so it was a busy place. You'd land and there would be a group of guys eagerly waiting for your plane, because that was their ride home. They'd actually shout 'replacements, replacements' at the fresh meat that was coming in."

Carl shook his head at the memory. He had done several tours of duty in Vietnam. As close as he was to his son, he seldom talked about that time in his life. He said it was because nothing very interesting happened to him. *It was mostly just boredom,* Carl had insisted. *You wouldn't be interested in any of it.* Derrick always wondered if there was more to it, but he respected his father's boundaries when it came to that long-ago conflict.

"Anyhow, I was coming into Ton Son Nhut for my third tour, so I knew my way around a little bit," Carl continued. "I was waiting for a Huey to take me into the boonies, but it was delayed for a few days by mechanical trouble or something. I was just wandering around the base when I came across the infirmary. They had—"

Carl stopped himself for a second to look away. The glow from the television, which was soundlessly tuned to the Orioles postgame show, reflected on his face.

"They had just accepted a medical chopper full of wounded civilians. It was the usual thing. A village had been harboring Vietcong and the air force had cooked it down with a load of napalm. It was just—"

Again, Carl had to compose himself.

"The thing about napalm is that it sticks to things. That was part of how it was designed. It sticks to houses, trees, human bodies. Even small bodies. And it burns so hot. Once it gets going, it's eight times hotter than boiling water. What that does to human flesh is . . . I mean, look, I had seen people burned with napalm before. But it was always combatants. And I didn't feel a lot of . . . I mean, I felt bad for them, I guess, but not too bad. When you got right down to it, it was either us or them, you know?

"But these civilians were something else. And you knew most of them weren't going to make it. People who burn up that bad linger a few days, but all the while their lungs are filling up with fluid. The body is trying to heal itself of these overwhelming injuries, but in doing so it actually begins to drown itself. A few survive, but most of them . . ."

Carl was shaking his head. His eyes were open, but Derrick got the sense they were now seeing things from long ago. "There was this little girl. From what I understood, she had lost her mother in the attack. And God knows where her father was. Probably in a tunnel somewhere, waiting to kill himself a GI. Anyway, she couldn't have been more than seven or eight. She was the sweetest little thing. One side of her face was perfect—olive eyes, high cheekbones. You could tell she was going to be a beautiful woman someday. Except the other side, it was just . . . it was ruined. The napalm had hit her on the left side and stuck to her. Her left arm had been completely burned off. Her ribs. Her leg. It had gotten everywhere. She was in so much pain.

"I visited her a few times, gave her chocolate bars from the PX to cheer her up, little dolls, that sort of thing. She tried to smile every time she saw me, even if she could only do it with half her face. The docs had her shot up with morphine, which helped some. But you could tell there were times when the morphine was wearing off and she didn't know how to ask for more. The pain had to be . . . I mean, you can't even imagine."

He brought the beer to his lips only to find it empty. Derrick tried to imagine what his father had looked like back then: his hair dark, his skin unlined. He would have been younger than Derrick was now. Young and powerful. And yet, in that moment, also powerless.

"Anyhow, the last night I was there, I had gone to visit her again. She just couldn't stop crying, the poor little thing. You could tell it hurt so bad. I ran to get a nurse to up the morphine, but they told me she was already getting the maximum dosage. So I just, I tried . . . I tried to cradle her. I mean, you could barely touch her, she was so fragile. But I wanted her to know that, damn it, someone still cared about her. Even someone from a country that had done this to her. I held her and she cried, and I held her some more. Eventually, she slipped into a coma, which was probably a blessing. And I kept holding her until . . ."

He didn't complete the thought, letting his voice trail off into the darkened living room.

"Anyway, when it was all over, I went straight to the Officer's Club to get as drunk as I knew how. I ended up sitting next to a young air force lieutenant, a Lieutenant Marlowe. I started talking about what I had just witnessed and it turned out he had been the one who airlifted the civilians there, so he had seen it, too. We started talking about the horrible things people did to each other, about war, and about the terrible irony that mankind was smart enough to be able to design these weapons and still dumb enough to use them on each other. You have to remember, this was the height of the Cold War, when the nuclear threat was still very real. And he said something like, *We just can't be trusted with certain weapons. There ought to be limits.* We promised each other that someday, if either of us ever got in a position of authority within the military, we'd use it to help enforce those limits."

Derrick nodded, pensively.

"Son, I'm an old man. I can't really do much to keep that promise anymore. But you can," Carl finished. "You have to do everything you can to get this weapon out of the hands of whoever has it. But you also have to make sure it doesn't fall into someone else's hands. Not even the United States. We can't be trusted, either."

"Okay," Derrick said. "Let's get to work."

TEN MINUTES LATER, CARL HAD BREWED A POT OF coffee. They were in the kitchen, which was perhaps the only one in tony Fairfax not to have undergone remodeling in the last thirty-odd years. It had been pulled from a time warp, all linoleum flooring and Formica countertops. The light fixture, which looked like something out of a seventies pizzeria, glowed brightly above them.

Derrick had his tablet lying on the table in front

of him. Carl had a laptop computer with a fresh legal pad and a sharpened pencil alongside it.

"At this point, we have to be thinking terrorist, yes?" Derrick said.

"Yes."

"What type are we focusing on? A group of violent 'true believers'? A lone wolf?"

"Any of the above. All of the above. The important thing to remember is terrorists come in all shapes and sizes. Sometimes they look like Osama bin Laden, yes. But Ted Kaczynski was a terrorist and he looked like half the computer science professors in this country. Timothy McVeigh was a terrorist and he looked like a pizza delivery boy. Sometimes they come in forms you don't expect."

"Right. And in this case, we still don't know what is motivating these terrorists or what they want. All we really know about them is what kind of weapon they used."

"This fancy laser," Carl said.

"That's right. A high-energy laser. That makes these terrorists different from Kaczynski or McVeigh. Those guys used fairly simple weapons, the kind that anyone with an Internet connection and half a brain could learn how to make in a few hours with stuff they could buy from a hardware store. A high-energy laser is a lot trickier. You can't find those parts at the Home Depot, and even if you could, your average wack job wouldn't know what to do with them. So the question becomes, how did these particular terrorists acquire that kind of expertise?"

"Could be a scientist or engineer who turned," Carl said.

"Could be. But anyone with those capabilities

would be highly valued by society. They would be well paid, well respected. Those people don't usually feel compelled to turn on the system that is rewarding them so well."

"Unless it's someone who feels like the system isn't rewarding them enough," Carl pointed out.

"Always a possibility. But I feel like it's more likely we're looking at some kind of situation where our expert is being forced against his or her will to help the terrorists. I think we're looking for a kidnapping."

Carl took a sip of his coffee, wincing at the beverage's temperature. "I don't know. Anyone who worked on a cutting-edge weapons project would need to have a pretty high security clearance. When I was at the bureau, one of the duties of the local field office was to keep an eye on people like that. If someone with a high clearance went missing, his or her boss would have made a big stink about it."

"So maybe it's not a kidnapping," Derrick said. "Maybe it's some form of blackmail. Or a member of the expert's family has been taken and is being held as collateral."

"I like that better as a theory. So how do we find the expert in trouble?"

Derrick stared into his coffee cup, as if the answer was floating somewhere in the black liquid. "We're looking at a fairly specialized field of study. There are probably no more than a few dozen people in the country who would have this kind of knowledge, if that. I bet as soon as we start looking, we'll see the same names, over and over. Let's dive into the literature, the academic journals and whatnot, and make a list of the possibilities, then start quietly checking in on them."

"Sounds good," Carl said.

Quietly, diligently, the Storm boys bent their heads over their respective devices. Carl Storm had joined the FBI before it went upscale, before movies and television made it trendy. He had gone off to work every day in thick-soled shoes and cheap suits. He believed in working a case from the ground up— no shortcuts, no slacking—and had raised Derrick to have the same investigative sensibilities.

As the hours passed, there were small bits of dialogue between them. *Would you check out . . . ? Don't bother with . . . Have you bumped across . . . ? I'm e-mailing you a pdf from . . .*

The sentences didn't even need to be completed. It was almost as if the men had joined brains, and it had not merely doubled their capacity. It had quadrupled it.

They worked steadily, without a break. Carl was the keeper of the list, which he inscribed in careful block letters on his legal pad. There didn't turn out to be as many names as Derrick thought there would be. Once they reached twenty, they just kept bumping into scientists they had already identified.

It was around 2 A.M. when Derrick said, "Okay. I feel like we've got a good start here. Let's divvy this up, start looking into these guys, and see if anything shakes out."

They did not have access to the kind of databases that Jedediah Jones's techs would be able to hack into. But as an ex–private investigator, Derrick knew his way around a public records search. And Carl was not so long-retired that he had lost his acuity.

Another hour went by. Carl made another pot of coffee, then heated up some frozen sticky buns, typical of the bachelor-inspired gourmet cooking

Derrick had grown up with. Even though he had since become something of an epicurean, Derrick still had a certain nostalgia for the frozen/canned/prepackaged gruel of his youth. It was his own odd version of comfort food.

Neither man made a noise about sleeping, or even being tired. The Storm stamina—willed from father to son—was legendary.

It was closing in on four o'clock when Derrick announced, "I got something. William McRae."

"The guy who had that piece in *Applied Physics Letters*?" Carl asked, as if he had a subscription to that publication coming to his mailbox for years.

"Yeah. Check this out."

Derrick spun his tablet around so his father could see it. The headline was from a weekly paper in Northern California called the *Hercules Express*: LOCAL SCIENTIST MISSING, WIFE SEEKS ANSWERS, it read.

"He disappeared three weeks ago," Derrick said. "He went out for a jog one day and didn't come back. You can read between the lines and tell the police did some stuff then, but basically treated him like a walk-away. Here's another piece."

Derrick tapped his tablet and another piece from the *Hercules Express* appeared: PUBLIC HELP SOUGHT TO FIND MISSING SCIENTIST.

As Carl's eyes scanned the piece, Derrick continued: "McRae fits. He went to MIT undergrad, Berkeley for his master's degree and doctorate in physics. He started working on solid-state lasers in the seventies at Lawrence Livermore National Laboratory, which has contracts to provide research to a variety of government agencies. McRae eventually became the director of the laser program, and while I'm sure a lot of his practical work was classified, his theoretical stuff was published all over. Three of the people he frequently coauthored with are on our list as well. The difference is they still work there. McRae had started his own consulting business and continued tinkering with this, but it looks like it was a hobby. He officially retired from Lawrence Livermore three years ago."

Carl snapped his fingers.

"That's why no one noticed him missing," he said. "Once he was retired, he lost his security clearance. Amazing how the world forgets about you when you get put out to pasture."

Derrick ignored the commentary. "So we're agreed that if you were a terrorist who wanted to kidnap someone who knew enough to help you build a big, scary laser beam—and you wanted it to be someone who was off the radar—this would be the guy. It seems the locals were at least somewhat thorough in their efforts to find the guy. Think they missed something?"

"I bet there's an anxious wife out in California who would love to tell you," Carl said.

"Yeah, there's just one problem."

"What's that?"

"Commercial flights are grounded."

"Can you take a train? Drive?"

"No time," Derrick said. "I have to call Jones. I'm sure the air force is still flying. He can get me on a military jet."

"You know how I feel about that snake."

"I know," Derrick said. "But right now I have no choice."

Carl grunted. He had made his displeasure with Jedediah Jones known many times. But even the most loving, protective father realizes he eventually needs to let his child make his—or her—own decisions. All the father can do is hope he has instilled enough of the right values in the child that those decisions are the right ones.

Derrick had gone back to his notes. "The only article William McRae published since his retirement was extolling the virtues of a promethium laser beam. It was an update of work he had done during the eighties and had come back to."

"Promethium? Sounds like something out of a comic book."

"No, it's a real element. I looked it up. Number sixty-one on your periodic table. Named after the titan in Greek mythology who stole fire from the gods and gave it to mankind."

"At times like this, I wish we could give it back," Carl said, then hoisted his coffee mug in the air. "To Lieutenant Marlowe, wherever he is. We're doing our best, buddy."

Carl drank, then set down his mug. And Derrick knew that his father's mind was once again wandering back to a little girl burned by napalm and the memory of her gasping for her final breaths.

CHAPTER 9

Marble wasn't supposed to sound hollow.

Katie Comely did not have a degree in geology, like Professor Raynes did, but she had spent enough weeks down in the crypt where she had been working to know exactly what noise the floor made when you dropped something on it.

It was solid. Like a *chunk*. Like there was nothing but a few hundred feet of sand under it, and then bedrock under that, and then the Earth's crust—all firm substances, all the way down to the molten core of the planet.

But that was not the timbre of the clanging that resulted when she dropped her hammer. It was more of a *thwok*. Like there was a pocket of air behind it; a small chamber, perhaps, or some kind of opening that echoed.

The first time she heard it, she almost didn't believe it. She assumed she had been underground too long and it was starting to play with her senses. So she picked up the hammer and dropped it again. Sure enough: *thwok*. She moved to another spot. *Chunk*. Back to the first spot. *Thwok*.

There was no doubt. Katie had been closing up a crate containing a set of common artifacts—some urns that would not generate much interest, tools employed by ancient construction workers, a chunk of wall with hieroglyphs proclaiming the greatness of a pharaoh who ruled Lower Egypt before it merged with Upper Egypt five thousand years ago. Outside the crypt, up on the surface, some of the dayworkers who were hired to take care of the heavy lifting were struggling with another crate at the direction of some of the graduate students.

She had the crypt to herself. She shoved a wisp of blond hair that had escaped her ponytail away from her face. Maybe she should go fetch the others before proceeding, except . . .

Well, maybe it was nothing, right?

Or maybe it was the greatest find since Tutankhamen.

Only one way to find out. She went to the corner where she kept a crowbar, and brought it over to the piece of marble in question. There were narrow slits around the sides of it where it met up with other pieces of marble. She worked the crowbar under gently, being careful not to damage the stone. She pulled.

The crowbar was long enough that it had leverage to lift the heavy piece, but only barely. She peered underneath, hopeful.

And, yes, there was an opening where the floor should have been. No question. But unless she got the stone moved out of the way, she wouldn't be able to see how deep it was. Her angle was wrong.

Her heart had started pumping double-time. Every archaeologist knew the story of Howard Carter, the man credited with finding Tutankhamen, the man who refused to believe that every tomb had been discovered and plundered. He spent years searching before going down what appeared to be a stairway to nowhere, finding a sealed door that led to the final resting spot of a little-known boy king who had been undisturbed for millennia.

Was this a similar situation? Would she long tell the story of dropping the hammer, hearing the hollow report of the stone, and having the hunch to investigate? Or would Raynes take all the credit, downplaying her role to the point where she would end up a mere footnote? *Who was that postdoc anyway?*

There would be more danger of that if she went up to the surface and asked for help to move the marble slab. Raynes might insist on being the first one in—him or one of the pushier male graduate students, who would argue his physicality was needed.

But if she got it shoved aside by herself and then made the find, there would be no danger of that.

She looked around the space where she had been working. Off in another corner there was a rolling jack the dayworkers used to help get the crates out. She retrieved it, wheeled it next to the slab, then crowbarred the marble up again with one hand. When it was just high enough, she used her other hand to slide the jack underneath.

Then she began pumping it upward, slowly raising the marble until there was enough space for her to crawl under. She was breathing heavily now. She wiped her brow and turned her flashlight on the hole. The beam disappeared into the darkness without reaching an end.

It was a passageway, for sure. But to what?

She went over to her backpack and grabbed her headlamp, securing it to her forehead and switching it on. This way, she could keep her hands free.

She lowered herself on her belly and slid toward it, preparing to crawl down the hole. She took one last nervous look at her jack. If it faltered—if the marble slipped away or some other unseen calamity hit it—she would be trapped underneath. There was no way she'd be able to lift so large a stone by herself. It might be a long, lonely time before someone found her.

If they found her. The thought occurred that she ought to tell someone what she was doing.

But then they might try to talk her out of it, or go in themselves, or . . .

Taking one last deep breath, she slunk under the slab, down through the opening headfirst. It was only slightly wider than she was—and Katie was slender—but that made it easier to hold on to the sides as she descended. After perhaps ten feet, she felt it beginning to turn, gradually flattening out. There was just enough room for Katie to slink forward on her belly.

The passageway—yes, it was a passageway—had been lined with clay, which had long ago hardened, forming an effective barrier against a cave-in. Katie kept her eyes on the tunnel ahead of her. The flashlight beam only went so far, and she found herself straining to see beyond it in the distance.

She was concentrating so hard on peering into the darkness that, at first, it didn't register that something was coming toward her. Her ears told her first. It sounded like snapping.

Then her light fell on an emperor scorpion. Katie shrieked. It was coming toward her. Fast. It had to be at least eight inches long. Its stinger was arched up behind it.

Raynes had warned all his students—in particular, the Americans who had no experience with the poisonous arthropods—to check their shoes and beds before sliding their feet or bodies inside. Scorpions loved to rest in dark, enclosed places, he said.

He had not given any instructions on what to do if one was shuffling toward you in a tunnel. One of the dayworkers had been stung on the forearm a few weeks earlier. The administering of the antidote had not prevented it from swelling up like a football, nor had it stopped the pain. The man's moaning could be heard all over camp. Last she heard, it had gotten infected, and the man was in danger of losing his arm.

The scorpion advanced. She screamed again, like it would do her any good. Could scorpions even hear?

She tried sliding backward, but the creature was coming at her faster than she could back up in such an enclosed space. She was probably disturbing its nest. It was clearly determined to fight.

Well, in that case, so was Katie. She had not come this far—to this country, to this crypt, to this hole—to be cowed by a bug. She balled up her hand and let the scorpion scuttle closer. Closer. Closer still.

Then, just as it was about to strike, Katie pounded it with her fist. She felt and heard the crunch of exoskeleton. She drew her fist back and mashed a second time, then a third, not waiting to see if its body was still moving. She was taking no chances.

When she was thoroughly satisfied that her hand felt too moist with scorpion guts for the thing to possibly still be alive, she allowed herself to look. Sure enough, the thing was flattened. A greenish-yellowish ooze leaked from one side. The stinger, still curled above it, twitched for a few seconds before it finally stilled.

She shuddered, then exhaled heavily. It took

considerable will to make herself move forward again, and the only thing that did it was the thought that now took hold: the scorpion had to be coming from somewhere.

Three turns later, Katie discovered where. Her headlamp illuminated a large opening of some sort. She could make out the far wall, but nothing underneath. Not until she was out of the tunnel. All she could tell was that the cavern was lined with clay, just like the tunnel had been, suggesting that whoever dug it had done so a long time ago. The more modern Egyptians lined interior chambers such as this with stone.

The fall from the tunnel to the floor was only a few feet, but she couldn't see much of where she was landing. For all she knew, it was covered with snapping, stinging scorpions. She dropped and came to her feet quickly, ready to stomp any of the little devils that dared come near her.

But the floor was bare. Satisfied she was out of danger for a moment, she focused her beam on her surroundings.

And nearly lost her breath.

It was another crypt. The hieroglyphs lining the walls told her as much. Her light panned over an open stone sarcophagus along the far wall. The lid, also stone, lay in several pieces on the floor next to it, suggesting tomb robbers had reached it at some point, perhaps in antiquity, before the entire complex had been buried under sand.

Keeping her eyes wide, walking gingerly so as not to disturb anything, she moved slowly toward the ancient coffin. She leaned over, and then peered inside.

And nearly lost her breath again.

There was a mummy, wrapped in brittle, yellow linen. The funeral mask, if there had ever been one, was long gone. But the body was still there. Intact. Perfect. The arms were folded, right over left.

This was not just any mummy.

This was a pharaoh.

"Oh, my God," she whispered, even though she had the place to herself.

It was a find that would change the trajectory of her career, a life-changing stroke of incredible good luck, potentially a discovery that would add to—or alter—what the world knew about one of its most important ancient civilizations.

But only if the mummy didn't suffer the same fate as her Khufu statue. She had to get it safely to the lab, or this would all amount to nothing.

NIGHT HAD COME TO THE DESERT. AND WITH THE night came the cold. Sand heated up quickly under the scorching solar glare, but it lost heat just as quickly once the sun set. Temperature swings of sixty degrees or more were not unusual.

Katie had a blanket wrapped around her as she stared into a fire, watching the flames waver and the sparks leap into the sky. Most nights, they didn't build a fire—wood was too scarce, and it would be like a signal flare for wandering bandits.

But Professor Raynes had declared that they would celebrate what just might be the most significant find of the whole expedition. And so they had built a great bonfire. Many toasts followed: to Katie, to Raynes, to Egypt, to the dig's sponsors, to anything anyone could think to raise a glass to.

All around her there were drunk and/or dozing

archaeologists. The graduate students had gone at it particularly hard.

Only Katie—supposedly the most celebrated of the celebrants—had not partaken.

And now she stared into the flames, lost in her thoughts. She had spent most of her life as a student, absorbing information that had been discovered and promulgated by others. But now she was poised on the brink of an important transition: she was going to be in a position to be a creator of information, to add to human knowledge—not just take from it. To actually be in a position to make a contribution to a field she loved so much was almost dizzying. And yet she also knew it could be snatched from her, quite literally at any second.

"Everything okay?"

The voice made her jump and gave her a shot of adrenaline. It had been quite a day for her nerves.

"You scared me," she said, bringing her hand to her chest.

Professor Raynes patted her shoulder. "Sorry, sorry. I thought you heard me coming."

She shook her head.

"You ought to be the drunkest among us," he said. "Why are you the most sober?"

"Because I'm worried."

"About what?"

She tilted her head toward some of the dayworkers, who were just out of earshot. "Them. They know exactly what was found down there. And I'm sure they can sense from the excitement how valuable it is. If one of them heads back to town and spreads the word that there's been a big discovery, how long is it going to take until we're seeing another dust cloud with thieves riding in front of it?"

Raynes nodded. "I've been thinking about that—"

"We have to do more than think!"

"Settle down, settle down," he said, putting both hands up like a crossing guard trying to halt school-children. "I'm already taking steps to deal with that."

"Don't tell me by hiring more guards. They turn tail and run the second we need them," she said, aware she was sounding whiny. "I'd rather try to shoot these bastards myself than rely on those jokers."

"No, no. We're through with them. I've con-tacted the IAPL."

"Umm . . . okay?" Katie said, her confusion plain.

"Sorry. International Art Protection League. It's an NGO that specializes in this sort of thing. They started in Bern, Switzerland, and focused on crack-ing down on museum theft in Europe, helping police agencies cooperate with each other across interna-tional boundaries. Too often pieces that were being stolen from one country would appear on the black market in another one, where they weren't even aware of the theft. They had some good successes early on and attracted some major donors, and now they've branched out into Asia and Africa."

"I don't want to catch these guys once the mummy is already on the black market, I want—"

"That's the thing that's made the IAPL so effec-tive. They realized a while back you had to be proactive as well as reactive. They send teams out, filled with—I don't know what you would call them—mercenaries, I guess. Soldiers of fortune. They're highly trained and they won't run the moment some guy in a pickup truck fires a few rounds in the air."

"And are they going to help us?"

"We'll see," the professor said. "We've made the request. We'll just have to hold tight and hope for the best. It'll take a few days to extract that mummy. Maybe they'll be here by then."

Katie's eyes returned to the fire. "I hope so," she said. "I really hope so."

CHAPTER 10

HERCULES, California

I f there was one good thing about working for Jedediah Jones, it was that most of the free world owed him favors.

Jones had traded one of them to get Derrick Storm a seat on a military cargo plane that had taken off from Andrews Air Force Base at first light.

The mood aboard had been tense. The speculation in the media was that terrorists were responsible for the flights that had gone down, even if no one could guess how they were doing it. The crew had decided that with commercial flights grounded, there was at least a 50 percent chance the terrorists would target military planes next.

"Don't worry, we're not going anywhere near Pennsylvania," the captain had assured Storm.

Storm had nodded, not wanting to tell the man that the weapon was most likely mobile, and that it could probably be wheeled anywhere. Nothing in the sky was safe until Storm could figure out who was doing this and why.

Jones had been typically taciturn when Storm had shared his thoughts about the laser beam and the missing scientist who might be behind it. "Sounds like we need to get you out to California," was all Jones had said.

The flight chased the sun across the country, making good time in empty airspace. It landed just as the Bay Area was purging itself of morning traffic. In an unmarked vehicle borrowed from the air force—another underpowered Chevrolet, unfortunately—Storm drove out to Hercules, a small town just north of Berkeley.

William McRae's onetime home was a large brown ranch with tan shutters set on a pretty piece of land near the top of a hill. Storm could see a deck on the back of the house that provided a commanding view of the valley spread below. On a clear day, he bet some of the tall buildings of San Francisco were visible. It was what realtors would call a million-dollar view. While Storm was no professional appraiser, he would not be surprised if the house would fetch something in that neighborhood if it was ever put on the market.

The lawn was immaculately maintained. The gardens were likewise spotless. There was an orderliness to the layout that suggested a logical mind was behind its creation.

An American flag hung by the front door. On an oak tree next to the driveway, someone had tied a yellow ribbon.

Storm parked on the street and walked up the driveway, hoping he might find some answers inside the house at the top of it.

He climbed the five slate steps that led to a small patio in front of what appeared to be the main door to the house. He pressed the doorbell button. It responded with an arpeggio-like chime. No one came to the door. He rang again. Nothing.

It wasn't like he had an appointment. Then again,

he also didn't have time to wait for one. He descended the steps and looked around. No sign of anyone. He walked back toward a garage he had passed on his way up. One of the garage doors was open. There were two cars inside.

He kept going, rounding the corner of the house and into the backyard. There, he found a white-haired woman hunched on her knees, digging in a well-mulched flower bed with a small trowel. She wore floral-patterned gloves with matching gardening clogs.

"Alida McRae?" Storm said.

"Yes." She looked up at him with steady blue eyes.

"My name is Derrick Storm. I'd like to ask some questions about your husband. Do you mind talking with me?"

"Are you with the state police?"

Storm wore a blazer and button-down shirt with jeans underneath. She was mistaking him for a plain-clothes cop.

"No, ma'am."

"The FBI?"

"No, ma'am."

She jammed the trowel in the ground. "Then who are you, exactly?"

"I'm a contractor for the government. It's best I don't say which part."

"And what is your interest, exactly?"

"Same as yours. I want to find your husband and see that he is returned home safely."

She stood, pulled off her gardening gloves, and let them drop to the grass. She drew a cell phone out of her pocket and began punching numbers.

"Ma'am?" Storm asked.

She didn't answer. She took a few steps farther away but spoke loudly enough that Storm had no trouble hearing. "Yes, Chief, this is Alida McRae. A strange man claiming to be from the government has shown up at my house and wants to ask me questions about my husband. Could you please send an officer out to the house immediately?" She waited for a reply. "Yes, I suppose you can send two if you'd like. The more the merrier. Thank you."

She hung up and faced him. Storm knotted his fingers in front of his body, thought about whistling. Jones had protocols in place to handle this sort of thing—numbers that could be called, cover stories at the ready, people who would vouch for Storm. He just wished he didn't have to waste the time right now.

"The police are coming right out," she said. "I'm going to have them check you out before I say a word."

"Okay."

She stood there, staring at him sternly, her fists jammed on her hips. "I'm sure they're going to ask for ID."

"Okay," Storm said again, rocking back on his heels.

"Their response times are quite good. They'll probably be here in three minutes."

"Good," Storm said.

"Good?"

"Yes, good. The sooner we get this over with, the sooner we can get on to finding your husband."

She stared at him just a bit longer. "And you said your name was Storm?"

"Yes, ma'am."

"Why don't you come up on the back deck. I'll make us some iced tea. We can talk there."

"Are you sure you don't want to wait for the police?"

She scooped up her gloves and gardening trowel. "I didn't really call the police. They've been no damn use to me anyway. I just wanted to see how you'd respond. I figured if you were legitimate you'd stay and if you were a con man you'd run."

Storm smiled. He liked Alida McRae already. "I'm legitimate enough," he said.

"To be honest, I don't really care who you are or which part of the government you work for. If you're trying to bring Billy home, you've got my full cooperation."

OVER THE NEXT TWENTY MINUTES, STORM SAT ON THE McRae family deck, iced tea in front of him, the Alhambra Valley laid out beneath him, and made Alida go through her version of her husband's disappearance.

There were no surprises. Her husband was gone. She didn't know why. None of his routines had changed in the days or weeks prior to it. Nothing in his behavior suggested he was going anywhere.

Storm asked some questions but didn't sense he was extracting any new insight out of her. Most of what she said had already been reported in the paper.

When he was satisfied she had nothing more to tell him about the mysterious vanishing of William McRae, Storm changed subjects. He told her about his suspicion, now twice-confirmed, that a high-energy laser beam had been responsible for knocking planes from flight over Pennsylvania, and his belief that the people responsible might have been forcing her husband to do their bidding.

Alida's face became graver the more he spoke. "He had done a lot of work on high-energy lasers," she said quietly.

"I know. I saw his name splashed across the literature. Would he know how to make one?"

She just nodded.

"The only paper Bill published in the last three years was about the feasibility of a promethium laser beam," Storm said. "Do you know anything about that?"

"I guess you could say so. I helped him write it."

Storm must have looked curious, because Alida answered the question he didn't even ask. "I helped him write all his papers. Billy is a scientist, through and through. Even with all the papers he's published, words have never been his strong point. I was an English major. I've been ghostwriting for him since graduate school."

"No shame in having a ghostwriter," Storm said. "Some of the best books published every year are penned by talented writers whose identity the public will never know."

"I enjoyed it. Bill's research is everything to him. If I wasn't conversant on it, there would have been whole decades of our marriage when we wouldn't have had much to talk about. Some of the other wives at the laboratory just throw their hands up and say they can't understand any of what their husbands do. I feel like they're giving up on a big chunk of their partners' lives. It's really not *that* incomprehensible once you get into it."

"Do you think you could explain it to me, Mrs. McRae?"

"First of all, call me Alida. When you call me Mrs. McRae it makes me feel like an old lady. Second of all: of course I can explain it to you. I wasn't asleep when I was writing all those papers, you know."

"Okay, Alida," Storm said, smiling. "Let's start with: why promethium?"

For the first time since they met, Alida smiled. "Do you like science fiction, Mr. Storm?"

"What red-blooded American boy raised on Ray Bradbury and Rod Serling doesn't?"

"In that case, I think you and Billy are kindred spirits. One of the reasons he wanted to pursue it was simply for the name. I mean, a promethium laser beam. It just sounds cool."

"It does."

"But there's also a scientific utility to it as well. How much do you know about solid-state lasers?"

"Perhaps I should have also mentioned *Star Trek* creator Gene Roddenberry? But that's about as far as it goes."

She smiled again. "Okay. I'll give you the non–science fiction primer. I'll try not to bore you with the details, but one of the big distinctions in the laser world is three-stage versus four-stage. There are only a small handful of elements that make four-stage lasers."

"What's the difference?"

"Four-stage is a hundred times more powerful than three-stage."

"Big difference," Storm said.

"Probably ninety percent of the solid-state lasers out there are made with neodymium, which happens to be next to promethium on the periodic table. They're both elements that are known as lanthanides, which are . . . I'm losing you, aren't I?"

"A little. I slept a lot in Mr. Menousek's chemistry class, which I regret. Most of the chemistry I know about deals with how to make and defuse bombs."

She let that pass without comment. "Lanthanides are better known as rare earth metals. They have all kinds of practical uses, especially in high-tech gadgetry. They're mined all over the world, from Sweden to South Africa to Australia to China. Anyhow, where was I?"

"Neodymium."

"Right. Most of the lasers are made with neodymium. But Bill had always had his eye on promethium. Every element has a different wavelength when you make a laser out of it. Remember ROY G BIV from science class? That's the color spectrum as it appears in nature. The lower wavelengths are red. The higher wavelengths are violet. Still with me?"

"Definitely."

"Okay, so promethium checks in at nine-hundred-thirty-three nanometers, which is not in the visible spectrum. But when you put a cesium filter on it, it radiates at four-hundred-fifty-nine nanometers, which is a very pure blue, the best blue you can get from a four-stage element."

"Are you sure you weren't the lead researcher on that paper?" Storm teased. "Your recall of those numbers is amazing."

"Have you ever published a scientific paper? You end up writing it and rewriting it and editing it so many times to please some idiotic review committee, you feel like you have the thing memorized by the end. Anyhow, four-hundred-fifty-nine nanometers is significant, because it turns out to be the perfect wavelength for slicing through the Earth's atmosphere, which is also very blue in the middle of the day. There's almost no loss of power."

"So if you were designing a high-energy laser beam that you wanted to use to, say, shoot down airplanes, this would be the stuff?"

"Bill always said that a high-energy promethium laser beam would be an incredible weapon," she confirmed.

Storm tapped his finger on the countertop. Sometimes he hated being right. She poured him an iced tea refill from a glass pitcher lightly beaded with sweat. Storm started posing his next question as she topped off his glass.

"Well, now, let me ask you this: if promethium is such dynamite stuff, why didn't he do more with it while he was at Lawrence Livermore? Why wasn't he trying to develop this for the military? Why wait until he retired?"

"Oh. Right. Promethium was . . . it was more of a hobby for Bill, I guess. For one thing, it's mildly radioactive, so it's a little difficult to deal with. It's easy enough to shield, so it's not like I worried much about it. They actually used promethium to power the batteries in some of the first pacemakers. But when lithium batteries came along, they were a lot lighter and smaller, so out goes promethium. But the biggest reason promethium had limitations was, well, remember how I mentioned promethium is a rare earth?"

"Yes."

"It's probably the rarest of the rare earths. Bill said there was no more than twelve pounds of the stuff spread out over the entire Earth's crust. No one has ever found a large deposit of promethium. Bill worked with very small amounts of it. I saw it when they shipped it to him, before he put it in crystal form. It was just this white powder in this little clear plastic bag, almost like it was a drug or something. Except it wasn't as fine. It was more granular."

"And someone had, what, found it in a mine somewhere?"

"Oh, no. It had been fabricated in a nuclear reactor. Promethium isn't found naturally. At least that's what Bill said. That's why all this stuff you're saying about a high-energy promethium laser is a little out there. High-energy laser beams require very large crystals—the larger the crystal, the more powerful the laser. Billy was the one who did the math, so I couldn't give you the exact number. But I do know you would need several hundred pounds of promethium to make a crystal big enough for a high-energy laser capable of doing the kind of damage you've described."

Storm looked at his iced tea, studying a lemon seed floating within the light brown liquid.

"Could someone with access to a nuclear reactor fabricate that much promethium?" he asked.

"I don't think so. You make it by splitting plutonium atoms, and it's not like that's easy to come by. It's also a pretty slow process. The promethium Bill used came from the Oak Ridge Laboratory in Tennessee. Even at their peak, when they were making promethium for those batteries, they didn't make more than about fifteen pounds a year. By the time you made a few hundred pounds' worth, the older stuff would have decayed. Even the most stable promethium has a half-life of less than three years."

"So how would someone get enough promethium to do this?"

Alida shook her head. "I don't know. The only good news is that whatever supply they have will only last so long. As the promethium degrades, it causes impurities in the crystal. The one Bill made for that paper he wrote eventually stopped working."

"How long did that take?"

"A few months."

"Meaning whoever has this weapon will be able to keep using it with impunity for the immediate future?"

"I'm afraid so."

"It would stop working after a few months. But then, if they had more promethium, they could make another weapon."

"That's right."

Storm took a sip from his tea. "In the most perverse way, that's good news for you."

"How so?"

"Because it means whoever has grabbed your husband will have to keep him alive. And if he's alive, I'll find him."

"You . . . you will? In your capacity as . . . a contractor for the government?"

"No. In my capacity as a human being."

Alida did not reply. She had placed a hand over her mouth. Storm noticed tears were pooling in the corners of her eyes.

JUST DOWN THE STREET, BEHIND A PARTIALLY DRAWN curtain, in an empty house with a FOR SALE sign out front, a man spoke into a Bluetooth device that was planted in his ear.

"Yeah, he's still there," he said in an accent that came from somewhere south of the Mason-Dixon Line.

The man had short-cropped hair, a nose that had been broken several times, and a jaw that was twice the size it needed to be. A loaded Bushmaster Carbon-15 with a Trijicon ACOG 4X32 scope leaned against the wall next to him. He wore a Colt .45 in a shoulder holster. And he kept a Buck knife in an ankle sheath.

But his most distinctive feature was a wine-colored stain that started just below his scalp and splashed down the right side of his face.

"How the hell am I supposed to know?" he said in reply to whatever question had just been posed to him. "What do you want me to do, knock on the door and ask him for a dang business card?"

The voice on the other end spoke. The man with the wine stain picked up the Bushmaster and used the scope like a pair of binoculars to study the Chevy that had taken Storm out to Hercules.

"Well, it's definitely a government car, that's for sure," the man said. "It's got the white tags and all that. But it ain't got no markings that—"

The man was interrupted. He listened for a moment then said, "No, no. That's what I'm try-ing to tell you. It ain't the locals. They're treating this whole thing like McRae just walked off. They haven't found nothing because there wasn't nothing to find. I keep telling you, we did that part real good. Plus, she always goes to them. They ain't come to her since the first couple days."

He lowered the gun. There was more talking on the other end.

"Beats me," he replied. "Maybe she called someone

who called someone who knows a fed? It don't look like FBI. They drive them big cars, Caprices and whatnot. I've been thinking maybe the car is military, but the guy who got out didn't look military. He was big like he was in the military—Special Forces big. But no uniform. And the hair was wrong. Hell, maybe he's from the census or something?"

The man listened to an instruction.

"Okay. I'll shoot him as he comes out."

Another pause from the other side of the conversation. He picked up the gun again, and was looking through the scope as he spoke.

"Yeah, yeah. You get the stuff I sent earlier?"

He got a quick affirmation, then continued: "No, I'm telling you, she didn't see nothing. She ain't laid eyes on me once. I was in my little hiding place when I took those, but it looks like I was right next to her. Ought to keep that scientist of yours plenty motivated. Just let me know if you want more."

He was nodding as more squawking came from his Bluetooth.

"Yeah, I'm straight. I can take her out anytime you want. You just give me the word and the old lady is as good as gone."

The voice on the other end began wrapping up the conversation, but the man cut it off. There was movement in his scope. The big guy who had come in the government car was coming down the front steps. The man with the wine stain trained his cross-hairs on the big guy's head.

"Hang on, hang on. I gotta go. He's coming out. I'll shoot him right now."

He kept the big guy in his scopes for another long second.

Then he lowered his gun and reached for his

camera, which was at his feet. It had a 300-millimeter lens, which he used to zoom in tight on the big guy. After the autofocus did its work, the man with the wine stain jammed down the shutter button. The camera motor clicked off two dozen shots in less than two seconds.

The man quickly peeked at the screen on the camera, ready to fire off a few more if need be.

But it wouldn't be necessary. He had captured this stranger—whoever he was—quite clearly. He plugged the camera into his laptop and began uploading them to his employer.

CHAPTER 11

SOMEWHERE IN THE MIDDLE EAST

Tall and angular, with close-set eyes, a nose that dominated his long face, a ratty beard that obscured his chin, and a white turban wound atop his head, Ahmed heard it all the time: he looked like a young Osama bin Laden.

He took it as a compliment. Many of the people who said it were admirers of bin Laden, even if they'd be careful around whom they'd admit that. They'd considered bin Laden a brave leader, even if they hadn't agreed with his ultimate tactics. Nothing wrong with being compared to someone like that.

Also, bin Laden had enjoyed the company of many wives. Ahmed wouldn't mind that part a bit. He didn't even have one.

He leaned back at his desk. People often thought men like Ahmed didn't have desks, that they spent their lives out crawling around in the sand like some oversized scarab beetle. But no, he had a desk and an office. It was a large office, with plenty of room for a television that he kept tuned to Al Jazeera and for the prayer mat that he reverently unrolled five times daily and turned in the direction of Mecca.

The room was located in a building that was older than Ahmed's great-great-grandfather, within a walled compound that had been in Ahmed's family for many generations before that.

It did not look like much now, he knew. Long ago, Ahmed's family owned all the land around it, giving the compound the look of an estate. But slowly, through the generations, his forefathers had sliced off one piece of land after another, until only a handful of acres were left. The area, which had once been rural, had slowly been developed until now it was a densely packed residential neighborhood. The compound was fronted by a narrow street that carried its share of traffic. Unremarkable houses, far younger than the one Ahmed sat in, ringed it on all sides.

Had any of his neighbors been asked, they would have said that Ahmed was a quiet businessman who mostly kept to himself.

They might have said they found the razor wire atop those walls to be a bit excessive, not that Ahmed was particularly interested in their opinions on the subject. They certainly wouldn't have known about the fully automatic rifles he kept at the ready. Or the men he hired to wield them. Or the things he asked those men to do with them. The guns would not have been in keeping with his businessman persona.

That was part of what the walls helped hide. Ahmed loved those walls for that reason and for others. The walls were what turned his house into a sanctuary. They had protected his great-great-grandfather and all the men in his family who had come since. Whatever havoc was going on in the world around him, the compound—its buildings and its land—could be protected.

And there had long been havoc here. This part of world was called the Fertile Crescent, the cradle of civilization. Many, many generations before, Ahmed's ancestors had been among the first humans to form sedentary agricultural settlements, domesticate animals, and cultivate grains. They made calendars by tracking the waxing and waning of the moon, learned to predict the floods of the mighty rivers, built trenches to irrigate their crops, made the land into something valuable.

And then they started fighting over it—and had been doing so ever since.

Ahmed's family had gotten out of the farming business long ago. There were better ways to make money. The land and climate had changed much. The Fertile Crescent was not as fertile as it had once been.

And yet still people fought over it. They fought because of religion, because the old maps had different lines on them than the current maps did, because new factions took over governments and used their power to make life miserable for old factions.

Ahmed was no mere bystander in these battles, of course. Far from it. War. Chaos. Confusion. These things were all good for Ahmed. If people in this part of the world ever stopped beating their plowshares into swords, it might be trouble for Ahmed. He was one with the sword-bearers. The peace that do-gooders kept thinking they could bring to the Middle East did not interest Ahmed in the slightest.

There was a knock at his door.

"Come in," Ahmed said at the start of a conversation that would take place in Arabic, both men's native tongue.

A young man with a long beard and a turban that matched Ahmed's entered the room. "We have the promethium secured," he said.

"Excellent. It is shielded, yes? I don't want my men getting sick from radiation poisoning."

"Yes, sir."

"How much did it end up being?"

"Three hundred and eighty-two pounds," he said.

Ahmed's eyes went wide. "You're sure? That's more than I was anticipating."

"I saw it register on the scale myself."

"And it is pure, yes? As pure as the other shipments?"

"Absolutely."

Ahmed smiled and leaned back. "Three hundred and eighty-two pounds of pure promethium. Praise be to Allah. The best yet. This will be good for us all."

"Praise be to Allah," the man replied.

"You may go now."

The young man complied with the order. Ahmed picked up the phone. There was much to be done.

CHAPTER 12

LANGLEY, Virginia

It was a good thing Jedediah Jones's people could only see his outsides.

Outwardly, he staked his position at the center of the cubby with his usual calm, assured demeanor. His face was a Venetian mask their eyes could not penetrate. His shirt, which he had changed sometime in the middle of the night, did not have a wrinkle on it.

It was his insides that were a rumpled mess.

His power was based on having made himself a go-to guy for other powerful men over the course of years and decades. Presidents. Senators. Cabinet members. Other parts of the CIA. They all came to Jones to fix their problems. They all needed Jones.

This was what drove him. His work ethic was something akin to a lifelong manic phase. His standards, unyielding for all those around him, were even higher where his own behavior was concerned. If an issue could be solved with hard work—and Jones believed more or less everything could be solved with hard work—he was equal to the task. He was the man who never let anyone down when it mattered.

Until now. Facing the most serious threat to national security since that horrible September day in 2001, Jones was foundering. It was now nearing twenty-four hours since planes had started falling from the sky, since the powerful men had turned to him for help, and he had no solutions for them.

What he had was Derrick Storm's conjecture that some kind of laser beam was causing this. Jones knew not to doubt Storm. If anyone could intuit from looking at one piece of metal what had happened to a whole plane, it was a man like Storm, a man whose intuition seemed to border on clairvoyance.

But Jones had also not taken Storm's theory to any of the powerful men. Not until Storm had more than just a piece of metal to go on. It was too unformed, too likely to be flawed. Jones had made a career out of not being wrong, and he didn't want to start now.

In the meantime, Jones had set agents in all corners of the globe to work. He had ordered them to break laws, confidences, bodies—whatever they had to do to get him information. He, himself, had not slept. The powerful men were depending on him, waiting for him to produce. And he was disappointing them.

What was the opposite of power? Impotence. That's what Jones felt. It was splashed across his face: the sheer misery that he wasn't doing enough, that he was slipping. It was the most horrible sensation imaginable.

Then it got worse.

Standing in the middle of the cubby, surveying his people at work, he recognized that something was wrong before he even knew what it was. One of the techs was sitting up in his chair, pounding furiously on his keyboard, horror in his countenance. He had headphones clamped over his ears and was perhaps unaware he was suddenly exuding stress from his body.

Jones reminded himself that he was the boss. His people needed his unflappable, steady leadership. They would be rattled if they saw him react in any overly demonstrable way. Making sure he was composed, he walked slowly over to the young man in question, and gently placed a hand on his shoulder.

"What is it, son?"

"Sir, the computers picked up unusual voice patterns from Emirates air traffic control. The number of discrete sounds per second went off the charts, much more than what you'd get for a sandstorm or a near miss. I had to backtrack the algorithm in order to switch from passive to active listening, but as soon as I tapped in I—"

"Spit it out, son."

"Sir, a plane has gone down."

"Where?"

"It was on approach to Dubai International Airport. It was approximately seventy nautical miles from the field and it went into a spin. Sir, York, Pennsylvania, is approximately seventy nautical miles from Dulles. Those planes also went into—"

"What are the coordinates of where it crashed?"

The tech pointed to a series of digits on his screen.

"Wallace," Jones said to another one of the nerds. "Get me eyes on 24.344057 north, 55.559553 east."

"Yes, sir," a voice from three desks away said.

"Put it up on the main screen when you have it."

The other techs were, by now, aware of what was unfolding. Jones could see their heads moving, their attention being ripped from their terminals. The volume in the room had increased threefold.

"What towns or cities are nearby?"

Another voice volunteered: "Sir, that's just outside Al-Ain, right near the border of Oman. Al-Ain is a city of a little more than a half million that's known for its—"

"I'm not going on vacation there, damn it!" Jones barked. "Tell me about the highways. If we're seeing a repeat of the Pennsylvania Three, the weapon will be near a highway."

"There are several major ones connecting Al-Ain to Abu Dhabi and Dubai. E-16, E-95, and E-66 go north. E-22 and E-30 go west. E-7 heads west into Oman. We'd need more information to narrow in on which one is being used."

At that moment, the thirty-foot screen at the front of the room blinked onto one image. In the middle of a tan, empty stretch of desert, there was the splintered husk of what had once been a commercial airliner. Several of the plane's pieces were strewn on the desert around it. Smoke poured from where one of the engines had come to a rest.

"Damn it," Jones said. "Bryan, who do we have on the ground in Dubai who might already be compromised?"

Kevin Bryan consulted the roster he kept in his head and spat out several names. Jones picked Michael Reed, a man whose bungling had led to his exposure to the Emirates intelligence community a few days earlier. Reed was due to ship out of the country before the Emirates special police force could gather enough evidence to arrest him.

"Tell Reed to alert UAE authorities immediately,"

Jones barked. "They have to get all planes off this flight path. If this is like Pennsylvania, any other plane coming in on this approach is in danger."

"Is it possible this crash is unconnected to the Pennsylvania Three?" Bryan asked.

"We'll find out in the next few minutes. In the meantime, it won't hurt to act like we're seeing the second act of this attack."

"Yes, sir," Bryan said.

Jones turned to another one of the techs. "Figure out which flight that is. Download its flight plan. Trace backward over the last fifty nautical miles from where it crashed and set a search grid of two miles along either side of the line. Pay particular attention to areas near highways. If Storm is right, there's going to be some kind of laser beam stationed somewhere in that grid. I want it found."

The tech balked. "Sir, that's . . . that's a needle in a haystack."

Jones glared at him. "Then you better sift through it until one of your fingers gets pricked. Understand?"

"Yes, sir."

Jones swore. All around him, the considerable computing power he had assembled—and the talent he had brought to the cubby to work it—was being strained to its limit. Jones realized his fists were balled. He forced himself to flex his fingers.

It was possible that plane had gone down due to natural causes. But Jones knew the odds. Commercial airline travel was, statistically speaking, about as safe as a walk across your living room. Maybe if it was a third-rate airline in a developing country that didn't have the money to maintain its fleet, there could be problems. But the Emirates was one of the most sophisticated countries in the Middle East, one that had smartly reinvested its oil money into infrastructure, education, and health care—things that would still be there even when the oil finally ran out.

A sick, sinking sensation was spreading to Jones's stomach. He realized he was holding his breath. He exhaled softly. The Pennsylvania Three went down within twelve minutes of each other, at 1:55, 1:58, and 2:07. It had already been seven minutes since the first plane was stricken. If they could just get through the next—

"Sir!" one of the techs called out. "Another plane over Al-Ain has gone badly off course. The tower in Dubai has lost contact. I'm listening in now. They're freaking out."

"Coordinates?" Jones asked.

"Twenty-four point four-nine-nine-six-four-six north, fifty-five point six-nine-six-five-oh-nine east."

"That's maybe fifteen miles from the first crash," Bryan said. "The first was just to the west of E-95 highway. This was just to the east of it."

"Narrow our search grid to the E-95 corridor," Jones ordered. "Can someone get me eyes on this plane?"

On the large screen, there came the satellite image of a plane in flight—but only barely. The sight was so incongruous as to even shock Jones: the aircraft's starboard wing was missing. What was left of the plane had entered a tight, clockwise spiral. There was not nearly enough lift coming from its one remaining wing to keep it in flight or on course. It was difficult to gauge its altitude from a two-dimensional picture, but whatever height it had, it was losing fast.

The cubby had gone silent. Some of the best and brightest computer jockeys in America had been reduced to horrified spectators. There was nothing any of them could do to save the doomed souls aboard.

All they could do was watch as the plane plowed into a dune in an empty stretch of desert. It kicked up an enormous cloud of sand that obscured their view of the aircraft breaking apart under the enormous force of hitting the ground at such a steep angle and such a high rate of speed.

Jones slammed his fist on a desk next to him. Several techs snapped their heads in his direction.

They had never seen him lose his cool.

THE NEXT THIRTEEN MINUTES WERE ONES JONES DID not want to ever relive.

Two more planes that had not been able to scramble away from the danger zone over Al-Ain were struck and fell to the desert like wounded birds.

Jones and his people could only sit and watch, cataloguing each disaster, trying to find patterns. The similarities to the Pennsylvania crashes were already obvious, except they were happening half a world away.

When it had stopped—partly because the UAE authorities, warned by Reed, had gotten all the planes out of the air—Jones sat in the chair at the desk he kept in the middle of the cubby. He buried his face in his hands. The Pennsylvania Three had been joined by the Emirates Four. And yet, even having narrowed their search grid, they had not been able to locate whatever was making it happen.

"Sir?" Bryan said, holding a phone toward him. "It's Storm."

"Jones," he said into the mouthpiece, his voice cracking slightly. "I assume you've heard about what just happened on the Arabian Peninsula."

"I have."

"Please tell me you know something."

Storm spent the next five minutes briefing Jones about his strengthening conviction that a high-energy laser was responsible for the crashes. Jones, in turn, told Storm more about what they had just witnessed taking place above the Arabian Desert.

"And you said you watched the whole thing from satellite?" Storm asked when he was done.

"That's right."

"I assume you saved that footage."

"Of course."

"How close a view could one of the nerds give me on that severed wing?"

"About as close as your nose is to your toes. You know that."

"Could you have them send the image to my phone?"

"Absolutely," Jones said.

Jones set the phone down for a moment, walked over to one of his techs, and asked her to comply with Storm's request.

"What are you thinking?" Jones asked when he returned to the line.

"I have an idea. I just want to be sure of something."

The woman whose desk Jones had just visited gave him the high sign.

"Okay," he said. "It should be landing on your phone any moment."

Storm paused, but only briefly. His phone was connected to the government's secret beta version of a 5G satellite network. It was a hundred times faster than 4G and didn't come with the blind spots of land-based networks.

"Yeah, I got it," Storm said. "Give me a moment."

Jones waited for Storm to study the picture. Storm had saved Jones from seemingly hopeless situations in the past. At this point, the head of Internal Division Enforcement could only pray that whatever Storm had forming in his mind would work the same kind of magic again.

"Okay," Storm said. "It's a laser. There's no doubt."

"Is it the same weapon that did the Pennsylvania Three?"

"I would imagine its specs are identical, but it's not the exact same unit. A weapon capable of producing a laser this powerful would be fairly large. The crystals themselves weigh several hundred pounds. And then there's the issue of heat displacement. A weapon like this gets incredibly hot when you fire it, and unless you divert that energy somewhere—a large pool of water, the ground, something—it would melt stuff you didn't want melted. The high-energy laser I saw demonstrated a few years ago needed a truck to haul it around, mostly because of the heat factor. Even if you had managed to miniaturize some of its parts, you'd still have something reasonably large. The fact that there seem to be highways near the crash sites suggest to me this weapon is being towed around by a car or truck. The only way to get something that size from Pennsylvania to the Middle East in a day would be to fly it. And all nonmilitary flights out of the U.S. have been grounded."

"Good point. So what's this idea of yours?"

"We go on the offensive. We have to. Right now, this guy can strike anywhere. He's been using highways because they provide quick access, but there's nothing to say he has to keep operating that way. If it's a large truck, all he needs is blacktop. If it's a light truck, he could even go off-road. No one flying over land is safe."

"I agree. But how do we go on the offensive?"

"We set a trap," Storm said. "Draw the enemy out."

"I'm listening."

"Whoever is doing this has two very powerful lasers on two continents, but they also have a problem."

"What's that?"

"A lack of targets. No one is going to be flying anywhere in the foreseeable future. Seven plane crashes in two days? Every airport in the world is going to be shuttered. That means our terrorist is out of business for the time being. And, bear in mind, whoever has this weapon knows his window of opportunity to use it is going to be somewhat limited. From what I'm told, promethium degrades naturally, which causes impurities in the crystal. Too many impurities and the crystal becomes worthless. So our bad guy is going to be itching to use this thing."

"I agree. How do we use this against him?"

"By giving him a target. A big fat one."

"What did you have in mind?"

"How about Air Force One?" Storm said.

"Are you out of your—"

"Not with the president on board, of course.

Hear me out. We have the White House make a big announcement: the United States is the mightiest nation in the world and does not bow to the will of terrorists. 'By executive order, domestic air travel will resume in two days. But in the meantime, as a show of faith to the American people, the president, several cabinet members, and a handful of brave members of Congress and the Senate are all going to hop aboard Air Force One at Andrews Air Force Base and fly in a big circle over the eastern United States before landing back at Andrews.' We'll show footage of them getting on board, waving and smiling and all that, and then have a dummy plane painted like Air Force One and being remotely piloted actually make the flight. There would be no one on board."

"But how do we—"

"I'm not done," Storm said. "We have to make our terrorists feel like they're earning this. So we give a fake flight plan to the press. The one we really fly will supposedly be a secret. But, of course, we'll stick it on the FAA's server."

"Which is secure, but is easy enough to hack into," Jones said. "The techs do it all the time. And we can assume whoever is carrying out these attacks has a similar capacity."

"Exactly. Then we make sure our circular flight plan has only one spot where it is both over land and seventy nautical miles away from Andrews. We monitor the area via satellite from the cubby, then make sure we hide enough boots on the ground to capture the weapon and whomever is operating it."

Jones was nodding, even though Storm couldn't see it.

"You think that'll work?" Jones asked.

"I don't know," Storm said. "But I do know one thing."

"What's that?"

"I've yet to hear anyone else come up with a better idea."

CHAPTER 13

KILMARNOCK, Virginia

They were doing it wrong. All wrong. Storm could have told them; but, of course, no one was asking him.

They had set up the operation exactly as Storm had specified. The White House had made its announcement. Both the real and the fake Air Force Ones had been readied. A host of faux-brave officials, from the president to the secretary of state to the Speaker of the House, had volunteered to pretend to be on board.

Then they made out the route, both the one announced to the press and the unannounced one planted on the FAA server. The unannounced one made its approach to Andrews from the south. At exactly seventy nautical miles from the field, it passed over Kilmarnock, a small town in the Tidewater part of Virginia. It was in a sleepy part of the state known as the Northern Neck, a peninsula bordered by the Potomac River to the north, the Chesapeake Bay to the east, the Rappahannock River to the south, and a whole bunch of farmland to the west.

It had been strategically chosen for its remoteness and its difficulty of access. The nearest highway, Interstate 95, was close to an hour away. There was only one main road running through the region north–south and only one running east–west. Both were single lane for much of the way. Getting in or out of the area involved crossing bridges. Storm was working under the assumption that the weapon was camouflaged to a certain extent. But, at the same time, it was large enough that it couldn't be completely hidden. Putting up roadblocks and checking vehicles—car-by-car, truck-by-truck—would be relatively easy. The weapon would not be able to escape.

The plan was perfect.

Then the bureaucrats had gotten involved.

They called it Operation Mockingbird, in apparent ignorance of the secret CIA campaign to influence the media during the 1950s that bore the same name. Still, Storm approved—if only because he so adored the Farrell Lee novel of a similar name. But then they decided neither Storm nor Jones would be allowed to run it. Being that it was on American soil and had to involve more people and equipment than even the CIA could reasonably expect to hide, Storm and Jones had been forced to hand execution of the plan over to the FBI, which had started making mistakes from the moment it took over.

First, they put a man named Jack Bronson in charge. Big, bald, and obstinate, Bronson was ex-military of the worst kind. Too hierarchical in his thinking. Too much enamored with chain of command. Too impressed with the fact that he was at the top of it.

Second, they had set up a task force that involved too many other agencies. The Department of Homeland Security. The Transportation Security Administration. The Federal Aviation Administration. The Department of Defense. The Federal Emergency Management Agency. It really started getting ridiculous when a pencil pusher from the

National Aeronautics and Space Administration showed up, making noises about how Operation Mockingbird's success was needed to keep a satellite launch on schedule. Storm half expected someone from the Department of Agriculture to show up and ask if they were taking proper care not to harm any crops. It was enough to make Storm yearn for another government shutdown.

Third, there was just too much noise. Storm had envisioned an operation where every single piece was undercover, made to blend with its surroundings. The Northern Neck was a quiet area, filled mostly with retirees, farmers, and the occasional Chesapeake Bay waterman who didn't want to give up on that way of life. Folks moved slow, talked slow, drove pickup trucks, and dressed comfortably in T-shirts and Crocs.

So it just felt wrong to have a bunch of government agents in sedans racing around, filling the air with urgent chatter, wearing tailored suits and sharp-toed shoes. Everyone involved in the operation stuck out as did every piece of equipment that had been brought in. Even if the terrorists were unfamiliar with American culture, they would be able to smell out the trap.

And, having ceded control to the FBI, there was nothing Storm could do about it. He was being allowed to "observe," with the implicit understanding that observation meant keeping his mouth shut.

Bronson had set up a temporary command post under a set of tents in the parking lot of a bowling alley just off Main Street. There was a thin, pathetic attempt to disguise it as a FEMA training exercise, but even the most guileless locals weren't fooled. FEMA wasn't known to have anti-personnel tanks in its arsenal. Some of Bronson's agents had skipped all pretenses and wore gear with "FBI" emblazoned on it. Storm wondered if Bronson's next step would be to engrave invitations announcing the task force's presence.

Storm had his hands in his pockets and, in a shoulder holster, his gun of choice: a Smith & Wesson 629 Stealth Hunter, a sleeker, modernized version of a .44 Magnum Clint Eastwood first made famous. Storm called it "Dirty Harry" in his honor.

Feeling both restless and bored, he roamed from tent to tent, looking at the FBI's gadgetry with only mild interest. Jones's stuff was cooler.

He had come in from California on a military transport plane that morning, grabbed his Taurus from the parking lot at Langley, and made impressive time down to Kilmarnock, passing a whole lot of slow-moving traffic on the single-lane roads.

He paused in front of a screen that had been set up in the communications center. There were two pieces of footage playing on a loop on CNN: first the president and other dignitaries boarding the plane, then the mock Air Force One taking off from Andrews.

The plane was scheduled to fly over Kilmarnock at 2 P.M.—which everyone agreed made sense, given that the terrorists seemed to like that time. It was 1:52 when Storm's journey took him back to the main tent. There he found Bronson, his face glued to his phone's small screen.

"Things still on schedule?" Storm asked.

"I imagine so," Bronson said, pointedly not looking at Storm.

Storm looked up in the sky, which was blue and

empty of air traffic any larger than a passing sparrow. "Where's the plane?"

"Not here."

"I can see that. Is it late? Will it be here soon?"

"Not unless this is Cape Charles."

"Excuse me?"

Bronson finally looked up. "It's a town at the tip of the Eastern Shore of Virginia."

"I've heard of it. But what does that have to do with the plane?"

"Oh, that's right. I forgot you weren't on that distribution list."

"What distribution list?"

"We changed the flight plan. We're bringing Mockingbird up the Eastern Shore instead of over this airspace. DoD didn't want to sacrifice a plane. Those things are expensive, you know. Boeings don't grow on trees."

Storm stared at the man hard. Airplanes were expensive, yes. But human lives were priceless. That's what the Department of Defense should have been prioritizing. Storm spoke through gritted teeth. "And when were you going to tell me this?"

"It was need to know."

"You're really going to pull a 'need to know' on me?"

"Yes. All of the people who needed to know did. And that didn't include the CIA or any of its semi-illegal contractors. It doesn't change the operation as far as you're concerned. We've got the roadblocks in place. We'll get the weapon before it gets very far."

"Please tell me you've also got people in place on the Eastern Shore."

"No need," Bronson said. "The FAA logged

several unauthorized attempts to breach its system coming from Damascus. One of the attempts was successful. The hacker went right for the phony flight plan."

Bronson bent his head toward his phone again. Storm stared at the top of Bronson's shaved pate for a moment. "Do you think we're dealing with idiots?"

"Hmm?"

"Do you really think that people who are smart enough to build a weapon that—"

He stopped himself. Storm figured he was only allotted so many words and so much breath in this lifetime. No sense in wasting either on a man like Bronson.

"Never mind," Storm said.

If Homeland Security, the TSA, the FAA, the DoD, FEMA, NASA, and untold other federal agencies were all aware of this plan, the terrorists surely were, too. All the people and equipment the FBI had clogging up this little town in Virginia might as well have been actors and stage props. They would not be needed. Not here, anyway.

Storm made a decision and started walking over toward an open field where an FBI helicopter sat idle. The pilot was sitting in the cockpit with the window open, oblivious. He was also paying more attention to his smartphone than anything around him.

Without bothering to speak, Storm reached up into the cockpit. The pilot finally looked at him, more curious than anything. Storm's hand was traveling for a spot on the side of the pilot's neck. Storm grabbed, squeezed, held. The pilot made a brief croaking noise, then slumped over.

"Sorry, friend," Storm said.

Storm quickly boarded the helicopter. He

removed the pilot's helmet and put it in the passenger seat. Storm then unbuckled the pilot's slumbering body and lowered it to the ground. He closed the helicopter's cargo door and window, then assumed the pilot's seat. In front of him was a dashboard crowded with dials, buttons, and switches. He grabbed the flight stick, his thumb naturally finding the trim switch.

An AS550 Fennec helicopter was, fundamentally, similar to an AS350 Ecureuil, which Storm had once flown through a typhoon in the Gulf of Tonkin. He figured flying this one on a balmy day over the Chesapeake Bay would be no problem.

Within two minutes, before anyone from the FBI could figure out why the rotors on the helicopter were whirring, Storm had lifted off and was on his way. The last thing he saw on the ground was a phalanx of stupefied FBI agents running toward him.

He paid them no mind. He had a laser to find.

IT IS A LITTLE-KNOWN FACT THAT THE GEOGRAPHIC feature now called the Chesapeake Bay was once a fairly narrow river, back when the world was colder and more of its water was locked in polar ice. And while in this warmer, wetter epoch, the bay is wide enough that a person standing on the shore near Kilmarnock cannot see the other side, it is not so wide that a Fennec Fox can't get across it rapidly.

Storm tilted the Fennec forward, accelerated to its top speed of 150 miles an hour, and was soon over water. The gas gauge was close to full. The stick felt comfortable in his hands. The chopper responded nicely to his commands.

He increased his altitude to one thousand feet

where the flying would be a bit smoother. He figured it would be eight minutes before he was back over land.

He used the time to call someone who might be able to tell him where he was going.

The voice of Javier Rodriguez soon filled Storm's Bluetooth: "Yo, bro, you don't happen to know who just stole a helicopter from the FBI, do you?"

"It wasn't stealing. It was borrowing without express permission," Storm corrected him. "I'll give it back when I'm done."

"From the chatter we're hearing on the fibbies' frequencies, you might want to do them a favor and fly it straight to Leavenworth. Because it sounds like that's where they want to send you right about now."

"Too bad I'm allergic to Kansas," Storm said. "They'll forgive me when I find their laser beam for them and then give them credit. I assume you're tracking the Mockingbird?"

"It's on our big screen right now. The only way I could get closer to that plane is if I was on board with a flight attendant serving me pretzels."

"Good. You got a fix on my location, too?"

"Yeah, I see you. You're the little funny-looking tweety bird that's about to get shot down by those F-16s that you should see closing in shortly from your three o'clock."

"I'll worry about that in a second. Can you tell me where Mockingbird will be when it's seventy nau—"

"Check your phone, bro. I already sent you a course correction."

Storm looked down at his phone and tugged the flight stick until he was heading in the proper direction.

Rodriguez continued: "You're heading near a little town on the Eastern Shore called Crisfield. I hear they got great crab cakes there. Pick some up for me and Bryan when you're done, huh?"

"Will do. In the meantime, can you do something about those F-16s?"

"Other than hope that you made me a beneficiary in your will? Not really. Jones is on the line with the air force right now, but so far they're not interested in anything we have to say on the subject. You seem to have crossed into a serious no-fly zone. They don't want to hear about anything in the air that doesn't have their stripes on it. Especially not stolen helicopters."

"Borrowed. It's borrowed," Storm said, aware that a pair of fighter jets was closing in fast above him. "Anyhow, looks like my friends are here. I'll talk to you later."

"I seriously hope so, bro," Rodriguez said.

Storm ended the call and took stock of his situation. A Fennec could be armed, but this one wasn't. And his 150 miles an hour, which had felt so fast moments earlier, suddenly seemed pokey. The two F-16 Fighting Falcons coming to join him could hit supersonic speeds without straining themselves. And he could see the full complement of sidewinder missiles on their wings.

The helmet was still sitting in the seat next to him. He could hear a voice chattering through the earpiece inside. He got the helmet on in time to make out the voice of what he presumed was one of the F-16 pilots.

"November-three-niner-zero-alpha-tango, identify yourself or you will be treated as hostile."

"Hostile!" Storm said. "You guys are the ones

with the missiles under your wings, and I'm the one who's hostile?"

"November-three-niner-zero-alpha-tango, identify yourself or you will be treated as hostile."

Storm realized the microphone in the helmet was switched off. He corrected the problem, then said: "I'm actually quite friendly once you get to know me."

The F-16 pilot did not seem convinced. "November-three-niner-zero-alpha-tango, be advised you are flying into restricted airspace. Identify yourself immediately."

"I'm just the orphaned nephew of a poor moisture farmer from the planet Tatooine. Tell Uncle Owen and Aunt Beru I'm not coming home for supper."

Storm was now bracketed by the F-16s. He could see inside their bubble canopies and look at their pilots, each shielded by the mirrored visors of their flight helmets. They were not looking back at him. They were also not impressed with his knowledge of Luke Skywalker's backstory.

"November-three-niner-zero-alpha-tango—"

"Look, fellas, I'm on your team, okay? I'm trying to find a terrorist who shoots down airliners for fun. Cut me some slack here."

"November-three-niner-zero-alpha-tango, be advised our orders are to get you out of this airspace by any means necessary, including force. Change heading immediately to signify your intent to comply."

Storm had no such intent. He looked down. He could again see land, both an island off to his left and the more substantial stretch of land that was

Maryland's Eastern Shore. The bay was dotted with pleasure boats and commercial watermen.

He put the helicopter into as steep a dive as he dared. He watched his airspeed indicator climb as his altimeter dropped. He still did not have the advantage of speed over these fighter jets. But by skimming the wave tops he could at least make himself a more difficult target. The F-16s wouldn't dare go much lower than they already were.

"The change in altitude isn't what we had in mind November-three-niner-zero-alpha-tango. Adjust to heading two-eight-niner immediately."

Storm leveled out at roughly twenty feet above the water. He had to adjust course a few times to make sure he missed the masts of some of the sailboats.

"Sorry, fellas," Storm said. "I've got a terrorist to stop. You can either join me or not. I could use your help."

"November-three-niner-zero-alpha-tango, be advised we have been given the order to fire. Change course immediately or we'll have no choice."

Storm banked hard toward land, now just a few hundred yards off his starboard side. The F-16s mirrored his move, but well above him. If anything, Storm thought they had increased altitude. It's not like they needed to be terribly close to him to shoot him down. Their missiles probably had a range of tens—if not hundreds—of miles, not to mention guidance systems that could deliver their warheads between the "N" and the "3" on his tail numbers, if they chose to.

He was over land now, flying just above the rooftops of the houses that dotted the shoreline. He hated using them for cover. But he also knew that, for whatever the pilots were saying to him, there was likely an air force commander somewhere telling them not to take a shot unless they were sure the falling helicopter wouldn't crash into a civilian's house.

"November-three-niner-zero-alpha-tango, we have achieved target lock. Change course now."

Storm saw the town of Crisfield in the distance. But he was now over what looked like wetlands or some kind of wildlife preserve. There were no houses. No cover.

"November-three-niner-zero-alpha-tango, this is your last warn—"

And then nothing. The line in Storm's helmet went dead.

Expecting a missile was now on its way, Storm veered toward a stretch of forest, desperately hoping he could get the warhead to detonate on a tree instead of his fuselage. He was nearing a stand of pine trees when he heard it.

It came from not far behind him.

A tremendous explosion.

Then another.

It sounded like planes crashing.

Storm craned his neck left, then right, trying to get a glimpse of whatever happened, but he couldn't see anything. Unlike fighter jets, which gave pilots a near-360-degree view of their surroundings, a chopper only let its flier see ahead and a limited amount to the side. He brought the helicopter up to a hundred feet, then set it into a hover. He slowly rotated its nose in a circle so he could survey everything around him.

Sure enough, there were two smoldering wrecks

of airplanes, separated by no more than a few hundred feet.

Something had shot down the F-16s.

And in one sickening second, Storm knew exactly what had done it.

STORM RIPPED OFF HIS HELMET, REACHED INTO HIS pocket, hit the number for the cubby.

"I got Derrick," Storm heard Rodriguez yelling, before he returned to a more normal tone to say, "Hang on, bro."

Storm consciously brought his breathing back under control, knowing it would help steady his heart rate. He was figuring it out fast: the lunatic manning the laser had seen the F-16s coming and decided they were either a threat or they made for good target practice.

And, thinking like a terrorist, there was no reason not to shoot them down. One of the advantages of a laser over, say, a missile was that the laser had essentially unlimited ammunition. As long as its power source was good, it could keep firing as often as it acquired a new target.

The only thing that had likely saved Storm was that he was flying low enough that the laser couldn't target him.

Which meant it had to be close by.

"Storm," the husky voice of Jedediah Jones filled his ear. "Do you see a water tower with a large red crab painted on it to your right?"

Storm's eyes went to a gray tower that loomed above the low-slung buildings of the town around it. To the right there was a cove filled with boats, their naked masts reaching upward like a series of white sticks that had been jammed into the water. "Yeah, I see it."

"Head straight for it. But stay low. Repeat: you must stay as low as possible."

"I copy."

"You'll be looking for a white truck that is currently located in a marina parking lot just short of the water tower as you approach it. Our techs have been studying satellite images of it. It is designed as a surface-to-air weapon, and based on their early estimates, its lowest angle of fire is thirty-five degrees. It effectively creates a blind spot that lowers the closer you get to it. Even staying as low as a hundred feet in the air, you can't get any closer than one hundred and sixty-three feet or you will be within the weapon's range."

"I don't exactly have a tape measure up here with me. I'd appreciate some help on ideas where to land this thing. I see some streets but they look too narrow. I'm not real keen to mess with those power lines alongside them, either," Storm said. He pushed the stick gingerly forward, not wanting to tempt the 163-foot circle of death.

Jones's voice again came into his ear. "Do you see a ferry dock? Should be dead ahead of you."

Storm's eyes focused on a slab of concrete jutting out into the water just to the left of the harbor inlet. "Yeah, I got it."

"Put her down there. Mockingbird is coming into the laser's range any moment. The terrorists will probably take their shot and make a run for it. But if you can get the chopper down and get on foot, you might be able to catch them."

"Will do," Storm said. He pushed the helicopter ahead. He was again over water. The down draft from the chopper's whirring rotors flattened the water as he passed over it, confusing the wave patterns.

He reached the ferry loading dock—empty, thankfully—and hovered over it for a moment, until he was sure his skids were parallel with the ground. Then he went hard for the concrete surface, not caring that his landing would have failed to impress an experienced pilot. At this point, he was all about speed, not style.

Storm cut the power to the rotors but did not wait for them to stop spinning. He unbuckled himself and spun toward the cargo door, throwing it open and hopping out. He began sprinting in the direction of the water tower, down the middle of Crisfield's main drag, a wide, four-lane road with a divider down the middle.

"Is the weapon still there?" Storm asked into his cell phone.

"Yes," Jones said.

"Guide me to it."

"You are currently on Main Street. Did you see Eleventh Street? You just passed a sign for it."

"Yes."

"Good. Go to Ninth Street, then take a right."

Storm did not bother to take stock of the houses and buildings that blurred in his peripheral vision as he ran. His eyes focused on the street signs: Tenth Street, Spruce Street, then Ninth. He rounded the corner at full speed, his arms and legs pumping.

"Slow down, slow down," Jones said. "As soon as you reach the end of that building on your left, the parking lot should be in view. The truck is on the far side of it. We have not seen any combatants yet so we assume they're inside. We also assume they're armed. Approach with caution."

Storm slowed as the parking lot came into view. It had space for well over a hundred cars, although only a smattering of the spots were being used. At the far end, without any other cars around it, Storm spied his target.

It was not just any truck. It was an ice cream truck, painted stark white, complete with decals of various tasty treats on the side. Storm could see a Nutty Buddy, a Strawberry Shortcake, a Chipwich. It could have fooled anyone. The only thing marring its authenticity was a retractable turret that had emerged from a split in the roof. On top of it, there was a metal cylinder with a glass-enclosed end pointed toward the sky. It looked a lot like one of the high-powered spotlights used to strafe the sky at a Hollywood movie premiere.

"I see it," Storm said, softly. Then he looked up and saw the contrail of an airliner, high overhead. It was the fake Air Force One. The Mockingbird, as the FBI was calling it.

"Good work. Now, listen to me, Storm: the laser is your objective. We're assuming the human operators are low-level foot soldiers. They are not of consequence. We'll either capture them or not. The laser is what we're after."

"But if all we capture is the laser, how will—"

Storm stopped himself. In that moment, he saw Jones's play. Jones was more interested in acquiring the United States government another weapon of mass destruction than he was in catching terrorists. The long-ago words that Lieutenant Marlowe had spoken to his father echoed in his head. *There ought to be limits.* Then he heard his father's words. *We can't be trusted, either.*

"Never mind," Storm corrected himself, then lied, "I'll do everything I can to secure the weapon."

"Excellent," Jones said.

Storm did a low run from the corner of the building toward one of the parked cars, keeping his eyes on the truck and, more to the point, any humans or gun muzzles that might be emerging from it. But there was no sign of movement coming from it, nor was there any indication they had noticed Storm's surge.

He hid behind the first car he reached. Picking his way from one vehicle to the next, he could slowly narrow the gap between himself and the truck. But that trick would only last so long. The ice cream truck had roughly 150 feet of open pavement surrounding it.

He began weaving from car to car, never letting his vision drop from the truck.

Which is why he saw the narrow beam of blue light coming from the turret.

It was both strikingly blue and blindingly bright. As a reflex, Storm turned away. He could feel the burn to his retinas from the few nanoseconds he had been focused on it. He blinked several times rapidly. There was a line in his vision, almost like he stared at the sun too long.

"Mockingbird has been hit," Jones said. "The wing is off. It's going down."

Storm blinked again. The line was fading. He looked up in the sky to see the smoking plane entering a death spiral. He dashed toward the parked vehicle closest to the truck and un-holstered his Dirty Harry gun.

"Okay," he said. "That means these guys have hit their target and are going to close up shop any second. I'm moving in."

"Don't harm the weap—"

Storm ended the call before Jones could complete his instruction. He had heard just about enough of that.

STORM CROUCHED BEHIND THE CLOSEST VEHICLE TO the ice cream truck, which he studied carefully. He was near enough now that he could see inside the cab. It was empty.

The terrorists had to be in back, which was a good development for Storm. There was only so much room in there, especially considering the laser itself had to take most of the space. That meant there were no more than three of them. Perhaps only one.

There were no signs of antipersonnel armaments on the truck, nothing more threatening than the aforementioned Nutty Buddy decal. Still, he did not feel he could approach any nearer. One hundred and fifty feet of open parking lot was too great a distance. He could cover the distance in less than six seconds, yes. But that was still six seconds when he would be totally exposed.

He had to know what—and whom—he was facing. Time to attack. He aimed Dirty Harry at the front-passenger tire and squeezed the trigger. The tire exploded. The truck, now partly disabled, lurched toward its front right.

Storm waited.

No response.

Maybe the people inside were so focused on the

laser they didn't feel it. It's possible they also might not have heard it, too. The inner compartment could be soundproof to a certain extent.

Storm aimed at the rear-passenger tire; shot it out, too. The truck was now leaning to its right at fifteen degrees. There was no way anyone inside could be unaware of the sudden incline.

They would be coming out any second to inspect what was happening. There was no door on the back. There was an opening on the right side—an awning that could be brought up, allowing ice cream to be sold from underneath. But that was bolted down. Storm was reasonably sure it was just for show.

No, the only way out of the interior would be through the cab. Storm trained his vision on that part of the truck. He counted to ten. There was no sign of movement. He counted to thirty. Still nothing.

He put three quick shots into the passenger-side door, in case anyone was crouching behind it. Storm was using hollow-tipped rounds, which were not ideal for penetrating thick armor. But the ice cream truck's side was only marginally thicker than a tin can. It was no match for the force of a .44 Magnum.

Storm counted to thirty again. The truck just sat there, forlornly, tilted to one side on its rims. It wasn't going anywhere; that was for sure. And the cautious thing for Storm to do would be to wait until he had backup. Jones was surely sending reinforcements.

But then the laser would be in Jones's hands by the end of the day. That outcome was unacceptable to Storm. He couldn't lose control of this situation. He had to handle this himself.

With Dirty Harry still drawn and ready to fire, Storm approached the truck in a low crouch. The wind stirred. The smell of brackish water filled his nose. From somewhere nearby, he heard the shrill cry of an osprey.

There was a stillness about the truck that was simply eerie. It was like the thing was being operated by ghosts. He was next to it now, his back flat against its side. He risked a quick glance in the cab.

Empty. For sure. He yanked the handle. The door opened. He climbed in.

The inside was remarkable only inasmuch as it kept faithfully to its pretense of being an ice cream truck. There was even a button to ring a bell that would alert children to the presence of frozen-dairy deliciousness coming near.

There was an opening between the two seats with a small door that a man would have to crouch to go through. This was the entrance to the laser area. Storm aimed at the top of it. If someone was crouched on the other side, lying in wait for him, that's where his head would be. Storm fired.

The noise of Dirty Harry discharging in such a close space was deafening. Storm couldn't suppress his flinch reflex. When he looked, he saw that the bullet had not penetrated the door. It had bounced off and buried itself in the dashboard on the other side.

The door was bulletproof. This was no ordinary ice cream truck after all.

Whoever was inside the trailer was now fully aware of his presence. Storm assumed they were laying an ambush for him. He couldn't risk being in the middle of the doorframe when he opened it.

He hopped over to the driver's seat, crouching on it. With his body out of the way, he pulled the door handle.

He half expected a bulletproof door would be locked, but it swung open easily. He three-quarters expected its opening might be greeted by a bullet coming out, but no projectiles passed. He fully expected to be met by some kind of resistance, but there was none.

Finally, he allowed himself to look in. What he saw was a marvel of engineering, for sure—a series of mirrors and crystals and engines whose purpose he could only guess. It was both exotic and beautiful, and a part of Storm wanted to spend all day studying it.

But in that moment, what he saw was not as pressing as what he didn't see. There were no human beings inside. There wasn't room for any amid all the machinery.

Storm had thought the laser was being operated by ghosts. It was actually being operated by remote control. The terrorists had moved the truck into place and were firing it from somewhere else. Perhaps somewhere nearby. Perhaps many miles away. Perhaps a bunker outside Jalālābād, Afghanistan.

From overhead, Storm heard the beating of helicopter rotors getting closer. The reinforcements were arriving. Perhaps they were Jones's people. Perhaps they were FBI.

To Storm, it didn't matter. They had their priorities. He had his. *We can't be trusted, either.*

He waded into the back of the truck, amid all that fancy, delicate hardware. As a lover of technology, he felt some small regret for what he was about to do. As a lover of humanity, he felt none.

He turned Dirty Harry around, gripping it by its still-warm barrel so it was less like a gun and more like a hammer. And then he started swinging.

The truck trailer was soon filled with the sound of glass shattering and metal being twisted. If his gun barrel wasn't strong enough to destroy something, his booted foot took over. Storm took three minutes to wreck as much as he could. The helicopter was getting closer the whole time.

When he was satisfied he had reduced the guts of the weapon to a shattered mess—beyond any hope of reconstruction or even comprehension—he stepped back outside the truck and called Jones.

"Storm!" he heard. "What's going on?"

"There's no one inside," Storm said. "They were operating it remotely."

"But we have the weapon."

"Yes and no. I think they must have been monitoring the truck and seen me coming. I heard a small charge go off inside as I was approaching," he lied. "They sabotaged their own weapon rather than let us get it. It's a mess inside."

Jones took a second to absorb this information. "Well," he said, philosophically. "I suppose we could have anticipated that. We'll get it back here and study what's left. In the meantime, I have another task for you. One of our agents picked up some chatter as to who might be behind this and why. But we can't afford to compromise him. I'm hoping you can go in and, ah, extract some information."

"Okay. Where am I going?"

"Panama."

CHAPTER 14

PANAMA CITY, Panama

Storm spent the first part of his flight studying the intelligence that had been gathered on the Emirates Four.

Not that it was much. As with the Pennsylvania Three, crash investigators had yet to make much sense out of the wreckage left on the ground.

Likewise, the victims were a scattershot cross-section of the kind of folks who might have reason to visit Dubai. Along with hundreds of little-known mothers and fathers, sons and daughters, and business travelers and vacationers, there were: Lyle Gomez, a professional golfer coming into the city for a tournament; Beth Bowling, the tennis player; Barbara Andersen, a celebrated cabaret singer; Viktor Schultz, the head of Tariffs and Trade for the European Union; Gunther Neubauer, who represented Schleswig-Holstein in the Bundestag, the German equivalent of Congress; and Adrienne Pellot, a leggy French supermodel best known for her *Vogue* cover shots.

The list went on. Until he made sense of why this was happening, all the information had the feeling of cosmic background noise, hissing on a low frequency for all eternity.

Storm soon drifted off. He was fortunate he slept well on airplanes. Lately, it seemed to be the only rest he was getting. He was jolted awake by the wheels of the Gulfstream IV touching down on Runway 03R/21L at Tocumen International Airport.

Like many of North America's air transit hubs, Tocumen was still mostly shut down, but it was slowly coming back to life. Commercial airlines were going to begin flying again soon. Private jet travel had been cleared for anyone brave enough to attempt it.

Storm entered on his own passport—something of a novelty for him when traveling on business—and quickly cleared customs. He was on the other side, in an otherwise empty arrivals area, when he was greeted by the only other soul there, a dashing man whose features appeared to be a mix of Spanish and Mesoamerican.

"And he sent by the hand of Nathan the prophet," the man said.

"And he called his name Jedediah, because of the LORD," Storm said, completing the passage from II Samuel.

"Greetings, Mr. Storm. Whatever you've been told my name is, you will call me Carlos Villante. You will remember at all times that I am the deputy director of the Autoridad del Canal de Panama. I work for a man named Nico Serrano, who is the director of the authority. And you are an American investor here to consider buying bonds issued by the authority. Are we clear?"

"Exceedingly."

"Good. Come with me. We have much to do and little time."

Storm followed Villante to the short-term parking area, where he walked straight for a Cadillac CTS.

"Nice ride," Storm said. "But isn't it a little too nice for the deputy director of a public agency?"

A knowing smile spread across Villante's cheeks. "Have you ever heard the story of the man with the bags of sand?"

"Can't say that I have."

"Please, get in and I'll tell you," Villante said, gesturing toward the passenger's side as he entered via the driver's side.

Villante buckled his seat belt, fired up the engine, and drove out of the parking garage as he spoke. "One morning at the border, a man on a bicycle approached a customs agent with two bulging saddlebags. The customs agent opened the bags to find they were filled with sand. The agent proceeded to dig through them, sure he would find drugs or jewels or some hidden contraband. He found nothing but sand, so he had no choice but to wave the man through.

"The next morning, the man on the bicycle came back. Again, his saddlebags were filled with sand. Again, the customs agent checked them thoroughly and, again, he found nothing. The same thing happened the next morning. And the morning after that. And every morning for weeks. The customs agent was growing increasingly frustrated. He started forcing the man to empty out the bags on a table, so he could search the sand grain by grain. Then he turned the bags inside out. Then he put the bags through an X-ray machine, sure he would see something. But there was never anything more than sand.

"Finally, one morning the man on the bicycle was coming through, and the customs agent said, 'Please, sir. I surrender. I will not report you, today or ever. But you must tell me: *what* are you smuggling into my country?' And the man said, 'Very well. I will tell you. I am smuggling bicycles.'"

Storm cracked a grin.

"So that is why I drive this car," Villante said. "People at the authority, people all over Panama City, they think I must be taking a bribe from somewhere. And they have searched high and low trying to figure out from whom and for what. As long as they remain determined in that search, they will never see what I am really doing."

"Good cover," Storm said.

"So far," Villante said. "Anyhow, I hope you are sufficiently impressed that I may now give you your briefing."

"Please do."

"Your target is named Eusebio Rivera. He lives on the seventieth-floor penthouse of Pearl Tower, one of the newest skyscrapers in the city. He is a very successful, very wealthy businessman. He is well connected among the class of businessmen who came to prominence in the years leading up to this country's takeover of the canal, and he only grew richer after it happened. But I assume Jones told you about the troubles of the expansion project and what that means for men like Rivera?"

"He did," Storm said. "But he said it was better to let you fill me in on your encounter with him."

Villante told Storm about his visit with Rivera on the day of the Pennsylvania Three. From his phone, Villante played a few clips of Rivera talking about Erik Vaughn. Villante was unable to bug Rivera's apartment, but he was able to get a tap put on his work phone. The recordings had made it clear:

Villante was not the only man Rivera had told about the dead congressman. He wasn't even the only man Rivera had invited over to toast Vaughn's death. In each case, the toast was the same: down with Erik Vaughn, up with Jared Stack.

When Villante finished, Storm said, "So he knew Erik Vaughn was dead before it was announced in the media."

"That's right."

"And did you ask him how he knew this?"

"I did. He was evasive. I couldn't press the issue without creating suspicion. The deputy director of the canal authority would not be interested in such things."

"Of course. But you're thinking he knows more than he's letting on."

"I suggested that perhaps he was involved and he responded by toasting Vaughn's death. Ordinarily, I might have disregarded such a gesture as posturing. Men like Eusebio Rivera are always trying to make themselves seem more important than they are. But you combine that with his seemingly insider knowledge about Vaughn's death *and* his insistence that the canal authority director, Nico Serrano, immediately go to Washington. . . . He seemed like a man very aware of the strings he was pulling. I have not played all of the wiretaps for you, but he made sure everyone in Panama City was aware of Congressman Vaughn's death and that they made plans to act accordingly."

Storm nodded. They were passing through palm tree–lined streets recently made wet by a brief rainstorm. It was pushing eleven o'clock at night. Panama City was a hardworking town. The sidewalks were empty. Most of the residents had to be at their jobs in the morning and had already turned in.

"So you need me to get him in a confessional mood," Storm said.

"I am told that's part of your expertise."

Storm just nodded. "How am I getting to him?"

"At this hour, he will be holed up at his penthouse in Pearl Tower."

"What's security like there?"

"Difficult," Villante said. "Pearl Tower is high-end residential. The poor in Panama have come a long way since the seventies, but there's still a pretty big gap between them and the rich. And for all the beautiful buildings you see around you, the slums are never far. It makes the rich fairly paranoid. Rightly so. They make sure they are well protected."

"Specifics, please?"

"There's a doorman outside the building, then a twenty-four-hour concierge just inside who eyeballs everyone who comes in. If the concierge doesn't like what he sees, he locks down the elevators and then radios their on-site security. There are anywhere from two to four of them, depending on the hour, and they're always armed."

"That doesn't sound difficult," Storm said. "If anything, that sounds like an open invitation to—"

"I'm not finished. Rivera has his own bodyguards, who are with him at all times. He keeps a staff of six, at least two of which are always on duty. The nightmen are named Hector and Cesar. They drive for him, stick near him whenever he's out in public. When he's at home, they have a feed of the building's security cameras that they keep an eye on. I have no doubt you can handle the rent-a-cops on the ground. But he's on the top floor. You'd have seventy stories to go up, either by elevator or stairwell.

They would have all the time they needed to prepare a nasty greeting for you."

"But being as you work for Jones, you've already thought of a clever way around all this."

"I have," Villante said. "Jones tells me you like . . . what did he call them . . . toys, yes?"

A gleam appeared in Storm's eyes. "Yes, yes I do. I like toys a lot."

"And he tells me you're an expert climber and that you are in good practice at the moment?"

"I am."

"Good. Because you've got quite the climb ahead of you."

A HALF HOUR LATER, STORM WAS ALREADY FORTY stories up the side of Pearl Tower.

On his hands were strapped two circular pads. Two similar pads were strapped to his knees. Using aligned carbon nanotubes—a technology that mimicked the microscopic hairs that let a gecko hang upside down with just one finger—the pads allowed him to cling to the side of the building. The pads were wirelessly linked to one another. Controls on the hand pads let Storm control when the pads gripped and when they slid. It meant that Storm could pull himself up with his hands while bracing against his knees; and then, while his hands held steady, he could slide his knees forward.

It was slowgoing, being that he could only go about three feet with each pull. It was unnerving, being that he had no net or harness. And it made him look like a giant inchworm.

But it made him feel like Spider-Man. Make that

Elvis Spider-Man. Villante had outfitted him in a white, one-piece suit that helped him blend into the side of the building, lest any passerby alert authorities that a skyscraper was being free-climbed by a lunatic.

And for as difficult as the climbing was, the thought of being Elvis Spider-Man cheered him enough—or distracted him enough—to keep going. That, and he needed the time to scheme. Villante had given him a rundown on the apartment, its layout and its contents. He directed Storm toward the bedroom, told him where the bodyguards would likely be, and generally gave him a sense of what he would face.

But it was up to Storm to come up with an exact plan, something he had not done by the time he reached the seventieth and final floor of his ascent. He was—not for the first time—going to have to make it up as he went along.

Secured to his back was a disc-shaped object roughly the size and shape of a children's snow saucer. It had been wrapped in white, for camouflage purposes.

That was the toy that he began putting into use when he stopped at Rivera's bedroom window. Removing his climbing pads and letting them stay stuck to the wall of the building, he shrugged the disc off his back, unwrapped it, and placed it on the window.

He pressed a button. Without making a sound, with only the slightest shred of vibration, a diamond-tipped blade inside the disc made a full circle, leaving a clean incision in its wake. Storm yanked away the disc, which retained the circular piece of glass, and quickly attached it to one of the climbing pads still stuck to the building.

Then came the dangerous part. Or, rather, it had all been dangerous; this was simply the part that was most dangerous. If the slumbering Mr. Rivera became aware that a warm, moist breeze was suddenly blowing through a hole in his bedroom window and decided to investigate—and then, further, to alert his bodyguards—Storm might be crawling through the hole to face the barrel of a gun.

His only hope was to move quickly. He affixed the one remaining hand pad to the glass and gripped it tight. He released the kneepads and swung himself inside.

In one fluid motion, he rolled and came up with his Dirty Harry Stealth Hunter drawn, a move he had practiced many times.

Except this was not one of the times he needed it. All he heard was a man snoring thunderously.

He crept toward the slumbering figure of Eusebio Rivera, who was on his back, mouth wide open. Each inhale was met with a noise loud enough to rattle the nightstand next to his bed. Storm had never heard such a cacophonous soft palate. The exhales merely sounded like a person being strangled.

Storm reached for his back pocket and a small, plastic container that resembled a package of Baby Wipes. He pulled out a handkerchief that was slightly damp—again, like Baby Wipes—except what had made it moist was not infant-safe: it had been doused with chloroform.

He held the cloth under Rivera's nose for exactly two inhales—enough to make sure he wouldn't wake up for a half hour or so, not so much that he would be unconscious all night.

Satisfied that Rivera had been properly dosed, Storm rolled the man on his side. The snoring stopped—to the relief of anyone within ten floors of Rivera's penthouse who hadn't been blessed either with earplugs or congenital deafness.

Storm walked lightly across the deep pile carpeting to the bedroom door. Outside, he could hear a soccer game—sorry, *futbol* game—playing softly on the television. It was a rerun of Panama's international friendly against Costa Rica, and it sounded like the ticos were not playing well, to the great relief of Panamanians throughout the isthmus.

For all Storm knew, only one of the guards was watching the television. Or neither one of them were. Making it foolish to open the door. He wished one of the toys Jones had given him made it possible to see through walls. Opening the door without knowing the location of his opposition was foolhardy.

Sure, he could swing open the door and shoot at anything that moved. But problem one, the entire building, including the armed guards far below, would be aware that all was not well in the penthouse. And problem two, he didn't feel like killing two men whose only sin was doing their job and protecting their boss.

This, admittedly, was more of an ethical problem. Perhaps even a stylistic problem. But still, a man had to have a code of operations, and Storm took his seriously.

Storm thought it through for a moment and decided on his plan. He replayed in his mind the sound of Rivera's voice on the wiretap recordings. Spanish was one of the eight languages Storm spoke. And owing to the influx of Spanish-speaking immigrants currently redefining American demographics, he had more of an opportunity to use it than he did, say, his Romanian.

He positioned himself on the right side of the door, the side away from the hinges. Trying to summon the feeling of gravel in his vocal cords, he called out, "Hector . . . Hector come in here, please," in his best imitation of the raspy voice he'd heard on the wiretaps.

Storm stood with his back against the wall. He transferred his gun from his right hand to his left. He heard footsteps coming his way. They were soft on the carpet, but the man who made them was heavy. Storm listened intently as they got closer.

Timing was essential. And Storm's was perfect. The moment the man's foot crossed the threshold, Storm swung his right elbow with all his force, bringing to bear not only his own momentum, moving backward, but also that of the bodyguard, who was walking forward. The man was shorter than Storm thought he would be. But Storm was able to adjust his aim at the last second such that the hardest part of his elbow still connected with the softest part of the man's nose.

Storm heard the crunch of cartilage. The man dropped heavily. Storm quickly hopped on him, smothering his face with the chloroform-dampened handkerchief. He dragged the man's body into the darkness of the bedroom.

One down.

Now, of course, Storm had another dilemma. He did not know where the other guard was. He eased out into the sitting area, Dirty Harry leading the way.

It was empty, save for its furnishings—two easy chairs; a love seat; and a low-slung, five-foot-long, brown coffee table that somehow reminded Storm of a dachshund. The flat-screen television was bolted to the wall.

Storm kept in his mind a loose floor plan of the apartment, one based on Villante's description. Beyond the sitting room, there was a great room that opened into a kitchen, a formal dining room next to the kitchen, a foyer leading to two spare bedrooms, a media room, a small library . . . and the other bodyguard, Cesar, who could be anywhere.

Then Storm heard a toilet flush. It came from just off the foyer.

Storm crossed the sitting room and passed quickly into the great room, knowing Cesar would have to pass through to get back to the television and the *futbol* game. Improvising now, Storm crouched behind an easy chair, ducking so his six-foot-two body was hidden by its suede-covered shape.

If Cesar the bodyguard had any inkling as to Storm's presence, it would have been a terrible move, going prone in a way that made him vulnerable to attack; and if the penthouse had hardwood floors, Storm wouldn't have been able to attempt the move that came next.

But all was in Storm's favor. Cesar walked through the great room with the easy stride of a man comfortable in familiar surroundings. And he didn't hear anything as Storm burst from his hiding spot and jumped on the bodyguard while simultaneously toeing the backs of his knees.

It was a tackle that would have made a Washington Redskins linebacker proud. Storm finished the move straddled on top of the man. Cesar let out a grunt, but his vision was soon filled by the muzzle of Storm's Dirty Harry gun.

"I would be very, very quiet if I were you," Storm said, in Spanish. "I wouldn't even say a word right now."

The guard lay on the ground, face down, either resigned to his defeat or uncertain of any other options he had. Storm again reached for his chloroform handkerchief.

But the moment his hand touched the cloth, he knew it wasn't going to work. The fabric was already dry. Once again, he cursed sleeping in Mr. Menousek's chemistry class. He should have remembered: chloroform was chemically similar to alcohol and shared its volatility, which meant it evaporated quickly.

"And now we have a situation," Storm said in hushed Spanish. "I don't want to kill you. Really, I don't. But I also can't have you bothering me. Your boss has done some bad things, and I need to be able to question him about them without your getting in my way and without your alerting all the neighbors. I can't think of how we're going to accomplish that unless I shoot you. But I'm guessing you don't want to be shot, do you?"

Storm had the gun barrel against Cesar's head, which shook slightly. Storm realized that due to his previous instruction—the part about staying quiet—the man was saying nothing.

So Storm said, "You can give me some input if you want to. I'm really at something of an impasse here."

Cesar cleared his throat and said softly, "You could tie me up. Bind me. Gag me."

"Yes!" Storm said. "Yes, that's an excellent idea. And it's one I might have come up with myself. Except I didn't bring any materials to do that and I've never been to this apartment before, so I don't even know if there's any rope or—"

"There's some duct tape in the utility room."

"There's a utility room? Vil . . . uh, I wasn't aware of that."

"Yes, yes," Cesar said, his voice growing excited. "You could keep your gun on me, make me keep my hands in the air. And I could walk to the utility room, get the duct tape. You could make me bind Hector first, then bind myself. This would be the intelligent thing for you to do, as otherwise I might be able to take advantage of a momentary lapse in your attention and disarm you."

Storm was nodding before he even realized he agreed with the man. "You make an excellent point. Okay. Let's do that."

Storm let Cesar up.

"Thank you," he said, putting his hands up.

"You are most welcome," Storm said, relieved that civility was not dead, after all.

TRUE TO HIS WORD, CESAR THE BODYGUARD PRO-duced a roll of duct tape, which he used to secure Hector to one of the chairs in the living room. He then went to work on himself. Storm assisted him in the final stages until he was satisfied the man wasn't going anywhere.

As a final act of mercy, Storm turned Cesar toward the *futbol* game. The man was bound and gagged, so he signaled his appreciation by blinking his eyes several times.

Storm shifted his attention to Eusebio Rivera, who had returned to sleeping on his back and to the window-shaking snores that emanated as a result. Having been busy with the bodyguards, Storm had yet to work out a precise plan of how he was going to force information out of Rivera when he woke up.

Then Storm's attention shifted to the twenty-foot-long fish tank that occupied one wall of the bedroom. Next to the tank was a small end table that held two fishnets—one small, the other larger—and a variety of fish food in canisters that ranged in size from a saltshaker to a tennis ball can.

Beside the table, there was a footstool that allowed access to the top of the tank, which came within about two feet of the ceiling. That, Storm reasoned, was for feeding of the piscine critters that were swimming aimlessly about inside.

Curiously, there was also a partition that separated a quarter of the tank from the other three quarters. On the left side of the partition there were dozens of species of saltwater fish. The right side appeared to be barren. It had the same fake coral, the same underwater vegetation. Just no fish.

Then Storm saw it wasn't barren, after all. Mostly hidden in one of the rocky crags, Storm saw the ghastly, ghoulish face of a moray eel, the biggest one he had ever seen in captivity.

And that's when he got his plan.

Storm returned to the sitting room, flipped over the dachshundlike coffee table, and, with four sweeping chops, sheared the legs off. He slid it along the carpet. It moved with relative ease. Storm grabbed the roll of duct tape, feeling Cesar's eyes on him the whole time. Hector remained insentient.

Taking what now resembled a paramedic's backboard into the bedroom, Storm laid it next to the still-slumbering Rivera. He rolled Rivera onto it, then began securing him to its surface with the duct tape, keeping his arms pinned at his side. As Storm turned him into a duct tape mummy, Rivera resumed his snoring, which had at least one benefit: any strange noises Storm might be making were inaudible next to that racket.

With Rivera properly tamped down—only his head and feet were uncovered—Storm slid his quarry and the impromptu backboard off the bed and onto the floor, then over toward the fish tank. The moray eel side of the fish tank. He removed the tank's lid and set it aside so it wouldn't get in the way of what came next.

He lifted the head end of the board so it was leaning against the side of the tank, then went around to the foot of it. With both hands, he lifted it and began shoving the leading edge up toward the top of the tank. Rivera was portly but small-statured. He probably didn't weigh more than about two hundred pounds. Storm routinely deadlifted far more.

When he got the top of the board aligned with the top of the tank, Storm kept shoving, walking up the footstool as he went, until the backboard was finally where he wanted it: resting on top of the lidless fish tank.

Storm's next task was to catch himself a fish. He selected the larger of the two nets and, standing on the footstool, dipped it into the fish-occupied side of the tank. The fish were not especially enamored of being caught, but eventually Storm was able to chase down a large, slow angelfish, which he brought out of the water, thrashing and flopping. He removed the fish from the net with his hand and brought it down to the end table, where it wriggled some more.

"Sorry about this, fish," Storm said, removing a utility knife from his back pocket. He unfolded a blade and stabbed just behind the fish's eye, putting it out of its misery.

He moved the footstool back over toward the

eel side of the tank, where Rivera was still prone. His snoring, however, had finally stopped. Storm climbed the stool and, with the utility knife, began disemboweling the fish, smearing the guts on Rivera's cheeks, forehead, and chin.

That's what Rivera was experiencing when he finally came to: the very foreign feeling of being strapped to a table and having his face covered in fish entrails by a perfect stranger, who was dressed in what appeared to be a white leisure suit.

"What the . . . what is this? Who are you?" Rivera demanded. "Why can't I—"

"Shhh. No noise, Mr. Rivera."

The man, perhaps sensing that he was at something of a disadvantage, quieted for a moment as Storm continued his job. But as Storm rubbed what might have been a fish pancreas—did fish have pancreases?—on his nose, Rivera could not help himself.

"What are you doing?"

"Preparing you for the eel," Storm said calmly. He tossed the pancreas, or whatever it was, aside. He had been careful not to let any of the fish parts fall into the tank. He didn't want the eel's appetite to be sated by an easy meal.

"What are you—"

"Eels have lousy eyesight but a tremendous sense of smell," Storm said. "They're like the bloodhounds of the sea. They let their noses tell them what to eat. I want to make sure your face smells absolutely wonderful to my friend hiding in the rocks down there. I'm betting if he's hungry enough, he'd strike at pretty much anything that smells good to him."

"Are you mad?" Rivera asked, struggling in vain against his duct tape binding.

"Some other eel facts: their teeth are razor-sharp, but what's really impressive about them are their jaws. Not just the bite force—that's something for sure. But also their stubbornness. Once a moray eel clamps on something, it doesn't let go. Even in death. It's something of a primitive design from an evolutionary standpoint, and I won't bore you with the mechanics. I'll just tell you that divers who have been bit by moray eels often have to pry the jaws off with pliers when they get back to land."

"What is your . . . ? What do you want?"

Storm did not answer. Rivera's face was now glistening with the slick residue of what had once been the insides of an angelfish. Storm climbed down the step stool and repositioned it so he could grab Rivera's feet. He lifted and, with the backboard sliding along the thick, beveled edge of the glass, lowered Rivera's head into the tank.

It was, essentially, waterboarding. Storm style. With a hungry eel to provide a little extra fear factor.

Storm counted to thirty before sliding Rivera out of the water. He emerged, gasping and spitting.

"Jesus, man," he said, between huge, hungry gulps of air. "What do you want? Money? You want money? I'll give you mo—"

Storm tilted the head of the board back in the water, submerging Rivera once again. This time, he counted to forty-five.

The eel had not yet made an appearance, a mild disappointment to Storm. If Villante was right, Rivera was responsible for the deaths of more than a thousand people worldwide. Having a moray eel eat his face ought to be the least of his punishment. Storm brought Rivera's head out again.

"God, please," he said, his eyes bolted open with

fear, his chest heaving as his lungs tried to recover from oxygen deficit.

"God is the least of your worries at the moment," Storm said, then put the man under again. This time, he counted to sixty. And, perhaps, he did it a little more slowly than the previous two times. Just to give the eel a chance.

When he brought Rivera back to the surface again, no words came out. He was now focused only on survival, not on begging, arguing, or cajoling. Which is exactly what Storm was waiting for.

"Erik Vaughn," Storm said. "I want you to tell me everything about how you had him killed."

"Vaughn? What are you . . . what are you—"

Storm sighed impatiently and jammed Rivera's head under again. Storm counted to ninety this time.

He worried he had perhaps overdone it. The man's thrashing slowly stilled. When Storm brought Rivera back up, he did not appear to be breathing anymore. Storm was just beginning to consider giving the man's diaphragm a quick pump when Rivera wretched out a stomach full of salt water, coughed several times, and resumed respiration.

"Please, please," he said, weakly. "I don't know what you're—"

"I'm talking about the promethium laser beam you used to shoot Congressman Erik Vaughn's plane out of the sky," Storm said. "You're going to tell me everything about it. Not only how you did it, but who you worked with and how you got the promethium. You're also going to tell me where you're hiding William McRae, the scientist you kidnapped. You're going to tell me all of this in an impressive level of detail so I know you're not just making it up, and you're going to do it right now."

Rivera just lay there, fighting pathetically for breath. Storm was sure he had broken the man's spirit. But perhaps a bit more convincing was required. He tilted the board to again submerge Rivera.

"No! No! Please!" the man howled. "I promise you, I know nothing about this. Nothing at—"

Storm put him under, but counted only to sixty this time, if only because he really, really did not want to have to administer mouth-to-mouth on Rivera. Not at any time. And especially not when his face had been covered in fish entrails.

"You seemed pretty happy Vaughn died," Storm said when he brought Rivera up again. "From what I understand, you've been toasting his death with everyone in Panama City."

"Yes, yes, I know," Rivera said, panting fiercely. "You are right. I was very happy. Congressman Vaughn has been an impediment to getting funding for the canal expansion project. I said some terrible things about him and I'm very, very sorry. But I didn't have him killed. I swear to you."

"Then how did you know he was dead before the media announced it?"

"I have a cousin who emigrated to America in the eighties. He is a citizen now. He works for the FAA."

"Who is he and what's his date of birth?"

Rivera quickly replied with a name and a date.

"I'm going to have that checked out," Storm said. "But in the meantime, I'm going to give the eel another chance to find your face."

Rivera went back under. Pulling out his satellite phone, Storm called the cubby and got one of the nerds to run a quick check on the FAA's employment records. Sure enough, Rivera's cousin checked out.

Storm brought Rivera back up. The eel had not yet shown itself. All the movement was probably scaring it, encouraging it to stay hidden. A shame.

"My people say you're lying," Storm said.

"No, please, please! I'm telling the truth, I swear it! Listen to me, I had nothing to do with this congressman dying, but I might be able to help you."

"I'm listening."

"You said this laser, it was promethium, yes?"

"Yes."

His voice came fast, and he forced the words out between large breaths. "I was at the locks a little while back, maybe three, four weeks ago, and one of my friends down there was talking. He was saying that a ship had come through that made the sensors go off, the nuclear sensors, what do you call them . . . ?"

"A Geiger counter?"

"Yes, the Geiger counter. This was big news at the locks. Everyone was talking about it. There is always the fear that terrorists will try something at the canal. They pulled the ship aside, searched it, and found the container that was setting off the counter. I don't know the details, but they tested what was inside and they found out it was promethium."

"Did they detain it?"

"They couldn't. That shipment, it was not intended for import into Panama, so there was nothing customs could do. They packed it back up, shielded it so the radiation wouldn't get any of the sailors sick, and sent it on its way. There are many hazardous substances we are allowed to detain, but promethium isn't on the list."

"So they let it through."

"Yes."

"And how are you thinking this is helpful to me?"

"Because I remember the name of the sender. It was printed on the forms, and my man at the locks told me what it was. It was a company out of Egypt called Ahmed Trades Metal."

"'Ahmed Trades Metal,'" Storm repeated, making sure he had heard it correctly.

"Yes, that's right. If you find that company, you will find the source of your promethium."

STORM LEFT THE BEDROOM WITHOUT ANOTHER WORD. He had no continuing use for Eusebio Rivera, but also no desire to have Rivera slow his exit by calling building security.

Still, Storm didn't lack compassion. He cut loose Hector, who signaled his profound thanks by slumping onto the floor, letting the drool continue to pour from his mouth and remaining in a deep sleep.

Eventually, Hector would wake up, remember having been tackled and wonder why his boss was perched atop a fish tank. But he would also cut everyone loose and let them go about their business. There was no harm done, except to Rivera's pride and to the fish Storm had to cut open. Collateral damage.

"Blink once if you want me to change the channel," Storm said to Cesar, who did not blink in return.

"Enjoy the game." Cesar acknowledged Storm's well wishes by smiling with his eyes.

Storm's exit from the building—which came via the elevator—was substantially faster than his entry into it. Villante was waiting for him in his Cadillac, which was parked on the street outside.

"Jones wants a report," Villante said as Storm climbed into the car. It was after two o'clock in the morning, which meant it was after three o'clock where Jones was. But, of course, the man would still be awake.

Storm pulled out his satellite phone, and prepared himself to lie. If the promethium had come from Ahmed Trades Metal, then the last thing Storm wanted was for Jones to know it. Whatever he discovered about the company, he would have to do without the help of anyone in the cubby.

"What do you have?" Jones asked.

"It's a dead end. Rivera knew nothing."

"Are you sure?"

"My methods were effective," Storm assured him.

"Well, I've got another lead for you to follow. You remember I mentioned Ingrid Karlsson?"

"Yes."

"Her reward offer has apparently netted some significant information," Jones said.

"What is it?"

"She wouldn't tell me over the phone. But she said she would share what she knows in person if I would send an agent I trusted."

"And instead you're sending me?"

"Exactly," Jones said. "She'll pick you up at Slip F-18 at the marina outside Casino de Monte-Carlo two mornings from now. A trip to Monaco won't trouble you too much, will it?"

"You know I will sacrifice for my craft if I must."

CHAPTER 15

MONTE CARLO, Monaco

The man who emerged onto the gaming floor at Casino de Monte-Carlo—refreshed, resplendent, and refined—owed a little something to the Boy Scout he had once been.

Derrick Storm's association with the Boy Scouts of America had resulted in some less-than-desirable outcomes, yes: a brief bout of pyromania around the age of twelve that nearly incinerated his father's car; a tendency to encourage younger boys to engage in snipe hunts, at least one of which ended with a Cub Scout getting lost in the woods overnight; and, later, during his time with the organization, a fascination with a certain Girl Scout camp across the lake that nearly led to his arrest.

But it had at least one positive result. Storm had been instilled with the virtue of self-reliance, having taken the Boy Scout motto, "Be Prepared," very much to heart.

And so whereas a lesser man might have foundered when faced with this emergency—a night in Monaco, one of the world's great human playgrounds, with nothing to do—Storm had found himself equal to the crisis.

Having the right friends helped in this matter. The moment he hung up with Jones, Storm calculated that it was nearing nine o'clock in the morning

Monaco time. He deemed that an acceptable time to ring Jean-François Vidal, the chief operating officer of the Société des bains de mer de Monaco, the company founded by the Grimaldis—the ruling family of Monaco—to run the principality's most important tourist properties.

He was also a man who owed his life—not to mention the non-bomb-marred façade of his most famous hotel—to the resourcefulness of a certain American intelligence operative.

So when Storm announced himself over his satellite phone, what he heard in response was Vidal half-speaking, half-singing, "Derrick, Derrick, Derrick! It is such an exquisite pleasure to receive your call. Please say you are coming to our small jewel of a city."

"I am."

"This is most wonderful news. Please say you are staying as my guest, for this will give me great joy."

"I am."

"Please say you will accept the services of the limousine I will send to the airport to greet you."

"I will."

"Please say I may prepare one of our finest suites at the Hôtel de Paris for you?"

"That would be lovely."

"Please say you are staying at least a week. A month, perhaps?"

"Alas, only a night."

"A shame. Is there anything else I can do for you?"

"I'm currently dressed in a white leisure suit that smells like fear and raw seafood. I suppose I could use an improvement on that."

"It is done," Vidal said. He did not ask Storm's size, what designers he might prefer, or whether he liked starch in his shirts. Vidal was the kind of man who knew such things and took care of them. "Is there anything else?" he asked.

"Nothing at the moment. Except that I hope you will join me for a drink later."

"It would be my honor and privilege."

"Oh, and Jean-François?"

"Yes, my dear Derrick?"

"I know you mean well, but no prostitutes."

Vidal had a tendency to overextend this aspect of his country's hospitality. It was legal in Monaco, of course. But it was still not Storm's style. "Of course not," Vidal assured him, then ended the call laughing about Americans and their prudishness.

Ten and a half hours later, pushed by a brisk tailwind, the same Gulfstream IV that had taken Storm to Panama City landed at Côte d'Azur International Airport in Nice, France. He was then whisked via a stretch Lexus limousine to Monaco and the Hôtel de Paris, where he walked past its low relief sculptures, through its towering colonnades, and into its marble-lined lobby, a bright, airy space that featured an arrangement of fresh flowers in the middle that was nearly as tall as Storm.

He was then shown to the Winston Churchill Diamond Suite, in which the former prime minister himself had stayed many times and was said to have helped furnish and decorate. Two of his prints still hung on the walls.

Once inside, Storm quickly saw Vidal had thought of everything. A Brioni tuxedo, custom-tailored to Storm's exact measurements, hung in the closet. A pair of a.testoni shoes was underneath. A towering fruit basket—not quite as tall as the lobby flower arrangement, but close—and a chilled bottle

of Goût de Diamants were set out in the living room.
The curtains had been drawn, giving Storm a magnificent, 270-degree view of the lights of the city
shining off the cliff and into the darkness of the
Mediterranean beyond.

Moments after he entered, a masseuse knocked on
his door and insisted on administering a brisk massage to work out the kinks from his long flight. That,
followed by a quick jog and a shower, had Storm feeling renewed in body and soul. No longer was he a
bedraggled world traveler who wore yesterday's bad
clothes and smelled vaguely of seafood. He was now
a suave, assured gentleman, dressed in habiliments
that signified to all that he belonged among the professional athletes, celebrities, royalty, and superrich.

It was shortly after ten P.M.—a time at which
Monaco's nightlife was just starting to tune itself into
a humming harmony—when Storm made his way
to the magnificent belle epoque edifice that housed
Place du Casino, Monaco's most famous gaming
destination. His appearance on the casino floor was
immediately greeted by Vidal, who kissed him on
both cheeks.

"You look wonderful as usual, Derrick."

"Thanks to you."

"I have extended a two hundred thousand euro
line of credit. You need only sign for it at the cashier
window. I trust that will be acceptable?"

"That will be fine. You are too kind, Jean-
François."

"Anything for you, Derrick. You know I am
indebted—"

"Your debt is nothing. Let's toast to your health."

. . .

TWO MARTINIS LATER—ENOUGH TO LUBRICATE BUT not inebriate—Storm settled into his first game of blackjack. The first two cards he received were an ace and a queen, which set the tone for the extraordinary run that followed.

For the next hour, Storm could do little wrong. He doubled-down on elevens, tens, nines, even some eights and sevens, all with success. He split sixes and won both hands. He hit on a sixteen against the dealer's jack and was rewarded with a five. He stood with a thirteen and watched the dealer bust.

His bets had started modest—he had no plan to test the boundaries of his two hundred thousand euro credit limit—but still his pile of chips grew, to the point where he was almost embarrassed by it. He kept changing smaller chips into larger ones to hide his success, not that it did much good. Without even trying to keep count, he knew he was up several hundred thousand euros. His tablemates, two older German gentlemen, actually began applauding his success, punctuating it with the occasional *"Gut, sehr gut!"* or a head-shaking *"Mein Gott, mein Gott."*

In the meantime, another game—parallel to the one he was playing at the table—had developed. A striking red-haired woman with high cheekbones and an aristocratic air two tables over kept glancing Storm's way. She wore very little makeup and needed even less. Her hair was up in an exquisitely sculpted twist atop her head. Her slender neck was decorated by a glittering necklace. Her ice-blue dress matched her eyes and plunged low enough that it couldn't really be said to even have a neckline. More of a navel line. Her body was a tribute to the benefits of plentiful exercise.

She was, in short, stunning.

She kept stealing ganders at her phone, like she was expecting something—a message, a call. But none came. Her brow, which was otherwise smooth and perfect, acquired a small indentation every time she brought it out of the tiny, jeweled purse next to her.

Yet to Storm, there was something else about her that made her seem like she wasn't comfortable in all of her luscious, pale skin. He sensed indecision in her. Hesitance. And it wasn't the kind that was calculated to be beguiling. Or was it?

The way the game seemed to be going is that Storm would glance in her direction and catch her staring. She would respond by looking away, as if her eyes had only fallen on him by accident. This happened several times before Storm finally accompanied his glance with a smile. This time, she blushed before turning away.

The pile of chips in front of her, which was small to start with, kept shrinking. She seemed unconcerned with it. Storm decided to ignore her for a time, to see how that would play. When he finally broke down and allowed her to enter his peripheral vision, he saw her gaze had not left him.

Then it returned to her phone. She checked once more for whatever it was she had been checking for this whole time. Once again, the phone seemed disappoint her. She shook her head. She stood. A decision had been made.

Storm returned his attention to his own table. The dealer had just given him two eights. He split them rather than deal with a sixteen against the dealer's seven. His eights were covered by a king and a four. He stood on the eighteen and asked for a hit on the twelve, which got a four on it. So much for avoiding a sixteen.

He opted to stand. The dealer flipped over a queen. It was a wash.

Storm was distracted enough by that action that he hadn't noticed the redhead was now behind him. She was even taller and more lithesome than Storm had first thought. Her hand rested lightly on his shoulder. Her pale, pink lips neared his ear.

No words left her mouth. She just passed behind him, leaving a faint smell of lavender in her wake, and walked out to the balcony.

Storm felt an involuntary twitch in his lower body. He signaled to Vidal, who had been nearby talking with one of his floor managers, and had seen the entire exchange. The Frenchman walked smoothly over to Storm's table. Storm withdrew his bet to signal to the dealer that he was sitting out this hand.

"I thought I told you no prostitutes," Storm said. Not because he actually thought she was a prostitute, but because Vidal would know for sure.

"She is no prostitute, my friend," Vidal assured him. "I do not know the woman. But I do know the jewelry she is wearing. That is a piece by one of the Mouawad brothers. Perhaps you have heard of them, yes? They recently sold a necklace called 'L'Incomparable' for fifty-five million U.S. dollars. That piece she is wearing is not quite as fine and without a loop I could not say for sure . . . but it is worth, say, two, three million euros?"

Storm let out a low whistle. Vidal finished: "All I am saying is, she is not a prostitute. She may be many other things, however. And at least one of the things she is, right now, is alone. Which seems a terrible waste."

Storm shoved a few chips back in front of him,

to show the dealer he wanted to resume play. He was rewarded with two jacks. The dealer had an ace showing and asked the players if they wanted insurance. Storm declined as did the Germans. They immediately regretted it when the dealer flipped over a king.

His luck was changing. Or at least it was in the game of blackjack. In the other game, it remained to be seen. He flipped a ten thousand euro chip at the dealer and shoved back from the table.

"Ah, the legendary Derrick Storm never disappoints the fairer sex, does he?" Vidal crooned.

"You don't mind having these taken care of, do you?" Storm said, gesturing at his chips. "I don't think I want to be encumbered this evening."

"Certainly. Would you like it in gold bullion, delivered to your suite? Euros? Dollars? Pounds? You know we aim to please."

"Just leave it on my account," Storm said. "You never know when it might come in handy. I like to be prepared."

"Very well," Vidal said, then nodded toward the balcony. "I hope you are prepared for that as well."

"We shall see, my friend," Storm said. "We shall see."

He clapped Vidal on the shoulder, and walked out to the balcony.

MONACO WAS THE KIND OF PLACE THAT WAS MORE likely to have a traffic jam at midnight than at noon, and as that late hour approached, the city was alive. But while the light reached the balcony, the noise did not. Only the music from a string quartet, which had just begun its set, leaked out of the open doors of the casino floor. From the nearby Mediterranean, a warm flow of salt-smelling air washed gently inland.

Storm walked up to the woman in the ice-blue dress, who was alone by the stone railing that looked out on the sea. She turned as he approached. A few stray strands of her red hair had slipped out of the twist and were being moved by the breeze. Up close, she was even more captivating than she had been from across a crowded casino room.

"Was it something on my tux?" Storm asked.

"Excuse me?"

"The way you kept looking at me. I thought perhaps I had spilled something on myself. I'm terribly clumsy that way."

"Oh. No. No, that wasn't it at all."

"Not my tux then. My face. I must have something on my face. You'll have to show me where."

He was moving in closer, as if to give her the opportunity to point out whatever flaw she had been staring at.

"No, no," she said.

He was very close now, close enough that the smell of lavender was again filling his nostrils, mixing with the faint hint of sea salt to form a wonderful fragrance. It was one no one could bottle. It was also one Storm would always associate with this moment, this woman, this place.

People sometimes thought that a man like Derrick Storm had been with so many women that one more was no great event. The opposite was, in fact, true. Each new experience was only heightened by the appreciation of past liaisons and the anticipation of future ones. He found the female side of the species endlessly fascinating, and was forever intrigued by its complexities.

"Well, perhaps if we get to know each other better, you'll be comfortable enough to tell me what it is. My name is Derrick Storm."

"I know," she said. "I saw you talking with the manager and I asked him your name. He said you are . . . a very generous man."

"That's a nice thing for him to say."

Their faces were inches apart. He could feel his own heart beating a little harder than was necessary for his current level of exertion, and he noticed a flushing under the faint dusting of makeup on her cheeks. Her heart must have been pounding, too.

"He said you saved the casino from destruction," she said.

"I'm sure he's exaggerating."

"He said you're a hero."

"To others I'm a rogue. It's all a matter of your perspective."

"What's your perspective?"

"My perspective is one that will be improved immeasurably when I kiss you."

He bent his head and brought his lips to hers. She responded by moving her body against his and placing a hand on his chest. Storm was something of a kissing connoisseur and therefore he knew that the first kiss—for all it had been romanticized in song and verse—was never really the best one. It was more like a promissory note, an indication of what the future payout might be, once a certain melding of kissing styles had been achieved. But, at least based on early returns, this one had real potential.

His hand was just beginning to stroke her jawline when she pushed him away.

"I have a boyfriend," she said, quickly.

"Is it me?" Storm asked. "Well, this is a bit

sudden, but, yes, I would be delighted to be your boyfriend."

"No, no," she said, flustered. "I mean, I'm seeing someone."

Storm made a show of looking around. "And yet I see no one. Is he a man blessed with the power of invisibility?"

"No. He was supposed to meet me here, but that was two hours ago."

"I see," Storm said. "Is this the first time he's been late?"

She shook her head.

"Is it the second time?"

She shook her head again.

"Do you have a reason to believe he is desperate to be here but is currently lying in a ditch, incapacitated and unable to signal you or anyone else his distress?"

Another headshake.

"He stands you up a lot, doesn't he?"

This time, a nod.

"Then he is a fool," Storm said. "And I don't say that simply because you're a beautiful woman and he's a fool to leave you alone. I say that because the love of a woman—any woman, no matter how beautiful or homely—is the most exceptional thing that can happen to a man, and he is a fool to treat that most precious commodity as if it were disposable."

Another nod.

"Can I tell you a quick story about love? I think you'll like it."

He intertwined his left hand with her right, and moved his right hand to the small of her back. It was a dancing position, though he was not yet dancing properly. Just swaying.

"I never really got to see my parents' relationship, because my mother died when I was young," he began. "But I got to see quite a bit of my grandparents'. My grandpa Storm was an old-fashioned gentleman. He escorted my grandmother by the arm everywhere they went, even if they were just walking into the grocery store. And he always held the door for her. Didn't matter what kind of door—a car door, a barn door, a bathroom door. If there was a door, Grandpa Storm was going to hold it for her. He loved my grandmother, and that was one of the small ways he showed how much he appreciated her.

"Anyhow, they were going into a restaurant one day when Grandpa was hit by a massive heart attack. It should have killed him on the spot. But there was a door to be opened. I don't know if he worried my grandmother didn't know how to open one or what. Somehow Grandpa managed to stumble to the door and hold it for my grandmother. It was literally his dying act. When the paramedics came, they had to drag him away from the doorway. At the funeral, I told everyone that I don't know whether or not there's a heaven. But if there is, Grandpa is there, holding the door for Grandma."

He had turned his swaying into dancing. Not ambitious dancing. Not yet. But dancing all the same.

"So that's what love is," he concluded. "Or at least that's what love is to me. Now, as for this supposed boyfriend of yours," Storm said, nodding in the direction of the small jeweled purse where she kept her phone, "how is he supposed to hold the door for you if he doesn't even show up?"

He gave her a quick twirl, expertly rejoining her at the end in perfect step.

"I think maybe he shouldn't be my boyfriend anymore," she said.

"I think that's wise."

"You're a very good dancer."

"Oh, we haven't even started dancing yet," he said, and then began in earnest.

They spun around the marble balcony, Storm confident in his lead, the woman sufficiently tutored by her finishing school or boarding school or debutante lessons—or wherever it was modern young women of a certain class learned such things—that she was a more-than-proficient follower. It took perhaps a song or two for them to learn to anticipate one another's movements, but then they settled into a marvelous synchronicity, to the point where he barely had to signify his intent and she barely felt her feet touching the floor.

Lost in the music and the movement, they did not speak for a while. When she finally opened her mouth to say something, it was not what Storm was expecting.

It was, "Jacque!"

A young man, his face bloated, his eyes glassy and red, his nose running, had stumbled out on the balcony. He had on what was easily a five-thousand-dollar tuxedo, but he wore it sloppily, with disregard for its splendor. The bow tie was askew. The shirt was loosely bloused over his midsection, which was also sloppy. The young man had a slender build but was already working on the beginnings of what would someday become a champion beer gut.

Fair or unfair, Storm immediately had the young man pegged. He was a common species here in Monaco and other places where the idle rich tended to congregate: he had been given a world-class education and every opportunity to succeed but was not availing himself of it; rather, he contented himself with spending money for which his great grandfather had worked very hard, making much of it disappear up his nose or down his throat.

"There you are, you whore," Jacque said in slurring French.

Storm started to reply in his own French. "Ease off on the name-calling my—"

"I'll handle this," Storm's dancing partner said quietly before squaring to face her soon-to-be-ex-boyfriend. "Jacque, you were supposed to be here more than two hours ago. I got tired of waiting for you here, just like I've gotten tired of waiting for you to grow up. We're through, Jacque."

"What, because of this dumb piece of meat?" Jacque said, not even looking at Storm. "How much did he cost you?"

Storm moved closer, ready to signify his displeasure with some pointed commentary, when the woman replied: "No, not because of this extraordinary gentleman. You want to know why? Because the only time you're ever nice to me is when you want to have sex or you want me to pick up the check. Because you talk about all these big ideas that you're going to accomplish but you never make a single move to do any of them. And because the only place you ever seem to be in a hurry is in bed."

"How dare you, you slut," Jacque said.

He brought his hands up. He reared back, fist balled, loading his weight onto his back foot. But he never got the chance to transfer it to his front foot and deliver the blow. Storm hit him with a sweeping kick to the midsection. He felt it compress several ribs, more than likely cracking them, and it sent

Jacque reeling backward into the outer wall of the casino. His head slammed against the stone and his body crumpled.

Storm closed in and had to restrain himself from lifting the man up and throwing him over the balcony. It would have been fun, yes; but if the young man really was from a prominent family, it would have caused trouble for Jean-François. And Storm didn't want that.

So, instead, Storm lifted the man's arm and checked his pulse.

"Darn it. Still beating," he said, then let the arm fall back to the man's side. "Shall we dance?"

"No, no," she said, still flushed. "We have to go."

"Why? This set probably has at least two or three more songs in—"

"You don't understand. Jacque's family, they keep a large security force. Well, they call it a security force, but they're really just thugs. When they find out what has happened—"

"I can handle myself."

"I'm sure you can," she said, and again slid close to him, filling his nose with her lavender scent. "But I don't want to waste this evening watching you fight every goon that comes out here. There are better ways to spend our time."

Storm did his best to keep his smile inward. "Yes, yes I suppose there are. We can retire to my suite at the Hôtel de Paris, if you wish."

"No. No. They might look for you in the hotel. And we can't go to my place, either. But my family has a little pied-à-terre not far from here that Jacque does not know about. It is small, but there is room enough for two, if you like."

"I like," he confirmed. "I like."

He was careful to hold every door for her on their way out.

HER FAMILY'S "LITTLE" PIED-À-TERRE TURNED OUT TO be a magnificent early-eighteenth-century baroque town house jutting out over a cliff that plunged into the sea. Its exterior offered an exuberant demonstration of that ornate style, its curvilinear shapes and dramatic forms suggesting both movement and sensuality.

It reminded Storm of one of his favorite bits of architectural advice: if it ain't *baroque*, don't fix it.

The inside was expensively decorated, though perhaps more rococo than baroque. It had an impersonal air to it and lacked a lived-in feel. This, truly, was just a rich family's crash pad, exhaustively maintained but seldom used.

The redhead, whose name he still did not know, gave Storm instructions to retire to the rooftop patio while she took care of a few things down below. From his perch, Storm could hear the Mediterranean crashing into the sheer cliff face several hundred feet below. It had a magical, almost hypnotic rhythm to it.

He peered across the sea, turning himself to face Africa and—if his sense of direction was right—the city of Tangier, in Morocco. For a while, that had been the place listed on the death certificate that Jedediah Jones had sent him. The document had been Jones's idea of a joke. Storm thought of the mission that had led him there and nearly killed him for real. He had gone to capture an operative named the Viper, only to be ambushed, betrayed by one of his own men. He wound up lying in a pool of his own blood on a cold tile floor, his guts riddled with bullets.

He had recuperated in the care of a man named Thami "Tommy" Harif, a salty U.S. Navy veteran who had dual American/Moroccan citizenship. His assistance—and his silence—had been bought by Jones in an exchange, the details of which Storm was glad to be ignorant. Storm had also learned not to ask questions about Tommy's other income streams, which supported his rather grand lifestyle. There had been one point during his convalescence that Storm had mistakenly stumbled upon a warehouse filled with ordnance. When he inquired its purpose, Tommy had piously said, "Why, it's for the cause of righteousness, of course." Storm decided at that moment he didn't want to know more.

Storm put Tommy out of his mind. He tried to put everything out of his mind. From up here, the worries of the world—terrible men with terrible weapons, airplanes falling from flight, whatever horrible secret Ingrid Karlsson was going to share—felt remote. He wished he could pretend they would stay that way, but he knew come morning he would have to face them again.

The only consolation was that morning was still a few hours off. Which meant he could keep pretending, if only for a little while longer.

After perhaps ten minutes, his date appeared carrying two glasses of red wine. She had discarded her ice-blue dress in favor of a simple spaghetti-strapped camisole and a small pair of men's boxer shorts from which her thighs emerged and seemed to keep going forever. She was barefoot. Her red hair had been let out of its cage and was now down, framing her face. She had scrubbed off her makeup.

Storm's original assessment of her—that she was stunning—was in need of an upgrade. She was easily one of the most beautiful women he had ever been near, and she wasn't even trying.

"Sorry. I just had to get a little more comfortable," she said, handing Storm one of the glasses.

Now that she was out of her evening wear, she appeared slightly younger than Storm had originally thought. Storm guessed that she was perhaps twenty-seven, the age at which some women are just finally getting around to purging the Jacques of the world out of their system; others, Storm knew, kept at it their whole lives.

They touched glasses and sat next to each other on a padded limestone bench that overlooked the sea.

"It's lovely up here," Storm said.

She breathed deeply. "I really ought to use this place more often," she said.

"If I owned a place like this, I'd probably never leave," Storm said, taking a small sip of his wine. He let the wine first hit the tip of his tongue, to taste sweetness; then he let it wash over the sides, so he could enjoy the tannins.

Her next words jolted him. "Did you really come up here to lie to me?"

"Excuse me?"

"You, sir, are a man of motion. I heard the stories about your saving the hotel. I saw how you handled Jacque. You would no sooner stay cooped up in a place like this, beautiful as it may be, than you would live underground in a bunker. You are a rover, an explorer. You require movement, action, great deeds. You are the man who saves the world, and you'll go wherever it needs to be saved at the moment."

He shrugged, remaining quiet. He knew she was

right. But there was no way to respond to such a statement without sounding immodest.

"So why do you do it?" she asked.

"Do what?"

"Don't be coy, Mr. Derrick Storm. Other people would hear that a bomb was going to wipe out a section of this city, and their first response would be to run out onto their yachts and get as far away as possible. I am told you ran toward the bomb and defused it. Why? Why are you the one who saves the world?"

"Because someone has to be?"

"Not good enough," she said. "You can do better."

Storm took another small sip of his wine. "You are familiar with Einstein and the theory of relativity, yes?" he asked.

"Of course."

"Well, I have no quarrel with the science of that. I have a quarrel with the people who don't leave Einstein to the physicists. People want to apply relativity to everything, even morality. They would have you believe that there are no absolutes in this world, that everything can only be defined in relationship to everything else. And that's well and good for them, but not for me. Because if you take that theory too far, then suddenly you're left with a world where there is no good, no evil, just different points of view.

"So, take the Nazis," he continued. "If you take moral relativism to its logical conclusion, suddenly you can't say the Nazis were bad. They were just a group of people who applied their worldview to the extreme, right? Well, that's not for me. I believe there is such a thing as absolute bad and absolute good. And, yes, there is a full spectrum of shades in between, which is where most people live. But when

I see things that are a lot closer to the bad end of the spectrum, and see that people who are a lot closer to the good end of the spectrum are going to be hurt, I feel I have to act."

"But again, why you?"

"Because I was the guy who was made bigger and stronger than most other guys. Because I've been trained in how to use that strength. Because my father remains one of the most decent men I've ever met, and I know he'd be disappointed in me if I didn't use my skills to protect good, innocent people. And mostly because if I don't respond to these situations, I'm not sure anyone else will, and I can't live with the guilt of knowing I could have done something but didn't. It's some combination of all that, plus a lot of other stuff I can't think of right now because this wine is going to my head a little bit."

She crossed her glorious legs and looked at him earnestly. It made her even more attractive to him, if that was possible. "But how do we judge what's bad and what's good?"

"With our basic sense of humanity. It's there, deep down in all of us. Or at least most of us. We just need to have the courage to listen to it and act accordingly."

"So what happens when you need to be saved? Who does that?"

"I don't know," Storm said. "Luckily, it doesn't happen all that often."

"Well, if you ever need someone to save you, I'll be happy to do it."

"Really?" Storm said, as much bemused as touched. "You have to be careful making offers like that. You never know when someone is going take you up on it."

She nodded thoughtfully, then held up her empty glass. "Drink up, Mr. Einstein. You're falling behind."

Storm tilted back his glass and took a Storm-sized swallow of the red wine. Then another, until the glass was done.

She was smiling at him the whole time. It was a pleasant, sweet smile, until it started going slanty.

Then, Storm realized, it wasn't just her lips that were getting crooked. Her whole face was. No, wait, it was the whole world.

Nausea hit him harder than any of the waves crashing far below. The glass slipped from his hand and he was dimly aware of it shattering on the marble.

He felt himself going over. He tried to yell, to fight it, to battle the gravity that was taking him over. But nothing in his body would respond. He wasn't even sure if the yell made it out.

The last thing he was cognizant of before it all went black was her reaching for her phone, picking it up, pressing a few buttons.

"He's down," she said into it. "You can come get him now."

CHAPTER 16

SOMEWHERE IN THE MEDITERRANEAN

There was a hand in his face. It was large and hairy. Useful looking, if a bit ugly. Its knuckles bore the marks of too many scrapes, too many punches. The palm had a long scar running along it that looked strangely familiar and . . .

Yes. That's because it was his own hand. He made an effort to flex it, and it moved. Not only was it his own hand, it was under his own control. This was a good start.

He was in a bed. It was a nice bed, with high thread-count satin sheets and a down comforter that provided ample protection against a blast of air-conditioning from above.

He blinked twice. Sunlight streamed through a set of windows to his left. When he looked out the windows, he could see only clouds. But the clouds were moving.

No. He was moving. He was in a vessel of some kind. A boat. Definitely a boat. It was a large one, but he could still feel the faint motion of the waves, the rumble of engines far below him.

He propped himself up on his elbows.

"There you are," a pleasant voice sang out.

It was the redhead from the previous night. She was wearing a blue knit top and white shorts that were just long enough to not cause a scandal when she bent over. Her hair was up in a ponytail. She was still stunning, but there was an officious air to her.

"Good morning, Mr. Storm," she said.

Storm made a grumbling noise that sounded like "wuueeaaaiii," but it went up in pitch slightly at the end. The woman took it as a question.

"You're aboard a boat called the *Warrior Princess*," she said. "It is owned by my employer, Ingrid Karlsson. My name is Tilda. I am Ms. Karlsson's personal assistant. You were brought here by helicopter last night shortly after you blacked out. I apologize for having to do it that way, but Ms. Karlsson is very security conscious. She never ties her boat up at port. She doesn't like people coming by and gawking at it. She feels it invades her privacy."

Storm sat all the way up, rubbed his eyes.

"I guess I needed saving sooner than I thought," he said.

"Oh, this doesn't count," she said. "And I'm sorry about how last night had to end. But, for what it's worth, I had a lovely time. You really are quite a magnificent dancer."

She giggled, brought her hand to her mouth. "And an outstanding kisser. Thank you for that."

Storm made a noise that was supposed to be "you're welcome," but it didn't quite come out right.

"The effects of the sedative we used should be wearing off shortly," she said. "If you like, I can have the ship's doctor prepare a mild amphetamine for you to help you perk up a little quicker."

"No drugs," he croaked.

"Very well. Perhaps some breakfast, then?"

He nodded. Moments later, he heard, "Good morning, Mr. Storm. What can I have the chef prepare for you?"

Storm's eyes struggled to focus. When they did, he saw that it was Jacque, from the previous night. Except he no longer looked like an indolent, spoiled cocaine addict. He was neatly attired in white pants and blue polo shirt. White and blue were apparently the staff uniform around here. He was a lot thinner than Storm remembered. No beer gut.

"You had a chest protector on," Storm said.

"Yes, sir," he said, smiling good-naturedly. "Though that was still a mighty good kick. I'm a little sore this morning."

"I'm just glad I didn't go for your face."

"Ms. Karlsson's security staff had studied your tendencies. They said if I brought my hands up and left my midsection exposed, that's where you would strike. Good thing they were right. Anyhow, what can I get you from the kitchen?"

"Eggs. Bacon. Toast. Coffee," Storm said, knowing that combination would restore his vitality more efficiently than any pill or potion from the ship's doctor.

"Yes, sir," he said, disappearing as quickly as he came.

Tilda showed Storm to the shower—though, sadly, did not join him—then pointed him toward a closet where several clothing choices were laid out for him. Storm went casual, selecting a black cashmere sports coat, a gray polo shirt, and a pair of jeans that fit his thighs and ass like they had been tailored for him. For all he knew, they had been.

After his breakfast, served to him on china that cost more than the first three cars Storm owned, Tilda led him on a long tour through the *Warrior Princess*, from the top of its glistening superstructure to the depths of its engine rooms. She let him have the run of the place, skipping only the crew's quarters—which weren't all that interesting—and Ingrid Karlsson's personal quarters, which were very interesting, but which were only open to guests who were invited by Ingrid herself.

Tilda stopped at her own stateroom, which was just off the main aft deck. He wasn't sure if it was just part of the tour or if it was a suggestion for later. He hoped it was the latter, but by now he recognized he didn't have much of a read on Ms. Karlsson's personal assistant.

As they continued, Storm got to take in some of its more entertaining features: a cinema with a screen as large as any he had seen at a commercial movie theater; a library that included Scandinavian crime-fiction masters Henning Mankell and Jo Nesbø, as well as Maj Sjöwall and Per Wahlöö, but not a trace of any hornet's-nest kicking, fire-playing tattooed girls; a three-level swimming pool complex that included a waterfall, a lagoon, and four hot tubs, from an intimate two-seater to one that looked like it could accommodate a full party; and an indoor health club that included an assortment of weight machines, cardiovascular contraptions, and courts for tennis and racquetball.

Some of the other recreational facilities included a retractable sea deck off the stern from which snorkelers and/or scuba divers could jump into the water when the ship was anchored; a floating dock that could be deployed for the launching of any one of several pleasure crafts, be they Jet Skis or powerboats appropriate for pulling water-skiers; and upper decks that could be used to entertain guests with skeet shooting, kite flying, or the opportunity to blast biodegradable golf balls into the great blue beyond. The helicopter pad—where, apparently, Storm had landed the night before—was on a deck near the stern, next to a sleek smokestack that was the ship's tallest feature.

There was also a variety of dining rooms, both covered and open, to serve all manner of meals to groups both large and small; a ship's commissary, where all the items were, naturally, free; and an inebriating assortment of bars, wet and dry, from which alcohol and other liquid concoctions could be prepared. More or less, every amenity that might be available to a person staying in a resort or on a cruise ship was accounted for.

Each room was decorated with a grandeur that staggered even Storm, no stranger to wealth or those who possessed it. Stylistically, each had its own design aesthetic, which varied widely, almost as if the boat's owner wanted to be able to pick the era that fit her mood. Victorian could give way to modern, which in turn could give way to cubism. Influences ranged from west to east, north to south, with Russian Imperial being followed by feng shui being followed by African folk art.

If there was a common theme, it was simply opulence. Everywhere he went Storm caught glimpses of rare antiquities, the finest furnishings or priceless artwork. Any one of the pieces might have been the jewel of another person's collection. Here, they were commonplace. At times, Storm could scarcely believe that everything he was seeing was floating on a ship that could go anywhere it wanted across 75 percent of the Earth's surface.

But, no, they were definitely on a boat. At one

point they passed another ship, calling out to it with three loud blasts of what sounded like a more mellow version of a trumpet.

"What is that supposed to be? A trombone?"

Tilda laughed. "You're close. That's actually meant to mimic the sound of a French horn. Ms. Karlsson loves the sound of a French horn and one of the touches she insisted on when commissioning this ship was that it signaled other ships with something that sounded like a French horn. She really did think of all the details."

The tour ended in the ship's bridge, which was, to a gearhead like Storm, the most impressive part. It was less a wheelhouse in the traditional sense and more of a command center, decked out with walls full of computers and digital screens. The *Warrior Princess*'s gadgetry was every bit as advanced as anything Storm had seen on a warship, in some cases even more advanced than the U.S. Navy vessels Storm had been aboard. Ingrid Karlsson obviously didn't have to worry about any sequesters.

The ship's defenses were particularly impressive. Like Xena herself, this *Warrior Princess* was equipped for a fight. There was the human security force, which consisted of barrel-chested men—Storm had seen three or four—wearing the blue-and-white uniforms that Karlsson favored. Storm was actually surprised there weren't more of them, but only until he was shown the electronic security, which was far more formidable.

Storm listened as the first mate ran through some of its features. Radar, of course. Sonar, both passive and active. Lidar for anything any of those systems missed. Surface-to-air missiles that could knock out anything that tried to approach from the air.

Torpedoes that could handle anything coming from the water, either on top of it or below it. And they were all linked to an automated advanced detection system that was at the ready 24-7, whether humans were monitoring it closely or not.

"We've had to tinker with some of the settings," said the first mate. "We've had some issues with schools of tuna tripping it, but we've kept it at a pretty sensitive level. Truth is, anything much larger than a dolphin tries to come at this ship and it'll have a warhead heading toward it. There was one time when we nearly blasted a whale out of the water."

"And that would *not* have made me happy," said an authoritative voice. "Even with the amount of money I give to Greenpeace, I never would have heard the end of it."

Storm turned to see a middle-aged woman, nearly six feet tall and well kept, with black hair cut in straight bangs across her forehead and lively gray-blue eyes.

It was the warrior princess herself.

THERE WERE PROPER INTRODUCTIONS, FOLLOWED BY a lively recounting of the previous evening's activities.

"I must apologize, again, for the method of extraction," Karlsson said when they were through. "In addition to my usual concerns about privacy, I felt the CIA's involvement required some extra care. If we had met at Slip F-18 as planned, we would have been practically begging for someone to tail us. Unleashing Tilda on you was the only way I could think of to prevent that."

"That's okay," Storm said, winking at Tilda. "There were benefits."

Storm and Karlsson left Tilda and the other crew members, retiring to a salon just off her private quarters.

As with other rooms in the ship, this one was decorated in its own style—in this case, Queen Anne. Storm recognized a classic example of portraiture of that era. The largest was of a man with a doughy face in knight's armor. He had a towering pouf of center-parted curly hair. It was a wig that would have made a Jersey girl proud.

Storm selected a high-backed walnut chair with swooping cabriole legs and sat.

"That's from the early eighteenth century," Karlsson told him. "It is believed that Queen Anne herself sat in that chair when she celebrated passage of the Acts of Union with Parliament. Are you familiar with the Acts of Union?"

Storm bit his lip rather than make a joke about the acts of union he personally preferred. "Not really," he said instead.

"They were two acts, passed by the parliaments of England and Scotland, that ended hundreds of years of bloody fighting between the English and the Scots with the stroke of a pen rather than the flash of a sword. What's interesting is that, unlike most treaties, both sides came away claiming to be the victor. But I would argue that's what happens when you erase national borders, which are human constructs that never should have been drawn in the first place. Everybody wins. That chair is a symbol of my hope for humanity."

"Should I stand instead?"

"No, no," she laughed. "I know my tastes are a bit eclectic, but it is done thoughtfully. I don't want to be a slave to one design style any more than I'd want to be a slave to one government. I don't want people to come here and say, 'Oh, a Swedish lady lives here' or even, 'Oh, here's a Swedish lady who's pretending to be Hindu.' I want the whole world represented on this ship. I want people to find something that's familiar and comfortable in one place, and then something that broadens their horizons or challenges their perspective in another."

"It's breathtaking," Storm said. "Every bit of it."

"Well, thank you," she said. "To tell you the truth, Brigitte had a very heavy influence on this room. She picked out several of the pieces. She loved the Michael Dahl portrait behind you."

Storm turned around and again appraised the painting of the guy with the Jersey-girl hair.

"That's Prince George of Denmark. He was Queen Anne's husband. Brigitte picked out that painting because of the kind of spouse Prince George was. He was always supportive of his wife in public, even when they disagreed privately. And unlike most men of that era, who would have tried to assert their dominance over their wives in some or all aspects, Prince George was quite content to let Queen Anne be the powerful woman that she was. You could say Queen Anne had the world's first truly modern mate, a person who was not fixated on gender roles."

Ingrid's voice trailed away. Storm could tell she was lost in a memory.

"You cared for her a lot, didn't you?" he said.

"Oh my, I . . . yes, of course. Brigitte and I were lovers, as you may have heard. She was . . . I won't say she made me realize I was a lesbian, because that's not true. I had figured out fairly early on I was not interested in a sexual relationship with a man. No offense."

"None taken. I'm not interested in a sexual relationship with a man, either."

Karlsson smiled and continued: "But even though I knew men weren't for me in the way that women were, I wasn't sure if I could ever really have a true relationship with a woman. Most of the women I was attracted to physically were not attractive to me in other ways. I wasn't really sure I could be a true-life partner with any of them. This sounds conceited, but I didn't think any of them could be my equal. I certainly wasn't ready to share equally with them, to give and take and compromise the way you have to if you are to succeed in a relationship. Then I met Brigitte and everything changed. She was what I had been looking for even before I knew I had been looking for it."

Her gaze again went distant. Then she returned her attention to the room and said, "Please don't share any of this with the press. These are not things I want to read in the tabloids."

"Wouldn't dream of it."

"Thank you. Brigitte and I talked frequently about living more openly, because we're proud of who we are. It's not like we were ashamed of anything. Our families certainly knew the nature of our relationship, as did our close friends. But we just didn't feel like it was anyone else's business. No one talks about the sexuality of the CEO of UPS or FedEx. Why should mine be an issue?"

"I understand," Storm said.

"Anyhow, we were not married in the legal sense, because neither of us wanted to recognize the hegemony of a nation-state, nor did we want the complications of a religious union. I'm not sure either of us could have decided which religion we actually practice"—she interrupted herself with a laugh—"but we were married in the emotional sense. There was never going to be another woman for me, or for her. And I don't think it ever occurred to me we wouldn't live to a ripe old age together. Then the plane crash . . ."

Storm shifted in his seat, which creaked with the ancientness of wood that had held many bodies before his. He could tell he had lost Ingrid to her thoughts again, so he brought her back by saying, "Which is, of course, why I'm here. Jedediah Jones tells me you've developed some information about who's behind this?"

"Yes. It turns out fifty million dollars buys a lot of cooperation from people who otherwise wouldn't be very helpful to anyone. These terrorists claim to be undyingly loyal to their causes and their ideals, but it's amazing how fast their fealty fades when you dangle enough money in front of them. Have you ever heard of the Medina Society?"

"The Medina Society. A violent splinter cell of the Muslim Brotherhood," Storm said, as if reciting from a textbook. "Named after the city in Saudi Arabia where the Prophet Muhammad fled after being forced from Mecca in the year 622. This journey, known as the hijra, is considered the beginning of the Islamic era. The siege of Medina was the first major military victory for Muhammad and his followers, who eventually conquered all of Arabia. Medina is also where Muhammad is buried, which makes it a holy place to followers of Islam, second only to Mecca in its importance. Non-Muslims are not allowed to enter portions of the city.

"Let's see here, what else . . . Much like the Muslim Brotherhood, the Medina Society promotes the Koran and the Hadith as being the only proper basis for a properly pious society. Also, like the Muslim Brotherhood, it rejects most forms of Westernization, modernization, or secularization. Unlike the Muslim Brotherhood, which has tried to gain power lawfully by putting up slates of candidates for election, the Medina Society attempts to accomplish its goals through force, fear, and intimidation. Among its objectives are the total elimination of the Israeli state, the reversion of Palestine to Muslim control, the banishment of non-Muslims from government, the reinstatement of Islamic theocracy . . . How am I doing so far?"

"Pretty good. You left out that they also favor the return of women to traditional roles, the widespread use of clitoridectomy to staunch female sexuality, and the legalization of honor killings."

"So, basically, they're a bunch of guys who make the Taliban look like moderates," Storm concluded.

"Very good. Jones has prepared you well."

"Nah, I just read the newspaper. Anyhow, what makes you think they're behind this?"

"Because as I said, fifty million dollars buys a lot of information. And it also buys offers of assistance. I've yet to infiltrate the Medina Society itself, but I've now had several groups contact the people I've put on the ground in the Middle East. I've now heard from three separate sources that the Medina Society is behind this. And . . . are you ready to suspend your disbelief for a moment, Derrick?"

Storm said, "Consider my disbelief disengaged."

Ingrid smiled and perched closer to the end of her seat. Her voice grew hushed. "According to my sources, the Medina Society has created an incredibly powerful, futuristic, high-energy laser beam. It is powered by a substance called promethium, which was previously thought to be so rare as to effectively not exist in nature. But they have apparently found a large store of it. It sounds sort of wild to me, but once again it is something we have confirmed through multiple sources."

Storm sighed. "Well, fortunately and/or unfortunately, my intelligence lines up with yours on this one. I can confirm they have made a promethium laser beam. I captured one myself. But, obviously, they have at least one other."

"From what I understand, they have the capacity and the materials to make more. The weapon that shot down the planes headed for Dubai is potentially just one of several. What I've yet to determine is how they have the expertise to make such a sophisticated weapon."

"I have," Storm said, who then told Karlsson about William McRae, the missing scientist.

"And no one in the United States government was even concerned this man was missing," she said, shaking her head. "It is so typical of government: once a citizen's usefulness is perceived to be through, the citizen is treated as disposable."

Storm let Karlsson's political diatribe go. "Let's focus back on the big picture. How do we stop these lunatics before they zap anything else? Have your informants told us where we can find this Medina Society?"

"That's the tricky part, apparently," she said. "According to what I've been told, the Medina Society is very savvy. It has learned not only from its own mistakes but also from the mistakes of others, everyone from Khalid Sheikh Mohammed to Osama bin Laden himself. It does not use the Internet to communicate, ever. Not even in code. It does not permit its members to use cell phones. Its leaders move around a lot and are hypervigilant about cloaking those movements. They know that the Americans have satellites powerful enough to see the dirt under their fingernails and they act accordingly. These are some of the smartest terrorists anyone has ever seen."

Storm realized he had been clenching his lower lip in his teeth. He released it. He was in a position where he had to make a snap judgment about someone he had just met—whether to trust her or not. It was the kind of position in which a spy often found himself, and sometimes it was a life-or-death call. This time, it wasn't just Storm's life that was in jeopardy. It was potentially thousands. Maybe millions.

"Ingrid," he said deliberately. "I know you and Jedediah Jones are . . . friends."

"Well, I wouldn't call us that," she said. "I would say we're people who have used each other for our mutual convenience from time to time. You are familiar with the story of the frog and the scorpion, I assume?"

"From *Aesop's Fables*, yes? The scorpion who cannot swim needs to cross the river and asks a frog to transport him to the other side. The frog says, 'No, you'll sting me.' The scorpion says, 'No, I won't, for if I do we'll both drown,'" Storm said. "The frog relents, but then halfway across, the scorpion stings the frog anyway. As they go down, the frog says, 'Why would you do this?' And the scorpion says, 'I am a scorpion. It is my nature.'"

"Very good. To me, Jones is the scorpion. But as long as you understand what his nature is, you can handle him accordingly."

Storm's smile was a knowing one. "I understand. Believe me, I understand. So I have to be honest with you: Jones's interest in this incident may not actually align fully with yours."

"Please explain."

"He wants the people using this weapon to be stopped. We all want that," Storm said. "But he also wants this technology and the resources behind it to be recovered for future military use by the United States government. And while I am a proud American citizen, that is not something I want my government to be able to deploy in the field of battle or anywhere else."

"I concur with you," she said. "My allegiance is not to any government but to humankind itself."

"Good. Then what I'm about to tell you can't reach Jones's ears. Agreed?"

She nodded.

"I may have a lead that will help us find the source of this promethium," he continued. "Have you or anyone in your network of informants ever heard of a company called Ahmed Trades Metal?"

Her shoulders actually slumped. "Why do you ask?"

"From what I've been able to learn, Ahmed Trades Metal may be the source of the promethium being used to power this laser beam."

She was now shaking her head. "Well, you're right and you're not right. I'm afraid 'Ahmed Trades Metal' is not a company. It's a rallying call for members of the Medina Society. It's like when Americans say 'Remember the Alamo' or 'Remember the *Maine*.' A man named Ahmed was one of their earliest martyrs. Some of their leaders have actually changed their names to Ahmed or named their children Ahmed, so it's become quite a common name within the movement. 'Trades metal' is one of their slang terms for making a bomb or improvised explosive device, because it's like trading metal with the enemy. 'Ahmed Trades Metal' is sort of their way of saying, 'Let's go blow up some stuff in the name of Allah.'"

Storm felt his own posture failing, too. "So I haven't really learned anything, have I?"

"Well, it's one more concrete indication that the Medina Society is behind this. But other than that? I'm afraid we are lost."

And then, in that uncanny way he had, Jedediah Jones inserted himself into the conversation via a buzzing in Storm's pocket.

"Well, look who it is," Storm said.

"I'll leave you to take the call," Ingrid said. "Find me when it's over and we'll discuss what to do next."

She rose and, as she reached the doorway, paused for a moment. "I asked Jones to send me his best man. I'm glad he sent me a good man as well."

AS THE WARRIOR PRINCESS DEPARTED THE ROOM, Storm pressed the button to receive Jones's call.

"Storm Investigations."

Jones did not bother with niceties or small talk: "Have you made any headway?"

Storm relayed the brief version of how he ended up a guest aboard the *Warrior Princess* and provided some of the details from his conversation with Karlsson Logistics's CEO.

"The Medina Society?" Jones said when Storm was through.

"You don't think they're behind it?"

Jones paused just a little. It was the delay that told Storm his boss was, as usual, hiding something. "No, actually, I'm not surprised," Jones said. "That explains why we've heard so little about this. If it was one of the other extremist groups over there, we would have had ten different agents who would have been able to put the schematics of this weapon up on a wall for us. The Medina Society is the nut we can't seem to crack. We have been completely unable to infiltrate their ranks."

"Yeah, not even Ingrid's money has been able to," Storm said. "They seem to be pretty careful, but they do have one vulnerability."

"What's that?"

"The promethium. It seems to be the limiting factor here. It's incredibly rare, and finding a large supply of it is what has enabled them to make this weapon. Yet because it has such a short half-life and decays so quickly, they'll constantly need more of it. They'll want continual access to their source. I say we go full-court press after the promethium. If we do that, it'll lead us to the Medina Society."

"Funny you should say that," Jones replied. "Because we had reached more or less the same conclusion over here. We brought the weapon you recovered back to the lab and have been crawling through every aspect of it. The weapon itself doesn't turn out to be that complicated. It's the promethium that makes it powerful. So we had our chemists study the promethium very closely. It turns out there may be a lead for us embedded within it."

"Do tell."

"Promethium is a metal, as you are aware. And,

like all metals, it has magnetic properties. The way it interacts with the Earth's magnetic field means that certain information about it is, in essence, recorded within it. If you study it under a powerful enough electron microscope, you can tell from the way the nuclei align themselves where the promethium was at the moment it came into its current form."

"Sort of like nature's version of a GPS," Storm said.

"Something like that. In any event, one of the techs is a whiz with this kind of stuff. And she was able to determine the approximate coordinates of where this promethium came into being. The promethium used to make that laser came from 25.77392 north, 31.84365 east. That's accurate to within plus or minus one point eight miles, within a ninety-nine percent confidence interval."

Storm quickly scribbled down the numbers. "And what did you find when you had the satellite look at those coordinates?"

"Nothing. Sand. That one-point-eight-mile radius means we're looking at ten square miles. We've looked at it as carefully as we could, but we could have missed something. It's a stretch of the Sahara Desert not far from the Nile River in Egypt. And, of course, that's just what's on top of the Earth in that spot. Most rare earths come from inside the Earth."

"Which means you need someone who probably looks a lot like me to go there and do some digging," Storm said.

"Precisely. I've got Clara Strike on her way."

Storm felt his brain hiccup on the name. He and Clara Strike had a complicated history, like two quarrelling clans whose members kept intermarrying.

Sometimes they made love. Sometimes they made war. The only constant was the passion behind both impulses.

All he said was, "Strike, huh?"

"Don't tell me you two are squabbling again."

"I don't know what we are at the moment," Storm said. "Anyhow, why don't you conjure up a helicopter and get me off this boat and on my way to Egypt? I'll make sure to tell Ingrid's people not to shoot it down."

"Good plan. I told Strike you would meet tonight in Luxor. That's the nearest big city to those coordinates. She'll have the rest of the details about the operation for you there."

Storm ended the call, then found Ingrid Karlsson, who was out on the foredeck watching the bow of her magnificent ship cut through the blue water of the Mediterranean.

"Egypt is a good place for you to be," she said when he was through explaining where he was heading. "It seems that the Medina Society has used the recent political instability there to strengthen its foothold. I will keep the money flowing to my contacts and will be in touch if I learn anything. And if you need anything from me—anything at all—please know all you have to do is ask."

"Of course. I appreciate your willingness to help."

Karlsson surprised Storm by grabbing both of his hands in hers. She fixed her blue-gray eyes on his, looking at him with the same intensity she used to turn a Swedish shipping company into a multi-national conglomerate.

"I often have railed against human beings pursuing

their more savage instincts, and yet I . . . I do want vengeance," she said. "I can't even explain why it will give me comfort. But whoever did this to Brigitte must pay."

"I'll do my best."

She gripped his hands even tighter. "And be careful of Jones. Please remember his nature."

CHAPTER 17

LUXOR, Egypt

He smelled her before he saw her.

Clara Strike had this perfume that, as far as Derrick Storm was concerned, ought to have been regulated by the Food and Drug Administration as a psychotic drug. Storm had once read in Alice Clark's book *Mating Rituals: A Field Guide to Relationships* that, much as in the animal kingdom, humans use their noses every bit as much as their eyes to pick a partner.

It sure worked when it came to Strike. Storm swore he could pick up even one molecule of her perfume, and he caught his first whiff of her even before he knew exactly where it was coming from.

Storm had been instructed to meet her in the bar at the Winter Palace hotel, the legendary British colonial–era establishment where Agatha Christie was said to have written *Death on the Nile*.

Storm felt like he could have used some of Hercule Poirot's cleverness as he neared the hostess stand and the scent of Strike grew stronger. In addition to their perilous personal past, there were professional complexities as well. Unlike Storm, who worked for himself, Strike was a CIA asset, through and through.

The last time he had seen her was in an abandoned

factory building in Bayonne, New Jersey. They had spoken of fresh starts, without saying exactly what that entailed. They had discussed a future, with no details as to when or how that future would take place. And then, in the midst of the mission, she had taken a bullet, albeit one that was stopped by her vest. It left Storm to chase a villain while Strike got whisked off for medical treatment. Then she had gone her way and he his, as usual. And—also, as usual—nothing had been solved.

He had gotten delayed in customs—traveling on his own passport was so tedious—and had not had time to check in before their rendezvous time, which had now arrived. The hostess led him through a large room whose furnishings looked like it hadn't changed much since Queen Victoria's time and whose chandeliers dripped with crystal. The next room was smaller, though no less opulent, and that was where Strike had selected a private sitting area.

She was dressed in what was clearly off-duty clothing: a yellow eyelet summer dress that cut off just above the knee, a garment that was both simple and, on Strike, spectacular. Her skin was a few shades darker than it normally would have been, suggesting she had either been on vacation or had just completed an assignment that involved less time than usual under fluorescent lighting. Her wavy brown hair had acquired a few natural highlights from the sun.

When she saw Storm, she stood and gave him a smile that nearly stopped his heart. Maybe it was that the rational part of his brain—the part that reminded him how poisonous they sometimes were together— was temporarily disabled, but he forgot how much he missed her.

"Derrick!" she said.

She came near and brushed her lips against his cheek, bringing the full effect of her perfume on his olfactory nerves. It was enough to make him light-headed. She drew back to look at him, then laughed. She had left a lipstick smudge on his cheek, which she wiped off with her thumb.

"God, you look good, Storm," she said. "It's great to see you."

She sat back in her chair, then crossed her legs. There were no more than a half dozen other men in the room. With that one movement, she had captivated all of them. Storm selected a seat across from her. There was an antique chessboard between them.

"I didn't tell Jones this, but I was thrilled when he told me you were heading out here," she said. "We never really got the chance to catch up after Bayonne. I had really thought I was going to get some time after that, and maybe we could disappear for a little bit. I've been dying to go back to your place in the Seychelles. Or another one of those weeks in Manhattan or, hell, anywhere. But then, you know, one thing led to another . . ."

He just nodded, unsure of what to say. How did he tell her that a week with her was the thing he most wanted and also the thing he most feared? The greatest love he had known had "Clara Strike" written on it, but so did the greatest heartbreak. She had died in his arms. It had been his fault. And she had let him live with that pain and guilt for years, never telling him that she was really alive and that it was all just Jedediah Jones's fakery. He could never fully forgive her for letting him go through that. And yet he also understood it as being a kind of bizarre occupational hazard: the emotional collateral damage that seemed to be a part of every big job.

"I heard about that thing with you and the plane over Pennsylvania. Crazy. If you had waited, what, five minutes longer, that death spiral would have been terminal. Those are some lucky passengers. I know Jones had your identity withheld from the press. Still, I feel like someone ought to throw a ticker tape parade for you or something."

A waiter appeared with a bottle of Château Carbonnieux Blanc, poured two glasses, then set the bottle in an ice bucket.

"I hope white is okay," she said. "It was just so hot and I spent the day . . . well, in the heat. It felt so good to get back here and have a shower. I swear, I must have knocked off about thirty pounds of dirt and sand. I found this little dress in the bottom of my suitcase, and it was like, yes, something that isn't either tactical clothing or a pantsuit. Between that and the air-conditioning, I feel like a new person."

Storm hadn't touched his wine. He hadn't moved. It was all so much: Strike being here, so close. Her looking so good. Him wondering what it was all about. Things were seldom unambiguous with Strike. Even when she seemed like she was coming straight on, that was usually just to hide the part that was coming from an angle. And yet—contradiction alert—that was part of what made her so damn good at her job, which was one of the things he admired about her.

He realized she was staring at him. "Storm, are you going to say anything, or are you just going to sit there like a big, gorgeous idiot?"

"Sorry, sorry," Storm said. "I just . . . I think the

only sleep I've gotten in the last few days has been aboard something that was moving."

"Isn't it a little early in the evening to start trying to get me in bed with you?" she teased. "Jeez. At least get me a little tipsy first."

He reached toward the chessboard in front of them, picked up the white pawn, and studied it. It was intricately carved ivory. An antique. Egypt had banned the ivory trade long ago. He placed it down two spaces ahead of where it had started, then raised an eyebrow at Strike.

"We haven't played chess since that time in Istanbul," she said.

"I've studied since then."

"I hope so," she said, selecting a black pawn one row over from Storm's and moving it out two spaces.

"So I assume Jones has given you the coordinates?" he asked, making his next move.

"I'm fully briefed, yes."

"So what do you say we have Jones airlift us a Humvee and head on out there tonight?" he asked, taking her pawn with his.

"Too good a chance we'd miss something at night," she said, beginning the first in a series of moves whose strategy Storm did not immediately recognize. "Whatever we're looking for—if, in fact, there's even anything to find—might be very small. We already know it's something that can't be seen from satellite, which means it might be some kind of subtle geological feature. Or it could be something that someone has camouflaged from the satellites. We know that the Medina Society is aware Uncle Sam has eyes in the sky that are always on them and they are known to take countermeasures.

"Besides," she finished, "the desert isn't safe at night. Local intel says that outlaw activity has been out of control lately."

"What are you afraid of? You've got big, strong me at your side."

" 'Big strong you' isn't impervious to bullets last time I checked. Do I need to remind you that there's no place to hide in a desert? Besides, we're not here to shoot up the countryside. This is a touchy time for the red, white, and blue in these parts."

She was the first to move her knight out and was using it to decimate some of his early defenses until he finally knocked it out with a bishop. Then, two turns later, she turned around and captured it with her queen.

"I'm not here to hide," Storm said.

"Then you need to change your thinking. If the guns-blazing approach worked with the Medina Society, we would have already wiped them out. These aren't your run-of-the-mill, towel-head wack jobs, Derrick. They're smart."

"So how are you proposing we move in on this?"

"You're not going to like it."

He was maneuvering one of her rooks into a trap. She was going to lose it for sure. One, maybe two moves from now. "I'm a big boy. I can handle it."

"Camels," she said.

His face fell. His left arm dropped to his side. "Aww, come on, seriously?"

"We have to go quietly. We go out there in whatever kind of big, fancy toy you want, and if anyone is out there, they'll be able to see us coming from nine miles away. We have to maintain the façade of being poor nomads. And poor nomads in this part of the world still use camels."

He looked down at the board. It turned out, while he thought he was trapping one of her rooks, she was really ensnaring one of his. He had to sacrifice it to save his queen.

"You know how I feel about those . . . things. They stink."

"So do you sometimes. Look, there's no choice. It's already set up. We're going to be meeting a truck with the camels just outside visual distance of the target zone. But once we're inside, it's camels."

Storm made a face and a noise that was only slightly more mature, under the circumstances, than what a second-grader might have done.

"Okay, but at least tell me we get to have real weapons," he said, watching as one of his knights fell to her queen.

"Oh, yeah. We're fully outfitted. I don't have a death wish, Storm. I'm just talking about exercising some caution in how we approach. We need to look like nomads from afar. What we keep hidden in our gear is a different matter."

"Good. Because other than Dirty Harry, I've got nothing on me."

"You and that gun," she said, shaking her head. "Oh, by the way, checkmate."

He looked down, alarmed. "Wait, no it's not," Storm said, staring desperately at the black and white spaces that surrounded his king, sure there had to be somewhere safe the piece could move.

She sighed, patiently letting him reach the conclusion that she had foreseen at least five moves earlier. Finally, he frowned and tipped over his king.

"Let's get some sleep," she said. "I've set a wake-up call for three A.M. I want to be in the target zone at first light. Hopefully we can find whatever there is to find before it gets to be a hundred and twenty degrees out there."

"Sounds good to me. Let me go check in."

"Oh, you don't have a reservation."

"Why not? Jones said—"

"I canceled it," she said quickly. "What with the sequester and all, I felt it would be in the best interests of fiscal austerity for us to share a room."

"So you're saying this is my patriotic duty," Storm said.

"It is."

"Well," Storm said, rising and offering Strike an arm. "In that case: God bless America."

She accepted his escort. Then they retired to her room and exercised their right to pursue happiness in a most vigorous fashion.

THE STARS WERE JUST BEGINNING TO FADE WHEN AN ancient, diesel-reeking livestock truck slowed to a stop by the side of a little-used road, air brakes hissing, suspension creaking.

In Arabic lettering on the side, Storm could make out H. MASSRI PROPRIETOR. In a much larger font were two words that Storm wished he had never seen put together: CAMEL RENTAL.

"Seriously?" Storm said. "Rent-a-camel?"

"Grow up," Strike said under her breath as she waved at the driver.

"Hello, hello!" Massri said in cheerful, accented English. "You are Mr. and Mrs. Sullivan, yes?"

"Sullivan?" Storm said. "You know, I've never liked the name Sullivan."

"Grow up faster," Strike said through clenched

teeth, then in a louder, more chipper voice said, "Yes, yes, that's us!"

Massri was already scurrying along the side of the truck, toward the trailer, where he opened up the back door to reveal two light brown, single-hump camels, one about seven feet high, and the other about six. A wall of stink poured out, assaulting their noses.

"Congratulations on your wedding, Mr. and Mrs. Sullivan. I am so pleased you have chosen to spend your honeymoon in this manner. It is my great honor to introduce you to Antony and Cleopatra. They are my most romantic camels."

Massri led the shorter one out first. "This is Cleopatra. She is a very sweet girl. The best I have. You know, the word 'camel' comes from an Arabic word that means 'beauty.' Isn't she beautiful? I have a mind to take her to the South Sinai Camel Festival, where I think she will have a most excellent chance to win a prize. You can go ahead and pet her if you like, Mrs. Sullivan."

Massri had led the female camel down the ramp and handed her reins to Strike, who lightly pet Cleopatra's muzzle. The camel responded by closing her eyes and stretching her neck to get her face closer to Strike's.

"I can tell she likes you very much. Most excellent," Massri said, then returned to the truck.

"And this is Antony," he said, grabbing the animal's halter and yanking. "He is also a most excellent camel. A champion camel in his own right. Very well trained. Very well bred. His father was one of the great racing camels of our time. This camel, he can run like the wind blows, Mr. Sullivan."

Storm could see that was true—but only if it was a very still day. Antony was not running. Or walking. Or planning to leave the trailer without a fight. The animal's rump was pinned against the back of the pen, and he kept it there even as Massri tugged his chin forward. Antony signaled his displeasure with a loud, growling belch.

"As you can see, I have already loaded the camels with everything you will need for a three-day journey in the desert," Massri said. "They should not need water during that time. But if you should happen upon an oasis, it is okay to let the camels drink. They can drink up to forty gallons in three minutes."

Antony still wasn't budging. The sound emanating from him had gotten deeper and more ominous-sounding.

"He has a little bit of a temper, especially this early," Massri said. "Not a morning camel, this one."

"A little bit of a temper?" Storm said. "What does he do when he really gets mad?"

"Oh, then he bites," Massri said, under his breath. Massri realized Storm had heard him and added, "But that never happens. Almost never happens. He is a good camel. He is just a little stubborn. This is not an unusual trait for a camel, you will find."

Massri finally succeeded in yanking Antony all the way down the ramp. Antony was making a noise that sounded like an outboard motor that had a small rodent stuck in it. A slab of pink flesh had slipped out the side of his mouth.

"Why is he sticking his tongue out at me?" Storm asked.

"That is not his tongue, Mr. Sullivan. That is called a 'dulla.' It is a large, inflatable sac that comes from his throat. It shows he is trying to assert his dominance over you. Or perhaps to mate with your female."

Strike whipped her head in their direction. "Excuse me?" she said.

"Oh, I would not be too concerned about that, Mrs. Sullivan. It is the wrong time of the year for him to be rutting. Besides, camels are unique among hoofed mammals in that they are the only ones to mate while sitting down. When he sits down, he is either too tired to continue or he is feeling amorous. As long as he remains on his feet, you have nothing to worry about."

Antony had finally stopped vocalizing, and was now just looking annoyed. Storm took one step toward the beast. It responded by growling and showing his teeth.

"And you said he never bites, huh?" Storm said.

"Almost never," Massri said, his smile having returned. "Ah, but Mr. Sullivan, never mind that. You should see him run. He is magical. Like a unicorn!"

"Without the horn," Storm said.

"Yes, without the horn."

"Which would make him, what, a Pegasus?" Storm said. Massri looked at him quizzically. Storm decided to drop the comparisons to mythical creatures.

"I just wish camels didn't smell like, you know, camels," Storm said, wrinkling his nose as the odor of the animal—some horrible and undetermined mix of urine, manure, and camel sweat—came even closer.

"Ah, well, you must remember, camels have very sensitive noses. Antony can smell water from three kilometers away. So it's possible you are far more offensive to him, Mr. Sullivan."

Storm looked at Antony, whose mouth was developing a thick beard of white, frothy foam that he was shaking into globs that fell onto the ground.

"I doubt that very seriously," Storm said.

Storm added to the beast's burden a few essential items that Strike had packed, which mostly consisted of weaponry that had been broken down for ease of storing. Each still had a concealed sidearm—Storm his Dirty Harry gun, and Strike a Smith & Wesson .500 Magnum, which billed itself as the most powerful revolver in production.

Collectively, the two guns packed a wallop. But Strike had added two longer rifles: a CheyTac M200 sniper rifle and time-worn Colt M16 that was conspicuously battle tested. In addition to some nicks and dings, the switch that allowed it to toggle from single shot to automatic had been set to automatic and then ripped off. Strike packed extra ammo to compensate for that anomaly.

Massri helped both Storm and Strike up onto their camels. Cleopatra remained docile, allowing Strike to mount her easily. Antony kept trying to turn and bite Storm's legs, which Massri was able to prevent only by whacking the camel's nose with a riding crop.

"Here, why don't you keep this," Massri said, handing Storm the crop when he was finally atop the beast. "It comes free with the rental. But I warn you, Mr. Sullivan, use it sparingly. This is the fastest camel in all the desert. A unicorn! A Pegasus! I would put this camel against even the fastest thoroughbred. He is the Secretariat of camels. You are most fortunate to ride such a champion."

Antony let out one final belch, then fell in behind Cleopatra, who had already started walking at a slow, dutiful pace toward the vast openness of the Sahara.

THEY HAD DECIDED TO TRAVEL INTO THE MIDDLE OF the target zone, to the exact coordinates given to them by Jones, and then begin a search pattern of concentric circles that radiated out from the epicenter.

The sun rose behind them as they rode west. Sunrises in the desert, to which Storm was no stranger, were hauntingly beautiful. At least at first, you could even convince yourself that this place—so infertile, so desolate—wasn't all that bad. Or at least that it got a bum rap. Storm watched their long shadows grow shorter.

Then the sun reached a certain altitude, high enough that its rays didn't have to slice through so much of the atmosphere. That's when Storm could start to feel it beating through the thin, earth-colored *thobe* that covered his body and the white keffiyeh wrapped around his head and neck.

The sand, which had cooled with the night, began to heat. It was slow at first, but it was incredible how quickly it happened. Storm wasn't bothering to check the temperature—what was the point?—but it felt like it was rising five degrees every fifteen minutes. A morning that had started out in the fifties was soon into the eighties. Storm felt the sweat popping on his body. He looked at his water bottle. Not yet. They had to conserve what they had.

The pretense of being nomads aside, Storm was glad for the glimpses he was able to sneak at his handheld GPS. The terrain was so featureless that he understood how it was that people ended up traveling in huge circles when they were lost in the desert. It was easy to get disoriented. The GPS kept them more or less on course.

But otherwise, they were traveling across the desert as humankind had for many millennia. On camel. In the heat. Baked by the murderous sun.

They said little. Both seemed to be conscious of conserving their energy, not wasting it on idle talk. For whatever Strike said about getting their task done before the heat of the day, that was clearly not possible. They had too far to travel.

Antony, for whatever initial recalcitrance he may have shown, had settled into a good rhythm. Frothing and spitting aside, this is what he had been bred for since his species was first domesticated in the days before the pharaohs.

It took three hours to near the coordinates Jones had provided. It was already above ninety, Storm was sure, and it was like the furnace was only beginning to roil. Storm was aware Strike was looking at him with increasing frequency as they closed in. He was allowing himself more time with the GPS out. They had locked in the proper northerly coordinate. They now just had to get far enough west.

Finally, they had arrived.

"This is it," Storm said, pulling on Antony's reins. In a rare fit of obedience, the camel came to a stop.

They shared a silent beat where they scanned the landscape. There was nothing. Just an ocean of sand that stretched seemingly without end on all sides. Somewhere within ten square miles, what they sought was hidden. The enormity of finding it was manifesting itself.

"Well, it's all clear to me now," Strike said, knowing Storm would get the sarcasm.

"It's damn inconsiderate of the terrorists not to at least plant a flag for us or something. I mean, we came all this way."

"Inhospitable terrorists. The worst. Next thing you know, they won't have pulled out the good china for us."

"I blame the parenting. People just don't know how to raise a good terrorist anymore," Storm said. "Let's head to the top of that dune over there, see what we can see."

Storm urged Antony forward, and Cleopatra fell in behind. When they reached the summit of what seemed to be the tallest mound of sand amid all the other mounds of sand, they again stopped. The camels stood side by side. Cleopatra nuzzled Antony, who let out a thunderous belch.

It was the only sound for miles.

"Oh, now it's *really* clear to me," Strike said, surveying a view that had changed only in elevation. "The silly thing is, I thought it would be easier once we got out here. If anything, it's more hopeless than when I was looking on the satellites. At least back then I didn't have sweat dripping down my cleavage."

"Man, I never thought I'd feel jealous of sweat," he said.

Strike said nothing, accustomed as she was to ignoring the fact that Storm seemed to think of sex every eight seconds.

Storm pulled out a pair of Steiner Marine 7x50 binoculars that Strike had been thoughtful enough to include in his backpack. He focused the viewfinder and began scanning the horizon. He made it a full 360 degrees around and started his way back.

He was perhaps halfway through when he saw a glint. It was sun striking off either glass or polished metal, neither one of which was known to be a surface naturally found in a desert. He noted the direction and removed the device from his face.

"There," he said, handing her the binoculars. "Look at two hundred and seven degrees."

"Two hundred and seven degrees is what it is out here," she said, taking a look. "Are you sure you're not just hallucinating?"

"No. That's why I'm having you look. Do you see that reflection?"

"Storm, I don't see anything but . . . Oh, never mind. Yeah. I got it now. Jones had mentioned there was something that looked like a Bedouin encampment, but he said it was outside the target zone so they didn't really pay too much attention to it. You think that's it?"

"Whatever it is, it's more interesting than anything else I see around here. I'm sure it's outside the target zone, but let's ditch the search pattern and go check it out."

"Sounds good to me," Strike said.

And off down the dune they went. In the Steiner glasses, the flash they saw had looked almost close enough to grab. In reality, it was nearly five miles away and took the better part of an hour to reach.

Again, they lapsed into quiet. The only sound was Antony's occasional bellowing. Camels have evolved with all kinds of clever features to help them beat the heat and preserve their hydration—blood cells that are circular instead of oval, noses that trap the moisture in their exhales and cycle it back to their body, dung that is so devoid of water it can be lit on fire. Humans have no such adaptations. And as the temperature surged above a hundred, Storm and Strike began suffering accordingly. The heat felt ubiquitous, like it had now filled every ounce of available space, spinning every atom into an inflamed tizzy. Whatever oxygen there was in the air seemed to have evaporated along with whatever water there was on the entire planet.

Neither complained. Storm said nothing because there was no point. Strike said nothing because, whether she acknowledged it or not, she always felt like she was in a kind of unspoken competition with Storm: who was tougher? Who was the better agent? Who could withstand more? Even if he was unaware of the contest, she didn't want to let him win.

As they neared what had been glinting in the distance, they saw it was not just a stray piece of metal lying in the sun. It was a settlement of some sort—a grouping of tents, some of them quite large, with trucks scattered around them. Storm kept his eye on it, watched as men in white and off-white clothing scurried from tent to tent, trying to stay in the sun as little as possible. He counted perhaps two dozen men, though it was difficult to account for duplicates at that distance.

They appeared to be doing work of some sort. What their purpose was, Storm couldn't guess. He saw one open-sided tent where several items, some of them quite large, had been secured in crates, perhaps for transport.

When they got to within perhaps a half a mile, Storm could hear excited shouting. The sound carried through the distance, and even though the words did not, Storm could surmise they had been spotted. There was more shouting, and when they got to within a few hundred yards, Storm saw a camel-mounted greeting party coming out to intercept them.

It was around that time when Storm was finally able to guess what was going on there. He saw an ancient block sandstone structure sticking out of the ground. It had an entrance that led underground. Most of the activity that wasn't focused on Storm and Strike seemed to be centered around that entrance.

"Any thoughts?" Strike said.

"It looks like some kind of archaeological dig to me."

"I agree. And ordinarily I would say that means they won't be belligerent toward us. Except I see guns on several of those men."

"Only because they're more scared of us than we are of them," Storm said. "Why don't you start talking to them? Hearing a woman's voice will calm them. I'm going to raise my hands real high, but I want you to keep yours under your burka, on the trigger of that little cannon you're carrying. Just in case. We good?"

"Got it," Strike said.

She began calling out in loud, friendly Arabic: "Good day, my friends. We are but peaceful travelers. We mean you no harm. Lower your weapons, please. Again, we come in peace."

Storm studied the muzzles trained on them and the guns behind them. They were old guns, probably inaccurate to start with and poorly maintained on top of it. Sand wreaked havoc on a weapon, especially one that wasn't properly cleaned. Even if these clowns wanted to shoot Storm and Strike, they'd probably fail.

Eventually, Strike's words had their intended effect. Storm watched as the muzzles lowered. They were close enough to be able to see the smiles on the men's faces.

And that one of them wasn't a man.

She also clearly wasn't Egyptian. Storm could see wisps of blond hair escaping from her loosely worn hijab. And freckles across the bridge of her nose. And bright blue eyes. And a certain posture and confidence that suggested a very attractive young woman was hidden underneath the swaddles of cloth that hid her from the sun and, at the moment, most of Storm's inquisitive examination.

"Hello, there," Storm said in English, directing his words toward her. "My name is . . . Talbot. Terry Talbot. And this is my partner. Her name is Sullivan. Sally Sullivan."

"Oh, hello," she said. "I'm Dr. Katie Comely."

"Pleased to meet you," Storm said, smiling.

"A little too pleased, I'd say," Strike grumbled under her breath, shooting him a look that could have been used to make the opening incision for heart surgery. Storm returned her glare with a blank face, a front affected throughout the world by men who are desperately trying to pretend they did not notice the attractiveness of another woman in their midst.

They had gotten close enough that their camels were now regarding each other at least as closely as the humans. Antony let out a groan and was again starting to slobber. Luckily, the humans seemed to be friendlier in their greeting. Storm watched as

Dr. Comely's eyes went wide for a second, and then seemed to fill with understanding.

"Are you with the I-A-P-L?"

"Sorry?" Storm said.

"The International Art Protection League. I just . . . I saw the gun sticking out of your pack there, and I—"

Strike was about to correct her, when Storm jumped in. "Yes. Yes, we're with the International Art Protection League. Sorry, normally when people refer to us by our acronym, they say 'i-apple,' kind of like iPhone, but, yes, we have guns. And camels. And we are here to protect you. Your art. You and your art."

"I'm so, so relieved you're here," Comely said. "We've been having the worst problems with bandits. They've stolen so many of our finds, I just can't even begin to . . ."

She turned and yelled to a man who was just coming out of camp on his camel. "Professor, it's the art protection people!"

Katie was smiling like she was a devout pilgrim and Storm and Strike were the Second Coming.

"May I present Dr. Stanford Raynes," she said.

The man road his camel with a jerky hesitance. He was tall and thin and had a haughty, academic air that Storm immediately disliked. Still, he smiled and again exchanged names.

"Won't you join us in camp?" Katie said.

"It would be our pleasure," Storm said, spitting out the words before Strike could find the language that went with her scowl.

"Wonderful, wonderful. You can even help us extract our latest find from the tombs. It is potentially very, very exciting. But it's also sort of heavy,"

Katie said, turning her full attention to Storm. "Not that it would be a problem for you. You look like you could lift a tank. You must work out a lot, Mr. Talbot."

"I've been known to," Storm said.

Strike now had murder in her eyes, but she said nothing.

"Well, come on then," Katie said. "We'll have a rest while we wait for that big ball of fire to go away, but then there's much to be done."

CHAPTER 18

SOMEWHERE IN THE MIDDLE EAST

On the far wall of Ahmed's office, there was a large painting of a scene from "The Three Apples," one of the tales related by Scheherazade in *One Thousand and One Nights*.

In it, a fisherman discovers an ornate trunk, which he sells to the caliph, the ruler of all Islam. When the caliph opens the trunk, he finds the body of a young woman, hacked to pieces. The caliph dispatches his wazir—his chief advisor—to find the murderer, giving the wazir three days to accomplish this task or else face death himself.

On the third day, the wazir has failed and is about to be executed when two men appear, both claiming to be the murderer. The story unfolds from there with a series of turns, each more unexpected than the next, made all the more extraordinary when you remember the teller of the tale, Scheherazade, was trying to save herself from beheading by a merciless king.

To modern scholars, "The Three Apples" is one of the earliest known examples of a thriller in literature, relying as it did on an unreliable narrator and a multitude of plot twists to enthrall readers.

To Ahmed, it was a reminder that no one can be trusted and nothing is as it seems.

Which was fitting, because the painting wasn't just a painting.

It was also a door that led to a secret place, a chamber tall enough for a man to stand in, deep enough to stash anything of value. One of Ahmed's ancestors had created it, to hide who-knows-what from who-knows-whom.

Ahmed had actually played in it as a boy. He'd steal some halva from the kitchen, fill an amphora with water, and scurry in early in the morning, before his father had finished his breakfast. Then, sufficiently provisioned, Ahmed would spend the day in there, spying on his father. The painting was transparent from the inside in a few places, allowing Ahmed to see out even though no one could see in. He would stay there, very quietly, listening intently to the conversations that passed between the men who came in.

Ahmed called the compartment *aman*, Arabic for safe.

Eventually, his father discovered what Ahmed was doing. But rather than scold his son, he praised the boy's cleverness. He bid Ahmed to cease entering *aman* surreptitiously. But, every now and then, he would invite his son in to eavesdrop on an important conversation.

Now pay attention to this, he'd say. *This man is going to ask me to sell to him for a hundred gineih a unit. I will tell him such thing is not possible, that no one could sell for so little, that I will not be able to feed my family on that amount. I will plead and be quite pitiful. Eventually, he will acquiesce and accept a hundred-and-twenty-five, never knowing that it only cost me fifty.*

Other times, it would be: *This man will begin*

by begging me for a special deal. He will cry about his own poverty. I will berate him for his weakness and then pretend to give him a very special price of a hundred and fifty gineih. He will say that his own children will go hungry. As a magnanimous gesture, I will give it to him for a hundred-and-twenty-five gineih. It still only cost me fifty.

Ahmed was amazed how often his father's predictions turned out to be accurate. He learned much about the world of men and business while secreted away in *aman*.

He never guessed that, someday, he would use the chamber to hide a store of something called promethium, a substance that could be used to make a weapon more powerful than anything his father could have dreamed of.

Nor did Ahmed guess that there were would be times he would ask members of his own security force to hide in there. Just in case. And only because Ahmed was not as gifted as his father at anticipating what visitors to the office might say and do.

And because those visitors tended to be more dangerous than the ones Ahmed's father had entertained.

Ahmed was looking at that painting, thinking of the lessons of "The Three Apples," remembering those long hours he had whiled away inside as a boy, when his phone rang.

"Yes?" he said in Arabic.

Ahmed's side of the conversation went as follows:

"Yes, I'm ready. I am always ready. You know that. . . .

"Any time you like. Would you like it to be tomorrow? I can make it tomorrow. . . .

"Yes, of course I will have the money. Have I ever failed you? . . .

"And we are agreed on the price? . . .

"No, no, no. That is not acceptable. Not at all. These complications you speak of, these are not my problem. . . .

"Well, so kill them if you have to kill them. What do you expect me to do, weep at their funeral? They mean nothing to me. . . .

"Well, then I will suggest to you the desert is a wonderful place to dispose of a body. You are aware of the saying we have about that, yes?"

Ahmed then laughed and said, "No, no. It is this: sand only surrenders that which it wants to. You take care of your problems. I'll take care of mine. I will see you in the morning, Allah be praised."

CHAPTER 19

WEST OF LUXOR, Egypt

Katie Comely's cheeks were flushed, and for once it wasn't only because of the heat.

"I just don't understand where your objections are coming from," she was saying to Professor Raynes. "These people are the answer to our dreams. Did you see the size of that guy? He could fit three Egyptians in his pocket. More importantly, did you see the size of his gun? And the woman looks like she can handle herself, too. Certainly a lot better than a bunch of so-called guards that run away the second someone gives them a cross look."

Katie and the professor had retired to his tent. The heat of the day was upon them. Outside, the mercury was climbing toward fifty degrees Celsius, more than 120 degrees Fahrenheit. Inside Raynes's tent, a solar-powered air-conditioning unit pumped in cool air that provided a hedge against the oppressiveness of the desert. Much of the cold leaked down through the wooden floor that Raynes had installed to lift his tent off the sand. The result was that the tent was merely lukewarm, as opposed to sweltering.

Still, it was a lot more posh than most of the archaeological digs Katie had been on. Raynes had all the latest equipment, plus generators to run it all. It helped give the camp at least a veneer of civilization amid the brutality of their surroundings.

"All I'm saying is, I'm not sure I trust these people, Katie," Professor Raynes said.

"How could you say that? They're from i-apple. They're here to protect us."

"Yes, yes, I know we *think* they're from i-apple. But normally people from the International Art Protection League don't just show up out of nowhere, on camels, without warning. They call ahead. They come in trucks. These people, they could be anyone."

Katie put her hands on her hips. "Why would they *say* they're from i-apple if they're not from i-apple? That just seems like a random thing to go claiming. If you're that worried, call up your contact in Bern."

"I will, I will," the professor said.

"It's just, we're so close. I've got Bouchard ready to move. He's coming out tonight."

She had taken to naming her mummy Bouchard, after Pierre-François Bouchard, the French army officer who found the Rosetta stone—the discovery that was considered to have launched the entire field of Egyptology. Until Katie was able to get the mummy back to the lab, she would get no closer to knowing his real name. Which of the many previously unfound ancient kings of Egypt was he?

"I know how much he means to you," the professor said, softening his tone.

"Anyone who says they want to help? As far as I'm concerned, I don't care if they are charlatans in

some way we don't yet realize. If they protect us, I'll
buy whatever snake oil they want to sell us or—"

"Katie, are you sure that's wise?"

"I just . . . I lost Khufu and if I lose this too . . .
I mean, this is my whole—" she began, then stopped
because she realized she was about to cry.

"Katie, Katie," the professor cooed.

He stood, walked around behind her, and began
rubbing her shoulders. It was the first time he had
ever touched her in a way that couldn't be considered
professional. She had a mind to fight it, to shrug it
off, and to chastise him for it. She knew about his
crush. It was wrong on many levels.

But then she reminded herself she needed all the
help she could get. There were worse things than
accepting an unsolicited back rub. If that's what kept
him on her side, she would allow it.

TWO TENTS OVER, THERE WERE NO BACK RUBS
going on.

"Oh, Mr. Talbot, you're so big and strong," Clara
Strike said in a mocking rendition of Katie Comely's
soprano voice. "You look like you could lift anything. As a matter of fact, why don't you come over
here and lift up my skirt?"

"Oh, stop."

"And when you're done, what do you say we dig
around in whatever you find there? I bet we could
really do some wonderful excavating."

"What are you suggesting?" Storm asked.

"What am I suggesting?" Strike said, returning
to her normal tone. "I'm not suggesting anything.
I'm saying she wants to play a game of hide the

hieroglyph with you, and from the way you're look-ing at her, the feeling is more than a little mutual."

"Come on now," Storm said. "You're just being silly."

"Silly, am I? Sorry; so it was just a coincidence that we went into the desert a newly and happily married couple—Mr. and Mrs. Sullivan, on their honeymoon, riding the most romantic camels in all of Egypt, deeply in love—and the next thing I know I'm actually an old maid, schlepping over sand dunes with some guy named Tommy Talbot."

"Terry Talbot. I told you I didn't like the name Sullivan."

"So you divorced me, just like that? The institu-tion of marriage is that meaningless to you?"

"I didn't div—

"I just don't know what I'm going to say to all our friends who came to the wedding. And all the money my parents spent. Can you return a wedding dress that's only been worn once?"

"Can I remind you we were not actually married?"

"Not anymore, apparently," Strike sniffed, hold-ing her chin up high.

"I was improvising, okay? I also told her we were international defenders of art, whatever the hell that means. I can't be held accountable that the young woman happens to be impressed with my physique."

"Yes, yes. I know. You're *sooooo* ruggedly handsome."

Storm brought a bandana to his face, dampening it with the sweat that was forming on his brow and lip. "Look, we're here, okay? And I don't know if you noticed, but this appears to be the only thing in the target-zone radius that's not a pile of sand. The promethium might well have been discovered here."

"By a bunch of archaeologists?"

"Or maybe by the people who were here before the archaeologists, I don't know. But, as you so vividly pointed out, there is a lot of excavation going on here. People who dig in the Earth tend to find things down there. Maybe things like promethium."

Strike uncrossed her arms, grabbed a water bottle, and took a swig. Storm could tell she was softening.

"Look, if you've got a better idea than hanging out here, I'm all for hearing it," Storm said. "But at the moment, I think this is our best bet. At the very least, I'm sure we can protect them from these bandits that are supposedly roving around out here. Who knows? Maybe the bandits are the ones behind it. Or maybe there are Medina Society members embedded here at the dig site, pretending to be part of the expedition when really they're secreting out the promethium every time they return to civilization? There are a host of possibilities."

Strike fingered the water bottle. "Okay, so what are you proposing?"

"First off, we maintain the cover of being Talbot and Sullivan from the International Art Protection League. There seems to be a lot going on tonight. You shadow Professor Plumb—"

"Professor Raynes."

"Yeah, whatever. As I was saying, you stick with him, see if you can work your charms on him to figure out what's really going on. Pay attention to the natives, too. They're the ones who are doing the heavy lifting, as Katie pointed out. But it still seems like Raynes is the head honcho of this dig site, so he'll probably know about anything that's been happening here. Meanwhile, I'll hang out with Dr. Comely."

"Terrible sacrifice for you that it is," Strike said, narrowing her eyes.

Storm did his best to look virtuous. "Why, Mrs. Sullivan, I'm sure I have no idea what you're talking about."

THE FEROCIOUS SUN HAD FINALLY BEGUN TO SETTLE in the sky, flooding the desert with mysterious reds and complex yellows. The sand released its heat with the same kind of speed it had soaked it up in the morning. And at the dig site, the teams of grad students, postdocs, professors, and local workers had shifted back into an active state.

"We basically have two work sessions a day," Katie Comely was explaining to Storm, who was patiently following behind her. "We're up before first light so we can take advantage of the morning hours. We take a siesta in the middle of the day. And then we work again at night, usually at least a few hours after sunset."

"When do the bandits strike?" Storm asked.

"The morning. It's almost like they know when we have something really valuable. I think one of the workers is tipping them off, probably getting paid for the information. But I don't know which one, and my Arabic isn't very good yet, so it's hard for me to make any headway in that area."

"And when they come, it's . . . on camels? In dune buggies? What?"

"Pickup trucks. They need the trucks to haul off our stuff. You can see them coming from a ways off, but there seems to be nothing we can do to defend ourselves. It's so disheartening. The professor has hired security, but they turn tail and run without firing a shot."

"Who are these bandits? Do you know anything about them?"

"Well, they cover their faces, of course. They're just . . . locals, I guess. Desperate locals. Egypt's economy has been in a real tailspin with all the political instability. Unemployment has spiked. Sometimes I wish I spoke better Arabic so I could talk to them. There has to be a way to get them to stop what they're doing. Maybe we could hire them to provide security for us, you know? Pay them protection money. Either that, or maybe I could convince them to, I don't know, find someone else to rob."

Katie had led him to the entrance of the tomb and was about to go underground when she paused.

"Oh my goodness, do you hear that?" she said.

Storm stopped behind her and tuned his ears to a sweet chirping sound. It was at once angelic and strangely uplifting, like nothing Storm had ever heard.

"What is that?" Storm asked, finally focusing on the small, yellow bird making the sound.

"That," Katie said, "is a very rare sight, indeed. That's a Jameson's Finch."

"It's lovely."

"Egyptians believe it's extraordinary good luck to see a Jameson's Finch," she said. "It's like the American equivalent of a rabbit's foot, a horseshoe, and a four-leaf clover, all in one. People who see a

Jameson's Finch are said to be on the brink of something very fortunate happening to them. The bird originally had a number of names. No one could seem to agree what to call it. Pharaohs actually kept the finches at their palaces so they could enjoy the songs. We've found mummified finches in the tombs of pharaohs who couldn't bear the thought of going to the afterlife without their favorite songbird."

"Poor bird."

"Actually, what made it a poor bird is that they were being hunted to extinction. These finches have a very narrow migratory path, stopping at just a few spots on their journey from the tip of South Africa up to Egypt each year. It made them an easy target for poachers.

"Then Jameson Rook, the famed magazine journalist, wrote a major story about the bird's plight and how it was going the way of the carrier pigeon if no one stepped in. Several governments in Africa, which normally couldn't agree on anything—even what name to give the finches—banned hunting of the finches and also set up some sanctuaries for them. And the finches' numbers rebounded to the point where they're now no longer considered endangered, merely threatened. The Egyptians were so thrilled not to lose the bird, they officially renamed it Jameson's Finch, in Mr. Rook's honor."

Storm listened to the bird's song, then mimicked it, pursing his lips and tweeting back at it in its own lilting song.

"Wow, that's pretty impressive," Katie said. "Maybe you're good luck, too?"

"We'll just have to hope so," Storm said.

As they went underground, she began narrating

the history of the dig site—how it had been discovered by Professor Raynes, using his advanced seismographic techniques; how a rotating team of archaeologists had been unearthing treasures from it for a year now; and then how she had happened upon the hollow stone and the hidden tunnel underneath.

Storm listened with half an ear. He was keeping an eye out for anything that seemed out of place or anyone acting strangely. For whatever he had said to Strike, he wasn't totally convinced the dig site had anything to do with the promethium. But it made sense to act as if it did. There was no downside of being wrong, and potentially great benefits to his investigation if he was right.

So he studied everything and everyone with great care. Even Katie Comely. If the Medina Society really was as clever as everyone thought, it very well might be using a fresh-scrubbed American girl as an operative.

Storm kept asking questions, being careful to stay true to his cover. The passageway Katie was leading him down had been widened and reinforced to prevent cave-in. Storm was able to walk—albeit in a crouch—down into the lowest tomb. Once there, Storm could stand. They had set up temporary lights that set the whole place aglow.

"Up until just a few days ago, it's very possible no human beings had laid eyes on any of this for five thousand years," Katie said, pointing out some of the hieroglyphics on the walls.

"And this," she finished, "is the mummy I've been calling Bouchard. Note the way his arms are crossed. Note how intricately the linen was bound around him and the care that was taken with every detail. We won't know until we unwrap him, but my guess is we'll find a very painstaking embalming. There's no doubt in my mind this was a pharaoh. But we have to be able to get it back to the lab so we can study it adequately."

Storm looked at Katie, then at the human-shaped pile of rags in front of him, trying to imagine what this king's world had been like and what kind of troubles he had faced. What would this king have felt about something like the Medina Society, a group that believed in killing and maiming to achieve its goals? He probably wouldn't have blinked an eye. Brutality was the norm back then. Power was taken by force. The losers were killed or enslaved. It was only modern humans who were supposed to be more evolved.

Katie was talking about the various scientific processes that would soon be applied to the mummy when Storm interrupted her.

"You're pretty geeked on this Egypt stuff, aren't you?"

She stopped herself, then smiled. "Yeah, I really am."

"How did that happen to a girl from . . . I'm guessing Missouri?"

"Kansas, actually. But you're on the right track. I grew up in this little farming town in Kansas where nothing ever happened and all anyone ever talked about was the weather, how the weather compared to what it had been in the past, and what that might mean for the corn crop. Oh, that and college basketball."

She laughed at herself and continued, scanning the walls as she spoke. "When I was seven, my parents took me to this traveling exhibition of Egyptian treasures that had somehow meandered its way to a museum in Kansas City. That was the first time I had ever really been confronted with the idea that there were these people who had lived a very long time ago in a very different place, that they had created this remarkable civilization, and that they had invented so many of the things we now take for granted. It seemed so exotic, so wonderful, so foreign in the best way. And it just fired my imagination.

"I started studying everything I could about it and never really stopped. Any time I had a project in school, I would find a way to make it about Egypt. I majored in archaeology with a minor in Egyptian Studies as an undergrad, then went on and got my graduate degree, then my doctorate. In some ways, the more I learn just makes me want to know that much more, and I . . . I'm sorry. This is really boring, isn't it?"

"Not at all," Storm insisted. "One of the reasons I decided to come work for i-apple was that I loved the passion people like you—artists, archaeologists, museum curators—have for their jobs. I would otherwise be a soldier of fortune, a hired gun who worked for whatever company offered the biggest paycheck. At least this way I work for people who are doing things for a higher cause."

Even though Storm said it to maintain his cover, there were pieces of his own truth hidden within the words.

Katie turned and looked at him with two big, blue eyes. "You're really going to help us, aren't you?"

"I'm certainly going to try," he said.

She hugged him with her whole body. "Thank you," she said. "Thank you so much."

He hugged her back, feeling the parts that had been made hard by her work and the parts that stayed soft. Her contours seemed to fit nicely into his. He didn't really think she was a terrorist.

Which might have made her a perfect one.

CHAPTER 20

A SECURED ROOM

William McRae came to slowly, with the same sense of dread he had felt every morning for, what, three weeks now? Four?

He was starting to lose track. When he was first abducted, snatched by a group headed by a man with a wine stain on his face and a gun on his hip, McRae had assumed his captivity would be brief. He thought he would either be killed, or released, or his ransom would be paid.

Instead, they had drugged him, keeping him in a narcotized stupor for perhaps several days. He had the sensation of almost constant motion, like he was being moved somewhere. Sometimes the movement would stop and he would think: okay, now the end is coming. Then it would resume. He often heard an engine. He thought, perhaps, it was a generator. Maybe they were somewhere off the grid, and the engine was what supplied them their power. Or maybe this was a large vehicle of some kind. It was all so disorienting.

Once he recovered from the effects of the sedatives, they put him to work, making it clear to him that they would hurt him badly if he refused. He had not yet tested them on whether they'd carry out this threat.

It never occurred to him that his captivity might stretch this long, that he would start to get confused about the passage of time to the point where he could no longer reliably say what day of the week it was. The things that used to anchor him to time—the busy retiree's schedule of volunteer activities, the weekly rhythms of the things he and Alida did together, the calendar in his office, and the cell phone in his pocket—had all been taken from him.

In truth, he had not been badly treated in some ways. His confines were comfortable. His bed had a pillow-top mattress and clean, fine sheets that were changed every few days. His "cell," such as it was, was a windowless interior room, yes. But it had plush carpeting and its own en suite bathroom with a shower, sink, and toilet. It also had a small sitting area, where he took all his meals.

He was given clothes that fit him well. If he ever needed something, there was an intercom in his room. He could press the button anytime, tell the guards what he needed, and someone would fulfill the request. When he had discovered a mild allergy to one of his pillows, it had been removed, and he had received prompt medical treatment for his discomfort. He was being well fed, even overfed, by food that was delicious and nutritive.

The trade-off was that they were working him constantly. Every day after breakfast, they led him from his bedroom, across the hall and to the left, to his workshop. It was also windowless. He was kept under constant guard and made to work all day and into the evening.

After McRae had made the first laser for them, he thought he was done. He actually had stalled on the work a bit, thinking that when it was through, he was through.

Then they came back and said: build another one. Then another.

At first, there was a part of him—the scientist in him—that was thrilled by the work. He had always theorized that given enough promethium, he could make the most powerful laser the world had ever seen. But because promethium had always been in such miniscule supply, with no hope of getting more, it remained nothing more than a theory.

Getting to put it in practice was satisfying, even as he fretted over what they might be doing with the weapons. He kept thinking they would soon run out of promethium—where *were* they getting so much from, anyhow?—and that when that happened he would get a rest.

It was just getting to be too much. He was not a young man anymore. They brought people in to help him with some of the more physical tasks, but some of it was still up to him. His hands, which had a tendency toward arthritis as it was, were getting sore. He worked each day well past the point where his fingers literally ached.

His body was just out of whack. He missed his daily jog, not only for the physical release it gave him, but also for the mental health aspect. The jog centered him, soothed him, made him feel healthy, and released all those wonderful endorphins in his bloodstream.

The absence of the jog, on the other hand, had been a disruption. He wasn't sleeping as well at night. He was more irritable. The windowless rooms were getting to him. His body craved the fresh air and the sunlight.

More than anything, he missed Alida. He missed her companionship, her steady good cheer, her laugh, her smile. He missed the way she smelled when she came in from gardening, like soil and sweat. He missed talking to her about his work, something that had started long ago and had become an ingrained part of their marriage. He found himself pretending to have those conversations with her, almost because he couldn't process information himself without thinking of how he'd explain it to Alida. She wasn't just his ghostwriter. She was his muse.

Some couples take each other for granted, especially after several decades of marriage; or they treat each other shabbily, neglecting to show each other the kindness they'd extend to strangers. William and Alida McRae had never done that. It had made their relationship strong, helped their love grow—rather than wither—through the years.

Being apart from her was, without question, the worst part of the whole ordeal for him. In their entire married life, forty-five years and counting, they had never been separated for more than maybe two, at most three nights—when he went to a conference on the East Coast to present a paper. Otherwise, they were inseparable.

He worried about how she was holding up without him. He worried about the effect her distress might be having on her health. He worried she was worried.

He begged his captors to let him call her, to tell her he was still alive. They had refused. What about an e-mail, he asked? A letter? No way, they said.

All the while, they kept working him. And now he was just tired: of toiling for these men, of his aching fingers, of agonizing over what they might be doing with the weapons he was making, of missing Alida.

He rolled over in bed, much as he wished he didn't have to. They watched him, he knew. Usually, they came in not long after he first stirred. Lately he'd taken to lying very still in the morning, milking a few extra minutes in bed. It's just that he was an old man and couldn't stay in the same position too long.

So he moved. And shortly thereafter, one of his captors came in. There were five of them. McRae assigned them each a Greek letter, based on where he thought each one ranked. This one was Delta.

"Good morning," Delta said gruffly. "What do you want for breakfast?"

"Nothing," he said, rolling back over.

Delta paused. He was younger than some of the other ones, which is why McRae had assigned him somewhat subordinate status. Like the others, he didn't bother hiding his face, which worried McRae: it meant none of them were concerned about him getting out alive to identify them.

"Come on, Dr. McRae, you have to eat."

"Forget it," McRae said. "I'm done working for you people."

The words just came out. He hadn't much considered their consequences. The man did not respond, just left the room. He heard the door click, as it always did. His captors did not leave anything to chance. McRae wondered if he'd even know what to do if the door didn't click. He hoped someday he'd get the chance to find out.

Three minutes later, another man came in. It was Alpha. McRae had decided he was the leader based on the deference the other men showed him and also because of his immense size. Alpha was at least six foot six and densely built, well north of three hundred pounds, most of it muscle. With blond hair and blue eyes, he looked like a modern-day Viking. He was carrying a manila envelope.

"Dr. McRae, I understand we have a bit of a problem this morning."

McRae just lay there, and said nothing. He was through. If they wanted to hurt him, fine. He wasn't building them any more lasers.

"Very well, if that's how it's going to be," Alpha said, sighing like this was nothing more than a minor inconvenience. He opened the manila envelope and began laying eight-by-ten glossy photos on the foot of the bed.

McRae didn't look at them. They were probably just gruesome pictures of some person they had mutilated. It was the lowest level of coercion. Perhaps the real torture would start soon. But McRae was betting it wouldn't. After all, if they damaged him, he wouldn't be able to work for them. This was his trump card, and he was finally playing it.

Then, out of the corner of his eye, he caught a glimpse of one of the photos being laid on his bed.

It wasn't some sick, blood-and-guts picture of some anguished prisoner.

It was Alida. Gardening.

McRae sat up, his heart pounding like a jackhammer against his rib cage.

"Nice pictures, aren't they?" Alpha said. "Really captures the care she puts into her work."

Alpha took out another photo. It was Alida, clutching the newspaper as she walked up the steps to their house. "I like this one, too. Action photo. And if you look very carefully, you'll see the date of the newspaper is yesterday. So it's very recent."

McRae's mouth was dry. He couldn't find any words.

"Let me talk this out for you, Mr. McRae, in case you're missing the point of all this. We have a man set up at your house, watching your dear Alida closely. If you refuse to work for us, we won't harm a hair on your scrawny little head. You're too valuable to us. We'll just hurt Alida instead. Are we clear?"

McRae nodded.

"I'm going to need to hear a word or two, Mr. McRae. Are we clear?"

"Yes," McRae said, hoarsely.

"Very good," Alpha said. "Now—and this time, I suggest you answer—what would you like for breakfast?"

CHAPTER 21

WEST OF LUXOR, Egypt

They had extracted Bouchard the mummy the night before, packing him in a crate with all the care they could to ready him for transport along with some of the other artifacts the expedition had unearthed.

Storm had kept his eyes open throughout the evening, still convinced there was more to the archaeological site than just some old bones. He was undeterred by his failure to find anything of significance. It was like the hieroglyphs on the walls: for years, no one knew what they meant; not until the other Bouchard, good ol' Pierre-François, tripped on that stone. Then it all became clear. Sometimes, in detective work as in life, you just had to be patient and wait for a break.

In the meantime, Storm immersed himself in the role of IAPL protector. He had pressed for leaving in the middle of the night and traveling through the desert under starlight. After all, if the bandits tended to attack in the morning, why wait?

But Professor Raynes nixed the idea. There were no roads where they were traveling, and the raw desert had too many furrows and trenches that would be hard to see at night. If they got stuck in one it could be disastrous.

Plus, the camels needed their sleep. Being familiar with the complications posed by an angry camel, Storm acquiesced. They planned a predawn departure and now, here it was: the first hint of light was glowing on the horizon when Raynes gave the order to move out.

Their caravan consisted of eight camels and three twenty-foot-long cargo trucks, one of which had been specially designated to carry Bouchard. The other two were more fully packed. Storm had not personally overseen the loading. That, he figured, was best left to the professionals.

But he did exert his influence on how the caravan would be organized. He placed the trucks, which were being driven by grad students, in the middle. He and the professor rode up front on their camels. The four hired guards were split between the two side flanks. Strike and Katie Comely brought up the rear.

As long as they were in the desert, they had to move slowly up and down the dunes. Their payload was too fragile and too valuable to risk jostling it. All it would take was one bump traversed a little too quickly to result in catastrophic damage to one of the pieces.

As a result, the cargo trucks were put on a strict speed limit of five miles an hour. Even the camels had to be reined back to match that torpid pace. It was fifteen miles to the nearest blacktopped road and the relative safety of Egypt's highway system. Once they reached it, they would be able to stable the camels and increase their speed for the remainder of the journey.

But they would not be getting there with any particular alacrity. Fifteen miles at five miles an hour. It didn't take a mathematical wizard to know that meant three hours—three hours during which time they would be fully exposed to anyone who wanted to take a shot at them or their precious cargo.

The International Art Protection League's unintentional stand-ins were more than ready for any outlaws who might try. Storm had assembled his CheyTac sniper rifle and wore it strapped across his back. Strike was, likewise, ready with her M16.

Just with those two weapons—and their proficiency at using them—they could repel a substantial force.

"So, Mr. Talbot, how is it you came to work for the International Art Protection League?" Raynes asked as they got under way.

"Friend of a friend recommended me. They pretty much hired me on the spot," Storm lied smoothly.

"There was no interview process?"

"I guess I've got that useful look about me," Storm said.

Antony punctuated Storm's boast with a loud belch. The camel had been his usual cantankerous self that morning. But at least he hadn't tried to mate with anyone.

"And how long have you been working there, Mr. Talbot?" the professor asked.

"About two years now. And, please, call me Terry."

"Two years. Impressive," Raynes said. "Have you ever bumped across a man named Ramon Russo there?"

Storm did not allow even the faintest wrinkle to appear on his face. With no access to the Internet, he had been unable to do any research on the International Art Protection League. But he had faked his way through many such conversations during his years undercover. The trick was to answer the question without answering it. Politicians called it a "pivot," and had usually perfected it by the time they finished their first campaign. Spies were no less masterful at it.

"You know, every time I hear the name Ramon Russo I think of the guy who played the part of the jock in *2 Cool for School* back in the nineties," Storm said. "Did you ever watch that show?"

"I can't say as I did."

"Oh, it was so funny. Every time this one character saw a pretty girl he'd say, 'Hubba-hubba.' So when you say the name Ramon Russo it makes me think, 'Hubba-hubba.'"

Storm let out a belly laugh and added, "Classic. Just classic. Hubba-hubba! Hey, you want to quote movie lines? It's a great way to pass the time. I'll say the line. You say the movie. Okay, here goes: 'Over? Was it over when the Germans bombed Pearl Harbor? Nothing's over until we say it is!' Okay, what's the movie? Come on, that's an easy one."

Storm caught Raynes looking at him with utter disdain and kept it going for the next hour, seldom letting the man cut in as he ran through the entire canon of *Animal House*, *Caddyshack*, *Vacation*, and other American film classics.

He was just getting into *My Cousin Vinny* when he saw a dust cloud rising in the distance. He cut off his version of Joe Pesci's rant about the biological clock to say, "Looks like we've got company."

STORM DIRECTED THE CARAVAN TO CLIMB TO THE TOP of a dune, where it would have the greatest visual and tactical advantage, then called for it to halt. He scrambled down off Antony, climbed to the top of one of the cargo truck's cabs, unslung the CheyTac, and began setting up its legs. Given the cowardice of Raynes's security forces, these bandits—assuming it was the same ones—had never encountered the slightest resistance. They had just stolen whatever they wanted, laughing the whole way. Things were about to change.

This was not, in the truest sense, his fight. It was surely not why he had come into the desert in the first place. But the basic framework of this confrontation offended his sense of decency. It was the strong picking on the weak. And to a man like Derrick Storm, that was always a fight worth having.

"What are you doing?" Raynes asked.

"In my experience, bullies are pretty much the same, the world over," Storm replied, continuing his preparations. "Whether it's the playground back home in America or the Sahara Desert, you need to punch them in the mouth before they take you seriously."

The bandits continued their approach. Storm almost thought of himself like a chemist running assays to identify an unknown element. This particular test involved making one of the bandit's heads explode like a target practice watermelon. Then he'd really see what these assailants were made of.

He was a good enough shot that, even with the raiding party closing in at fifty miles an hour, he was reasonably sure he could drop one of them at five hundred yards. He could then retarget and take out another one by the time they were within three hundred yards.

Then see how brave they were.

With his rifle set, Storm began a deep breathing exercise that would slow his heart rate. It was one of the first things an elite sniper learned: you had to pull the trigger in between beats. The slower your heart, the more of a window you had to squeeze off a shot.

Storm quickly got himself down to where he was going at least a second between beats. He decided his first target would be in the lead car, the one that was at the point of the rough V shape in which the bandits were approaching.

Storm drew a bead on the man's head. It was a harder shot than going for center mass, yes. But it would also have a more dramatic effect—head shots being bloodier, more spectacular, and less unambiguous. A guy slumping over from being hit in the chest could have just fallen down. It scared no one. The same guy losing a chunk of brain matter before he dropped tended to take his comrades' swagger away in a hurry.

There was no wind, which helped. Storm did some quick, rough math, judging how far the bullet would drop over the course of those five hundred yards. He set the crosshairs of his scope just above the man's head, knowing gravity would bring the bullet down to hit him square between the eyes. He put his finger on the trigger, felt his heart. It was a rhythm thing. Storm always liked to pull the trigger after the third beat. *Thump*, pause, *thump*, pause, *thump* . . .

"Wait! Don't shoot!" Raynes shouted.

"Why not?" Storm asked, without moving himself.

"Because I had a suspicion this would happen,"

he said. "I had the workers replace all of the valuable finds with garbage."

"Including Bouchard?"

"Especially Bouchard. That's actually a box of sand in that truck. There's nothing of value worth protecting. Let's just give it to them. We'll get Bouchard out another way."

Storm lifted his head from his gun. The bandits were getting closer. Four hundred yards now. Whatever advantage Storm had being able to pick them off at a distance wasn't going to last. According to Katie, the bandits had AK-47s. It was a weapon that grew vastly more effective at shorter range.

"I don't care what's in those trucks," Storm said. "We have to send them a message."

Storm moved his eye back to his scope.

"No! With all due respect, Terry, we are an archaeological expedition here to venerate this country's great history, not a bunch of outlaws ourselves. We are here as guests of the Supreme Council of Antiquities. Part of the agreement we sign with the Supreme Council of Antiquities is that we will be law-abiding and peaceful. We're not even supposed to have firearms. Please! There's no point in shedding blood to protect a pile of sand. Let me just talk to them."

The professor urged his camel toward the oncoming bandits. He raised his hands high in the air as the camel made a slow walk out.

"I don't like this," Storm said to Strike, who had come up from the rear on Cleopatra, with Katie trailing not far behind.

"This isn't your party, Storm," she said in a hush. "And, remember, we're not really here to protect anyone's art. Would you at least *try* to keep a low profile and not go shooting up the citizenry? If Doctor Dolittle thinks he can talk to the animals, let him try."

Raynes and the raiders came to a stop about fifty yards away. There were four enemy pickup trucks with seven armed assailants standing in the backs of the flatbeds. The professor kept his hands in the air and began chattering in Arabic with the man who appeared to be the head bandit. The conversation was, to say the least, tense in tone and body language.

But then Storm began dialing in on what was actually being said.

"Start shouting at me, point the gun at me, and sound really angry," the professor said in smooth, easy Arabic, never realizing that the boob who was just quoting Ferris Bueller was, in fact, quite fluent in the language.

The lead bandit, a tall man with a prominent nose, complied with the professor's instructions, lifting the muzzle of his gun and shouting something about how the professor had better stop playing games, saying it loud enough that everyone could hear it.

"Very good," the professor said calmly. "Now take a swing at me with the butt of your rifle. But for God's sake, Ahmed, would you miss this time? It hurt like hell last time."

The lead bandit—whose name was, apparently, Ahmed—unleashed another angry burst of words, punctuating it by swinging his rifle like an axe, coming within two inches of his head.

Strike, who also spoke Arabic, turned to Storm and asked, "Are you getting this?"

Storm nodded. He wanted to see how it would

unfold. He trained his ears back toward the distant conversation.

"Okay, thank you," the professor said, his hands still raised. "Now, I'm going to give it to you for the same price as last time, but next time the price is going up, understand?"

"We'll see about that," Ahmed replied. "Let's just worry about this time."

"Very well. But we'll have to talk about next time," the professor said. "In the meantime, what you've come for is in the second truck. You're going to have to make a show of taking it forcefully, of course. You might want to be particularly careful of the big guy on top of the cab of the truck there. Keep a gun trained on him in case he tries anything. Shoot him if you want to. But otherwise you'll find everything wrapped real nicely for you."

Ahmed said something Storm couldn't quite make out—his accent was thicker than the professor's. But, at this point, Storm didn't need to hear more.

"Katie, I've got bad news for you," Storm said. "What you're seeing isn't a stickup. It's more like a negotiation. Professor Raynes has been selling you out."

"What?" Katie said.

"He and the bandits are in cahoots. I'm sorry."

Katie was, at first, too stunned to form a full sentence. Instead, she sputtered, "What do you . . . He's . . . But that's not . . ."

"Katie, who owns the stuff you guys dig up?" Strike asked.

"Well, ultimately, the Egyptian people," Katie answered. "That's part of the agreement we sign with the Supreme Council of Antiquities."

"That's why he's selling you out," Strike said. "He doesn't see a dime if these pieces end up in a museum somewhere, but I bet these bandits are giving him a nice percentage of what they get for this stuff on the black market."

"So what are we supposed to do?" Katie asked.

Storm didn't answer. He had already resumed his position in front of the CheyTac, where he began counting heartbeats.

HE DID NOT AIM FOR HEADS.

He aimed for shoulders. Right shoulders, in particular. Storm knew the left hand was seen as unsanitary in Islamic culture. He was therefore betting all seven of the armed men in front of him shot with their right.

Unless they got shot first. A wound to the right shoulder would not be fatal for any of these men; and, truly, they did not deserve to die for the crime of being poor, desperate desert bandits. But it would certainly keep them from shooting back.

Storm trained his sights on Ahmed, the lead bandit, and squeezed the trigger. Ahmed crumpled, clutching his right shoulder as he went down. Storm quickly targeted the goon next to him. *Thump*, pause, *thump*, pause, *thump*, BANG. The goon joined his boss in agony.

By this point, the other bandits were looking wildly around, trying to ascertain where the gunfire was coming from. For as hostile as they pretended to be, they had not anticipated any resistance from this ragtag group of scientists. Especially when they probably all knew this was just a business deal in disguise.

Storm used this time of confusion to drop a third. Three of the men had, by this point, taken cover in their pickup trucks. One was still somewhat exposed. Storm buried a bullet in his bicep. Technically, it was a miss. But it would do the job.

The professor had put his hands down and now had his hands on the reins of his camel, which was braying loudly and running in a pattern that had no discernible sense to it.

The bandits were, likewise, in full panic. Their shouts were filled with confusion. Storm could tell, in that instinctive way he had, that the chief thought on all of their minds was, *How the hell do we get out of here?*

He just had to give the drivers of the pickup trucks a little more incentive. So he switched his scope from shoulders to a far easier target: windshields.

From just fifty yards, aiming at such a relatively large mark, he didn't bother counting heartbeats. He was just careful enough to make sure he didn't hit anyone sitting behind the windshield and started squeezing off rounds.

The first one shattered. Then the second one. By the time he was fixed on the third one, the trucks were already starting to move out, spinning sand in their haste to escape. Just for emphasis—and to give an enterprising windshield repair shop some extra business—Storm sent one more round hurtling out of the CheyTac.

With the bandits in retreat, Storm hopped off the roof of the cargo truck and was heading for the back of it. Katie, who had dismounted from her camel, appeared to be in shock more than anything. Strike was having a hard time steadying Cleopatra, whose gentle disposition did not appreciate gunfire.

Antony, standing still with unusual serenity amid all the excitement, was perhaps the only living creature that seemed genuinely unconcerned about the commotion.

"My goodness gracious," Raynes was saying as he rode back toward the group. "That was amazing! Did you see that? You were right, Mr. Talbot. Bullies *do* need to be punched in the mouth!"

Storm ignored the man. He unhooked the trailer door to the middle cargo truck, the one that had supposedly been carrying Bouchard but was now—allegedly—carrying rocks. Hopping up, Storm found a hammer that had been left on the floor and began prying open the crate inside.

"I don't know whether to curse you or thank you," the professor was yammering, having dismounted next to Katie. "But I will say it doesn't look like we'll have to worry about those ruffians again. So I guess I'll thank you."

The crate top was off now. It was not rocks. It was a large metal box with clasps on the sides. Storm opened the clasps, lifted the top, then peered inside.

It was a large pile of white powder.

A granular, white powder.

Which is exactly what Alida McRae said raw promethium looked like before it was refined.

A Geiger counter could confirm it, but Storm didn't need sensitive instrumentation to figure out what was going on. The archaeological dig was just a front. The professor was really running a promethium-mining operation. The men Storm had just shot at weren't bandits. They were terrorists who had come to buy it.

"I will have to write a very positive letter to the

International Art Protection League about your performance here today," Raynes said.

Storm hopped down from the truck and rounded the corner to confront Raynes.

"Drop the act, professor," Storm said. "There's no such thing as the International Art Protection League. You knew it from the moment my colleague and I appeared in your camp. I only figured it out when you let me quote movies for an hour instead of pressing me for more details about my employment."

Then Storm switched to Arabic: "Besides, I heard everything you said just now. And I know exactly what's going on here. You've been selling promethium to terrorists."

The word *promethium* made Strike's head whip in Storm's direction. Even Katie Comely, with her limited language skills, seemed to understand.

Raynes's face twitched. Then, with a speed that surprised even Storm, he produced a small pistol from the folds of his *thobe* and aimed it at Katie's head from point-blank range.

"Don't move," he said in a deadly calm voice. "If you try anything, I'll kill her."

CHAPTER 22

C arlos Villante pulled his Cadillac into the parking garage underneath the skyscraper that contained the offices of the Autoridad del Canal de Panama. He found his reserved spot—marked with, C. VILLANTE, DEPUTY DIRECTOR and parked there. Using his electric fob, he locked the car as he walked away, allowing himself one final smirk before entering the elevators.

He was ready for another day of smuggling bicycles.

While he considered himself, first and foremost, an employee of the United States government—that was certainly where his largest paycheck came from—the day-to-day reality of his existence was that he really did have to maintain the veneer of being a high-level bureaucrat within the canal authority.

It was no small chore. It was, in actuality, quite a bit of work: endless meetings, site visits, contracts to pore over, details to check. And whereas he didn't want to do his job so well that someone decided to make him the authority director, he did have to do it well enough not to get fired.

On this morning, that meant arriving an hour earlier for a meeting with his boss, Nico Serrano, the authority director, who had sent him a text message the night before, saying they needed to conference first thing.

I thought you were still in Washington, Villante had texted back.

Just landed.

Do you need me to prepare anything for this meeting? Villante wrote, ever the dutiful bureaucrat.

No. But be ready to hear some bad news, Serrano had replied.

So it was Villante wiped off whatever smile had been on his face as he rode up the elevator with all the other men and women who were girding themselves for another day of earnest paper pushing.

He set his briefcase down in his office, fixed himself a cup of coffee, and then walked by the corner office. Serrano was already there.

Villante tapped on the frame of the open door. "Would you like to meet now?" he asked.

Serrano looked up from his computer screen. There were dark smudges under his eyes. The lines on his face seemed deeper than the last time Villante had seen him, even though that had been only a week earlier.

"Yes, yes, come in," Serrano replied, rubbing his eyes.

"Would you like me to get you some coffee first? You look like you could use it."

"Thank you, but I've already had three cups. Sit down, please."

As Villante complied, Serrano asked, "How are things?"

Villante had no reason to lie. "Not very good. I went out to visit Parades yesterday," he said, referencing the name of one of his contractors, a man

Serrano knew well. "Parades says if the funding for the expansion project doesn't resume, he is going to have to default on his largest loan. It will probably mean bankruptcy."

Serrano bowed his head and squeezed his forehead, like this news had exacerbated an existing headache. Men like Parades had led the charge of Panamanian prosperity that had transformed their country. It was no exaggeration to say that if men like Parades were in trouble, it boded ill for the nation.

"I assume he is not alone?" Serrano asked.

"I'm afraid not. Grupa de 2000, Eusebio Rivera's outfit, is struggling, too. Most of the companies I'm dealing with are teetering on the brink right now, Nico. They're all in the same situation. They are relying on us to get the funding flowing again. I'm sorry, I'm telling you things you already know."

"Yes," he said. "But I . . . I keep hoping that somehow it's not the case."

"I thought our situation was about to improve with the Americans."

"So did I," Serrano said. "But I spoke with Congressman Jared Stack personally while I was in Washington. I was, of course, full of condolences about the death of his predecessor, Congressman Vaughn. And I expressed outrage over the attacks. I wanted to make it very clear there is no joy in Panama over the senselessness of this act of terrorism."

"Of course."

"But then the conversation moved along, and I reminded him of the importance of the canal to U.S. commerce. I brought out all the reports we prepared about how the widening of the canal would be a financial boon for everyone. I reminded him of the difficulties we are having here with financing. And do you know what he said?"

Serrano shook his head and continued. "He said that he and Congressman Vaughn were very close friends, and that while they didn't always see eye to eye, it would dishonor Vaughn's memory to fund the canal expansion when Vaughn had been such a staunch opponent of it."

"But that's . . . that's absurd!" Villante burst, his outrage real even if his identity wasn't. "The Americans are cutting off their noses to spite their faces."

"I had thought good sense would prevail now that Vaughn was gone. We all did. But, apparently, that is not the case. Good sense seems to be in very short supply in that town."

Villante balled his fists, then unclenched them. Again, it was not an act. He was genuinely upset by the stupidity of his government and wished he could express his anger to someone who might be able to do something about it. If there even was such a person.

"So what can I do?" Villante asked.

"This is going to get out. It always does. And when it does, there is going to be great despair here. Please just tell Parades and Rivera to hang on and not lose hope. If companies like theirs start filing for bankruptcy, it will be a tremendous disruption to our economy. You have to tell them we *will* get the money flowing again. It's just going to take a little longer."

"Do you have a plan, Nico?"

"I do."

"What is it?"

"It's best I not say. All you need to know is we are not yet out of options. I have another card to play."

"Okay, my friend," Villante said. "I will deliver your message of hope."

Villante stood and excused himself from Serrano's office. As he walked back to his own, he was already thinking of whether he should report this to Jones at Langley. As a deeply embedded asset, one who had invested years in establishing the most credible cover imaginable, Villante often heard bits of information that he was unsure of how to handle. He was constantly weighing the value of the information against the risk that sharing it might inadvertently expose him.

In this case, he decided he didn't have anything definitive enough to report. He would root around a little more, keep his ears open, and see how things played out.

CHAPTER 23

The gun was old and small for a revolver. It took Storm a moment to recognize it. It was a Colt Pocket Police, a gun coveted by Civil War buffs because generals on both sides had carried them.

Yet being an antique made it no less deadly when fired from point-blank range. Raynes had the weapon pressed against Katie Comely's temple. He was using her as a shield from the rest of the party.

"Hands up," Raynes ordered. "All of you, hands up. Nothing crazy here, or she dies."

Storm, the three graduate students who had been driving the cargo trucks, and the four guards slowly raised their hands. The only one who didn't comply was Strike. She had brought the M16 up to her shoulder and was aiming it at Raynes from perhaps thirty feet away.

"I've got the shot, Storm," she said calmly.

"Don't," Storm said.

"I can take him out," she insisted.

"No! For God's sake, you're on a camel and that gun is stuck on automatic. There's no way you'll be able to control your aim or the muzzle climb. There's too great a chance you'd hit them both."

"Better listen to your boyfriend, Ms. Sullivan—or

whatever your name is," Raynes said, hiding more of himself behind his terrified postdoc.

"I've. Got. The. Shot," Strike said again, not lowering the weapon.

"And Katie has got a family in Kansas," Storm said.

"Drop the weapon! Drop it, now!" Raynes was shouting as Storm spoke, pressing the barrel of the Pocket Police tighter against the side of Katie's head.

Storm wished he could place his body between Strike and her target. But she was too high up on the camel. All he had were words. The ones he chose were soft: "Clara. Please. Not for her. For me."

Strike took a deep breath, moved her finger to the trigger, tightened her grip on the gun . . .

Then tossed it on the desert sand below her.

"Damn it," she said.

"All right," Raynes said. "And while you're at it, let's get rid of those handguns you have, too. I've seen what's in those shoulder holsters. Do it real, real slow. If I even think you're making a move to draw, I'll shoot first and ask questions later."

Storm and Strike slowly discarded their sidearms, moving deliberately so their actions could not be misinterpreted.

"Okay, all of you, over there, away from the trucks," Raynes barked. "That's right. And let's keep those hands up."

Storm, Strike, and the others herded themselves into a small clump a short distance away from Raynes, who still had his gun trained on the side of Katie's head.

When he felt the group was a sufficient distance away, Raynes moved just slightly away from Katie.

"Okay," he said. "Now you're going to keep your hands up, but you're going to sit down."

Exchanging glances, the nine people who suddenly found themselves at gunpoint reached the conclusion that they didn't have much of a choice and took a seat on the sand.

"Very good," Raynes said. "Katie, there's a bunch of rope in the truck. You're going to go get it and use it to tie up all of these people. Start with Mr. Talbot here. Then Ms. Sullivan. And you had better make it tight."

Raynes shadowed Katie's movements as she went to the cargo truck, retrieved the rope, and began tying up her friends and colleagues. He stayed within a few feet of her, never letting the gun drop.

Storm and Strike communicated with their eyes only. At one point, Storm—as if responding to a suggestion Strike had made aloud—shook his head.

"We'll be fine," he said.

"No talking!" Raynes ordered. "And let's keep those hands up."

"But my arms are getting sore," one of the graduate students complained.

"A bullet will hurt a lot worse," Raynes snarled.

Katie, who was finally recovering from her shock, began fuming. "It's been you, all along. You're the one who told the bandits what we've dug up. You've been telling them when to make their raids. All as a front for selling this . . . this promethium, whatever *that* is. How could you *do* this to us?"

"You're very naïve, Katie. All this equipment. All these supplies. All these workers. You think I've been getting that kind of money from the university? Please."

"But . . . why just dig it up and let someone else take it?"

"Because if these people didn't take it, the Egyptian government would. Either way, I don't see a dime of it."

"But you get credit for the discovery!"

"Oh, fabulous, credit," Raynes said with a scoff as Katie continued her knot work. "Let me explain to you how credit works in the real world, my young postdoc. You make these amazing finds. You publish them, like a good academic should. You get all this quote-unquote credit. And then the university chancellor says, 'That's wonderful, professor. Congratulations. But, sorry, we have to cut your funding.'

"And then there are the foundations. Oh, let me tell you about them. They make you travel halfway across the globe to grovel at the feet of their almighty boards. And they tell you how fantastic you are. And then a week later, the executive director calls you up and says, 'Sorry, our portfolio didn't perform as well as we hoped this year. But we'll fund your dig two years from now, for sure. Good luck keeping it going.'"

Raynes punctuated this by lobbing out a few words that cannot be said on network television.

"And so there I was, slowly sinking, watching my budget and my staff whittle down to nothing, losing everything I had worked for. And then, one day, I noticed an unusual geological formation in one of the seismograms. I dug just a little and found a limestone cave that had a deposit of something that wasn't limestone. I had it tested and, lo and behold, it was this thing called promethium, the rarest of the rare earths. It sells for three thousand dollars an ounce. And what was I supposed to do at that point? Tell the Egyptian government, which would immediately claim mineral rights and take it all for themselves? No way."

Katie had furious tears streaming down her face. "You're a monster," she spat.

"Am I? I didn't hear you complaining when you were collecting that postdoc stipend and padding out your resume so you could get yourself a tenure-track job back in the States. Where do you think that money came from?"

Katie did not reply. Raynes went over to her and cupped the back of her head.

"Don't touch me," she said, jerking herself away.

"I was going to let Bouchard through. You know that, right? All the truly important finds got through. I just . . . I needed the bandits as a cover. I couldn't risk selling the promethium on the open market. I would have lost it all and we would have had to close the dig."

"So instead you sell it to terrorists," Storm said.

"Shut up!" Raynes said, briefly swiveling his gun in Storm's direction. "I sell it to a man named Ahmed. What he does with it is his business."

"He's using it to make a weapon that blows up commercial airliners laden with innocent people," Storm said. "But, hey, you've got a dig to fund, so what do you care?"

Raynes ignored him. Katie had bound the nine other members of the expedition.

"Very good. Now get in that truck," he said, pointing to the middle cargo truck, the one with the promethium still in back.

"I'm not coming with you," she said indignantly.

"Oh, yes you are. You're my insurance plan in case anyone here gets any ideas about playing hero.

Actually, sorry, you're the second part of my insurance plan. This is the first part."

He walked to the front of the first truck, aimed the Pocket Police at the front left tire, and shot it. The truck jolted down. He followed suit by shooting out the front right tire. Then he went to the back truck and similarly disabled it with two well-aimed shots.

Raynes returned to Katie, who needed a little extra cajoling to enter the passenger seat of the truck. Raynes got into the driver's side, turned the engine over, then rolled down the window.

His last words before putting the truck in gear and driving away were: "If any of you even have a thought about coming after us, know that it will cost Dr. Comely her life."

Storm waited until the truck had disappeared down into the valley of the dune, then sprung to his feet.

He ran over to the corner of one of the remaining trucks, using its sharp edge to hack into the rope that bound him, not caring that when he missed he was gouging his arms.

"Jesus, Storm. Slow down. What's your hurry?" Strike asked.

"I've got an Egyptologist to rescue."

"Just let her go. You didn't let me take the shot when I had the shot. Why endanger her now?"

"Didn't you notice?" Storm asked, with the rope already fraying.

"Notice what?"

"That revolver of his. It's a Colt Pocket Police. The Pocket Police was unusual for mass production revolvers in that it had four cylinders. That, plus one in the chamber means he only has five shots. He used four of them to shoot the trucks. He's only got one left."

"So?"

"So if he uses it to shoot Katie, he'd essentially be inviting me to kill him. And I can think of ten ways off the top of my head I could do it."

"Yeah, but what if he uses that one bullet to shoot you?"

"I'll take my chances," Storm said, the ropes now loose enough that he could slip free of them.

"Storm, seriously, you'll never be able to catch them."

Storm dashed over to pick up Dirty Harry, which he holstered. Then he ran to Antony and leapt up on the camel.

"Wanna bet?" Storm said, removing the riding crop from his pack and holding it aloft. "Hyah!"

Storm did not even have to hit the beast. As soon as Antony saw the crop's cruel whiplike end out of the corner of his eye, he let out a mighty bellow.

And then he began to run.

Like the wind—on a blustery day.

Like a Pegasus taking flight.

Like no camel ever has.

IT TOOK ALL OF STORM'S STRENGTH JUST TO HOLD ON at first. He never knew that a camel was capable of exerting such extreme g-forces on its rider.

But soon he was able to get hunched down in his saddle and lean forward as Antony, his ears pinned against his head, reached top speed.

"Hyah, hyah!" Storm said, keeping the crop in

his hand and outstretched—where Antony could see it—but not using it.

The cargo truck, which soon came into view, had perhaps a half-mile head start. Relieved of having to pretend there were precious artifacts in the back, Raynes was pushing the ungainly vehicle across the rugged terrain as fast as it could go, which was about thirty miles an hour.

Unfortunately for him, a champion racing camel can hit forty. And unlike a truck, the camel was bred to run in the desert.

Antony closed the gap fast. After a minute, he had cut the distance between himself and the truck down by a third. Two minutes in, he was less than a thousand feet away. After three minutes, he was within ten feet.

Raynes had started making an effort at performing evasive maneuvers, to little effect. In addition to being faster than the truck, Antony was also significantly more agile. Storm had no trouble countering Raynes's futile efforts as he drew even with the back of the trailer.

This, of course, was around exactly the time Antony decided he was getting less interested in chasing this silly truck. Storm could feel the animal slowing.

"Come on, Antony, hyah! Hyah!"

Storm reached forward so the crop was in the animal's face. Antony responded with one last burst of speed. Storm jumped from the camel to the truck just as Antony quit for good. The camel went from sprinting to walking to sitting down within a few short yards.

Raynes responded to the presence of another

passenger by swerving a few times, trying to shake Storm off the top of the trailer. But Storm hung on easily. His days of urban surfing had started long ago in suburban Washington, D.C. There was nothing this truck could throw at him that Storm and his daredevil friends hadn't conquered long ago.

Once he was sure of his purchase on the truck, Storm began crawling toward the cab. He was just starting to make progress when Raynes slammed on the brakes.

Storm gripped his fingers into the metal to avoid being tossed over the front of the truck and run over—if that was, in fact, Raynes's intention.

But, no, the professor had a different plan. As soon as the truck came to a stop, Katie spilled out of the truck's passenger side as if kicked. Raynes dove out after her and resumed a position he was rapidly perfecting: using Dr. Comely as a shield.

Storm had already drawn his weapon and was lying prone atop the truck, which meant he was also not within range of his enemy's gun.

"I told you not to come after us," Raynes screamed. Storm could hear him panting. Katie squealed, but he couldn't see what the cause of it was.

"Yes, and then you used four of your five bullets to shoot out our tires," Storm said, his voice steady. "Leaving you with just one and an interesting dilemma. If you use it to shoot Katie, I'll have you dead before she even hits the ground. But if you try to use it on me, you might miss. Or you might hit me but, with that little peashooter, not fully incapacitate me. And I assure you, neither of those outcomes will end well for you."

"Ah, yes, but you also have a dilemma, Mr.

Talbot. As long as I'm holding this gun to Katie's head, you can't dare make a move on me. Because if you do, her death will be on your conscience."

"True," Storm said. "So we are at something of an impasse, then. Are we not?"

"We are."

"In that case, I propose a deal."

"I'm listening."

"It's really quite simple, professor," Storm said. "You're going to leave Katie with me, and I'm going to let you go. You'll never be able to work in academia again, of course. And the Egyptian authorities might have quite a beef with you if they can ever catch you. It might be in your best interests to leave the country immediately and go to some place that doesn't have an extradition treaty with Egypt, because you had better believe I'm going to tell them you've been stealing antiquities and illegally mining promethium. I'm also going to see to it they keep a close eye on this area, because I know otherwise you're going to try to come back here and mine more. So you're through here. Trust me when I tell you, you're through.

"But, on the positive side, you get to keep your life and all that promethium in the back of that truck. That was, what, about three hundred pounds back there? Four hundred? You can't get top dollar for it dealing on the black market, but I'm betting you're still able to command at least a thousand dollars an ounce. So that's something in the neighborhood of five or six million dollars I'm giving you as a retirement plan. You should be able to live quite comfortably on that for the rest of your miserable life."

"How do I know if I let her go you won't just come after me again?"

"Because she and I are going to walk away. You've got the truck. We can't catch you on foot."

"Balderdash. You can just get on that speed-demon camel of yours anytime you want."

Storm laughed. "Do you see my speed-demon camel back there in the distance?"

"I do."

"Then you'll see he's sitting down. If you know anything about camels in general, or mine in particular, you'll know they only sit down when they're horny or when they've decided they're just not going anywhere for a while. Either way, you should have plenty of time to escape."

"And if I refuse your deal?"

Storm crept forward slightly on the roof of the truck, enough that Raynes could see Dirty Harry and little else. "Then we remain at an impasse. I will be holding you at gunpoint. And you will be holding Dr. Comely at gunpoint. But time is on my side, professor. It won't take long for my colleague, Ms. Sullivan, to get back to civilization and form a major search operation for us. We are not with the International Art Protection League, because there's no such thing. But we are with an organization that has all the resources needed to track down this truck in a desert and apprehend it."

"Okay, deal," Raynes said. "I'm getting back in the truck now, but I'm keeping Katie close. When I'm back behind the wheel, I want you to throw your gun as far as you can. When you do, I'll release Dr. Comely."

"Very well," Storm said.

He hopped down off the truck, on the opposite side from where Raynes was. Quickly, making sure the professor didn't see him do it, Storm jammed his satellite phone in one of the cargo truck's wheel wells.

"Okay, here goes my gun," Storm said, heaving the weapon into the distance.

Moments after it landed, Storm heard the truck revving. As it started moving, Katie leapt from it. She fell and rolled on the ground.

Storm didn't think Raynes would attempt a parting shot, but he kept in the truck's blind spot just in case. Then he walked over to Katie, who was already up and dusting sand off her pants.

"I don't suppose 'thank you' suffices?" she said.

"It'll do just fine," Storm said.

"I can probably do better a little later," she said.

Storm just smiled.

TRUE TO FORM, ANTONY THE CAMEL HAD SPENT HIS energy on his mad dash and could not be persuaded to carry passengers without trying to bite them first.

So it was Dr. Comely and Storm made the roughly three-mile walk back toward the others with the camel in tow.

Katie was quiet during the first part of the journey. Storm let her have her thoughts.

Finally, she said, "I should have known."

"No, you really shouldn't. If you lived suspecting everyone in the world was capable of that kind of evil, you'd be a paranoid, unhappy person."

"But there were clues," she said. "First of all, he did seem to have too much money. Most digs you go on, you subsist on ramen noodles and Pop-Tarts. You almost pride yourself on how rough you have it. But with Raynes, there was all this fresh food brought in. And the air conditioners. And the generators. And the wood floors on the tents. And all you had to do if you needed something was ask."

"I still don't think you should be blaming yourself," Storm said.

"No, but there's more. Every other day, he would just wander off in the late afternoon, just when it was starting to cool off a little. He would walk due east with a backpack on. And then he would come back two hours later, like nothing had happened. I asked him about it, and he said he was just getting some exercise, enjoying a walk. But, seriously, who just walks through the desert for two hours for no reason?"

"Yes, but as a wise man once said, 'Hindsight is fifty-fifty.'"

"You mean, 'hindsight is twenty-twenty,'" she corrected.

"No. That's what makes it wise. Hindsight is fifty-fifty. There's no greater expression of the arbitrary, random nature of the universe than saying something is fifty-fifty. It means you have an equal chance of being wrong and being right, of winning or of losing. There's no way to game fifty-fifty. You also can't second-guess it, because how were you supposed to know which way to go? That's the wisdom of 'hindsight is fifty-fifty.' It means you can't go back and beat yourself up over an outcome that only seems preordained after it happened."

"Are you sure you haven't been in the sun too long?" Katie asked.

Storm laughed. They were within sight of the disabled cargo trucks.

"So there's really no such thing as the International Art Protection League?" Katie asked.

"No. And yet we protected you anyway. That's called irony, in case you're wondering."

"So who are you?"

Any potential answer was interrupted when Strike became aware of their approach. She walked out to meet them.

"Where's the promethium?" she demanded.

Storm made note of the question. It was not *where's the professor?* Not *how are you?* Not *how did you get her free?* It was *where's the promethium?* At least he knew, once again, what Jones's—and, therefore Strike's—priorities were.

"It's in the back of the truck, as far as I know," Storm said.

"Fine. Where's the truck?"

Storm looked at his watch. "By now? It's probably on the highway."

"What? You let it go?"

"It was the only way to get him to free Dr. Comely."

Storm had enough history with Clara Strike to know her tells. Outwardly, there were few signs of activity—perhaps a slight flaring of the nostrils and a barely perceptible widening of the eyes. Inside, within her wiring, there were circuit breakers tripping.

Very evenly, Strike said, "You let the promethium go just to save a piece of ass?"

Katie's jaw dropped. Storm didn't back down. "I don't know if you noticed, but that ass actually has a human being attached to it."

"Our orders were to stop the terrorists and secure the promethium."

"No, *your* orders involved getting the promethium. I want no part of that scavenger hunt, even if it's abundantly clear that's all Jones really cares about."

"Don't be absurd. He wants those terrorists' heads on a platter. You should have heard him talk after the Pennsylvania Three."

"Really? You think I'm being that absurd? Seriously, if it came down to imprisoning terrorists or adding to the U.S. military's arsenal, which do you think Jones would choose?"

"It's not that simple," Strike said. "This is not a case of either or. We do our job right, we accomplish both."

"I'll bet you, right here and now, that Jones would let the terrorists skate free in exchange for a truckload of promethium."

"I'm not getting into theoretical debates with you, Storm."

"There might come a time when it's not theoretical. What's it going to be? Justice for all or weapons for generals?"

"It . . . it doesn't matter. We've got orders to follow."

"Orders," Storm scoffed. "You're going to hide behind orders?"

"It's not hiding. It's called doing my job," she shot back. "But I guess you're going to choose this moment to remind me that you don't really work for the CIA."

It was not their first go-around with this particular argument. And yet Storm felt himself sinking into his usual role. "Well, now that you mention it—"

"And then, after that, you're going to make it clear that what I want and what you want are, as usual, not fully compatible."

"This isn't about us. Stop making it about us. It's about mission objectives."

"To you it's not about us," Strike said. "To me,

it's always about us. That's the part you never seem to get. So let me be clear: it's about us. Are you going to help me or not?"

Was it about them? Or was it just her way of manipulating him, like she had done so many times in the past? Storm held her glare and said nothing.

Strike turned and stalked off. The anger wasn't faked. Storm couldn't help wondering if the reason for it was.

CHAPTER 24

HERCULES, California

The man with the wine stain was loving this job, mostly because he was charging by the hour.

It was going on four weeks now. Four weeks of 24-7 surveillance, billing out at $125 an hour, and his employer hadn't even blinked at the money. It was being deposited in his account weekly, without hesitation and without a sign of cessation.

And, yeah, it was a little boring, watching this old lady, Alida McWhatshername, shuffle around. But for that kind of money, who cared? He hoped the job never ended. As long as no realtors decided to show the empty house he was using, he could stay here forever.

He had his Buck knife out and was using it to dig some dirt out from under his fingernails. It was the most work the knife had gotten.

Whenever it ended—and all good things did, right?—he was going to go out and buy himself a new truck. His truck now was fine. But it was a little wimpy. He wanted something big. Something nice. A half ton, for sure. Maybe three-quarter ton. With leather seats. And a bitchin' stereo system.

Hell, if this job kept up, he could have whatever truck he wanted. He could even jack up the suspension and . . .

His phone was ringing in his pocket. He took it out and looked down. It was his employer, the man William McRae called Alpha.

"Hey," the man with the wine stain said.

"Anything to report?"

"Not really. She's just doing her thing. She goes to bed at the same time, wakes up at the same time, goes out in her garden. The usual. Most exciting thing she's done is go to the grocery store."

"Have you seen the large visitor again?"

"Naw. He ain't been back."

"Good. What about any other signs of law enforcement?"

"Nothing. She ain't gone to the sheriff in a few days now."

"Excellent," Alpha said. "And is she aware of your presence?"

"Nuh-uh. I don't have to leave the house. Most of the time, she don't know whether to wind her ass or scratch her watch."

"Ah, you southerners and your colloquialisms. They are so amusing. But what I am dealing with is not. Dr. McRae is getting a little testy. He's showing the first signs of balking at his work, giving us a little trouble."

"Oh, yeah?" the man with the wine stain said, sitting up a little. This was the most interesting thing that had happened since the big guy had left. "You want me to, I don't know, rough her up a bit? Put a little scare into her?"

He looked over at the Bushmaster propped against the wall. The .45 was in its holster. Not that he'd need that kind of firepower to scare an old lady. He could knock her around a little bit, hold the knife under her nose, make a big show out of it.

"No, we don't want you making contact until it's necessary. She might try to run if she knows she's being watched. Or she might attract more law enforcement attention."

"Okay."

"At this point, we just need some more pictures," Alpha said. "In case Dr. McRae gets more ideas."

"You sure that's all?" he asked. "I could mark her up a bit and *then* take pictures. You know, two birds with one stone and all that."

Alpha paused like he was considering this. "No," he said, eventually. "Just pictures for now."

"All right," the man with the wine stain said. "I'll upload some more in a bit. She don't lower her blinds at night. I can shoot some of her eating supper. When I get the angle right, there's this calendar in the background that shows the date."

"Perfect. Talk to you soon."

The man with the wine stain put his phone back in his pocket, lifted the 300-millimeter lens, and went to work.

CHAPTER 25

WEST OF LUXOR, Egypt

The helicopter came to get Strike an hour later. Its pilot was thoughtful enough to land just outside camp, so the sand stirred up by the rotors didn't lash into everyone. There was nothing he or anyone else could do to save Storm from the emotional whipping he felt as he watched Strike go.

This was how it went for them, he knew. For as close as they seemed that night at the hotel in Luxor, for as much as he yearned to be with her, for as strong as his feelings for her were, there was always another cataclysm waiting to ruin it all.

Someday there would be a reunion. Perhaps. And Storm would always be wondering whether it was fueled by personal feelings or professional necessity.

Storm watched the helicopter lift away. As it grew small in the distance, he was aware that Katie Comely was approaching behind him. Lightly, she put a hand on his back.

"You okay?" she asked.

He turned to face her. The heat of the day was upon them—it was at least 120 degrees—but her blue eyes had a coolness about them he found inviting. There was a hesitant smile on her freckled cheeks.

"Yeah. Perfect," he said.

All around them, parts of the camp were

breaking up. Word had gone out that the professor had taken off. The workers had done the math and figured out they were no longer going to get paid. They were departing with due haste. The academics were mostly just moping around, gossiping in small groups, bemoaning their fate, worrying about what would happen now that their funding was gone.

"This is none of my business, of course, but are you two together?" she asked, shifting her eyes in the direction of the helicopter. "I thought you were just colleagues when you first arrived, but then the way she responded to me earlier was, well, I think it's safe to say there were some feelings there. A woman doesn't usually call another woman a 'piece of ass' unless, you know."

"Yeah, that was just . . . actually, I don't know exactly how to describe that. And I'm not sure how to answer your question, either. We have been together in the past. I guess that's obvious. We are also pretty obviously not together right now."

"And the future?"

"Got me," Storm said quite honestly.

"Well, you're welcome to stay here as long as you like. It doesn't look like anyone is going to be using Professor Raynes's tent. And we could certainly use someone like you around."

"We?" Storm said.

She took a step closer and said, "Well, maybe just me."

Storm inhaled deeply, then expelled the breath slowly. "That is a wonderful, wonderful offer, Dr. Comely. And under different circumstances, I would be happy to take you up on it."

"But?" she said, the freckled smile dimming just a little.

"But I came here to do a job, and it's not done yet."

"I understand. I really do, but . . ." she looked down at the sand for a second, then looked back up at him and blurted, "Would you like to come back to my tent with me right now?"

She seemed so surprised the words had come out of her mouth, she hastened to add: "I mean, I don't want you to think I'm a . . . This isn't something I normally do. I just . . . Having that gun point at my head and . . . I don't know."

Storm leaned down and kissed her. On the cheek. "That is also a wonderful offer," he said.

"But?" she said shyly.

"Yeah. But."

"Okay. I understand."

Storm stepped back, but Katie walked toward him, rose up on her tiptoes, and kissed him. On the lips.

Psychologists have done double-blind, controlled experiments that have proven, scientifically, that in the immediate aftermath of surviving a traumatic event, feelings of passion are heightened. Storm didn't need to read any of the research. He was experiencing all the confirmation he needed.

"Thank you," she said, when it was done.

"Thank *you*," he said. "And now I'm going to have to go, because it's getting more difficult to do the right thing with each passing second."

It took every ounce of his self-control to walk away.

STORM PURPOSEFULLY AVOIDED ANY PROLONGED good-byes on his way out of camp. He simply got

Antony fed and watered, loaded him with what he hoped would be a sufficient amount of supplies, and hopped on.

"Wait! Where are you going?" Katie asked when she saw Storm heading out.

"Due east," he said.

She looked confused for a moment; then Storm saw understanding reach her face. "Good luck," she said.

"Could you do me two favors?"

"Anything."

"First, could you please contact the Supreme Council of Antiquities? They need to know what's been happening so they can take the appropriate steps, put a warrant out for Raynes's arrest. They might even be able to help you with Bouchard."

"That's a good idea. What's the second favor?"

"Strange question, but: how much does a camel cost?"

She again looked confused. "I don't know. Maybe, gosh, ten thousand gineih?"

"Okay." Storm reached into his wallet and took double that amount in American greenbacks, a currency still very much in favor in Egypt. He held it out for Katie. "Could you please see this gets to a local camel renter named Massri? I somehow suspect I won't be able to return his camels to him and I hate to leave him in the lurch."

"Will do," she said, accepting the money and smiling again.

Storm blew her a kiss, then urged Antony forward. He rode on without looking back. He had come to the desert to find the source of the promethium, and he wasn't going to leave until he did.

In some ways, his task had gotten slightly easier.

He at least knew what he was looking for now: some kind of opening into an underground limestone cave.

But in other ways, it was just as daunting. The opening did not need to be any larger than what one man could crawl into. And he was looking for it in a desert that had gotten no less vast.

Storm was missing the air-conditioning—and was getting even more wistful about passing on the offer Katie had made—before he even got out of sight of the camp. The heat was searing, and Storm could feel himself losing water by the liter: anything he sweated out seemed to evaporate instantly.

Still, in a strange way, the sun was his friend. He needed it to have any chance of finding this cave. He would not have the luxury of working at night, like the archaeologists did.

As he rode, he occupied his mind with math. Katie said Professor Raynes would disappear for two hours every other day. That meant he was likely walking for a little less than one hour out to the cave, digging out as much promethium as he could carry—which probably didn't take too long—then walking back.

Moving at a brisk pace, someone with long legs and in decent shape, like Raynes, could cover four miles in an hour. But that was on asphalt. Sand would slow him down a bit. Climbing up and down dunes would slow him further.

So Storm decided, somewhat arbitrarily, that three miles felt like about the right distance. Walk three miles in fifty minutes. Spend twenty minutes collecting promethium. Walk three miles back. It made sense.

Antony was in no special hurry, but he still covered the three miles in far less time than a human could. When Storm's GPS told him they had traveled due east three miles, he stopped and looked around.

They were now back within the target zone that the nerds had originally given Storm, but it was looking no less bleak and empty. Sand dunes stretched in every direction. Other than a few scrubby plants, there was no sign of life.

Storm decided to form a mile-square search grid with his current position as the center. In his mind, he cut the grid into two-hundred-foot strips, which meant he would pass within one hundred feet of every inch of this one square mile of desert. He just hoped that would bring him close enough to spot what might be a fairly small entrance.

Really, it was Antony who was doing the hard work. Slicing a 5,280-foot-wide grid into 26.4 mile-long lines meant Antony would have to travel 27.4 miles to cover it all. But camels were bred for such things, and Antony was no more or less disagreeable than usual, doing the usual amount of bellowing but plowing onward all the same.

They were ten miles into their back-and-forth journey when Storm hit pay dirt. It was a rocky outcropping that Storm had already passed two or three times. Each time, he had wanted to break off his route to explore it more closely, but he forced himself to stay disciplined.

Finally, on his closest pass, he saw something that didn't belong. It was a sheet of plywood, attached to the sheer side of the outcropping. The plywood was roughly the same tan color as the rock around it. It was crude but effective camouflage. Certainly, it couldn't be seen from satellite, owing to the angle as much as anything.

Storm dismounted from Antony and looked for something to use as a camel hitch. There was nothing, at least nothing that would stop Antony from doing as he pleased if he got it in his camel brain to run off.

"Stay," Storm said.

Antony belched at him.

"Good boy," Storm said.

He approached the plywood slowly. There were three hinges at the top of the sheet that had been bolted into the rock. He pulled at the bottom of the wood. It came up perhaps an inch, then stopped.

Storm frowned at it for a second, then saw the reason: it was secured in place by a bolt that slid into a hole that had been bored into the rock. The bolt had been painted the color of sand, as was the padlock that secured it.

It was a security system that might thwart a desert nomad, but not a man with Storm's skills. The lock was a cheap, mass-produced brand. Storm considered shooting it off—two bullets would have done it—but opted for the more elegant approach.

He lowered his ear to the lock and slowly turned the dial until he heard the first pin drop into place. On a more expensive lock, the sound is dampened to prevent exactly what Storm was doing. On this brand, it sounded like thunder. After he got the third number, he quickly spun the entire combination.

The lock opened easily. Storm swung the door upward, revealing a hole in the rock.

Storm walked back toward Antony and retrieved a flashlight from his pack. Properly armed, he returned to the plywood and lifted it again. He aimed the flashlight beam into the darkness underneath.

The entrance was only slightly smaller than the

sheet of plywood. He could see where footprints—presumably Raynes's—had been left in the sand.

Storm followed those impressions as the tunnel quickly narrowed down to a diameter that was a fairly tight squeeze for a man of his size. Raynes was tall, like Storm, but a lot thinner. Before long, Storm had to turn sideways.

The tunnel began to slope gradually downward and widen. Storm could tell, simply from the way that the echoes from his footfalls were coming back at him, that there was a large, open space somewhere ahead of him. He shifted his flashlight beam in that direction.

For a while, the beam was reflecting back from the sides of the tunnel. Then, suddenly, it was disappearing into the darkness. Storm quickened his pace and was soon shining the flashlight beam into a large, irregularly shaped cavern, perhaps twenty-five feet at its highest point and eighty feet at its widest.

Storm inspected the limestone walls. Whereas the tunnel had been chiseled by whatever instrument Raynes had used, these walls were different. They were smooth, like they had been carved by water many epochs long ago, when global climate was different and the Sahara received far more rainfall.

A thin layer of dust and sand covered the flatter parts of the floor. In some places, it was undisturbed. In others, it was a patchwork of scuffs and scrapes. Storm could easily make out the path that Raynes had repeatedly walked and continued following it.

It led him to the far side of the chamber and a wall that was unlike anything Storm had ever seen. It was pure white and stretched fifteen feet at a seventy-five-degree angle until it disappeared into the ceiling above it. Storm had heard miners talk about finding veins or lodes of minerals and how they ran in jagged layers through other types of rock. He realized he was seeing such a vein.

And this one happened to be made of pure promethium. The substance, which was some kind of promethium salt, was almost chalky in consistency. There were flakes of it lying in piles at the base of the wall. Storm realized the promethium he had seen had already been ground up, perhaps because it made it easier for transporting.

He reached out with his finger and touched the wall. It was hard, although if he dug his fingernails into some of the looser parts, he could break pieces off with his hands. Raynes had likely used a small pick. It wouldn't take very long to break off, say, fifty pounds of the stuff, which was probably about as much as Raynes could comfortably carry in a backpack across three miles of desert.

Still, going on the one-thousand-dollars-an-ounce estimate, that was a roughly eight-hundred-thousand-dollar walk.

And there was a lot more where that came from. Storm could see one spot where Raynes had worked through the entire thickness of the vein. Behind it was a substance with a subtly different consistency. That must have been whatever substance promethium degraded into. Or perhaps it was the substance that was the precursor to promethium.

Whatever the case, the wall was an incredibly rare—perhaps unique—geological oddity: naturally occurring promethium. It was something McRae and other researches thought didn't exist. Turns out they just hadn't been patient enough. Or lucky enough. Or perhaps unlucky enough. Nevertheless, there it was, this brief moment in this ore's life span when it happened to take the form of promethium.

Bearing in mind that the substance was mildly radioactive, Storm stepped away from it. He shined his flashlight on it one last time, then retraced his steps out of the cave.

Once back in the hot sun, which was blinding after having been under the earth, Storm buttoned the door back up. He made sure to note his precise location on his GPS. He imprinted the coordinates in his head.

Before long, he was back atop Antony, heading for the highway.

He had some terrorists to track down. And if his phone was still where he had wedged it, Professor Raynes was going to lead him right to them.

CHAPTER 26

SOMEWHERE IN THE MIDDLE EAST

He didn't have the address. He didn't have a map. He was more or less groping his way there on feel, telling himself with each turn that his route still looked familiar.

The only things going for Professor Raynes were that the cargo truck had been fully gassed up and that he had been to Ahmed's place twice before.

The gas was good, because already his credit card wasn't working. It told him the Egyptian authorities were on to him and were taking steps to make his movements more difficult.

And his faint recognition of his route was good because he couldn't waste time reaching Ahmed. Raynes had concluded that the man who had let him run off—Talbot, or whatever his name was—was actually quite correct. The promethium in back was a fine retirement plan. He would cash it in and disappear to somewhere no one would be looking for him. Maybe somewhere in the Mediterranean. Like Elba. If it was good enough for Napoleon, it was good enough for Professor Raynes.

He could feel his desperation growing as the time clicked on and he still hadn't arrived. He was sure he was lost at least twice, then he would recognize another landmark, telling him he was on the right track.

Then, finally, as the sun began to set and the lights of the suburban neighborhood he was crawling around started to come on, he found it: the narrow road that led to the walled compound where Ahmed conducted his business.

He saw the familiar sign—AHMED TRADES METAL, it said in Arabic—outside the gated entrance, which had a guard shack next to it. He was greeted by a man with an AK-47 hanging from a strap in front of him.

Raynes announced himself, and said he was there to talk to Ahmed. The man then spoke into a two-way radio. Raynes could hear angry words pouring out of it. The name Stanford Raynes had become an unpopular one in this place.

But eventually the man with the rifle said, "Okay. Come on."

The man got out of the guard shack, opened the gate, and waved Raynes to a spot just off the driveway, not far from the main house, under the long shadow of a tall eucalyptus tree.

"Wait in the truck. Someone will come for you," the man said, then returned to the guard shack, closing the gate behind him.

Raynes did as instructed, cutting the truck's engine. He gazed at the inside of the compound. All around him, heaping piles of scrap metal sat, slowly oxidizing. He recognized a mound that was strictly junk cars. Another was primarily refrigerators and other abandoned household goods. Yet another was tangles of wire of varying gauges.

Raynes had never given much thought to who Ahmed was or what he did with the promethium. He had assumed, quite simply, that Ahmed was nothing more than the proprietor of a business called Ahmed Trades Metal. Was he really a terrorist, as Talbot suggested? Or was that something Talbot was just saying to throw Raynes off?

At this point, Raynes didn't particularly care. He had worked too hard throughout his life to end up penniless and imprisoned. He'd sell to the devil himself. And if he already had? Well, so be it.

After five minutes or so, a man appeared. It was one of the men from the botched promethium exchange earlier in the day. He had a bandage on his bicep with a dapple of blood soaking through. He winced as he walked, glaring at Raynes the whole time. There was no question who he blamed for his discomfort.

"Come on," he said. "This way."

The man led Raynes to the main house and into Ahmed's office, where he and Ahmed had conducted business before. Ahmed was not there yet.

"Sit," the bandaged man said, as he then departed the room.

Raynes selected one of the two chairs in front of Ahmed's desk. In the corner, there was a flat-screen television playing Al Jazeera with the sound off. The professor's gaze shifted to the large painting that covered most of the east wall of the room. It was a man—a fisherman, by the looks of him—wading into a river to retrieve an ornate trunk. It was obviously a scene from a fable or piece of Middle Eastern mythology, but Raynes wasn't immediately familiar with it.

Two minutes later, Ahmed himself walked into the room. He had a bandage on his shoulder. He did not sit down, but stood where he could tower over Raynes.

"You have a lot of nerve showing up here," Ahmed said.

"That wasn't my man shooting at you, and I'm sorry he did," Raynes replied. "I told him specifically not to. He was acting on his own."

Ahmed narrowed his eyes. "Why should I believe that you didn't set us up? Why should I believe that your plan wasn't to kill us all and take my money?"

"Because, believe me, if that man wanted to kill you, you would be dead right now. And, besides, I'm here now."

"That's only because your plan failed. I should have one of my men come in and shoot you in the head right now."

"Slow down, slow down," Raynes said, his voice calm. "Think it through. Why would I want to harm you or your men? We have a very profitable business relationship. You pay me good money for my promethium. To my knowledge, you are the only man who has cultivated a large market for promethium here in Egypt. But, at the same time, I'm your only source for that promethium. We need each other."

Ahmed glowered down at Raynes for a moment more, then walked over and sat behind his desk. "So, yes, you are here. Why?"

"Because I want to complete the transaction," Raynes said.

"Very well. I'll have my men remove the promethium from the truck and replace it with the money. The bills are unmarked, as you requested."

With his left hand, the only one that was working very well at the moment, Ahmed reached for a two-way radio.

"Not so fast," Raynes said. "It has to be more."

"More? More what?"

"More money."

Ahmed furrowed his brow. "That's not our deal. You have the nerve to shoot my men and then demand more money?"

"Promethium sells for three thousand dollars an ounce."

"On open channels," Ahmed said. "We both know the private market is a different matter."

"Still, I've been giving it to you for nine hundred. I want a bigger cut."

"How much bigger?"

"Eighteen hundred."

"That's outrageous!"

"That's now the price," Raynes said, leaning back in the chair, keeping his gaze steady.

Ahmed returned it. He no longer had his hand on his radio. He was now stroking his beard. It made him look thoughtful.

"You are doubling the price because this is your last shipment," Ahmed declared.

"No, no. That's not it. I'm just . . . I think it's fair I get a bigger slice of the action. You're still getting the promethium you want."

Raynes could hear his own voice faltering and hated the sound of it.

"My father taught me long ago how to spot a liar sitting in that chair, and you are lying," Ahmed said, growing more sure of himself. "That man who shot at us is now in control of your encampment. And if he is in control of your encampment, he is in control of your promethium."

"That's . . . that's not true. I mean, yes, the dig site is . . . it is lost to me. But the promethium, I can get back to it. The man who shot you doesn't know where it is. It is well hidden."

"I don't believe you," Ahmed said. "In any event, I'm changing the deal. I am not buying promethium from you today. You are giving me this shipment, as a sign of good faith and as compensation for the wounds my men and I have suffered. When you return with a new shipment—as you say you are capable of doing—we can negotiate a fair price. Perhaps even a small increase. But this one is, as you Americans say, 'on the house.'"

Raynes could feel his panic rising. He couldn't give away his retirement plan. Without it, he'd have nothing. His credit card was already frozen. His bank accounts probably had been, too.

"No. Absolutely not. Fine, I'll . . . I'll stick with nine hundred. A deal is a deal."

Ahmed was smiling. "I'm sorry. The deal has already changed."

Raynes stared hard at Ahmed. Then he reached into his *thobe* and pulled out the Pocket Police. Ahmed didn't know Raynes was down to one bullet. He aimed it in the direction of Ahmed's turban-wrapped head.

"I'm not here to be pushed around," Raynes said.

"I wouldn't do that, if I were you," Ahmed said. "That's not good business."

"Yeah? And what are you going to do about it?" Raynes demanded.

Ahmed held up two fingers. "This," he said.

From the chamber behind the painting of the fisherman, from within Ahmed's beloved *aman*—his safe place—came a single bullet. It entered the left side of Raynes's skull and exited the right, followed by a thick spray of blood and brain matter.

Ahmed clapped and two men appeared. "Clean this up," Ahmed said. "And take the body to the smelter. We'll burn it in the morning."

CHAPTER 27

ASYŪT, Egypt

Not for the first time in his life, Derrick Storm was grateful he had installed the Find My Phone app.

Often, it led him no farther than his couch cushions. This time, he was hoping it would direct him to a place substantially more foreign and infinitely more dangerous: what was either a cell of— or the world headquarters of—the Medina Society.

His task, once he got there, was to disable the cell's capacity and gather what information he could about the rest of the network, so he could disable that, too.

He had little inkling of how he would accomplish this.

First he had to get himself outfitted, which took him the remainder of the afternoon and into the evening. Under ordinary circumstances, he would have merely bumbled his way out of the desert and into the arms of the nearest CIA station agent, dropped the name Jedediah Jones, and known that within fifteen minutes he would have one new car, two new weapons, and three new gadgets, at least one of which would be showing him satellite imagery that would allow him to count the hair follicles on his target's head.

This time, he had to do it like a civilian, without Jones's resources. The alternative—appealing to Jones for help—was too likely to lead to at least one shipment of promethium falling into Jones's hands. And that wasn't a possibility Storm could allow.

So he was roughing it. He ditched Antony—donating him to a family who promised not to turn him into camel stew—and changed his mode of transportation. This time, he left the ungulate order in favor of something manufactured by the Ford Motor Company. He found a Sixt rental car company that outfitted him in a Ford Mondeo—the closest he could get to a Taurus. Even roughing it, there were limits to what a man could withstand, and an underpowered foreign car was not among them.

His next stop was a clothing store, where he ditched his *thobe* and keffiyeh in favor of Western clothing. He went with black cargo pants, black boots, and a tight black T-shirt—not because he was particularly keen to show off his physique, but because an Egyptian men's extra large, the largest size he could find, was the equivalent of a medium in America.

With the transportation and clothing taken care of, he set about improving on his digital capabilities. He drove to an electronics retailer of perhaps dubious repute and purchased himself an iPad with a data plan. Compared to the technology he was used to, it was like being perhaps one step more evolved than the first primate who picked up a rock and used it to bash off a piece of tree bark.

Still, it allowed him to tap into the Find My Phone app and harness its detection skills. He plugged the coordinates it gave him into his newly installed

Google Maps app. He then checked out the address on Google Earth. Again, compared to the toys Jones gave him, it was like being an ancient sailor following nautical charts that had been roughed out on papyrus.

But Storm at least now knew his phone was inside what appeared to be a walled compound. Several buildings—a main house and other structures—were visible in the closest view on Google Earth.

That was good news. It meant his biggest worry—that his phone had fallen out of the truck's wheel well at some point during the journey, and that therefore Find My Phone would lead him to a roadside ditch somewhere—had not come to pass.

He set out from Luxor, following both the Nile River and the pulsing blue dot on Google Maps. As he drove, he tuned into news radio. Now that he was cut off from Jones—especially once Strike ratted him out—Storm was now relying on the media for information about the laser attacks. There was nothing new. The radio was mostly filled with talk about how a rare tropical cyclone was brewing in the eastern Mediterranean. The medicane—as meteorologists called a Mediterranean hurricane—was already threatening Italy with eighty-mile-an-hour winds and huge seas.

Storm turned off the radio as he arrived in a suburban neighborhood on the outskirts of Asyūt, a medium-sized city along the banks of the Nile River in the middle of Egypt. He negotiated a warren of haphazardly laid out streets until he arrived at a fifteen-foot-high wall with razor wire topping it.

The razor wire was actually an encouraging sign. People didn't put up razor wire unless they were trying to keep others out. Or, sometimes, in. Either way, it suggested something nefarious was going on. And nefarious was what Storm wanted. He wasn't hunting bunny rabbits, after all. He was hunting terrorists.

He parked his Ford on a side street and walked the perimeter of the wall on foot. His suspicion that he had found the right place was confirmed when he spied the sign outside the main gate. AHMED TRADES METAL it read in Arabic.

Storm felt his resolve steeling. This was it. He had found the terrorists' den. Perhaps this was the Medina Society's nerve center. Perhaps it was just one cell among many.

Either way, he was confident the cargo truck was inside those walls, hopefully still laden with its precious promethium load.

Storm checked the time on his iPad. It was ten minutes after 10 P.M. There was still activity inside the walls: lights on, men talking to each other, vehicles moving around. He tried counting the number of distinct voices he could make out. There were perhaps eight.

That didn't count men who were still inside the main house or any of the other buildings he had seen on Google Earth. But it gave him some sketchy idea of the odds facing him: eight to one, at least. Probably more like twelve to one or sixteen to one, thinking that some number of men—including the leaders—were likely to be inside.

Storm hunkered down behind a tree just outside the wall, down the street from the entrance gate, where he could see but not be seen.

There was no question in his mind he had to move on the compound before sunrise. Yes, he could plan a better operation if he had a full day to do reconnaissance. But giving the terrorists an extra day—during which time they might attempt to move the promethium, or shoot down more airplanes, or create other unimaginable mayhem—was out of the question.

He would just have to go on what he had, which was not much. Eight distinct voices. A compound with several buildings. An as-yet-undetermined connection to the larger network of the Medina Society.

Then, from behind his tree, Storm watched something he did not expect: the odds kept improving. As the hour grew later, men were leaving, one by one. Some of them were men he had shot earlier in the day—they had the telltale bandages on their shoulders. Others were uninjured.

Either way, they all followed a more-or-less similar pattern. They went to the main gate and announced themselves to the man in the guard shack. The guard came out with a key ring, selected one, and unlocked the gate. There was no automatic gate lift. He held it open for them as they passed through, then closed it behind them.

Some left on bicycles. Others walked to their cars, which were parked near the walls, in the neighborhood. It was like watching factory workers at the end of a shift, heading back home.

Maybe this was one of the Medina Society's tricks: never stay assembled in large numbers for very long.

Or maybe there was still a horde of men holed up quietly inside, and this was barely more than a slivering of the force Storm would soon have to face.

At eleven o'clock, there was a changing of the guard. The new man received the AK-47 like a baton in a relay. The man being relieved went to his car and drove off, just like the other men had. There was a routine feeling to what Storm was seeing. This had happened many times before.

By midnight, the exodus had stopped. All told, eleven men had departed. Storm waited another hour anyway, just to see what might transpire. Nothing did. Silence had settled onto the compound.

Sometime after one, with a quarter moon struggling up from the horizon, Storm rose from his hiding spot and prepared for his assault.

It was one man against . . . well, he was about to find out.

WHILE THERE WERE ANY NUMBER OF VULNERABLE points along the wall—mostly places where trees had grown tall enough to allow easy scaling and where the razor wire could have been clipped open—Storm decided to go in through the front, past the guard shack.

It just made sense. He would have to deal with the guard eventually: if not on the way in, then on the way out. There was no sense in procrastinating.

Dressed in his black clothing, Storm moved in the shadows toward the shack, which was lit by a single, dim bulb in the ceiling. The little building was elevated on concrete blocks and had a window that slid open, allowing the guard to be on eye level with entering trucks. Next to the window, there was a closed door with stairs leading up to it.

From inside, Storm could hear a small television. The volume was muffled, but it was tuned to what sounded like an infomercial. If that didn't qualify as a cure for insomnia, he didn't know what did. And yet the guard appeared to be awake.

The setup presented problems. Storm couldn't risk using his gun. The noise would alert the troops inside that something was happening. And while there were quiet ways of dealing with the guard, they all involved physical contact—which was impossible when the man was high up in the shack, protected by a door that was more than likely locked.

He was now across the narrow street from the shack, still shrouded by trees. Behind him was a new house being framed, which gave him an idea. Retreating quietly into the construction site, he eventually found what he was looking for: a scrap piece of two-by-four, about three feet long, not unlike a Louisville Slugger.

Storm departed the house from the side, which allowed him to circle in behind the guard shack, where he wouldn't be seen. He then shuffled silently up to the corner of the shack, sucked in a lungful of air, and pursed his lips.

What came out was an imitation of a Jameson's Finch. It was more than just passable. It was, if Storm said so himself, spot on. He paused, took another breath, then unleashed another chorus of the bird's optimistic, cheery song.

The television inside the guard shack suddenly went mute. Storm grinned, then whistled again.

There was a creaking sound as the door to the shack opened. Storm could hear one foot being put on the top tread of the stairs. He tweeted as if he was the happiest Jameson's Finch that ever lived, then cut it off.

Now there were footsteps coming down the

small flight of steps, and the gritty crunch of feet walking on a sidewalk that was covered in a light layer of sand. The guard was moving as if he was looking high and low, and left and right for the bird.

Storm chirped one last time, to give the guard a final fix on his location. He gripped the two-by-four in both hands and raised it behind his right shoulder. The guard had now zeroed in and was rounding the corner, sure he was about to see a Jameson's Finch that would bring him great good fortune.

Instead, it brought him a headache. The moment the guard appeared, Storm swung the two-by-four with all he had. Its flat side connected just above the man's ear with a percussive thud. He fell as if every bone in his body had turned to putty.

Storm was ready to give him one more shot, but it wasn't necessary. The man was out. Storm took the guard's AK-47 and draped its strap over his own torso. Then he grabbed the guard under the arms and dragged him quickly back into the shack. There was no rope or tape inside, so he yanked the cord out of the back of the television, using it to bind the guard's wrists behind his back.

The guard was wearing a turban, which Storm hastily unwrapped, exposing a matted mess of curly dark hair. Storm tore the garment into three strips, using one part to gag the man, another to secure his legs, and a third to tie the leg restraint to the hands, trussing him up like a Thanksgiving turkey.

It was not, to be sure, the most secure binding Storm had ever devised. But it would take the guard some time to get out when he came to. Storm planned to be long gone before that happened.

Storm's final act before exiting was to take the

key ring off a hook by the door. He approached the gate, which was as tall as the wall on either side of it and made of wrought iron. It was secured by a thick bolt that went deep into the ground.

He was impressed. A tank could have gotten through. But any other vehicle wouldn't have been able to get enough speed on the narrow street to ram it open, nor would it be able to gain the proper angle to hit it head-on.

That said, the gate was no match for the thin piece of metal now in Storm's hand. He slid the key into a well-oiled lock, which slid easily. Storm lifted the bolt, squeezed through a narrow opening in the gate, then left it ajar—enough that it wouldn't impede his exit, if that exit had to be speedy; but, hopefully, not enough that anyone inside would notice.

He was in. As far as he knew, he was the first American ever to penetrate a Medina Society cell. And what worried him more than anything was that, at least so far, it wasn't that difficult.

Which, in itself, seemed all wrong.

THIS BEING HIS FIRST CHANCE TO STUDY THE INSIDE of the compound in real life—not on Google Earth— Storm hastily slid to his left and found shelter behind an accumulation of scrap metal.

From that area of relative safety, he assessed his surroundings. There was a large, open area between the wall and what appeared to be the main house. Except to call it "open" was a misstatement. It was a cluttered mess, with heaps of metal everywhere, some several stories high. In the dim light under the quarter moon, it was difficult to say what all of them were. More than anything, Storm could discern the darkened outlines of shapes jutting out from the piles: rectangles at strange angles, circles looming in the sky, triangles heaped atop parallelograms. Storm wondered if the Medina Society had used some of these metal pieces to make the laser that shot down the planes in the Emirates.

Some of the piles had large cranes or dump trucks next to them. His nose told him there was a smelter somewhere nearby. He could smell its faint but sharp odor, its acrid scent still present even though it was not currently in operation.

Storm found himself smiling at the clever, perhaps intentional double entendre of the Ahmed Trades Metal rallying cry. This cell—or training camp, or whatever significance it held within the Medina Society network—was a scrapyard where metal was traded all day long.

Except now, in the dark of night, those mountains of metal were just one aspect of the terrain he could use to his tactical advantage. If the several hundred yards of space between the gate and the main house had been truly open, covering it would have been a suicide mission. Anyone inside who happened to be looking out could have picked him off at leisure.

Instead, Storm was able to slink from one mound to the next in relative safety. He had closed the gap between himself and the house significantly when he reached the smelter, an older brick building topped by a tall chimney.

He was leaving it when he tripped on something in the darkness. In his peripheral vision, he saw that it was a human leg. He whirled and drew Dirty Harry, ready to fire in case what he had tripped on was a sleeping insurgent.

But no. This particular human's mortality had already been taken. Storm saw the top of the man's head had a rather large chunk missing.

Then he saw the eyes, the mouth, the pointy chin. He recognized Professor Stanford Raynes. Or, rather, what was left of him after his apparent run-in with Ahmed and his men.

Storm took no great pleasure in Raynes's death. But it did solve one problem: the secret of the promethium's location had more than likely died with him. Now Storm was the only holder of that secret, and he did not plan to give it up.

Leaving the body, Storm had worked his way to within about fifty yards of the main house when he saw the cargo truck. It was sitting just off the driveway, under a towering eucalyptus tree, by itself.

Storm sprinted to it, taking the risk of being fully exposed for perhaps three seconds, relying on his black clothing to conceal him. He reached the rear bumper and moved his hand toward the catch that would allow him to lift the trailer door. If he could remove the box with the promethium and hide it somewhere, it might not solve the whole problem, but it would be at least one less load of the stuff that could be used to make a weapon.

But the door was padlocked. And unlike the cheap, drugstore lock Raynes had used on the cave, this appeared to be of a more substantial variety. The dial went from one to a hundred, not one to forty. Storm brought his ear to it, gave it several turns in both directions, listening intently the whole time.

He did not hear anything like a pin falling into place. The better locks were cushioned that way.

Any of the other strategies he might have used to thwart the lock involved making noise. And noise, at this point in his mission, was the enemy. For all Storm knew, one of the buildings he had seen was a barracks, filled with terrorists-in-waiting, any one of whom would love to have an American agent as a trophy, or any one of whom would be willing to martyr himself in the effort, knowing all the while that seventy-two virgins awaited him in heaven.

Storm's primary defense—explaining to the young men that virgins were vastly overrated as sexual partners—seemed inadequate.

So he decided to keep quiet. He slunk around to the wheel well where he had stuck his phone a day earlier, and retrieved it. Then he went to the driver's side of the truck and pulled on the door handle. It was locked, too. He would have to deal with it and its payload later. Worst case, he'd break the window, climb in, and hot-wire the thing. Best case, he'd find a way to blow it up.

With the truck out of his mind, he focused on the main house. It was a sprawling, one-story adobe residence that looked like it had once been a farmhouse.

Storm began searching for access points, but saw nothing that thrilled him. Like many houses in that latitude, the windows were small and high. Adding to the difficulty factor, their glass panes appeared to be constructed from crosshatched metal bars that had been anchored into the structure itself.

So the windows were not an option. The roof, which was made of sturdy, terra-cotta tiles, was likewise impenetrable. There was a chimney, but it was capped and, in any event, Storm was not feeling like Santa Claus.

That left the front porch, which faced the driveway. It was something of a novel concept for Storm, actually trying to enter a house through the front door. But at the moment it looked like his best—and only—choice.

There were, broadly speaking, two ways to approach the house: slow or fast. Slow had its benefits, in that it would give him more time to study his target as he slunk slowly along the ground. It would also be far less detectable by anyone inside the house who happened to be looking outside.

But fast had the advantage of being over with quickly. It also would make him a harder target to hit. And since his previous dash did not seem to have been noticed, Storm gambled that past equaled precedent.

It was roughly a hundred feet from the front of the truck to the front of the house. Storm felt the wind against his ears as he sprinted the distance, pulling up to the side of the steps, where he couldn't be seen from within the house.

There was no response to his mad dash. The house—the whole property, for that matter—remained dark and still. It was getting to be almost eerie, how unguarded everything inside seemed to be and how little opposition he had met.

Storm paused, listened. Nothing. Definitely nothing.

He turned and crept up the steps. The front porch was not especially tidy, littered with a random assortment of stuff that could not unfairly

be categorized as junk. There were a few AHMED
TRADES METAL signs. There were metal chairs that
may or may not have been heading for the smelter.
Standing next to the door was a tall sculpture that
had been roughly welded together out of scrap
metal. To Storm, it looked like the Tin Man, though
he wasn't sure if *The Wizard of Oz* was central in
Egypt's cultural lexicon.

"There's no place like home," Storm whispered
to himself as he walked across the porch.

He had Dirty Harry out now, held low at his
side. He was ready to raise and fire it at the slightest
provocation.

There was just nothing to shoot. He reached
for the screen door, then opened it. His hand went
to the handle of the main door. It turned easily. Was
this really happening? Was he really going to be able
to just walk right into the front door of a Medina
Society hangout?

The door was wooden and just slightly swollen
against its doorframe. Storm had to put a little extra
weight behind it, but it budged easily enough.

And then, without warning, it was like the world
caught fire.

BEING THAT LIGHT TRAVELS FASTER THAN SOUND,
Storm first became aware that illumination was
suddenly pouring out of every orifice of the house,
including some floodlights attached to the roof that
he hadn't seen before.

Nanoseconds later, the noise hit: a wailing,
shrieking, ear-splitting alarm.

Storm reacted instinctively. He grabbed the Tin
Man and tossed him across the door's threshold.

Then he rocketed himself through the maze of junk to his right and over the side of the porch railing. He flattened himself against some half-broken lattice-work that kept animals from crawling under the porch, keeping Dirty Harry tight against his chest.

As the siren continued pulsing at a volume that could have shaken a pharaoh from a four-thousand-year slumber, Storm stayed hidden in the shadow of the porch. He waited for the cavalry to emerge—dozens of future jihadists, swarming to protect their liege's castle.

No one came. After a minute or so, the alarm stopped. The lights stayed on. Storm heard cursing and the sound of someone tossing the Tin Man aside. Storm dared to turn and peek through the bottom slat of the porch railing.

What he saw, backlit against the bright glow of the house, was one of the men he had shot earlier in the day. It was Ahmed, the leader of what Storm had thought was just a motley gang of desert bandits. When Storm had heard Raynes say the name Ahmed, it hadn't triggered any bells. Ahmed was a common name in this part of the world. Had Storm known who the man really was, he would have taken care of all of this in the desert.

Yet another example of hindsight being fifty-fifty.

Ahmed took one step out on the porch, but no more. His head was bare, without its usual turban. His long, salt-and-pepper hair was greasy and unkempt. He was dressed in an ankle-length night-gown. He wore nothing on his feet. His right arm was tucked in a sling. His left arm carried a sawed-off shotgun.

He was letting the shotgun lead the way. He swung the muzzle from left to right, back to the middle, again to the right, and then to the left. Storm stayed absolutely still, knowing he was effectively invisible in the shadow of the porch, with all that junk to serve as cover.

Ahmed walked to the edge of the porch, swiveled the gun some more. He was mostly looking in the direction of the guard shack, where there was no activity.

"Wake up, you lazy dog," he yelled in Arabic, but of course got no response.

"You're fired," he added, to no greater impact.

Storm had a perfect shot at that moment. He could have dropped Ahmed easily. But if he killed Ahmed, he would have no more intelligence about the Medina Society's structure or organization, and certainly no idea of how to stop its current plot.

As a result, Storm maintained his hiding spot. Ahmed muttered a few choice Arabic words that ventured some unkind descriptions of the guard's mother. Then Ahmed turned and walked back in the house.

It was finally dawning on Storm that there was no one else here. There was no cavalry, no bloodthirsty true believers coming to the leader's aid. It was just the guard—who wasn't going to be an issue—and Ahmed.

Well, them and the Tin Man. But Storm didn't think the Tin Man would put up much of a fight. No heart.

Mostly, Storm couldn't believe his luck: a Medina Society leader, ripe for the taking.

All he needed was some patience.

He leaned back down against the latticework and watched as, one by one, the lights in the house went out. Then the floodlights followed suit. He removed the AK-47 from his back. He would not need to lay down a heavy blanket of fire against just one man.

Storm's eyes slowly adjusted to the darkness again and he began formulating his plan. Eventually, the leader—convinced that the Tin Man had been the cause of the false alarm—would fall back asleep. Storm just needed to be able to get into the house without tripping off all that sound and fury.

What kind of system was it? Knowing was the key to defeating it. Back in his days as a private eye— when he was barely scraping out enough business to cover the rent on his tiny strip mall office—one of the services he offered his clients was consulting on alarm systems. Another one was defeating alarm systems so he could snoop in his target subjects' homes, not that he advertised that particular offering in his literature.

He was not the world's foremost expert on the subject. But he knew enough to get by. In his mind, he replayed the scene of himself opening the door. It had happened so fast the first time. But by concentrating on it, he began to slow it down. Each replaying got just a little longer. Details that he had missed the first time began to pop out, almost like a form of self-hypnosis.

Once he got the picture moving slowly enough, Storm caught what he was looking for: there were two pressure sensors in the doorframe, one just above eye level, the other down around his shins. He knew well enough how they worked. They were nothing more than small semicircles of plastic attached to springs. As long as they remained depressed, the alarm system believed the door was still closed. When the springs extended, the system knew the door had opened.

He just needed to keep them down. Back in his private eye days, he used chewing gum, tape, Silly Putty—whatever he had available. He just didn't happen to have any of those things on him at the moment.

Then he remembered the eucalyptus tree that the cargo truck was parked under. Still moving cautiously, Storm crept around the other side of the porch. Then he made the sprint to the tree, running until he was on the opposite side of the trunk from the house.

He searched for old cuts and scratches in the tree, found several, and began pulling off the gum that had hardened there. He stuffed it in his mouth, where he began working it so it wasn't quite so stiff. It tasted terrible—Wrigley's had nothing to fear from untreated eucalyptus gum—but the consistency was right. He waited until he had a decent-sized mouthful of the goo, then moved back toward the house.

All was again quiet. The only thing that had changed about the house from the first time was that the Tin Man was now lying forlornly on his side. Storm crept up the steps, across the porch. He opened the screen door, then turned the handle on the main door.

But this time, he didn't shove. He slowly nudged it partway open, then held it there with one hand. He bit off a hunk of eucalyptus gum and with his other hand, wedged a lump of it over the top sensor. It held nicely.

He repeated the maneuver with the lower sensor. Gingerly, he opened the door just a little further, so that now the entire doorjamb was exposed. He used the remaining gum in his mouth to completely cover both sensors, packing them tightly so there would be no chance their springs would extend as the gum dried.

He opened the door the entire way. The alarm did not go off. Storm exhaled. He took one step into the house and closed the door behind him.

His eyes were already well accustomed to the dark, but they had not yet focused on the dim recesses of the foyer when he heard one of the more unmistakable noises in the modern world. It resonated straight from its source to some deep, reptilian part of Storm's brain. It was an authoritative *chuck* followed by an even more convincing *chick*.

It was the sound of a shotgun slide being racked from about fifteen feet away.

THE SAWED-OFF SHOTGUN IS THE MOST EFFECTIVE short-range antipersonnel weapon ever devised by man. In addition to the massive force of fire, its multitude of projectiles spread upon exiting the muzzle, meaning it only needs to be aimed in a very general sense. There is no such thing as surviving a shotgun blast from point-blank range without significant— and, most likely, terminal—injuries.

The only thing that saved Derrick Storm's life was that pumping a shotgun requires two fully functioning arms. And Ahmed, with only one, had to brace the shotgun stock against the floor in order to rack the slide before bringing the muzzle back up.

That small delay, no more than two seconds in duration, was all Storm needed. As Ahmed brought the gun back up and fired, Storm was diving to his right. The deadly blast of pellets sailed over his head and to his left, hitting only the air where Storm had once been standing and then the door behind him.

Storm rolled and came up with Dirty Harry drawn, as he had trained himself to do. From the light of the quarter moon that leaked in the small windows, he could make out Ahmed pumping the shotgun, ejecting one cartridge and loading the next one. He again was bracing it against the floor as he performed this maneuver. Storm didn't give him the chance to fire it again. He aimed for the man's left shoulder and squeezed the trigger.

The impact from the bullet spun Ahmed in a counterclockwise direction. He fell back and to his left, slamming into the wall before ending up on the floor. The shotgun was still within his grasp, but Ahmed didn't have a working arm with which to reach for it.

Storm covered the ground between them in three strides. He kicked the shotgun across the room, then went for a light switch.

The room was bathed in a sallow glow. Storm went over to Ahmed, who was desperately struggling to get into a sitting position. But it was difficult without either arm to prop himself up. The pain from the wound had to be excruciating, yet the man did not make a sound.

Blood was already soaking his nightgown. If only to speed things up, Storm reached under the man's armpits and propped him against the wall. He yelped in agony.

Storm pointed the gun at his large nose.

"Please, please don't," Ahmed whimpered, then

got his first good look at Storm. "You're . . . you're the man from the desert. You're the one who shot all my men."

Storm did not reply. He reached down and tore away Ahmed's sleeve, exposing his badly mangled left shoulder. Dirty Harry had made a neat mess of it.

"Please, sir, please," Ahmed was rambling from somewhere above his two ruined arms. "What is it you want? Do you want the promethium? You can have it. It's still in the truck. Please, sir, whatever harm I have done to you, I beg your forgiveness. Perhaps we can make an arrangement of some kind? I have a lot of money. It is yours for the asking. Just, please, let me live."

Storm ripped the sleeve into two long strips. "Your ulnar artery is severed," he said calmly. "You're already in shock. If I don't stop the bleeding, in ten minutes your blood pressure will start to fall rapidly. In twenty, you'll probably be dead. I'm making a tourniquet right now, but I'm only using it if you tell me exactly what I want to hear."

Ahmed greeted this news by bursting into tears. "Oh, Allah, it hurts so bad. I will tell you anything."

"Very good," Storm said. "Tell me about the Medina Society."

Pain was no longer the dominant emotion on Ahmed's face. Confusion was. Confusion with, perhaps, a dash of desperation.

"The Medina . . . the Medina Society?" he said. "But I don't . . . I don't know anything about—"

"Playing dumb isn't going to help you, Ahmed. And you may have less than ten minutes before it's all over. That was just an estimate on my part. But

I'm no doctor and you're losing blood pretty fast. So, again, tell me about the Medina Society."

He was breathing heavily, hyperventilating slightly and shivering as the shock plunged his body's temperature. "Okay, okay . . . The Medina Society . . . They are a group of extremists who want to set my country back two hundred years. . . . They . . . they don't seem to like women very much. . . . They are giving Islam, a very gentle, peace-loving religion, a very bad reputation. I don't know, is this what you're looking for?"

"You really don't have time to play cute with me, Ahmed. I know you think right now that maybe your life isn't worth saving. But depending on how good your information is and how cooperative you're willing to be, you could have a very good second career as an informant. I already know most of it. The Medina Society has been using the promethium to make the high-energy laser beam that has been shooting down airplanes. Just tell me how the society is organized and where the headquarters are."

The tears were coming harder now. "Please, sir. I am not trying to be cute. I just don't know what you're talking about. I can't inform on anyone. I am a scrap-metal dealer. I know nothing about these terrorists."

"Then what's with the Ahmed Trades Metal signs everywhere? I know what that means."

"I'm not sure what you're talking about. My name is Ahmed. I trade metal. My family has traded metal for several generations now. Before that, we were farmers. That is all."

"Yeah, sure it is. You want to explain that truck full of promethium sitting in your driveway?"

"Yes, yes, happily. The professor, Dr. Raynes, he sells it to me. He has sold me many hundreds of pounds of it. I don't know where he is getting it from, but he has found a great amount of it."

"And what do you do with it?"

"I resell it for a nice profit, of course. I did not know anyone was using it to shoot down airplanes. Please, sir, I am telling you the truth. I am a metal dealer, that is all. Please, sir. Please help me."

Storm looked down at the pathetic figure slumped beneath him. Much as he told himself he shouldn't believe these lies, there was a part of him that couldn't help it. It wasn't so much what Ahmed was saying as it was everything Storm had seen and done over the last few hours.

Taking out the guard had been too easy. Getting in the compound had been too easy. Breaching the house—despite the little hiccup with the security system—had been too easy. Taking out Ahmed had been too easy.

At every turn, he had met far too little resistance. He knew it while it was happening, but he hadn't been able to quite make sense out of it. Now he could. If the Medina Society really was so savvy that it had successfully resisted penetration by the combined might of the Central Intelligence Agency and the United States military for several decades, there was no way Storm would have been able to waltz in and take over one of its cells using little more than an iPad, a two-by-four, and some foul-tasting chewing gum. If it was that straightforward, a group of Green Berets would have done it a long time ago. The real Medina Society would have protected its assets far more fiercely.

What's more, there was Ahmed's behavior. If he was really a terrorist, would he be sniveling and begging for this life? No, he'd be saying his prayers to Allah, preparing to meet twelve and threescore virgins—with an emphasis on the *score*.

"So, if you're just a metal dealer, then you shouldn't mind telling me: who is your buyer for all this promethium?"

"I . . . I don't know for sure. They always insisted I wear a blindfold."

"You're going to have to do a lot better than that," Storm said.

"I'm trying . . . I'm trying, please. They . . . they arranged all the meetings. Always different places. I just followed their instructions. I would talk to them on the phone. I talked to a man if it was a matter of where and when to make a delivery. But if it was a matter of money, I talked to a woman. I got the sense she was the one in charge. The buyer was a woman."

"A woman. So you've narrowed the potential identity of your buyer from seven billion to three point five billion. You really want to bleed out, don't you, Ahmed?"

Ahmed was shivering more violently. His entire lower half was covered in blood, which was now pooling on the ground beneath him. "No, no, please. Wait. It was a woman, and sometimes she would be outside when she spoke. I got the sense she was on a boat. A very large boat. You could hear the waves and engine. And one time I heard a horn blast of some kind. It was a very distinctive sound. I asked her, 'Is that a trumpet?' and she said, no, it was made to sound like a French horn. Then she talked about how much she enjoyed the sound of a French horn."

Storm was momentarily frozen. A woman on a large boat that signaled to other boats with something that sounded like a French horn. Ahmed had, in a very short time, taken the suspect pool from 7 billion to 3.5 billion to exactly one.

"Your buyer is a very wealthy Swedish woman named Ingrid Karlsson," Storm said. "I just . . . I can barely believe it myself. One of those planes that got shot down was carrying her lover, Brigitte Bildt."

This seemed to excite Ahmed. "Yes, yes," he said. "One of the times we spoke, she had to take a call on another line. I think she thought she had muted our call, but I could still hear. She said two things that didn't make sense to me. But now, maybe they do. The first was something about getting rid of Brigitte. She said she had to get rid of Brigitte because Brigitte was going to the United States to speak to a man named Jedediah, who would expose her. I didn't know who Brigitte was. I thought maybe it was an employee she had fired. But maybe this was the lover who was on the airplane?"

Storm absorbed this information. Just as there was only one woman who had a French horn for a signal on her boat, there was only one man named Jedediah in the high reaches of the American intelligence community. Was Brigitte Bildt coming to America to reveal to Jones what her boss was about to do with the laser? It made sense.

"Keep going," Storm said. "What was the other thing?"

"She said that someone named Jared Stack would be dealt with. That is all I heard. At the time, I felt guilty, because it sounded to me like this Jared Stack was in trouble. But I don't know who Jared Stack is."

Storm did. Jared Stack was the congressman who had taken over for Erik Vaughn as the head of the Ways and Means committee. As far as Storm knew, Stack was still alive. But maybe—if Ahmed was telling the truth—that was only because whoever Ingrid Karlsson had sent to kill him had failed.

There was one quick way to check. Storm pulled out his phone, and dialed Javier Rodriguez in the cubby.

"What's up, bro?" Rodriguez said. "You still hangin' with Strike?"

"No time for gossip," Storm said. "I was wondering if you've heard anything about an attempt being made on Congressman Jared Stack's life?"

"Hang on, let me check."

Storm put the phone on speaker, then set it down. He took the strip of cloth he had ripped off Ahmed's nightgown and tied it as tight as he could around the upper part of the metal dealer's arm. Storm walked quickly into a nearby bathroom, found some towels that looked clean enough, and returned to Ahmed, using them to further staunch the bleeding.

"Thank you, thank you," Ahmed was muttering. "May Allah bring blessings to you."

Storm was finishing his rudimentary first aid job just as Rodriguez returned to the phone.

"This is freaky, bro," Rodriguez said. "D.C. cops just found Jared Stack strangled to death behind a crack house in Southeast. They haven't said a word about it to the media yet because it just happened. How the hell did you know about it?"

"Long story," Storm said. "I'll tell you later."

He disconnected the call then thought about what his father said that night they had first stumbled on William McRae and his work on promethium. Carl

Storm had warned his son that terrorists came in all shapes and sizes. Sometimes, he said, they looked like Osama bin Laden. Sometimes they looked like Ted Kaczynski.

And sometimes they looked like Xena: Warrior Princess.

CHAPTER 28

A SECURED ROOM

William McRae flexed his fingers, groaning when they creaked back at him.

There must have been a storm coming. A big one, judging from the pain he was in. He could feel the drop in air pressure in his aching joints, as well as or better than any barometer. He also noted a slight increase in the humidity of the air being pumped into his room, like it was ever-so-slightly more tropical.

He sat up in bed, dreading the day's toil ahead of him. He kept thinking that the men he was working for would run out of promethium, eventually. They had to. There simply wasn't this much of the stuff in the world.

But every five to seven days, they'd come in with more of it and McRae would start the process over again, turning the promethium into crystal, setting the crystals in the sequence needed to get enough power to the laser.

The newest shipment hadn't yet arrived. It was due any day now. He still had enough from the last shipment to keep him busy. Alpha had shown him a new round of Alida pictures the night before, just to keep him motivated.

It was the usual stuff: Alida heading out to the grocery store, Alida checking the mail, Alida doing all the little routine things he suddenly missed being a part of so desperately.

The one that had really broken his heart was of Alida sitting by herself, eating supper. He felt lonely for her just looking at the picture. She was a bright, engaging woman who felt that meals—and especially the evening meal—were a time for conversation and for sharing. He wished she would start inviting friends over. He couldn't bear the thought of her just sitting there by herself.

Alpha had made it a point to show William that behind Alida in that particular photo was a calendar that showed the date. The calendar had broken William's heart, too. Not because it proved they still had a man stalking her, but because of the content.

It was her fake daily-inspirations calendar. The sayings in it were just like Alida: smart, sassy, a little irreverent, but full of humor. The one for the day in question was, "Some people say you're racially intolerant. I just say you're an a-hole."

McRae smiled at the thought. It was one of the rare ones that had graced his face over the last month. Now that he was upright, his wakefulness clear to the cameras, it didn't take long for one of his captors to appear. This time it was the one McRae called Epsilon. McRae assigned him the lowest rank in his imaginary pecking order simply because he wasn't quite as sharp as the others.

"Good morning, Dr. McRae," he said officiously. "I'm here to get your breakfast order."

McRae yawned. Lately, he had taken to asking for more elaborate breakfasts, because he noticed they didn't put him to work until after he had eaten. It was a pathetic stall tactic, yes, but it felt like a small victory.

"I'd really like some waffles, if your chef can handle that," McRae said. "And maybe some fruit on the side. Strawberries, perhaps. Oh, and some grapefruit. But make sure he cuts out the sections this time. Unless you fellas want to give me a knife, someone needs to cut my grapefruit for me."

"Okay," Epsilon said, then turned and departed.

McRae listened for the click that always accompanied a guard's departure.

Except—were his ears failing him?—this time it didn't come. He quickly swung his legs down off the bed and studied the door. It had stuck against the doorframe without closing all the way. The humidity must have swollen the wood a little.

He scrambled over to the chair where he had draped his pants and pulled them on, then jammed his feet into his shoes. He waited another thirty seconds, just to make sure Epsilon was gone, then tentatively opened the door.

The hallway was empty. Every day, he had been led down that hallway to the left, toward his workshop. That and his cell were the only two rooms he had seen during his captivity.

He was glad he had asked for waffles. Mixing the dry ingredients, then the wet ones; separating the egg whites, beating them stiff; combining all of the above ingredients, then cooking them in a waffle maker. It would take at least fifteen minutes. Maybe twenty. No one would be looking for him during that time. They would think he was just lingering in the shower. There were no cameras in the bathroom.

This was his chance to make a break for it. Wedging the door barely open with one of his socks—so he could rush back in if he felt the need—he turned right down the hallway. When he reached the end, there was a metal door on the left.

Again with great caution, he shoved it open. It was a narrow staircase that only led up. McRae climbed the stairs to the top, where there was a small landing and another door.

But this one had a window.

It was the first time in a month that McRae had been able to look at the world outside his confines, and he could barely believe the view.

It was water. He was at sea. This was a boat. An enormous boat.

It all suddenly made sense: the motion he sometimes felt was from the waves, but only at the rare times when they got large enough to actually rock a boat that size; the rumble of the engine, which he thought was some kind of generator, had actually been powering the boat on its journey.

He opened the door and stepped out onto a narrow corridor that ran along the outer part of the deck. On one side was the ship's superstructure. On the other side were the waves, which were getting to be of the size that rocked the ship. He peered over the edge. It was a significant drop into the water, even though this was one of the lowest decks. He had half a thought to simply jump into the water. He was reasonably sure he could survive the fall.

But then what? He didn't know where they were. Even though the air felt warm, the water could be cold. Even relatively warm ocean water could cause hypothermia within a few hours. He could see land, but only barely. It had to be at least ten miles away. He wasn't that good a swimmer. Plus, there was that storm coming, the one he felt in his bones. He'd never last.

Maybe he could find a lifeboat. Or a smaller vessel attached to this boat—didn't super-yachts have stuff like that? Maybe then he'd have a chance.

Or maybe he'd have to recognize he was a prisoner on this boat until someone decided to let him go. Or, more likely, kill him.

McRae scampered along the corridor until he reached another door. He turned in. This hallway was very different from the one he had been in before. His hallway, the one he had seen every day for a month now, was very plain, almost institutional for its lack of decoration. This one was lavishly adorned. There were paintings every few feet, little end tables with jewel-covered lamps, elaborate woodwork, gilded trim.

He turned blindly into one of the doors off the hallway. It was a guest room—one of many, given the size of this boat. He was about to turn out of the room and leave it when he spied an old-fashioned, rotary-style telephone, sitting on one of the desks.

Was it just another decoration or . . .

One way to find out. He picked it up. Sure enough, it had a dial tone. He stuck his finger in the 0—the first number in the 011 he'd need to start an international call—and cranked it all the way around to the STOP. Remarkably, it returned not a series of clicks, like a rotary phone, but a beeping sound. Like a normal, modern touch-tone phone.

He kept dialing, getting almost feverish in his haste to complete the number. It was one he knew by heart, one he had dialed countless thousands of times, one that led him to a voice that was, to him, the sweetest in all the world.

The line went silent as faraway computers started making their efforts to connect two phone lines that were even more distant. After what felt like an infinite stretching of time, he heard a ringing.

"Hello?" said that dulcet voice. It was Alida. He was so choked with emotion, he could barely make himself reply.

"Honey, it's me."

"Billy?!?" she said, her volume rising. "Billy?!? Is that you? Oh my God, oh my God!"

She was crying. He was, too. They had, during their forty-five years of marriage, never gone a day without talking. Now, after a month of not communicating, neither could push out a single syllable.

Finally, William overcame the lump with a torrent of words: "I love you. I've missed you so much and no matter what happens, I want you to know you were the most wonderful part of my life. Being married to you has been the best thing I've ever done. And if I don't make it back, I want you to know that I loved you right until the very last breath I took. And if there is something after that, the first thing I'll do when I get there is to start loving you all over again, you hear? Do you hear me Alida May McRae? I love you."

She was sobbing now. Whatever effort she was making at a reply wasn't coming out as words.

"Also, I want you to remarry. I don't want you to be some sad widow who lives the rest of her life alone. Keep my picture somewhere and look at it every now and then. But not on your nightstand, you hear? I don't want you to be pining away for ol' Billy McRae. I've had a great life with you, and that's enough. But even if mine ends, yours has to go on. You've got a lot of good years left. I want you to find a new guy who treats you really well and takes care of you the way I should have. I'm so sorry, Alida May. I'm so sorry this happened. I miss you so much. And the thought that I'll never get to see you again is—"

"Billy, stop with that talk," Alida said, now that she had finally been able to control her breathing. "Where are you? We're going to get you out of there."

"I don't know. I'm on a boat somewhere. It's a very large boat, like a cruise ship but without other passengers. Listen, that doesn't matter. I've got something else to say that's very important. You have to get out of the house. These men who have kidnapped me, they're watching you all the time. They're taking pictures of you. They say they're going to hurt you if I don't do exactly as they say. So you have to run. Go to the police station or the FBI or whatever. Just make sure you've gone somewhere safe and that no one is following you, you hear?"

"I will, Billy, I will. But now you listen to me. A man came asking about you. His name was Derrick Storm. He called himself a contractor for the government, but I got the sense he was . . . something more than that. He promised me he'd find you. Just tell me where you are and I'll let him know. He'll rescue you."

"You don't understand," William said. "They snatched me while I was jogging and then they drugged me and took me somewhere. They've been keeping me in rooms without windows. I managed to escape my room, but . . . I didn't even know I was on a boat until just now. So I'm on a boat in a body of water, but I can't even tell you what body of water."

"Please, Billy. You have to try. Can you see land? Is there a city with a skyline you recognize or maybe some kind of landmark or something?"

William looked out the window, his eyes scanning the distant shoreline. It was so far away, he couldn't really see any of the structures. There were some cliffs. Some other spots were treelined. He more just had a sense that land was there. But it could be California or England or . . .

"Wait!" he said, having to suppress the urge to shout. "Yes, yes I see something, it's . . . My God, I think that's the Rock of Gibraltar. Yes, yes, it is. I swear, that's it. We're in the Mediterranean, in the Strait of Gibraltar, maybe ten miles from the coast. South of the Rock of Gibraltar. Does that help?"

"Yes, it does. Oh, Billy, we're going to get you home. And when we do, I'm going to hold you forever and never let you—"

"Someone's coming," he cut her off. "I love you."

And then he hung up. He ran through the bedroom, into the bathroom. But he could already hear the bedroom door opening. Out of the scores of rooms on this boat, how did they know he was in this one?

The cameras. They must have seen him on one of the monitors in the hallway and known exactly where to look. He just hoped that they didn't know he had used his time in the room to call Alida. He didn't want to put her in any more jeopardy than she was already in.

He slid back the shower curtain and quickly dove into the bathtub. It was the only place to hide. He quieted his breathing, hoping against hope that maybe they'd overlook him.

But no. The light came on in the bathroom. The shower curtain was being peeled back. McRae closed his eyes, almost like a child who thought that if he couldn't see the bad guys, the bad guys couldn't see him.

"There you are."

It was Alpha. McRae opened his eyes. The Viking-like man loomed large over him.

"Let's go, Dr. McRae. You've been a bad boy and there will be a punishment."

Alpha slapped one enormous hand on McRae's back, bunched up a huge handful of pajama, and used it as a handle to lift McRae out of the tub. McRae allowed himself to be shoved/led back to his quarters. For as devastated as he was that his brief escape had come to an end, for as much as he feared whatever reprisal he was about to face, it had been worth it.

For one thing, he didn't see any hiding places for cameras on his way out of the bedroom. So his captors didn't know about the phone call he had made.

For another, he now knew Alida would be safe.

He was just glad he had gotten to hear her sweet voice one last time.

CHAPTER 29

CAIRO, Egypt

The 6 October Bridge had been called "the spinal cord of Cairo," snaking as it did from the west bank of the Nile, through Gezira Island, over the river itself, and then on to the airport.

Its main span was 423 feet long, and Derrick Storm waited until he was nearly in the middle to slowly apply his brakes and bring the cargo truck to a stop, ignoring the angry beeps from the driver behind him.

This was the spot he had been looking for. The river was deep. The current was swift.

Just right.

He had sped through the night to get here. Having departed shortly before an ambulance arrived to care for Ahmed—and untied the guard in the shack on his way out—he had taken the cargo truck and the promethium, which he and Ahmed agreed was the best course of action. Well, it was more Storm's idea than Ahmed's. But Ahmed wasn't exactly in a position to argue. Nor did he quibble when Storm asked him to have someone return his rental car. Men on the brink of bleeding to death tended to be quite suggestible.

The long drive north had given Storm time to work out a lot of things relating to Ingrid Karlsson, allowing him to untangle the twisted mix of ideology and ambition that fueled her madness. She was a woman who shunned the beliefs that fueled much of humanity's violence toward itself. She was the citizen of the world, the one who rejected the concept of national boundaries or government intervention in markets or any of the people who would impose their way on others.

But that was, of course, its own kind of rigid doctrine. It turned out she was just as aggressive about promoting it as the religious zealots or the jingoistic nationalists. And in the promethium laser beam, she had found a weapon that helped her enforce her agenda.

He had been foolish in trusting her. The only person who had told him that Ahmed Trades Metal had any connection to the Medina Society was Ingrid. Ordinarily, he was scrupulous about being more suspicious toward information that came from only one source. And yet because Eusebio Rivera told him about seeing Ahmed Trades Metal on the promethium shipment going through the Panama Canal, it had felt to Storm like he had a second source.

And, of course, he had never checked it against existing CIA intelligence because, one, the CIA didn't have much intelligence on the Medina Society; and, two, he had been forced to play it so close to the vest with Jones.

So that was his main mistake. But now that he had Karlsson in his sights, other seemingly unconnected strands began tying together. The victims of the airline crashes, for example, started making a lot more sense.

Start with Erik Vaughn. The man was a sworn enemy of the Panama Canal expansion. Storm called and quizzed Carlos Villante, catching the purported deputy director of the Autoridad del Canal de Panama just as he was going to bed. Villante had confirmed that Karlsson Logistics had more canal-related shipping routes than any other company, and therefore had the most to gain from the canal's expansion.

Furthermore, Villante had said, Karlsson Logistics's own explosion from a small Swedish shipping company into a global behemoth had left it highly leveraged. It was likely that without the canal's expansion, the company would struggle to maintain the revenue growth that allowed it to meet an aggressive and rapidly increasing series of debt payments.

Jared Stack, who had unexpectedly taken Vaughn's place as an impediment to funding for the canal expansion, had also become an enemy to Ingrid Karlsson. And he was also now dead—the victim of what was supposed to look like a tawdry death for a misbehaving congressman and would have been investigated as such had no one been the wiser.

Sometime midway through the trip north, Storm's phone started ringing. When he checked the caller ID, it came up as restricted. The cubby. He ignored it and kept flipping through a mental Rolodex of other plane crash victims and finding others, both in Pennsylvania and the Emirates, who would have raised Ingrid Karlsson's ire.

One was Viktor Schultz. As the head of Tariffs and Trade for the European Union, he had pushed relentlessly for higher excises on goods coming into the EU. In doing so, he had made himself an anathema to Karlsson, who was a free trade fanatic.

Another was Gunther Neubauer. The legislator

had been called the Ted Cruz of Germany for his uncompromising stances on issues of great importance to him. His agenda was similarly reactionary: he was the leading voice calling for Germany to completely withdraw from the European Union. Many believed that if he succeeded, the EU itself would fold. That would have been a crushing blow to Karlsson's vision of a world without borders.

There were others with no real connection to Ingrid Karlsson—like Pi, the fruitarian cult leader. Not that anyone would miss him.

But that was part of what made Karlsson's attack so cunning. It was nearly impossible to separate the real targets from the collateral damage.

How she had known what planes they would be on—and where those planes would be—was no special mystery. The world's aviation authorities had some of the more easily hacked computer systems. And the airlines weren't much better. Meshing passenger manifests and flight plans was not especially difficult, especially when both were in their respective databases well ahead of time. It was possible Ingrid Karlsson had a vast enemies list and that she had picked off the few who happened to be in the air on the days she decided to use the laser. This may have merely been the start of a massive cleansing.

At the top of that list, it now seemed clear, was Brigitte Bildt, the woman who knew about her boss's plan, the woman who had been traveling to the United States to expose everything. Storm wondered how much Jones really knew about her visit and what she was going to say when she arrived. Probably a lot more than he let on, as usual. Probably everything.

By the time Storm arrived in Cairo—at roughly the same time as the rising sun—he felt like he had it figured out. And yet before he went full tilt after the Warrior Princess, he had one last errand to complete.

That was why he had come to the middle of 6 October Bridge. He quickly disembarked from the truck's cab and went around to the trailer, which he had already unlocked. It turned out the combination was Ahmed's date of birth: 12-23-74.

Storm pulled the metal box that contained the promethium out of the back of the trailer. He lowered it from the bed of the truck onto the pavement. His actions were being accompanied by what was now a line of drivers honking at him for clogging a lane of traffic. This, Storm knew, was ordinarily how right-of-way was established in many Middle Eastern countries: the car with the loudest horn got to go first.

But he was ignoring their ire. His phone rang again. He ignored that, too. He dragged the metal box up onto a small sidewalk, then hefted its leading edge up to the railing, so it was tilted at a fifty-degree angle. He was already breathing hard from the effort, but he didn't mind the exertion. It had been a few days since he had gotten to lift weights. This scratched that itch.

He removed the box's lid, tossing it quickly to the side, then lifted the back up so the container was now parallel to the ground. One end was still perched on the railing. The other was supported by Storm.

Then, slowly, so as to give the mighty Nile plenty of chance to sweep it away, he began pouring the promethium over the side of the bridge.

It took a little while, but Storm did not want to rush this. He took a kind of perverse pleasure in it: watching 382 pounds of pure promethium—with a fair market value of seventeen million dollars and a military value far greater—pouring off the bridge into the fast-rushing current below.

Chaos theory being what it was, some of those promethium molecules would sink at that spot, others a half mile away. Still others would be carried all the way to the sea.

The point was, no one would be able to recover them. They were effectively scattered to oblivion. Which, according to Storm—be it Derrick or Carl—was where they belonged.

AS STORM GOT BACK IN THE TRUCK AND GOT IT UNDER way, his phone rang again. He was going to ignore it once more, but this time the caller ID identified it as coming from MCRAE, WILLIAM.

He answered on the second ring. "Derrick Storm."

"Mr. Storm, this is Alida McRae, I'm the wife of—"

"Of course I remember you, Alida. It's nice to hear from you."

"I'm sorry to trouble you. But I just got a phone call from Billy, and I thought you'd like to—"

"Did he say where he is?" Storm cut her off again.

"He's on board a boat. He said it was a big boat, the size of a cruise ship."

Storm was off the bridge now, heading toward the airport. He pressed down the accelerator. "That boat is called the *Warrior Princess*," he said. "It's owned by a woman named Ingrid Karlsson."

"Ingrid Karlsson . . . You mean of Karlsson Logistics? *That* Ingrid Karlsson?"

"That's right."

"But why would she want to make laser beams

and shoot down airplanes and do all this other crazy stuff?"

"Ideology. She pretends not to have one. But really, she's driven by it. I'll explain it to you in detail sometime, if you're really all that interested."

"Well, I suppose I don't care. I just want Billy back. Right before he got cut off, he said the boat was in the Strait of Gibraltar, about ten miles south of that famous rock. I know you said you worked for the government in some capacity and I was wondering if you—"

"I'm on it," he said.

"Just like that?"

"Just like that."

"Can I help?

"Yes. Bake a cake for your husband."

"A . . . a cake? What . . . what kind of a cake?"

"Banana cream."

"Why banana cream?"

"Because banana cream cakes are delicious. That doesn't matter as much as what you're going to write on it. It should say, 'Welcome Home, William.' He'll be home to eat it in a few days."

Alida was getting wound up in professing her thankfulness when Storm cut her off one final time. "Mrs. McRae, I appreciate your gratitude. But I have work to do. Just bake that cake. A man always likes a good cake."

She wished him good luck, and he ended the call. Then he pulled off the highway and into a parking lot. He slid out his iPad, thankful that the airports were now open again and, furthermore, that the crashes had created a world full of jittery travelers. It meant the flight from Cairo to Tangier, Morocco, was only half full. He booked himself a ticket on it.

Tangier was located directly across a narrow strip of water from the Rock of Gibraltar. He had some ghosts there, yes. But he also had at least one friend who would be able to help him.

It just so happened to be a friend who would need some money. Storm typed out a quick e-mail to Jean-François Vidal, asking the chief operating officer of the Société des bains de mer de Monaco to have one hundred thousand euros worth of the recent winnings resting in the Derrick Storm account sent via wire transfer to an account in Morocco—an account owned by one Thami Harif.

He then sent a quick e-mail to his buddy Tommy, informing him that he was about to receive a visitor.

With that task settled, Storm got back under way. His flight left in two hours, but he was only a few miles from the airport. He turned the radio back on. The medicane had torn across Italy and was now regaining strength as it churned over the warm waters of the western Mediterranean.

Storm's phone blurped at him, telling him he had a call. Storm peeked at the caller ID. RESTRICTED. It was surely the cubby again. But Storm decided it was time to deal with that annoyance.

"Derrick Storm."

"You want to tell me what's going on?" Jedediah Jones asked. His voice had its usual tone: calm but insistent.

"Not sure what you're talking about, sir."

"Well, let's start with Jared Stack. How did you know about him?"

"Jared Stack?"

"Don't play dumb. It doesn't suit you. Rodriguez tried to cover for you, but I listened to a recording of the call. You're not going to weasel out of this one."

"Hmm," is all Storm said for a moment as he tried to formulate a lie. The last thing he wanted was for Jones to know about Ahmed. Storm doubted very seriously that Ahmed knew precisely where the promethium was coming from. He also doubted the man was harboring any additional product—he would have sold whatever he could to Ingrid Karlsson just as soon as he laid his hands on it. Still, there was the general rule of doling out information to Jones: the less, the better.

"Ah, yes, Jared Stack. Sorry, my mind blanked for a second," Storm said. "The contact you hooked me up with in Panama, Villante? He picked up some chatter that Jared Stack might be in trouble and he passed it on, knowing my interest in the case. You may be aware Stack had taken Erik Vaughn's place as the biggest legislative impediment to the funding of the Panama Canal expansion."

"I see," Jones said. "Well, moving on, Strike said the two of you were forced to split up and she lost contact with you. Have you made any progress on recovering the promethium that was stolen from the desert?"

Storm smiled. Clara hadn't ratted Storm out, after all. She was probably still pissed at him. But that wasn't exactly a first, nor would it be a last. At least she had covered for him with Jones. Or perhaps she was only covering for herself. Either way, it helped.

"No, sir, I'm sorry. I tried, but I failed. I have no idea where it is."

He could have easily passed a polygraph test on the last part—inasmuch as he was unsure which sections of the river bottom over which the promethium would eventually spread itself once it was done floating on the current.

"Well, to a certain extent it doesn't matter anymore," Jones said. "Strike came through for us, big time. She told us about how the promethium was coming from the desert. One of our techs was able to apply a beta version of a rasterized video search algorithm to our archived satellite footage. The computer was able to crunch the data and find one of the previous trucks that had made the shipment. Our tech was able to latch on to that truck and trace it all the way from its source to its destination. It was a helluva piece of work on his part, let me tell you. Really impressive stuff."

Storm knew from the way Jones was talking that everything being said was fiction. Jones was selling the story too hard, throwing in details that he ordinarily would have skipped, sounding more like a cheerleader than the hardened operative he was.

The fact is, for as good as his satellites were, they did not record every inch of the entire world at all times. The cameras had to be told where to look, and unless they had been focused on the archaeological dig site at the aforementioned times, there would be no archival record created.

"Anyhow," Jones continued, "we followed that truck's payload all the way to, of all places, the *Warrior Princess*. It turns out this was all being done by Ingrid Karlsson. We're not sure what exactly is in that woman's head or what she thought she was going to accomplish. But Agent Bryan went through our dossier of plane-crash victims and he was able to confirm there was any number of people who had made themselves inconvenient to Ms. Karlsson. I'm sure this all comes as quite a surprise to you."

Jones had dangled the last sentence out there as a bizarre kind of peace offering. Both men knew the other was lying. It was Jones's way of saying, *I know this is garbage. But let's just bury it and move on.* And maybe a younger Derrick Storm—the one who had not yet been scalded by Jones's "killing" of Clara Strike and then letting Storm believe she was actually dead—would have accepted the olive branch with a halfhearted, "Oh, yes, I'm stunned."

But not this Derrick Storm.

"You knew about Brigitte Bildt, didn't you," Storm said, evenly, in a way that was not to be confused with a question. "She told you why she was coming to America. The moment she was shot down, you knew Ingrid Karlsson was behind it. The reason you didn't tell me or anyone else immediately was because you didn't care as much about stopping her as you did about recovering the promethium, because you knew it would earn you a big pile of favors from the Joint Chiefs and an even bigger budget to boot."

"Hmm," Jones said, followed by his own pause. Eventually, he seemed to reach the conclusion that there was no point in trying to concoct a cover. "Well, look, you can tell yourself whatever bedtime stories you want to, Storm. It's all above your pay grade anyway. I was just calling to tell you your involvement in this matter is now over. Your orders are to stand down. Do you understand?"

"I do."

"So that plane ticket you just bought to Morocco, the one the techs just alerted me about, you're not going to use that, are you?"

Storm paused. "Actually, I probably will. I've got an old buddy in Tangier I've been wanting to see. We promised each other we'd have a good two- or three-day drunk a while back. This feels like the perfect time to celebrate the end of a successful mission. You have a problem with that?"

"No, I suppose not," Jones said. "Enjoy yourself."

"Thanks," Storm said. "We'll be sure to hoist one in your honor."

STORM ENDED THE CALL AND WAS ABOUT TO GET going again when he saw a new e-mail had arrived on his iPad. It was encrypted and asked for a password.

Storm just stared at it dumbly. Maybe whoever sent it to him had confidence he would be able to guess the password. But there was still a world of possibilities. He was about to start with some of the more obvious ones.

Then another e-mail arrived. It was from, of all people, cstrike@cia.gov.

I was just thinking about the game we played in Luxor, Clara wrote. *That was a lot of fun. I hope we can play again sometime. I like the way it ended.*

Storm stared at it for a second, then returned to the encrypted e-mail. It was from Strike, obviously. And she was trying to give him a clue about the password.

The game we played in Luxor. He typed in *chess* and hit ENTER. He got nothing. He entered the name of every chess piece on the board, from *king* down to *pawn.* Still nothing.

He looked back at Strike's e-mail. *I hope we can play again sometime. I like the way it ended.*

He grinned. He got it now. He typed in *check-mate.* The message opened:

> *You were right about Jones. He's made some kind of deal with Ingrid Karlsson*

where she gets to go free in exchange for the promethium. He's assembling a team to send to the Warrior Princess *as I type this. As far as I can see, the only way to stop this is if you get there first. Good luck.*
Love,
Me

CHAPTER 30

TANGIER, Morocco

The announcement went out over the loud-speaker not twenty minutes after Storm's plane had landed: as was forecast, the tropical cyclone had taken a left turn away from the French Riviera and was now barreling down on the Strait of Gibraltar. The eye was expected to pass very near Tangier. Ibn Battouta Airport, which had just opened up again, would officially be closing down. All flights in and out would be canceled until further notice.

As a smattering of departing passengers groaned, Storm actually pumped his fist in celebration. Whatever team Jones was arranging to take the *Warrior Princess*, their operation would be delayed until after the storm passed. There would have been no reason for them to take the unnecessary risk of carrying out the mission in the middle of a hurricane. They believed Ingrid Karlsson and the *Warrior Princess* would still be there when the weather calmed.

It gave Storm the narrow window of time he needed.

Get there, evade the *Warrior Princess*'s sophisticated sea/air defenses, defeat its well-trained security personnel, destroy the promethium, get Dr. McRae out safely, and arrest Ingrid Karlsson so that she could stand trial for her crimes.

All in the midst of a hurricane.

Storm was sure he had accomplished more impossible tasks. Just none that came to mind at this particular moment.

He walked quickly through the baggage area, still in disbelief he was back in Tangier. Long a haven for spies, writers, and other disreputable types, it had been under Moroccan control for more than fifty years. Yet it retained a distinctly international flavor from having been batted about between rulers for several thousand years. It had started out as a Phoenician trading post, then became a Carthaginian settlement. Then the Romans took over, setting the stage for it to be conquered and reconquered over the centuries: the Vandals, the Byzantines, the Arabs, the Portuguese, the Spanish, the British, and the French had all left their mark on the city and its history.

Then there was Storm's own history here. But that was something he was trying to forget.

He walked outside the airport into the passenger-pickup area. It was covered, but the steady rain that was falling was being blown under the roof by the wind. The first tentacles of the storm were already lashing the area. Storm looked at the sky and saw nothing but gray. He shoved his hands in his pockets. He was still wearing the black T-shirt and pants he had bought in Asyūt, which didn't provide much protection from the wet gusts.

Still, the moisture felt good. Refreshing even. He had grabbed a nap during his flight— and didn't mind nature's shower reviving him further.

As he scanned the cars waiting under the protected area, a camouflage-painted Hummer emerged from a nearby entrance ramp and made a line toward

Storm. It slowed as it approached. The passenger-side window was rolling down.

Inside, Storm could already see the driver. Thami Harif—"Tommy," to all his American pals—had a bushy head of silver hair, olive skin, and a scar that stretched across his left cheek, a memento from a knife fight. Ethnically, his father was of some undetermined mix of North African, Spanish, French, Portuguese, and perhaps other unknown strains, much like Tangier itself. His mother was a librarian from Bettendorf, Iowa, which meant Tommy had a full command of American English and all its idioms.

Storm knew Tommy would be driving with his left leg, if only because the right leg wasn't an option. He had lost it to an explosion long ago. He had a rotating selection of prosthetics that he changed to suit his mood and he nearly always wore shorts, so the world could enjoy them, too. Storm's favorite was a crude wooden stump made to look like a pirate's peg leg. Just because Tommy Harif made his living as a shady international arms dealer didn't mean he lacked a sense of humor.

Storm grinned and stuck out his thumb. Tommy's booming voice was already emerging from the window.

"I received a notification this morning that a hundred thousand euros had been deposited in one of my accounts," he said. "I made some inquiries and learned it came from a man named Derrick Storm. 'Derrick Storm?' I said. 'That's impossible. He's dead.'"

Storm's smile went wider as the Hummer came to a stop. "Those reports have been greatly exaggerated."

"He might as well be dead. I already spent half of

his hundred grand on hookers and booze. The other half, I wasted."

"It's good to see you, Tommy." Storm stuck his hand through the window and exchanged a vigorous shake with the man who had, quite literally, nursed him back from death's door.

"Get in," Tommy said. "Haven't you heard there's a hurricane coming? I hear it's going to be a real wild storm."

Storm opened the passenger door and climbed in. "Some people like a wild storm," he said.

"Count me among them," Tommy said.

"I missed you, Tommy," Storm said, clapping the man on the shoulder.

"You look a lot healthier than the last time I saw you. Fewer bullet holes."

"Well, we can't all be supermodels like you, but I try," Storm said. His gaze shifted down to Tommy's right leg, which was a utilitarian titanium model. Tommy was all business on this day. "No pirate leg today?"

"I know how much you like it, but I get lousy traction with that one," he said glumly. "It's no good in the rain. Plus, it gets stuck in the mud."

They took a moment of silence over this predicament. Then Tommy said, "So what brings you to my little city by the strait? A dangerous mission you can only tell me about if you kill me first, or however that little chestnut goes?"

"Something like that," Storm said as Tommy got the Hummer under way. "I was actually hoping you could take me to your, ah, little warehouse for a quick shopping trip."

Tommy said nothing for a moment. But Storm

knew he was being studied out of the corner of Tommy's eye. "Are you asking in the capacity of your work for Jedediah Jones?" Tommy eventually inquired.

"Not exactly. As a matter of fact, as far as Jones is concerned, you haven't seen me."

"I understand. So are you asking in the capacity of your work for some other part of the United States government?"

"Can't say as I am."

"Then who are you working for?"

"Why, Tommy, for the cause of righteousness, of course."

Storm delivered the line with the same gee-whiz earnestness that Tommy had once used on him, causing Tommy to erupt in laughter. "I understand, my friend. I guess what I'm asking is, can I count on you for a certain amount of discretion where the United States government is concerned? Uncle Sam . . . might not approve of some of my possessions."

"Do you even have to ask?"

"Where Jedediah Jones is potentially involved? Yes."

"Okay. Well, then I can confirm for you I am totally off the books, operating completely on my own, without the backing or authority of the Central Intelligence Agency or any other portion of my government."

Satisfied, Tommy continued driving them toward his home, a former Moorish castle set on a cliff just outside the city of Ceuta. It was about twenty miles from Tangier on a straight line, slightly longer on the N16, the highway that traced the shoreline of the Strait of Gibraltar.

As they traveled, Storm filled him in on all that

had been happening, and what the true nature of his visit was. He did this, in part, to gain the man's trust. But he also was eventually going to want Tommy's input. Tommy was not without expertise when it came to the use of force, brute or otherwise.

By the time they arrived, it was midafternoon and the sky was a bruised purple. The rain and wind had slowly ratcheted up in intensity during the course of the half hour drive. Storm could see the huge ocean swells rolling in the strait below.

Storm felt a familiar pang as the Hummer climbed the stone-lined driveway toward Tommy's residence. The main keep had been well maintained. Some of the parapets and balustrades had crumbled a bit since he last saw them, during the days of his convalescence. And while it was not a time in his life he particularly cared to revisit, he still felt nostalgia's grip.

Waiting for them on arrival was the meal Tommy had his chef prepare: couscous topped with lamb and vegetables. Storm demurred, saying he didn't have time; but Tommy insisted, pointing out that he had to wait until darkness to approach the ship anyway. Storm capitulated easily enough. It didn't help his resolve that he had eaten nothing more than airline food and that his mouth had started watering as soon as he walked in the door.

They continued talking throughout the meal, and as it reached its conclusion, Tommy summed up the obstacles facing Storm: "So, if I have this all straight, there is no way to approach this ship by air or sea, because anything much larger than a dolphin will be automatically spotted by the ship's detection systems. Even if you could get close, getting on board would be nearly impossible, because the boat will be thrashing around in heavy seas. And yet you can't wait for things to calm down because then Jones's goons will beat you to the punch."

"Right," Storm said.

"And then, even if you can somehow get on board, there are an undetermined number of highly motivated security professionals patrolling the decks. You have no idea where on the ship the captive is being kept, nor any idea where the promethium is being kept, nor any reconnaissance on Ms. Karlsson's personal quarters, including what special security measures might be installed there. Finally, even if you manage to defeat security, subdue Ms. Karlsson, destroy the promethium, and find the captive, you have to get them all off the boat in one piece?"

"That's about the size of it yeah. Any ideas?"

"Well, I do have one."

"Please share."

"Don't go," Tommy said. "Stay here with me. This is madness, even for a man of your abilities. Let's ride out the storm drinking fine wine and then hit Tangier in a day or two and spend some of your new fortune in style. You came inches away from death the last time you came to this country. Are you really that eager to make that last step into the grave this time? Forget everything you'll face once you get on board that boat; it's suicide even to head out in this."

"No, it's perfect. They'll never see me coming."

"That's not the point. Look, just let Jones win this one. Yeah, so the U.S. military gets a scary new toy and Ingrid Karlsson gets away. So what? What does it really matter to you? And don't give me this 'cause of righteousness' crap. That's my line, not yours. Why can't you just let this go?"

Storm shifted a well-gnawed bone around on his plate. "Because the Pennsylvania Three were actually supposed to be the Pennsylvania Four. I was on that fourth plane, sitting in seat 2B. I saw all the people on my flight, people she was going to let die without a second thought. They weren't anyone's enemy, Tommy. They didn't care about the width of the Panama Canal or the excise tax on auto parts heading into Germany. Their only sin was wanting to get back to their families to live a peaceful, happy life. I'm sure the people on the other planes were the same, and yet today their loved ones are burying whatever little broken pieces of them the authorities can recover from a catastrophic crash. The woman who caused all that pain has to face justice. She can't be allowed to escape punishment simply because she has something that the Joint Chiefs really want."

Tommy sighed. "Well, I tried. So what is it I can do for you, my friend, other than start planning your funeral?"

"Well, I need a gun. Some explosives. A knife."

"The basics. What else?"

"Well, let's make a visit to that warehouse of yours and find out. I assume a hundred thousand euro will buy me quite a shopping spree?"

"That it will," Tommy said. "That it will."

CHAPTER 31

THE MEDITERRANEAN SEA, SOUTH OF GIBRALTAR

The twin 220-horsepower engines underneath Thami Harif's thirty-five-foot cabin cruiser—named the *One-Legged Bandit*, in ode to his anatomical deficit—churned with only limited effectiveness in a sea that kept slipping out from under them with the passing of each wave.

From afar, Storm had thought the swells were thirty feet. Now that he was out in it, they were more like forty. From the bottom of one wave, the peak of the next wave felt like a small mountain about to crash on their heads. They'd climb until the height was vertiginous. And then they'd begin their drop back to the trough, which made Storm sure they were going to keep plummeting until they reached the bottom of the ocean.

Tommy had buttoned up every part of the boat that could be buttoned and jettisoned as much equipment as he could, both because he didn't want it to get swept away by the furious sea and because they needed every bit of buoyancy they could muster. About every twenty waves or so, a particularly large swell would come along and turn the boat into a submarine for a moment or two. The cabin was watertight, so Storm and Tommy would be treated to the surreal sight of watching the water close around them, then overtop of them.

Each time, a tiny, worried voice in Storm would swear this was the wave that was going to overwhelm them; or knock out the engines, rendering them powerless against drifting to wherever the hurricane wanted to blow them; or tear off some important piece of the boat and sink them without mercy.

And yet each time, the *One-Legged Bandit* would somehow float up to the top, its propellers still spinning through the wind-whipped fury. From underneath, Storm could hear the bilge pumps working double-time to excrete the water that was managing to find its way into the hull.

Tommy was hanging on to the wheel for all he was worth, his old seaman's arms tested to the limit of their strength. His titanium leg was braced against one side of the bulkhead. His flesh leg was curled tightly around the captain's chair.

Storm was, likewise, using a considerable amount of energy just to hang on through the unending roller-coaster ride. His task was made more difficult by the gear he had strapped on: scuba apparatus on his back; a modest amount of C-4 taped to the inside of his left leg; blasting caps and a small wireless detonator taped to the inside of the right one; a KA-BAR in a sheath on his right ankle; a bulletproof vest snug around his torso; a dry bag that included a grappling gun, a ring of single-loop plastic restraints, a Sig Sauer P229, and enough bullets to take on whatever hostile personnel he encountered once on board. It weighed him down, but it was a necessary concession. Getting equipped on a small boat in the middle of this maelstrom would have been impossible.

On flat seas, the *One-Legged Bandit* could have easily covered the distance it needed to travel in fifteen minutes. In these conditions, it had been fighting for two hours with no promise of an end. They had left with what Storm thought was plenty of time before dark. Now he wasn't so sure.

There was no conversation between the passengers. Each man was simply concentrating on surviving the next wave.

Every once in a while, at the crest of a wave, Storm's eyes would flit to the anemometer on the dashboard. He had yet to see the wind speed dip below seventy miles per hour. Most of the time it was in the eighties. The device topped out at a hundred. One or two gusts pushed the needle against its stop. The noise alone was deafening.

Finally, when they reached the peak of one particularly colossal wave, Tommy shouted over the howling, "I think I see it. We're heading right for it. Look at your one o'clock."

Storm had to wait for seven waves to pass until they again got high enough that he could make out a glimpse of Ingrid Karlsson's billion-dollar ocean liner. It was still roughly two miles off, which was the extent of the visibility in this tempest.

"Think they've seen us?" Storm asked.

"I hope not. I didn't make this thing torpedo-proof."

"That was poor planning."

"Look, Storm, not that this hasn't been a lot of fun, but this is about as close as I want to go."

"I understand. I'll take my leave of you now."

"Okay, my friend. Good luck."

They plunged down a particularly steep slope of a wave and sank underwater for three terrifying seconds. Storm held his breath until they popped up again, then clapped Tommy twice on the shoulder.

"Thanks, my friend. I owe you one. Again."

"You owe me nothing," he shouted. "Or at least nothing that those hundred thousand euros didn't take care of."

Storm could not reply. He had already pulled down his scuba mask and strapped it as tight as it would go to his head. The mask had the regulator built in. Storm twisted a knob and the oxygen started flowing.

With one hand steadying himself, he used his other hand to unstrap the diver propulsion vehicle from the side of the cabin. The DPV was the latest in individual underwater propulsion, a slick little unit developed for military purposes that delivered both speed and durability, along with lights, a navigation system, and other useful features. Storm didn't want to know how Tommy had procured one. He got it loose, then gripped it tight.

Then he crabbed over to the cabin door and timed his exit. If he opened it at the wrong moment—or, more accurately, if he didn't get it closed quickly— the cabin would be inundated with Tommy inside it. Without the buoyancy of the air-filled cabin, the boat might not make it up from one of the larger depressions.

Storm waited until the boat had rolled through off one of the smaller troughs and was heading for one of the peaks. Just as soon as he was confident enough water had rolled off the decks, he opened the door and ran through it, slamming it shut with all his strength.

From there, gravity did the rest. The boat's stern was tilted down at forty-five degrees. Storm followed the slope at an involuntary run, leaping when he reached the gunwale so he could clear over the side.

He was immediately in near total darkness. For one sickening moment, he thought the DPV had been ripped out of his hand by the force of his entry. Then he realized it was still tight in his fist.

As he sank in the water, breathing comfortably the whole time, he got his other hand on the DPV and switched it on. He let his weight belt take him fifty feet below the lowest trough, pressurizing his ears every ten feet or so, then filled his buoyancy regulator.

He switched on the headlight, and next took a look at the navigation system to make sure he was pointed in the correct heading. Then he turned on the propellers and started his journey toward the *Warrior Princess*.

NOTES FOR TRAVELING IN A HURRICANE: STAYING under the waves makes progress infinitely easier than trying to fight it out on top of them.

Fifty feet down, Storm was still dimly aware of the frothy, white-capped bedlam above him. But it did not impede his progress.

As he neared his target, Storm started aiming more erratically, but doing so purposefully. To the *Warrior Princess*'s great variety of sensors, he wanted to seem more like a seven-foot-long, four-hundred-pound tuna meandering through the depths than a six-foot-two, two-hundred-thirty-pound man about to mount a raid.

He had ninety minutes of oxygen. He used sixty of it, knowing that would be enough for full darkness to set in. His dry suit kept him warm enough, with its insulated layer of air allowing his body to keep enough of its heat so that hypothermia was not an issue.

By the time he resurfaced, about thirty yards from the *Warrior Princess*, the dim traces of daylight that had been penetrating the cloud cover were gone. It was now fully nighttime.

The edges of the boat were lit from stem to stern. Only a few of the staterooms were illuminated. She was not being tossed about like Tommy's small craft, but she was still feeling every inch of those forty-foot swells. According to her technical specifications, the *Warrior Princess* could withstand a Category 5 hurricane. That didn't mean riding out a Category 1 or 2 storm was a lot of fun. Certainly, no one was on the upper deck, shooting skeet.

No one was topside at all. And that was to Storm's advantage. He didn't worry about being spotted while he was in the water—he was just one tiny head bobbing in the huge waves.

But he did worry about being spotted while doing what came next. Releasing his grip on the DPV and letting it sink slowly to the bottom of the strait—a thirty-thousand-dollar piece of military equipment turned into another piece of trash on the ocean floor—he swam to within ten yards of the ship. The *Warrior Princess*'s engines were going just fast enough to keep her pointed into the waves and prevent her from getting broadsided. But she wasn't really going anywhere. It made her easy enough to keep up with, for as much as swimming in a hurricane was ever easy.

The closer Storm got to the boat, the more he felt

her hull looming over him as the waves bucked her about. It was difficult to quell the fear the boat was simply going to fall on top of him in the wild seas.

Eventually, he got close enough. Pumping up his buoyancy regulator until it was acting as a powerful life vest, floating him like a cork, he unzipped his watertight bag and withdrew the first of its treasures: a grappling gun.

Lofting its pronged hook over his head, he fired it at the railing of the lowest deck. He overshot it. But as he retracted the line, the hook ended up grabbing the rail on the way back. Storm tugged a few times. The line was firm.

He hit the retract button and let it slowly draw him toward the boat until he got his boots on the sheer side of the hull. Then he began walking his way up. It was just like climbing in the Alps, only it was a lot wetter, and the mountain was being tossed about by enormous waves.

About halfway up, he lost his footing. He went the rest of the way hand over hand, a process made a lot slower by sixty extra pounds of scuba gear.

When he reached the top, he flung himself over the side and went into a crouch. There was still no one about. Not even the security staff was doing patrols outside, possibly on the theory that no one would be stupid enough to try and board a mega-yacht during a hurricane.

Storm quickly shed the scuba gear and tossed it over the side—more expensive trash. Then he peeled off the dry suit and jettisoned it as well. The only item he retained was the dry bag.

Dressed in the same black-and-black outfit he had worn since Egypt and now with his sea legs underneath him, he made his way toward the main aft deck and one special door, behind which he hoped there would be the assistance he would need to succeed in this mad mission.

It was the door to the stateroom that belonged to Tilda, the redhead who had danced with him, drugged him, and now—he prayed—would aid him.

Storm and Tommy had talked out this particular tactical decision and agreed the job was nearly impossible without inside help. After all, Storm didn't know where Dr. William McRae was being kept. But Tilda did. Storm didn't know the layout of Ingrid Karlsson's quarters. But Tilda did. Tilda would know everything about the ship and its vulnerabilities.

She had said she would help save him sometime. This was her chance to prove it.

It was a gamble, yes. But so was getting up each morning. Storm just had to convince her he was, all kidding with Tommy aside, on the side of righteousness. He sensed goodness in her. He hoped he wasn't wrong.

The rain, which was falling in sheets, quickly soaked him. He walked normally, trying not to look suspicious. He was assuming there were cameras. He mostly was just gambling no one was watching them carefully in the middle of a hurricane. But if they were, he was trying to look like just another crew member, albeit one out of uniform.

He reached the door to Tilda's room, then listened for a moment. It was pointless. The wind was roaring at a volume that obscured anything else. There were no windows on this side of the stateroom. He was going in blind.

The door was not locked. He twisted the handle and burst into the room. It was empty. No Tilda.

He stood there for a moment, dripping on the carpet. This was not part of his plan.

Then, from the bathroom, he heard a faint hissing sound. It was a shower running. Showering in the middle of a hurricane: that was luxury.

Storm set the dry bag down on the bed, crept toward the door to the bathroom, and cracked it open. Tilda was warbling the tune to what sounded like a Swedish pop song. Storm wedged the door open a little further, giving himself a glimpse inside, feeling altogether too much like a stalker.

The shower was a stand-up stall, encased by an opaque door with a small gap above it. Steam poured out the gap. He slipped into the bathroom, then grabbed a towel off the rack. The singing continued.

In one quick movement, Storm threw open the shower door, shut off the water, threw the towel roughly around Tilda's torso then put his hand over her mouth to stifle the scream that was surely no more than half a second away. He took his other arm and grabbed her from behind, by the shoulders.

Tilda was too stunned to struggle. Her hands had automatically gone to keeping up the towel and not to attacking Storm. Modesty was a powerful force.

"Please be very, very quiet," Storm said. "I really, really don't want to have to hurt you. But if you make noise, you'll give me no choice. Do you understand?"

She nodded her head.

"All you have to do for a moment is just listen to me. Can you do that?"

Another nod. His hand was still clamped on her mouth.

"Thank you. Now, you remember on the rooftop

of the place in Monaco, we were talking about good and evil and Einstein and all that stuff?"

Nod.

"Well, you're going to have to take my word for it that it turns out your boss, Ms. Karlsson, is one of the bad guys. You've probably noticed something rather large being airlifted out of here several times in the last few weeks."

A hesitation. Then a nod.

"That was a laser beam, made by a very rare substance called promethium. She kidnapped a scientist and forced him to make it for her, then used it to shoot down those airplanes you've probably heard about."

She spoke into his hand. It was too muffled for Storm to make out. Storm lifted his hand so she could repeat herself. "Say that again?" he said.

"I said, 'That was Ingrid?'"

"Yes, I'm afraid it was."

"But that's not . . . all she ever talks about is how humankind ought to live peacefully."

"And she's willing to use force to make it happen, strange as that sounds. She thinks what she's doing is right for humanity, whether humanity wants it or not. I have no doubt she feels justified in her actions."

"But how do you know Ingrid is behind this?"

"Because I found the man who sold her the promethium. And it turned out the person I'm working for knew it all along. Brigitte Bildt was coming to the United States to warn my government about Ingrid. She just never got there. The Karlsson Logistics plane was one of the first ones shot down."

"She did that to Brigitte on purpose?"

"Yes."

She hitched the towel up under her arms. He felt her body relaxing in his grip. "I'm sorry, I just . . . I mean, part of me wants to say that it's not possible, that Ingrid would never do that—especially not to Brigitte of all people. But . . . I mean, I've heard some things I wasn't supposed to hear. Just little pieces. I kept telling myself it wasn't possible, that I must have just misheard or misunderstood."

"What have you heard?"

"Enough," is all she said.

"Enough that you know it's true."

She nodded. "So what do you want with me?"

He released her. She turned around.

"I need your help," he said. "I need you to be one of the good guys."

AS TILDA GOT DRESSED, STORM AVERTED HIS EYES and explained the rest of what she needed to know. They agreed they would free William McRae first, then confront Ingrid Karlsson.

Eight minutes later, they were heading for the door of her stateroom when she stopped him.

"Wait. Your clothes."

"What about them?"

"If anyone sees you on camera, they'll know you don't belong here. I can improve on them."

She went quickly to her closet and emerged with white pants and a blue shirt—the preferred regalia of the *Warrior Princess*. They were clearly not her size. They were made for a man even larger than Storm.

"A little big for you, aren't they?" Storm asked.

"A, uh, friend of mine left these here."

Storm eyed them then cracked a smile. "Must be a good friend."

"More like a convenient friend. It gets lonely in the middle of the ocean."

She tossed him the clothes. Storm ducked into the bathroom, shucked off his black clothes, and donned the Karlsson colors. His new outfit fairly swam on him. Especially the pants. He cinched the belt to keep them from slipping off his hips, then he bent over to roll up the hem.

"I could always use another friend, you know," she said from the other room. "Especially one who dances and kisses well."

"Have you ever been to the Seychelles?" Storm asked.

"No."

"We'll have to fix that," Storm said.

He emerged back into the bedroom to see Tilda gripping his Sig Sauer by the muzzle, having retrieved it from the dry bag. She had retreated to the far side of the stateroom, by the door.

"What's this?" she said, with measured disrespect. She was holding it like it was the most offensive refuse imaginable.

"Well, it's a gun, darling," Storm said.

"I can see that. Do you really need it?"

"Unless I can surprise everyone else on this boat while they're in the shower? Yes."

She was shaking her head. "You're with me now. You're not shooting up everyone on board this boat. They're good people. I'll tell them you're on the side of the angels. They'll listen to me, especially if they see you're not armed. No one needs to get hurt."

Storm paused, thought about his alternatives. He had assumed he would need to take the boat by coercion, that Tilda could be converted but that the rest of Ingrid's employees would be loyal to their boss. He felt naked without a gun. But Tilda had a point. Winning the people's hearts and minds might be easier than shooting them. It was certainly more humane.

"The man who owns those pants is named Laird Nelsson. He's the chief of security. He'll do what I tell him," Tilda continued. "The people on board this boat are my friends. I can't put them in danger. If you want my help, no gun."

"Well, it's hard not to like a guy named Laird," Storm said. "But what about Ingrid? I've got many admirable qualities. Being bulletproof isn't one of them. This vest is nice, but if she starts shooting at me, I want to be able to shoot back."

"She abhors guns. I think if she could reverse one human invention—other than the nation-state—it would be gunpowder. She had to be talked into even letting her security force have them. And even then it took Barbary pirates running amok in the Mediterranean to convince her."

"I'd still feel more comfortable with a firearm."

Tilda's answer was to quickly open the door and fling the gun out, end over end, boomerang style. Except, unlike a boomerang, this weapon wasn't coming back. Storm watched it arc over the side of the boat.

"And I feel more comfortable without one," she said.

"I wish you hadn't done that."

She crossed the room, raised herself on her tiptoes and planted a hard kiss on his lips. "Well, it's done now. Come on, let's go."

Storm sighed and followed. They went around to the boat's portside and a covered corridor that had nevertheless become very slick from the torrential wind-driven rain. The footing was treacherous, and every once in a while they had to stop and simply hang on as the *Warrior Princess* crested a particularly large wave.

She reached a door with a small window set into it, opened it, and turned down a narrow staircase that led below deck. At the bottom, she opened another door, which led to a hallway. Storm continued following. Unlike the rest of the ship, with its lavish decorations, this part of the boat was spare. Crew's quarters, Storm guessed.

Tilda reached one of the doors and tried the handle. It was locked. She knocked, rapping the door several times until it could be heard over the wind. "Laird, it's me," she said.

As she waited for a response, she turned toward Storm and asked, "Do you speak Swedish?"

"Enough to order in a restaurant, maybe," he said. "But not much more than that."

"Then you better let me do the talking. Laird speaks fine English, but it'll be faster in Swedish."

Finally, the door opened. Storm found himself looking at collarbones. Laird Nelsson was an immense man, at least a half a head taller than Storm, with blond hair, blue eyes, and bulk everywhere Storm looked.

Tilda herded Storm into the room and began talking in rapid Swedish, too rapid for Storm to follow—other than the names. He heard "Ingrid," "Brigitte," and his own name. Laird was in off-duty clothing and kept nodding as Tilda spoke. Storm felt like it was going well. Every once in a while, Laird's eyes would shift to Storm, who tried to look friendly.

When Tilda finished, Laird nodded one final time. "One moment please," he said, in English, as he reached into his nightstand.

He came up with a Beretta, which looked small in his bearlike paws. He pointed the weapon at Storm.

"Hands up," Laird said. "Come on."

Storm experienced a sinking feeling in his stomach as he slowly raised his hands.

"Ingrid Karlsson is a visionary in a way a mercenary like you could never understand," Tilda spat at him. "Don't you see? Someday, we'll all be citizens of the world. Ingrid is leading us there."

"And the people who don't want to walk her path get sent to their graves, is that it?"

Tilda ignored him and turned to Laird. "He doesn't have a gun. I saw to that. But he does have a knife. I saw an ankle sheath bulging from his calf."

"Very well. You will now remove your knife and set it on the bureau there," Laird ordered. "Do it slowly, please."

Storm complied. Out of the corner of his eye, he could see Tilda smiling savagely.

CHAPTER 32

ABOARD THE *WARRIOR PRINCESS*

While Derrick Storm didn't know much Swedish, he did know the word *mörda*. It's a verb. Its English translation is "to kill."

Storm heard *mörda* at least four times as Tilda and Laird debated what they were going to do with their new captive.

Eventually they decided to wait, for reasons Storm could not quite determine. Perhaps they wanted to let the empress, Ingrid Karlsson, give the ultimate thumbs-up/thumbs-down on his fate. Maybe Storm was to be used as a bargaining chip of some sort. Or maybe they just wanted to wait until the hurricane passed so they could dump his body without worrying about it being blown to land.

Whatever it was, Storm was soon led to the only room aboard the *Warrior Princess* that was designed to contain prisoners. It was the one just down the hall from Laird and the other guards, the one where Dr. William McRae had been kept for a month now.

Storm walked there with his hands still up and Laird pointing the Beretta at his back. Tilda inserted the key and opened the door.

"Get in there," Laird said.

Storm did as he was told. The door immediately clicked behind him.

Lying on top of the covers was a man of about seventy. He was trim, with a small amount of gray hair that looked like it was overdue for a buzz cut. He was reading a book by the late, great master of medical thrillers, Michael Palmer.

As Storm let his hands drop to his side, the man asked, "Who are you?"

"Hello, Dr. McRae. My name is Derrick Storm. I'm here to rescue you."

"You're the man Alida mentioned," he said, brightly. Then he considered Storm for another second. "Although, to be honest, she made it seem like you would be a little better at this whole rescue thing."

"I admit, this is not among my finest efforts so far. But this is just a temporary setback. We'll get you out of here somehow."

"Mr. Storm, I don't want to discourage you, but I'm not sure it's possible."

"Really? Why?"

McRae set down the book and sat up. "Because I've been in here for a month now and only managed to get out once. And it hasn't been for lack of effort. The one time I got out was only because a guard slipped up and left the door open. That's when I called Alida. But the other guards tracked me down pretty quickly. They've got cameras everywhere, including in this room. And I don't know if you noticed, but that door you just came through doesn't have a handle on the inside. That's just one of the details that makes the room escape proof. I've spent a month trying to figure out something and you'll notice I'm still here."

Storm nodded thoughtfully. "Are you familiar with Enrico Fermi, Dr. McRae?"

"Of course I am. What does he matter?"

"Well, he was one of the leading practical physicists of his time, as you know. Good enough that he won the Nobel Prize in 1938. We're talking about a supersmart guy. And yet when he joined the Manhattan Project, people told him his method of creating an atomic bomb was impossible, because you couldn't get the neutrons that resulted from the splitting of one atom to then split other atoms. And if you couldn't do that, there was no way the bomb would work. Fermi kept trying and failing, but with each so-called 'failure,' he was really getting closer to the solution. Fast-forward to 1942, and Enrico Fermi was the man who directed the first controlled nuclear chain reaction. How? Because he kept his belief in himself and didn't let past failure deter him. The point is, if you work hard enough, nothing is impossible."

"That's a lovely speech, Mr. Storm, but—"

"Also, I've got C-4 strapped to my leg."

"Oh. Why didn't you start with that?"

"Because I wanted to give the speech first, so you'd be impressed with my knowledge of physics."

McRae smiled. "I should have known Alida was right about you. The last time she was wrong about something was 1978, and she swore it wasn't going to happen again."

"She's one of a kind all right," Storm said. "Now let's get out of here."

Storm began surveying the room, assessing it in a clinical manner, going low to high, then high to low. The walls and ceilings were brushed steel, riveted into what were likely girders. He tapped it here and there. It felt thick. Certainly thicker than standard Sheetrock walls.

He pulled up a corner of the carpet to reveal a metallic subfloor. Then he went into the bathroom and gave it the same kind of inspection. The place really was designed to be a cell.

When he returned to the bedroom, he said, "You said there are cameras in here. What about the bathroom?"

"No. None."

"Excellent. And, tell me, you must have a laboratory or workshop where you've been putting the lasers together."

"Yes."

"Where is it?"

"Just down the hall and across the way."

"Are there cameras in there?"

"Not that I'm aware of. They always had a man in there with me, to make sure I wasn't sabotaging any of the equipment or doing anything else they wouldn't like."

"Perfect. In that case, I think you're getting a little seasick, Dr. McRae."

"Actually I feel fine."

"No, trust me, you're looking quite peaked."

"My stomach is iron, I never get motion—"

"The guards answer when you press this button, yes?" Storm said, walking over to the intercom.

"Yes, that's right."

Storm hit the button, waited. A voice came promptly to the line. "Yes?"

"Dr. McRae is feeling seasick. He says he's about to lose it. Is there any Dramamine aboard?"

"We'll be right there," the voice said.

Storm turned so his back was to the camera he had spied in the near corner. "When they come in, I expect seasickness. I'm talking Academy Award-worthy, you've-just-watched-Kevin-Costner-in-*Waterworld* seasickness. And it had better end with your head in a toilet, making a really nasty retching sound."

FIVE MINUTES LATER, THE DOOR OPENED. THERE WERE two of them: Laird, who had the Beretta drawn, and one of the underlings, the one McRae called Delta.

McRae had closed his eyes and was on the bed, moaning.

"He's suffering," said Storm, summoning his inner Clara Barton. "How long until this storm blows through?"

"The worst of it has already passed," Laird said. "It's still going to be bad for a few more hours, but the marine forecast says the seas should be down below twenty feet by morning. That won't budge this boat much."

"Uhhhhh. I'm not gonna make it," McRae moaned and launched himself into the bathroom, where he began making heaving noises.

Laird and Delta looked appropriately grossed out. "Just toss the medicine on the bed," Storm said. "I'll make sure he's okay. Sometimes you just need to get it out of your system. Did he have a big dinner?"

"Two helpings," Laird said. "Spaghetti and meatballs."

"Eww. That is *not* going to look good coming back up. All right. This might be a while. I'll hit the intercom if we need anything."

McRae chose that moment—a brief lull in conversation—to begin a new fake assault on the toilet. Delta tossed the Dramamine on the bed then joined Laird in full retreat.

Storm went straight for the bathroom, where

McRae was already reaching for the toilet handle to flush away the vomit that didn't exist. Storm waited a moment, then returned to the bedroom to grab the medicine.

By then, the door had closed. Laird and Delta were gone. To anyone watching on the camera—if anyone even was—it would look like Storm had simply forgotten the Dramamine and now, having retrieved it, returned to the bathroom to continue his ministrations.

Instead, he shut the bathroom door, then stood up on the sink and lowered his pants. He un-taped the C-4 and studied it for a moment.

"Have you ever worked with explosives?" he asked McRae, who had stopped with the dramatics and was watching Storm.

"Not really. Why?"

"I'm just wondering how much of this stuff to use. I don't really know the thickness of this ceiling. I want to make sure I use enough to get through it, but I need to save some for later."

"I suggest a SWAG."

"SWAG?"

"Yeah," McRae said. "It stands for Scientific Wild-Ass Guess."

Storm shrugged, then broke off half his hunk of the C-4. He freed several of the blasting caps from where they were taped on his other leg, and then took hold of the wireless detonator. He molded the plastic explosive halfway between rivet lines, figuring there would be a hollow space behind it.

He fixed the blasting caps into the plastic, then climbed down off the sink. He opened the door to the shower, which was similar to the one in Tilda's bathroom.

"In you go," Storm said to McRae. "This is as close as we're going to get to a bomb shelter."

"Some blast door," McRae said, tapping the opaque plastic on his way in. "Is this how Enrico Fermi did it?"

"No. But I'm told Robert Oppenheimer did his best thinking in the shower. So we're probably on to something."

Storm closed the door behind McRae. "You ready?"

"As I'll ever be."

"Wait, don't forget your high-tech ear protection," Storm said, sticking his fingers in his ear canals. McRae followed suit.

Storm set the wireless detonator on a built-in ledge that was supposed to serve as a soap dish.

"Three, two, one," Storm mouthed, then hit the two buttons he needed to depress on the detonator with his pinkies.

There was a *whump*, followed by the sound of pieces of metal crashing against other pieces of metal. It was loud, but nothing compared to the eighty-plus-mile-per-hour winds still raging outside.

Storm opened the shower door to see a gaping hole that had been blown up into the ceiling.

"Success," Storm said.

He climbed up on the sink, stood, and chose a spot where the metal had shorn completely away from the girder—and where, therefore, there was no jagged metal to avoid. He jumped up into the ductwork above the ceiling. He wormed his way around until he was being supported by the girder and could reach down a hand for McRae.

"Come on, Doc," Storm said.

"Where are we going?"

"To your laboratory. By my count, you've got about twenty minutes to make me a laser."

"A laser? What for?"

"Because otherwise the only way I can beat these guards is by challenging them to an arm wrestling contest, and I figure they'll just shoot me instead. But if I have a laser, I can shoot them first."

"But—"

"Don't say it's impossible. It wasn't impossible for Erico Fermi, remember?"

"No, no. It's not that. It's . . . Look, the lasers I've been making for these people are very powerful. Certainly powerful enough to take out any of those guards. But they're also very large. They get taken out a bay door on the side of the workshop. They're not especially portable."

"That's okay. I don't need anything nearly that powerful or that lethal. I've read about laser beams being used to blind pilots. Could you make me something powerful enough to cause temporary blindness?"

McRae suddenly was wearing the look of a chef in a fully stocked kitchen who was being asked if he could whip up a little snack. "Yeah, of course I could."

He got up on the sink and accepted Storm's assistance up into the ceiling.

"Which way?" Storm said.

McRae pointed to the left. "Right over there would probably be good."

The men began crawling across girders, in the tight space under the floor above them. When McRae gestured that they had reached the workshop, Storm was relieved to see a normal drop ceiling. No metal here. Storm easily stomped out one of the panels, helped McRae drop down into the workshop, and then followed him down.

"You were making up that thing about Oppenheimer and the shower, weren't you?" McRae asked.

"Not at all," Storm lied.

The truth was, he was mostly making up the thing about Fermi, too. But this hardly seemed like the time to mention it.

THE RESULT OF MCRAE'S TWENTY MINUTES OF FURI-ous jury-rigging was not anything that would geek the Star Trek crowd for its design.

It didn't boast any kind of sleek housing, nor did it have a handle or a trigger. To Storm's untrained eye, it was basically a sheet of metal supporting some electronic stuff and a piece of cylindrical glass, all of which McRae had hastily soldered or taped into place. It was roughly the size of two toasters, placed end to end.

When it came time to test the device, McRae donned dark, wraparound glasses and had Storm do the same.

He fired it just once, activating it by briefly depressing the rubber tip on a piece of metal, bringing it into contact with another piece of metal. An intense blue beam—less striking than the one Storm had seen demonstrated in Maryland, but still quite vivid—leapt from the device and into the wall behind them.

"Okay," McRae said. "You've got yourself a laser beam."

"Brilliant," Storm said, and meant it.

"A couple of things. One, this is just a fraction of the power of the ones that I've been making.

You'll see there is only one crystal, as opposed to the sequence of crystals I used on the other ones. And it's a lot smaller, made from cast-off pieces I used in some of my early testing. But if blindness is what you want, blindness is what you'll get. This is the aperture the beam will come out of," he said, pointing to a glass-covered slit at the front of the contraption. "The way I've got this set, the laser will actually spread as it propagates. That makes it less powerful, but it also makes it easier to aim. If you can get this going anywhere near a guard's face and he doesn't have eye protection? It'll be like he stared directly into the sun for way, way too long. He'll be blind for anywhere from twenty-four to forty-eight hours."

"Terrific."

"But, look, you have to careful. It's very fragile. I didn't exactly have time to make it battle rugged, you know? And it's also not going to last very long. I've got a few batteries here," McRae said, showing Storm a plastic-covered power pack with wires coming out of it. "But this laser will drain down those batteries very quickly."

"How quickly?"

"If I had to give it a SWAG, I'd say you've got maybe twenty-five or thirty seconds of laser time."

"Can you give me replacement batteries?"

"This isn't a kid's remote control car," McRae said. "I'm afraid these batteries are the only ones I have. Once they're gone, they're gone."

"All right, great work," Storm said, stuffing the safety glasses into one of his pants pockets. "Now, before we head out and face the guards, we've got one more thing to take care of."

"What's that?"

"The promethium. I assume you still have a supply of it?"

McRae nodded.

"We have to get rid of it," Storm said. "I've seen to it that the supply coming in here is cut off. But I want to make sure no matter what happens to us, there's not enough left to make another laser beam."

"Okay. It's over there," McRae said, pointing toward a large metal container that looked like a refrigerator.

"How would you recommend disposing of it?"

"Well, extreme heat would do it. If you cook promethium at a high enough temperature—I'd have to look up the exact number, but it's around a thousand degrees Fahrenheit—it changes the internal structure. Essentially, it turns into a big blob and ruins it for the purpose of turning it into a crystal for a laser beam."

"Do you have something in here that could generate that kind of heat?"

"No."

"So . . ."

"Or we could just pour it into this sink with hot water running," McRae said, pointing to an industrial-sized slop sink. "This promethium is in salt form. It'll dissolve easily in water."

"Why didn't you start with that?"

"Because I wanted to impress you with my knowledge of chemistry the same way you impressed me with your physics."

Storm cracked a grin. "I guess that's fair. Where does the water go after it leaves the sink?"

"I've been told it drains into the bilge tank. But right now, in this storm, I'm sure the bilge pumps are operating overtime. Essentially, we'll be pumping this right into the ocean."

"All right. Let's get that tap running."

It took just a few minutes for Storm and McRae, working in concert, to empty the promethium bin. For the second time in a day, Storm watched as millions of dollars worth of the planet's rarest rare earth disappeared into a flow of water.

He was relieved to see it go. He was the only person who knew where to find the remaining cache of promethium. And what McRae said about ruining promethium by heating it had given Storm an idea about how he could make sure no one could ever again use that cache.

As the last of the promethium swirled down the drain, Storm said, "Okay, let's go," and made for the door to the laboratory. The handle didn't budge.

"It's always locked from the inside," McRae said. "I'm sure a little bit of your C-4 stuck near the hinges would—"

"No," Storm said. "I want to preserve the element of surprise as long as possible. It's time for the patient to make an appearance back in his sickbed."

THEY RETRACED THEIR CEILING SLINK, COMING BACK through the hole in McRae's bathroom.

Once they were through the door into the bedroom, Storm made a great display of helping a hunched-over McRae back into bed. It was a show for anyone who happened to be watching on the display, yes. But it also helped Storm use his body to shield the laser from the camera without looking suspicious.

Keeping his body between the lens and the laser, Storm went over to the intercom and pressed the button.

"Yes?"

"Hi. I'm sorry to trouble you again. But Dr. McRae just puked up a lung. It's stopped for now, but he could really use some antinausea medication to make sure it doesn't start up again."

"Be right there."

Storm put on his dark glasses. "Close your eyes," he instructed McRae.

The door opened. There was only one guard this time, the one McRae called Delta. Storm activated the laser, aimed it in the general direction of Delta's face, and held the contact down for four seconds.

Delta wailed and fell to his knees. He had not moved from the doorway. Storm set the laser down on the bed, walked over to Delta, and gave him a swift kick in the head. The guard fell to the floor, face-first. Storm wrenched Delta's arms behind his back and secured them there with his plastic hand restraints. Storm checked the man for weapons. Delta had been unarmed.

"One down," Storm said. "How many are there, anyhow?"

"I've only ever seen five. I named them after the letters of the Greek alphabet. The one you just took out was Delta."

"Well, in that case, we've got Alpha, Beta, Gamma, and Epsilon. It'll be like a regular frat party in here. Hopefully it'll be just as much fun."

Storm retrieved the laser off the bed and went back to the door, where Delta's inert form made for a very effective stop. Storm expected his attack would have been seen on the cameras and would provoke a response. He positioned himself in a place where he could see up the hallway but where his own body was not exposed.

He waited. Thirty seconds. Sixty. Ninety.

"What's happening?" McRae asked.

Storm didn't reply, because he didn't know himself.

Then, finally, the door at the far end of the hallway, the one that led to the stairs, went just slightly ajar. Epsilon emerged first, followed by Beta and Gamma. They came in a low crouch, with two on the near side of the hallway and one on the far side. Their guns were drawn.

Storm put the laser at their eye level, then brought it from around the side of the door. The men started firing the moment the device emerged, but so did Storm. And whereas their weapons needed to be aimed with great accuracy, Storm's did not. He held down the button for fifteen seconds, making sure he hit both sides of the hallway.

Their cries were nearly as loud as their gunfire. So was their anguished Swedish, which even a non-Swedish speaker like Storm could recognize as curses.

They kept firing blindly. Storm heard the bullets whizzing by, hitting the walls and floor until, one by one, they began dry-firing their weapons.

Storm took a furtive glance out the door. They were midway down the hallway, still cursing. Two of them were rubbing their eyes with their non-gun hands in a futile attempt to massage their worthless eyes back to sight. The other was groping toward his pants pockets, perhaps to find a clip to reload. Storm set the laser down, sprinted at them, his footfalls all but inaudible on the carpet.

He choreographed his moves in his mind as he ran, and when he arrived, executed them skillfully. He took down Gamma with an elbow to the head. Beta got a kick to the face. He finished by snapping the hardest part of his forehead into the softest part of Epsilon's temple.

Storm began fastening plastic restraints on each downed man.

"Wow. You're good at this rescue thing after all," McRae said, peeking cautiously from around the door to his room.

"Oh, what, this? I learned this from watching Alida attack dandelions," said Storm.

"Those are some ugly dandelions."

"Eh, they grow on you," Storm said. "Come on."

"But what about Alpha?"

"You mean Laird Nelsson? The chief of security."

"Yes. The huge towhead."

"My guess is that he and Tilda, the tall redhead you may have seen around the ship, are currently with Ingrid Karlsson, deciding how best to get rid of me."

"Wait, Ingrid Karlsson? This is her boat? *The* Ingrid Karlsson?"

"Sure is. Why?"

He was shaking his head. "I read her autobiography, *Citizen of the World*."

"Don't tell me you really liked it and that you secretly align yourself with all its goals and aims and that now you're going to turn on me, because that's already happened to me once today."

"No. It was rambling crap. I bought it out of a

remainder bin for five bucks," McRae said. "When I get home, I think I'm going to ask for my money back."

STORM RETRIEVED THE LASER, WHICH HAD ANYWHERE from six to eleven seconds of fire time left, depending on the accuracy of McRae's guesswork. He passed the guards again. Gamma, the one who had taken the elbow, was groaning.

Storm gave him a kick in the head as he passed. It wasn't very sporting. But this wasn't a game. He quickly checked each man for extra clips. Finding none, he did not bother to tear their weapons from their hands, He didn't want an empty weapon that badly.

With McRae following him, Storm climbed the stairs, training the laser on the door at the top. Anyone who opened that door was going to get a blue blast in the face.

But no one did. They reached the top of the staircase and Storm announced, "Ingrid's quarters are in the front of the ship. We'll take a right out of here and walk toward the bow. Just stay behind me and watch your footing. It's nasty out there and this deck is sort of narrow. There's a railing, yes, but I don't need to tell you how dim your chance of rescue is if you fall in that water. If you feel like you can't make it, just stay here and I'll come back for you."

The moment Storm budged the door open, the wind caught it and pinned it back, nearly tearing it off its hinges. Storm stuck his head out. There was no one on the deck.

Bending into the full force of the gale, he began trudging forward. Each step was an effort. He had to cradle the laser like a football to prevent it from being torn from his grasp. His dark glasses were quickly covered by rain and sea spray being blown at him. He lowered them on his nose so he could peer over them, then had to squint as the full blast of the wind-driven water hit him.

He was aware McRae was struggling behind him somewhere. But when he looked back, he saw the scientist had retreated back into the stairwell. It was probably for the best. No point in getting Alida's husband hurt.

Storm had made it approximately halfway to where he could turn toward Ingrid Karlsson's quarters when the sizeable figure of Laird Nelsson rounded the corner.

The man McRae knew as Alpha was actually startled. He had obviously been talking with Ingrid, not manning the security cameras. He had no idea the prisoners were on the loose.

The delay gave Storm a chance to swing the bulky laser upward as Nelsson reached for his shoulder holster. Storm had the laser flat at eye level by the time Nelsson was drawing his gun.

As Nelsson aimed his weapon, Storm raised his safety glasses and pressed down the metal contact. A brilliant blue beam leapt from the device and struck Nelsson full in the face. Storm planned to hold down the button for four seconds.

Three seconds in, two things happened more or less simultaneously. First, the beam cut off, its battery spent. McRae's guess had been off by one second.

Second, the bullet fired by Nelsson struck Storm. Nelsson had been aiming for center mass and his targeting was true. The bullet hit Storm's vest just below the sternum, knocking the wind out of him and throwing him on his backside.

But, in some ways, it was the best thing that could have happened. Because it meant Nelsson's three succeeding bullets missed high.

Storm could hear Nelsson bellowing over the clamor from the hurricane. He had brought his hand to his eyes and was furiously swiping at his face, like he could somehow clear away the effects from the laser.

When he finally figured out he couldn't, he brought the gun back up and began firing it wildly down the deck, in the general area of where Storm had once been.

Storm had let go of the laser, ripped off the glasses and hunkered down as flat as he could against the floor. His chest felt like it had a fire spreading in it and breath was still not coming easily to him. As he began crawling forward—so he was no longer in the last spot where Nelsson had seen him—he was struggling to grab gulps of air.

Nelsson was coming down the deck toward him, in part because that was the direction the wind was taking him. Storm could tell from the way he was walking there that the man was sightless. But he was still dangerous. He was swinging the gun around and firing it sporadically.

Then suddenly he wasn't firing. He was reaching into his pants, as if going for another clip. That's when Storm sprung up and bull-rushed him. Storm was not eager to physically confront a man who outweighed him by at least eighty pounds. But it was either that or take his chances with fifteen more eight-gram bullets, which were capable of far greater damage.

Storm charged ahead, his speed slowed by the force of the wind. At the last moment, Nelsson seemed to become aware he was about to get tackled. He brought his hands up to defend himself, but Storm barreled into his midsection, driving Nelsson onto his back. The Beretta went flying from his hands.

Whatever thought Storm had about getting up and chasing after the gun didn't last long. Nelsson had grabbed him and wasn't letting go. Ingrid Karlsson's chief of security had already figured out the essence of this confrontation: a blind man is at a significant disadvantage in hand-to-hand fighting once he's no longer touching his opponent. But as long as he keeps contact, it's a fairly even fight. There's a reason blind high school wrestlers have won state titles.

Nelsson reached for Storm's face, or where he thought Storm's face would be. His fingers were trying to claw and gouge anything they could touch. Storm landed a punch, but it was one without much force behind it. They were too close. And yet there was no escaping. There were not many men large enough or strong enough to keep hold of Derrick Storm. But this was one of them.

Storm tried pulling away again. It was like trying to break free from an enraged octopus. He kept having to defend his face from Nelsson's savage attacks, while trying to mount his own meager offense. He got in a few more punches, none of them very convincing.

He was so distracted by his inability to hurt Nelsson that he hadn't fully braced himself for what came next. In one deft move, Nelsson flipped Storm over and got his hands on Storm's throat. The enormous Swede wrapped his fingers around Storm's neck and was squeezing, his forearms bulging.

They were now turned sideways on the narrow deck. Storm reached toward Nelsson's sightless eyes and scratched at them. But Nelsson didn't seem to care. He had already lost that sense.

Suddenly, Storm was losing his. Nelsson was bringing his immense weight to bear on Storm's neck and it was staunching the blood flow to his brain. Blackness was closing in around the edges of his vision. His brain was starving for oxygen.

With every joule of energy he had left, Storm gathered his legs against Nelsson's chest and then straightened them. It was a classic weight lifting move; for as strong as his opponent was, Storm's squat thrust was far more powerful than Nelsson's grip.

The huge man was propelled upward, toward the railing, which was marginally shorter than Storm's fully extended legs. Nelsson blindly grasped for something, anything to keep him from going over— Storm's feet, the railing, whatever. But without his eyes to guide his hands, he only succeeded in flailing at the air.

He caught briefly on the side, but his momentum kept carrying him over. Storm hopped up, raced over to the railing, and peered over. The last thing he saw of the erstwhile Alpha, Laird Nelsson, was a patch of blond hair going under a huge wave far below.

AFTER A BRIEF SWEEP OF THE DECK, STORM LOCATED the gun the chief of security had dropped.

Storm ejected the clip and gave it a hopeful inspection. It was, alas, empty.

The only thing Storm had to his advantage was

that he was the only one who knew it. He stashed the gun in his waistband and continued on toward Ingrid's quarters.

Storm took his final turn, then went inside, grateful to get out of the elements. His chest was aching and his larynx felt like someone had put it in a vise and turned the screws.

He paused to gather himself for a moment in the sitting room, the one that had Prince George of Denmark—and his bouffant of Jersey-girl hair— keeping silent guard. He thought of Brigitte and her fondness for the painting.

"Not so easy to be married to the queen after all, is it big guy?" Storm asked.

George offered no opinion on the subject, which is what had made him a good husband in the first place.

"Yeah, that's what I thought," Storm said, then went for the double doors that led to Ingrid's inner sanctum. They opened easily.

There was no one there, at least no one Storm could see. He recognized the room. It was Ingrid's office, the one he and millions of others had first seen on a YouTube video, with its antique rug, its mahogany desk, and all the other near-priceless baubles arranged around it.

Through another set of double doors, from the next room, Ingrid spoke a sentence or two of testy Swedish. She started with the name Laird. Then Storm heard his own name and the word *mörda* again.

He could guess at the translation: *Laird, are you back so soon? Have you killed Derrick Storm already?*

"I'm sorry, Laird isn't here right now," Storm

said. "He decided to take a swim. But, actually, it looked like he doesn't do that very well. So I guess I should say Laird decided to take a sink."

There was no reply. Storm crept cautiously farther into the room. He drew the Beretta, even though it was little more than a stage prop.

Tilda had said that Ingrid abhorred guns, but Tilda had proven to be a less-than-reliable narrator. Storm fully expected that Ingrid had a cannon waiting for him in the next room.

Or maybe she didn't. But, in this case, Storm decided there was little danger to being wrong about assuming Ingrid was armed. At most, it would just slow him down a little. The alternative—assuming she was unarmed and being wrong—was far worse.

He reached the double doors and listened for movement. There was none. He allowed himself a quick glimpse around the edge, then withdrew. It was definitely Ingrid Karlsson's bedroom. The dominant feature was a large canopy bed. There were also antique bureaus and wardrobes, ornate mirrors, marble statuary, and a thousand other details that Storm hadn't been able to register in that one brief glance.

The only thing missing was Ingrid. She was obviously hiding, planning to ambush him somewhere—from a closet, from the bathroom, from behind any one of those pieces of furniture.

Storm could afford to be patient, but only to a point. He knew Jones's teams. Middle-of-the-night and predawn raids were their specialty. Two o'clock in the morning. Three o'clock. Those were their preferred hours of operation.

It was already nearing midnight. Within a few hours, the wind would let up enough and they would be here. And then this would be their show—and, more accurately, Jedediah Jones's show. At that point, the negotiations would begin and the only people without a seat at the table would be the families of all the people Ingrid had killed.

Storm looked around to see what he could use to create a distraction and/or provoke a reaction. He spied a vase. It was china, probably late Ming dynasty, probably worth countless thousands of dollars. He picked it up and threw it into the next room. It glanced off one of the slats of the canopy bed and onto the edge of a bureau, where it exploded into several hundred pieces.

There was no response. Storm took a chunk of ivory that had been carved into a Madonna and threw that into the room. It struck a mirror, shattering it.

Still nothing.

Storm was trying to determine his next move when, from somewhere up on deck, he heard a rhythmic sound. It was hard to make out—what with the wind still whistling through, under, around, and over every exposed crevice of the ship—but it sounded almost like a large drum beating. It started slow but quickly gained speed.

Then Storm realized it wasn't a drum. It was helicopter rotors.

Ingrid Karlsson obviously had another way out of her bedroom. And now the former stunt-plane pilot was trying to escape by the only means available to her, hurricane be damned.

In the split second between when Storm made that realization and when he decided what to do about it, the layout of the ship appeared in his brain. The helicopter pad was on the top deck in the aft of the ship, almost the exact opposite locale of where he was right now, in the most forward deck. The *Warrior Princess* was 565 feet long. He'd have to cover at least four hundred of it to reach where Ingrid was now.

Still, it wasn't like he had a choice. If Ingrid got away from him, she had more than enough resources to disappear forever. She would never see the inside of a courtroom.

Storm sprinted out of Ingrid's quarters and down the walkway where he had nearly had the life choked out of him. With the wind now aiding him, he flew past the door to McRae's cell and the guards' rooms. It was still pinned open by the wind. There was no sign of the scientist.

The rotors were getting louder now. The only thing in Storm's favor was that it would take a minute or so for the turbines to begin pumping hard enough to allow for flight.

His legs burned as he willed them to push him beyond their maximum power. He passed Tilda's bedroom—he would have to leave her to Jones's people, who would surely appreciate the gift—and charged up two flights of exterior stairs on the outside of the ship. He did not look down at the waves, which had begun to subside but were still formidable mountains of water. His entire focus was on keeping his footing on the slippery steps. One stumble might cost him the time he needed to catch the chopper.

As he reached the edge of the helicopter pad, Ingrid was pulling back on the flight stick, lifting the aircraft off the ground. With one final burst of speed, Storm dashed across the last forty feet of the pad. The helicopter was now airborne. He could see the look of concentration on Ingrid Karlsson's face as she pulled back on the stick. He knew she saw him coming. He didn't care. At this point, he wasn't exactly trying to sneak up on her.

Storm fixed his eyes on the helicopter skid nearest to him and timed his jump.

DUNKING A BASKETBALL REQUIRES A HUMAN BEING to be able to reach roughly ten feet eight inches in the air: ten feet to reach the rim, plus another eight inches to allow enough of the ball to clear the top.

By the time Storm reached the helicopter, the skid he was aiming for was eleven feet in the air.

Fortunately, Derrick Storm could dunk a basketball with room to spare. He leapt, and the outstretched fingers of his right hand grasped the slick metal bar beneath the helicopter and held tight.

The chopper lurched for a moment as Storm's weight hit it, but it had enough lift to compensate for those extra 230 pounds. As it quickly gained altitude, the wind from the hurricane took it and pushed it back violently away from the boat.

To say Storm was hanging on for dear life was no mere expression. He was now over the frothing Strait of Gibraltar, dangling by one hand. Back when he had a dry suit and a buoyancy compensator—and a grappling hook to lift him out of it when the time came—he could handle the sea's rage. In nothing more than Laird Nelsson's borrowed clothing, he stood no chance of surviving until morning.

As the helicopter pitched and bucked, Storm managed to swing his left hand onto the skid. He started trying to pull himself up, but it was not easy. Whether Karlsson was intentionally flying wildly—like a rodeo steer trying to kick off its rider—or whether the hurricane made her fly that way, the effect was the same.

Under ordinary circumstances, Storm could rip off twenty or thirty pull-ups without much strain. In these conditions, it was a Herculean task just to do one.

But slowly, finally, he got himself up. It helped that Ingrid had finally secured the helicopter and that it was under better control; she now had a better feel for the stick as she ascended into steadier, more predictable winds—as opposed to the gusts that bounced chaotically off the huge waves.

Storm expected she would continue climbing, perhaps even until she was above the hurricane. Altitude was definitely her friend, Storm's enemy. Helicopters had a ceiling above which the air got too thin for the rotors to maintain their lift, but it was a high one. Ingrid just might go for it.

Instead, she did the last thing Storm expected: she flew back over the ship, traveling beyond its bow so she was actually out in front of it. She was flying lower, plunging back into turbulence that could kill them both if she crashed. Storm could not guess what she was up to.

Then she began circling around, and he figured it out: she was flying straight toward the top of the *Warrior Princess*'s superstructure. She was going to bash Storm against some piece of it. Perhaps the tallest part, a large smokestack located three-quarters of the way back.

Storm's arms were wrapped around the skid, but his legs were still hanging down. He redoubled his efforts to pull himself up as the helicopter plunged toward the ship. He wrapped one leg up and over, and then the other.

Hazarding a glimpse above him, Storm saw the chopper's cargo door. Its handle was his goal, perhaps his only salvation, depending on how good Ingrid's aim was.

He managed to get himself in a sitting position, his legs straddling the skid, one hand braced against the belly of the chopper. It got him closer to the door handle, but it was still out of reach.

The chopper was now directly over the bow of the ship and, with the wind pushing it, was closing in on the smokestack at a murderous speed. There was no more time for caution. He had to make a jump for the handle, which meant he had to get his feet on the skid.

At that point, he'd essentially have nothing to hang on to. He could lean a little into the side of the chopper, but was mostly relying on his balance. This was like urban surfing, only it was at a difficulty level even a reckless suburban Washington, D.C., kid had never attempted.

Gripping the skid with both hands, Storm placed his feet behind him somehow, then underneath him, before standing fully. He braced himself against the helicopter's fuselage, for what little help that was. If Ingrid had chosen that moment to roll right, Storm would have plunged to his death on the deck below.

But, with her aim set on the smokestack, she flew straight. She was now mere yards away from it.

At the last possible second, Storm jumped for the handle. He felt its rounded metal and closed both hands around it, using it to hoist himself off the skid just as Ingrid rammed it into the smokestack.

The air was filled by the shrieking of metal hitting metal, then of the skid being ripped away. The helicopter spun crazily, rotating 480 degrees and nearly losing control. Storm was now hanging on by the door handle alone.

And the handle was no longer stationary. The door to the chopper had swung open. Storm's head, outstretched arms, and shoulders were slammed against the side of the helicopter. Storm reacted the only way he could: by gripping tighter as he absorbed the impact, like a wide receiver who is about to be mashed by an onrushing strong safety but somehow hangs on to the ball.

Ingrid was again gaining altitude. The door started swinging closed. Storm shook off the effects of what was likely a minor concussion, and unhooked his right hand from the door handle. He used it to grab whatever he could on the inside of the helicopter before the door slammed shut.

His hand hit what felt like netting of some kind. Storm grasped it. His right arm was now keeping the door open. He stayed like that for a few seconds— half in the helicopter, half outside it—until, to his horror, the door started coming off its hinge. The joint was not designed to hold the weight of a fully grown man, swinging around on it like a jungle orangutan.

As the screws popped out one by one, Storm lunged desperately into the bay of the helicopter. He gripped the leg of a passenger seat against the back wall of the chopper and placed his legs inside as well.

The door was still swinging back and forth, banging around until it sheared off for good. Storm did not bother to watch it fall into the sea below. He was panting hard, grateful for the solid floor of the helicopter.

He did not stay there long. He had just gotten to his hands and knees when Ingrid, having set the chopper on hover and activated the autopilot, emerged from pilot's chair.

She had an ugly sneer on her face. In her left hand was a dagger. It had a blade ten inches long that was curved and cruel and lethal.

CONVENTIONAL FIGHTING WISDOM SAYS IT IS ACTU-ally quite difficult to kill someone with a knife. It requires the ability to overpower one's opponent, and even then it's hard work. Stabbing victims will often have dozens of knife wounds, and what kills them is not any one of them—it's the blood loss.

Then again, conventional fighting wisdom didn't have to face an enraged Swedish woman of Amazonian proportions in a hurricane-tossed helicopter.

Ingrid did not hesitate to begin her attack. She slashed at Storm's head, missing only because Storm rolled out of the way at the last nanosecond.

He hopped to his feet and immediately assumed a crouch, both hands out in front of him. Ingrid was no idiot. Yes, the knife gave her an edge—as it were—but Storm had advantages in size, strength, and speed. She had to stay out of his grasp.

Storm feinted to his right, seeing if Ingrid would go after him in that direction and get herself off balance; but she didn't go for the fake. He lunged for the knife, but she stepped back, then countered by stabbing toward his belly. Storm narrowly dodged it.

She brought the dagger high and chopped downward. Storm tried to step back but ran into the far side of the helicopter. He brought his arms up to shield himself. Ingrid's knife opened a gash in his right forearm. She slashed again. Another wound, this time near his elbow.

Storm planted his left leg and kicked with his right, catching Ingrid in the solar plexus and propelling her backward into the other side of the narrow chopper, the side closest to the door. From that distance, about ten feet, they considered each other for a brief moment.

"Jones and I had a deal," Ingrid said through ragged breath.

"I'm sure you did," Storm said. "It doesn't apply to me."

"You're a fool. Don't you see that by trying to stop me you're standing in the way of history? Nations and the lines they scrawl across the globe are going by the wayside. The governments of the world are impediments to a better way of life for all humanity."

"Why don't you let humanity decide that for itself?"

"Because most people are too stupid to know what's good for them," she snarled. "They need a real leader who can show them the way. I'm that leader."

"You're deranged."

"What? You think your American president is really someone who can make the planet a better place the way I can? You think your vice president or your secretary of state can do it? I was thinking about it when I ordered Air Force One to be shot down, how very un-tragic that crash would be. A plane full of the world's most powerful leaders, and yet there wasn't one person who could really make progress happen the way I can. It's just a shame that turned out to be a fake. You Americans would have eventually seen I was doing you a big favor."

"Don't you see the fallacy of your approach? Revolutions don't happen because one person believes something. That's how you get despots. Revolutions happen because thousands and millions of people come to believe something. You can't force your version of the future on people."

"You just don't get it," she said. "Your vision is clouded."

"No, it's actually working perfectly. And where I see you heading next is jail."

"That will never happen," she said, before following her assertion by charging at Storm, who deftly eluded her.

The result was nothing more than a switching of sides. From behind him, he could feel the rush of air from the opening where the cargo door had once been.

He crouched again, ready for Ingrid's next charge, which came quickly. But this time, Storm held his ground. As she closed in on him, he grabbed the blade of the knife with his left hand, roaring as it sliced his palm. But the pain had a gain: he managed to grab her left wrist with his right hand.

From there, it was just a question of using her momentum against her. Like a seasoned bullfighter, he shuffled his body to the side at the last possible second.

Suddenly, there was nothing separating Ingrid from the outside of the helicopter but moist tropical air. She hurtled into the space behind Storm and began the sickening drop into the sea hundreds of feet below.

All that saved her was that Storm had not relinquished his grip on her wrist. As she fell, he dropped to his belly, spreading his legs out wide to give him some purchase on the floor of the chopper and not get carried out the door himself.

For a few seconds, Ingrid just dangled high above the waves, her legs kicking pointlessly. The skid on that side of the helicopter had been shorn off by the earlier collision with the ship's smokestack. There was nothing for her feet to find. She soon stopped struggling and hung there, with Storm keeping a tight grasp on her.

She still had the knife in her right hand. The way Storm was gripping her, the interior of his right wrist was fully exposed. The ulnar and radial arteries on his wrists—the one suicidal people will try to sever—bulged.

At more or less the same moment, both Storm and Ingrid knew what she was going to do.

"Ingrid, don't do it," Storm yelled.

Ingrid was looking up at him with pure hatred.

"Ingrid, there's no way you'll survive the fall or the swim," he pleaded. "I might or might not die, but there'd be no question what would happen to you. You'd be dead."

She curled her lip, showing him her teeth. There was a lot of noise at that particular moment. The driving rain. The crackling wind. The churning rotors. But Storm could still very easily make out the words that came out of Ingrid Karlsson's mouth:

"It is my nature," she said.

The knife flashed toward Storm's wrist.

"No," he bellowed.

He blocked the knife with the back of his left hand. The knife point plunged in for a moment, then hit some bone. The unexpected resistance caused Ingrid to lose her grip on the weapon. It quickly disappeared into the sea below.

Storm began the slow process of pulling her up.

He was bleeding, and the wounds would require stitches. But none of them was fatal.

The only fatality was Ingrid's twisted ambition. Storm got her up into the chopper. She struggled a little, but ultimately, for all her fitness, she was a fifty-something-year-old with limited strength and energy. Storm subdued her easily.

Straddled atop her, he used his plastic restraints to bind her hands, then her feet. She yelled and cursed as Storm trussed her up, but eventually she quieted. Storm located some rope and tied her to one of the back-passenger chairs, lest she get any ideas about throwing herself out the open bay.

Storm located the chopper's first aid kit and dressed the worst of his wounds until they at least stopped bleeding.

Then he settled into the pilot's seat and began flying them toward The Hague.

The chief clerk at the International Court of Justice would be more than happy to receive Storm's passenger.

CHAPTER 33

BALTIMORE, Maryland

The first Major League Baseball game Derrick Storm ever attended was at the old Memorial Stadium, deep in a crumbling, blue-collar neighborhood of this town, far from the gentrification that was beginning to take place down at the harbor.

If Storm ever started to lose his mind to Alzheimer's disease or any of the other maladies of old age, he knew for sure this would be the last memory to go: him as a seven-year-old, walking up the ramp at Memorial Stadium, seeing the field stretched out before him like an impossibly perfect emerald blanket, gripping his father's hand tightly the whole time.

This particular Orioles game, which Storm attended with his father about two weeks later, was a close second. He didn't hold Carl Storm's hand this time. But he did put his arm around the old man before they walked down to their seats. By that point, Carl had heard all he wanted and more about his son's most recent adventure.

"It's great to be here with you," Derrick said. "Sorry we had to delay it a little bit."

"Come on," Carl Storm said. "We don't want to miss the first pitch."

The last two weeks had been hectic, a nonstop stream of investigators and lawyers and judges, all asking for the story "from the beginning."

Eventually, Storm had left Ingrid Karlsson in the custody of the International Court of Justice, where she, her assistant Tilda, and more than a dozen of the people she had hired to carry out her orders on two continents would face more than a thousand counts of murder in the first degree. Among the coconspirators was Nico Serrano, the director of the Autoridad del Canal de Panama, who was currently being extradited from Panama for his role in the plot.

William McRae had been found, safe and sound, by a team of CIA agents, who were being called a hostage rescue team as a result of Jones's relentless spin operation. Before he was reunited with his loving wife, Alida, McRae happily sold his designs for the laser to the U.S. government. Without the promethium to fuel it, the designs were nothing more than drawings on paper. Still, it funded an ambitious garden expansion for the McRaes, to say nothing of their grandchildren's college educations.

The day McRae was rescued, another arrest was made: the Hercules police moved in on a man with a wine-stained face and slapped him with a variety of charges; among them were breaking and entering, possession of an unlicensed firearm, trespassing, and invasion of privacy—the result of a camera found to be filled with pictures of an elderly woman gardening.

Storm, meanwhile, had received no less than four banana cream cakes from a local bakery during his time in The Hague. All of them also contained thank-you notes from Alida, each note growing in length until Storm finally had time to acknowledge her, thank her, and ask her to stop.

Storm had returned home in time to catch the image of Katie Comely being splashed across the front page of the *Washington Post*—and scores of other newspapers around the country—for what was being hailed as one of the most significant Egyptian finds of the last two decades. Her mummy turned out to be Narmer, the ancient pharaoh who united Upper and Lower Egypt into one kingdom. She was currently deciding between tenure-track positions at Princeton University, Harvard University, and Dartmouth College, though she was thought to be leaning toward Dartmouth.

As they walked down the stairs toward their seats at the game, Storm's phone rang. Recognizing the number as coming from the Pentagon, Storm answered it.

"Yes?" he said.

He listened for a moment, then said, "So it's done, then? Good. Thank you very much for letting me know. I appreciate it."

"Who was that?" Carl Storm asked as his son ended the call.

"That was the former Lieutenant Marlowe. He's now General Marlowe, third in line at the air force. He was just calling to tell me about the terrible error the air force just made. They mistakenly dropped a thirty-thousand-pound bunker-buster bomb not far from Luxor, Egypt. You may or may not know it, but bunker busters like that get incredibly hot when they detonate—many, many thousands of degrees. Good thing they dropped on an empty piece of the Sahara Desert with no significance whatsoever."

"Good thing," Carl said, grinning.

They reached Row B.

"You want the aisle?" Carl asked.

"No, that's okay, you take it," Derrick Storm said. "Seat 2B has been pretty good to me."

If you enjoyed
Wild Storm,
be sure to catch
Raging Heat,
Richard Castle's latest
Nikki Heat thriller.

An excerpt,
Chapter One,
follows.

ONE

Nikki Heat wondered if her mother hadn't been murdered what her life would have been. Would she be hoofing it like this from her police precinct to a crime scene, or would she instead be on Broadway rehearsing a Chekov revival or some cutting-edge relationship exploration with whispers of a Tony? At Columbus Avenue she paused for the walk signal. Life might have intervened in other ways, too. Fate could have just as easily made her that gourmet mom sitting in the Starbucks window to her right, helping her preschooler negotiate a hot chocolate. Or made her a panhandler, like that guy shaking his Dixie cup of coins outside the wine store across the street. She didn't see a Steely Dan backup singer anywhere around her, but she would enthusiastically be open to that possibility, also.

A swirl of urban wind lifted some gutter trash in a mini twister, and Nikki watched a plastic grocery bag, candy wrappers, and a newspaper ad spin south from Eighty-second until the spectacle lost its center and came apart into something more mundane: random garbage. It was only half past ten A.M. Why would somebody beg outside a wine shop that was closed?

She turned back to regard the panhandler, but he turned away from her and shuffled uptown. Heat got the light and crossed. One corner down, the traffic detail chopped the air with gloved hands to keep the gawkers moving past the street barricade. But they would let her through. The NYPD's top homicide detective had a corpse to meet.

The radio call from the first uniforms on-scene had carried a spoiler. "Don't eat or drink anything en route. Seriously." One part defiance, one part caffeine jones, Heat brought along the remnants of the vanilla latte cooling on her desk and polished it off before she reached the cordon. She lobbed the cup into a city can and flashed tin at the patrolman guarding the caution tape.

Inside the barrier, Nikki paused. To anyone else, it looked as if she were stopping to adjust her holster, which she did. But that was cover. The interval was her own moment, a ritual of one deep breath to honor the loss of a life and to connect her own experience with tragedy. Even though Heat had closed her mother's case two years ago, she still meditated on her simple pledge every time she encountered a new body: victims deserved justice; loved ones deserved smart cops. Duly acknowledged, she exhaled and moved forward.

Scanning Eighty-first Street with beginner's eyes, she vacuumed details and opened herself to critical first impressions. Seasoned investigators were most vulnerable to missing clues because it all got workaday, if they let it. So Heat downshifted to rookie mode, playing her walk-up as if this were her first case ever.

Nikki's first ping registered a half block from the planetarium. The paramedics out front were busy. Usually medical first responders were idle by the time she arrived because the victim was dead at the scene. Occasionally, a shooting or a knife rampage left a collateral victim or two requiring treatment or transport. But this morning, the reflection of bright emergency lights bouncing off the wet pavement was broken by middle school field trippers huddled around three ambulances. Even from a distance Nikki noted the signs of emotional trauma—sobs, giddiness, faraway stares. A teenage boy sat on a gurney inside one ambulance, vomiting. Outside it, a pair of girls stood holding each other, wiping tears.

She passed a coach bus with Edmonton plates idling at the curb. About two dozen Canadian seniors clustered near its door, muttering gravely in the drizzle and craning for a view of the action through the trees of Theodore Roosevelt Park. By instinct, Heat looked the opposite way, behind them. Her inspection tracked east from the Excelsior Hotel along the block of grand apartment buildings to The Beresford, whose rooftop towers blurred eerily into the low clouds and resembled a ghost castle lurking in the mist twenty-three floors overhead. Many of the street's windows were filled with rubberneckers, some of who held up smartphones to live-Tweet the carnage from their three-million-dollar condos. She got out her own cell and snapped off some shots so, later, she could pinpoint where to send her squad to interview eyewits.

High above the gray blanket, the lazy rumble of a jet on approach to one of the airports made her think of him. Six more days, he'd be back. God, these months felt like forever. Nikki shook off the distraction and once again told her longing to take a seat.

At the cobblestone driveway to the museum's main entrance she saw it for herself and stopped cold. Riveted, Nikki stood among the evacuees and stared like everyone else. Then muttered a curse.

The mammoth six-story glass box that encases the Hayden Planetarium looked as if a meteor had smashed through the roof. But what had punched a hole in the top of the massive cube had left an explosion of blood at the jagged circle in the ceiling. On the inside wall, tongues of red extended earthward, translucent paths streaking thirty feet or more down the glass curtain. Detective Heat didn't need to role-play beginner's eyes. This went down as a first.

———————

"Watch where you walk, Detective," said the medical examiner. But Heat had already paused on the bottom step leading down to the lower level of the giant atrium. Dr. Lauren Parry knelt on the floor in her moon suit marking evidence under Alpha Centauri. "Got pieces of this body everywhere. Some still falling. Or dripping's more like it."

Nikki tilted her head back. A hundred feet above her, drizzle and unfiltered gray light seeped through the puncture a human cannonball had made. The hole created a ragged bull's-eye in the glazed strip that framed the outer edges of the roof. Beneath the impact splatter, more blood—mixed with chunks of tissue—had not only trickled down the window, but also on one half of the giant orb nested inside the Hall of the Universe. Jupiter took a hit, too. The nearest model planet of the array suspended by wires in the cube now wore vertical streaks of red crossing its latitudinal stripes.

Elsewhere, bits of shredded clothing hung from structural tension rods where they had snagged on descent. As she looked, a gob of viscera dripped off one of the tatters and plummeted three stories, meeting the white marble floor with a splat as loud as a handclap. When it landed Detective Feller called out a long "Whooooaa!" which was followed by a chorus of rowdy guffaws from the three uniforms standing with him over near the gift shop. This time

Heat wouldn't reprimand him for his habitual lack of decorum. If ever a crime scene allowed for gallows humor to dissipate trauma, this was it. And with no family, media, or civilian bystanders around to offend, she let it slide.

Heat stepped carefully into the great hall, avoiding nuggets of glass and following the route suggested by the numbered yellow markers left behind by the ME on her way across the floor. When she reached her friend, Nikki asked, "Doesn't figure as a jumper, does it?"

"First of all, you know better than to ask me that so soon. And second, thank you for not contaminating my crime scene."

"I think I know where to walk, Lauren."

"Then I have trained you well. Unlike your Detective Ochoa, who managed to slip on a piece of tendon his first minute on-scene and land on his ass. When you see Miguel, you can inform him that he is my soon-to-be-ex-boyfriend."

Nikki scanned the neighboring buildings, all visible outside of the glass. "I don't see anyplace close enough to make this drop."

"You're going to press this until I answer, aren't you?" Dr. Parry stood and stretched her back. "Last week I worked a jumper up in the Bronx at the Castle Hill Houses. The rooftops of those projects are about the same height as these, OK? My victim had split open at the neck and abdomen and had gross organ protrusion, but she was, otherwise, an intact corpse.

"So there are not only no buildings close enough to reach this place, there's no structure around here high enough for a fall to do this to a body. Injuries this massive are more consistent with falls from hundred-story-plus skyscrapers."

"What about ID?"

"Our best bet will be DNA. If we get lucky, we may find extremities or teeth. Any more questions before I get back to work?"

"Just one. Are you going to chill out before tonight? Because I don't want to sit through *Perks of Being a Wallflower* with you harrumphing all through it."

"*Perks of Being a Wallflower*? I wanted to see Jeremy Renner as Bourne."

"A: there is only one Jason Bourne, and, B: it's my turn to pick, so deal, lady." Nikki gave her the kind of serious look that neither could take seriously. During Rook's two-month absence on assignment for his magazine, Nikki and Lauren had set a movie night once a week, a pleasant distraction for Heat but a weak substitute for having him near. Dr. Parry signaled her acceptance of *Perks* by telling Detective Heat to get out her notebook.

"Victim is, as yet, unidentifiable with no recovered parts sizeable enough to distinguish. We have tagged one shoe, a New Balance men's trainer that landed up on the First-Level elevator bridge, so we are open to the victim being male but cannot confirm without a DNA match."

"But a safe guess."

The medical examiner shrugged. "Otherwise, it's the floor on hands and knees, or cherry pickers to search the rigging. That's all I got."

"Then you'll be interested in this," said Detective Ochoa, painstakingly tracing Heat's path through the scattered remains and glass shards. Behind him, his partner, Detective Raley, followed, matching footfalls. "Found it over near Group Tickets." The duo, affectionately known as Roach, a mash-up of their last names, both turned to indicate the counter across the hall. "It's a piece of a finger."

"Or maybe a toe," added Raley.

The three detectives stood behind Parry while she crouched, examining the specimen with a magnifier. "Tip of a finger. Dark skinned."

Heat knelt and put a cheek near the floor for a closer look. "Let's assume black male, putting this with the men's shoe. Any chance for a print?"

The medical examiner cautiously rolled the specimen a half-turn with the blunt end of her tweezers. It reminded Nikki of checking the edge of a pancake for doneness. "Promising. We'll sure try."

"Nice one, Roach," said Heat as she stood.

Lauren tweaked her boyfriend. "Might even make up for your booty fall, Detective Clumsy."

While Ochoa made a face at her, his partner said, "Amazing. I mean that we got a whole piece like that."

"Not so unusual." Dr. Parry placed an evidence cone then bagged the fingertip. "When the human body experiences catastrophic blunt-force trauma like this, it separates at the joints first as it explodes."

"Giving the planetarium a brand-new exhibit for the Big Bang Theory," said the familiar voice behind them. By reflex, Heat rolled her eyes and thought, Rook. Always clowning aro—?! Heat spun, and there he stood, ten feet away, grinning that Rook wiseass grin. Nikki tried to collect herself, but all she could do was manage a breathless, "Rook?"

"Listen, if this is a bad time. . . ." He gestured widely to the carnage. "Last thing you need is somebody else just dropping in on you."

She rushed to him, wanting so much to forget who she was and where she was and just throw herself at him and kiss him. Instead, the homicide squad leader clung to her professionalism and said, "You weren't supposed to be back until—"

"—Next week, I know. Surprise."

"Uh, understatement." She took both his hands in hers and squeezed, then, frustrated, snapped off her nitrile gloves and held him again, this time feeling the warmth of his flesh. Soon a familiar rush filled her; the same intense magnetism that drew Heat to Rook three years before when he first came into her life. Nikki often reflected on how their relationship almost didn't happen. A damn journalist assigned to her for a research ride-along? No, thank you, she'd thought.

But soon enough Heat went from trying to get him reassigned because his pigtail-pulling wisecracks annoyed her, to yearning for his companionship so much she let him stay around. In time they not only became a couple, trading nights at each other's apartments, but Jameson Rook evolved into a valued collaborator on her toughest cases, notably solving the homicide of a celebrity gossip columnist, exposing a killer at the highest levels of the NYPD, helping her nail her mother's murderers, and even in saving the city from a bioterror plot. Oh, sure there had been some romantic ups and downs, including a few trial separations, but they didn't last. The pull— the magnetism—the rightness of their togetherness always prevailed. And, of course, there was the sex. Yes, the sex.

Nikki studied him. In two months he had grown thinner, tanner, more fit. And something else was different. "So. A beard?"

"Like it?" He struck a pose.

She stepped back and smiled broadly. "No. Hell, no."

"You'll get used to it."

"No I won't. You look like . . . you look like the Jameson Rook action figure."

He withdrew one hand and felt his chin to assess.

"Who told you I was here?" she asked.

"Sorry, an undisclosed source protected by my rights under the First Amendment. OK, it was Raley." The detective gave her a sheepish wave. When she turned back to Rook, he leaned in close enough for her to inhale his scent and whispered, "I thought I'd kidnap you for an early lunch. Say, someplace with room service?"

What Heat wanted to do was exactly that. Only screw room service; just race across the street to the Excelsior and leave a trail of clothes from the DO NOT DISTURB sign to the bed. But she said, "A terrific idea. If I weren't kinda busy investigating a suspicious death, and all."

"If your job is your priority."

"Says the man who left me eight weeks ago to write a magazine article."

"Two magazine articles. Or, as my editor prefers to call them, in-depth investigations. And seven weeks. I came back early. See?" He spread his arms wide and turned a circle, which made her laugh. Damned Rook, he could always make her laugh. The other thing he always did was understand how dedication translated into deferred gratification. So without complaint, he hoisted his duffel onto the counter at Coat Check, which sat unattended but full of backpacks and raincoats left behind in the hasty evacuation.

Since the morning rain had let up, Heat decided to convene her squad meeting outside and yield the interior to OCME and Forensics, who seemed less than thrilled by all those extra personnel contaminating their scene. She and Detectives Raley, Ochoa, Feller, and Rhymer formed a loose circle on the entrance plaza between the revolving doors and the circular driveway. Rook sat on a stone bench off to the side, making no attempt to stifle his jet lag yawns. Up the grass slope, evacuated tourists milled on the sidewalk behind the wrought iron fence. Predictably the news vans had arrived. Their raised snorkels formed portable forests at both ends of Eighty-first.

"I don't know why we got bounced out here," said Feller. "Didn't we find that finger for them?"

"We?" replied Roach, in near unison. And then Ochoa added, "Here, homes, I've got a finger for you, too."

Feller came back with, "I'm touched, Miguel. You even took it out of your nose," bringing a volley of chuckles that Heat clamped a lid on.

"Gentlemen, may I remind you we are in public at a death scene? Let's not find ourselves laughing it up on the cover of this afternoon's *Ledger*." She surveyed the street, and, sure enough, her eye caught a man snapping shots of them with a long lens. But as Nikki turned back toward her group, it occurred to her that, even though the guy seemed familiar, she didn't see a credential or recognize him as one of the usual press photogs. Where had she seen him before? Glancing again, she caught the back of his jacket getting swallowed by the crowd and shrugged it off. This was New York. The sidewalks were full of puzzler faces.

"Let's all remember," she began, "open minds. This could turn out to be an accidental, not a homicide. Either way, we are going to go about this case a little differently."

"As in, we're not looking for lurkers or suspicious persons fleeing the area," said Detective Feller. Like his colleagues, he had jettisoned the grab ass and gone all business.

"Exactly. Let's focus our efforts instead on establishing what happened. Starting with two priorities: victim ID and mode of death."

Rook raised a hand. "I'm going with *kersplat*." God, how Nikki hated and loved having him back. He read their reactions and, instead of backing off, joined the circle and doubled down. "Indelicate perhaps, but come on. The guy was basically a bug on a windshield. Except this bug actually went through the windshield, so he must have been going, what . . . five hundred miles an hour?"

"No way," said Ochoa.

"For a lawman, you seem quick to doubt the laws of gravity, Detective." He appealed to Nikki, "What height did Dr. Parry say the injuries were consistent with?"

Heat felt wary of having her briefing hijacked but answered, "Over one hundred stories."

"So we're talking an altitude of at least one thousand feet. I'm surprised he didn't achieve Mach 1."

"Doubtful, Rook. An object falls at thirty-two feet per second per second until it reaches terminal velocity." Ochoa turned a few heads with that one. "What? Back in the service, I was Airborne. Trust me, before you go jumping out a cargo door you buddy-up with ol' Ike Newton."

Rook couldn't let it go. "I don't doubt your courage, but aren't we splitting hairs here?"

The detective smiled to himself, then recited, "Mach 1 is the speed of sound, which is seven hundred sixteen miles per hour. Terminal velocity for the average human in free fall is one hundred twenty MPH and takes approximately twelve seconds to reach."

After absorbing his calculus beatdown, Rook paused and said, " 'Approximately.' I see."

"The variable is the drag coefficient. Drag is created by things like clothing, body position . . ."

". . . Facial hair, such as a G.I. Joe beard," said Detective Rhymer.

Heat jumped in. "All right. I know how much you guys like to measure and whatnot, but can we just stipulate our victim fell from a height that suggests an aircraft and leave it there?" They all nodded. Then, when Rook opened his mouth, she said, "Moving on" and he closed it and gave her a smiling salute with his forefinger.

Nikki assigned Rhymer to scrub the Missing Persons database for an ID on the John Doe. "Obviously start with New York City and the tri-state," she said, "but since this poor guy probably came from an aircraft, tap the FBI and Homeland, too. Also, do a run of prison escapees and active NYPD, county, state, and federal manhunts."

She gave Randall Feller the neighborhood to canvass beginning with the tourists being held between the sawhorses on Eighty-first. "What am I looking for, though?" he asked. "I mean, since we're not seeking a lead on a perp."

"This is one of those times that we won't know until we find it," she replied. "It's the lottery. All it takes to learn something is one person who saw the fall."

"Or heard something," added Raley.

Heat nodded. "Sean's right. Plane in distress, a

scream, a gunshot, whatever. And take a platoon of uniforms to knock on doors in those apartments." She gestured to the block of pale stone encasing the Upper West Side's most fortunate and texted him her iPhone shots of the looky-loos in their windows. Next she turned to Detective Raley and said, "Make a guess."

"Show me: video cams."

"Ding-ding-ding." Rales wore the crown as the squad's King of All Surveillance Media. Over the years he had excelled at scrubbing hours of sleep-inducing closed-circuit television footage of everything from neighborhood traffic cams to bank and jewelry store lipsticks, and scored major breaks in their cases. Today Nikki tasked him with finding CCTV mounts at the planetarium and the surrounding businesses and residences.

"There's a plus side," she said. "What you're looking for happens within a very tight time window.

"Detective Ochoa, I'm going to split you off from your partner to work the skies." He flipped open his notebook and took notes as she directed him to contact the FAA and Air Traffic Control for any Maydays, distress calls, or unusual activity in the local airspace. "Get a list of all aircraft—commercial and general aviation—that came anywhere near here around ten this morning; anything that might have veered off course or acted erratically or raised notice from other pilots."

"Like did they see anything up there or hear something on the radio that was freaky, got it."

"And don't forget the helicopters. Not just NYPD but the TV, radio, tourist, and commuter choppers." Heat looked up. The sky was brightening but still oystery. "Not sure how many of them got up in that, but if they did, somebody might have registered something."

Rook raised a hand but didn't wait to be called on. "Stowaways. Every once in a while you hear about dudes hitching a ride in the wheel well of an airliner. The pilot opens the landing gear and . . . well, you get the idea."

"Won't hurt to check, Miguel."

"Oh, and skydivers. Write that down." Rook annoyed Ochoa by tapping his finger on his notepad.

"No helmet or parachute turned up," said Heat.

"Maybe the plane banked and he fell out. Or jumped." Feeling their stares, he added. "Did anyone here see *Point Break*? Keanu Reeves dives out of a plane to chase Patrick Swayze, who left with the last parachute? Anybody?"

Ochoa clicked his pen and winked at Raley. "Skydiver one word or two?"

———

Heat knew it was time to send Rook home when she asked the group if they had any other theories about the victim and he didn't chime in. No speculation about an untoward application of the Monty Python cow catapult. No conjecture about a boozy wing walker stumbling off a biplane. No nothing. In fact, he had returned unnoticed to his spot on the stone bench and sat with a fixed vacant stare into the middle distance.

"Maybe you should get a nap," she told him when the others had dispersed. Logging thirty-six hours from Central Africa to Paris to JFK to that bench had finally taken its toll. He nodded blankly and she watched him amble away with his duffel after giving her an unsteady hug and a vow to catch up with her after some shut-eye. That bastard knew she was looking, too, because, at the top of the driveway, he lifted the vent of his sport coat and shook his ass. "Welcome home," she said to herself.

Back inside, Dr. Parry looked up at Heat over a grim container of human morsels and declared she would be at this for hours and that movie night was definitely off. "Although I had already assumed so now that handsome's back. Go ahead, you fickle bee-otch. Have fun."

"I will. Think I'll take him to see the new Bourne movie." Nikki turned and walked off to hide her grin.

As the detectives began to filter into the bull pen to report at the end of shift, Heat was surprised to see Rook arrive with them. "Not much of a nap," she said when he took a seat on her desktop.

"A nap'll kill ya. You want to know how an experienced traveler blows the gum out of the carburetor? Hit the treadmill, instead. Three miles and a hot shower, I'm good for, oh, another twenty minutes." He scanned the squad room. "What's with the empty desk?"

"We, um, lost one of our detectives this week." Before he could follow up, she cut him off. "A little sensitive, a little public right now, all right?"

"We won't discuss it here, then." He nodded, but continued, "Let me guess. Do I smell the handiwork of one Captain Wally Irons?" She gave him a sharp look and he put up both palms. "I think we best not discuss this here, if it's all right with you."

Detective Ochoa came over, turning pages to the

front of his notebook. "No hits at the FAA or ATC. No commercial air traffic over this part of Manhattan at that time. One outbound from LaGuardia over the Bronx ten minutes before and two JFK approaches: one, five minutes after—that was over the Hudson; the second traversed the West Side at about ten-thirty." Nikki recalled the sound of that plane on her walk-up, then asked about general aviation. "Nada. Same for Maydays, distress calls. And yes, Rook, I did inquire about stowaways. None reported, plus they said it wouldn't be procedure to drop landing gear this far out."

According to Rhymer, Missing Persons didn't kick out any matches. "And still waiting on callbacks from various law enforcement on fugitives and escapees." Mindful of the polite Southern nature that had earned Rhymer the nickname of Opie, Heat directed him to be a pain in the ass with those agencies. She also suggested he widen the window on Missing Persons to include the past week; you never knew.

"Sure thing. And I'll check MP reports throughout the evening, just in case somebody comes home tonight and finds it empty by surprise." When he said it, it sounded buttery, like "bah supprahs." Opie in the big city.

Rook stood. "Hang glider."

Ochoa shook his head. "From where, the Empire State Building?"

"You're right. He'd have to get it up there undetected." But Rook kept going with it. "How about the big skyscraper they're erecting on West Fifty-seventh."

"And what happened to the actual hang glider?" asked Heat. "Rook, you should have taken a nap instead."

Rhymer beamed. "A wing suit could do it."

"*Madre de dios*, it's contagious." Ochoa stared at the ceiling tiles, shaking his head.

Rook clamped an arm around Opie's shoulder. "You know something? The halls of this precinct are going to ring with sweet laughter when one of our brainstorms leads to a break in this case."

Detectives Feller and Raley strode in together, urgency on their faces. "You're going to want to see this," said the King of All Surveillance Media.

———

The six of them could barely fit into the storage closet Raley had converted into his digital domain, which basically consisted of two tables resting on filing cabinets, a scrounged assortment of yesteryear's technology, and a cardboard Burger King crown, presented to him years before by a grateful homicide squad leader. "While I was canvassing the crowd for eyewits, some old dude from Canada is getting real freaked over near the tour bus, so I check him out," said Detective Feller. "He and his wife—by the way, I'm betting she's a recent trade-up, if you catch my meaning—anyway, the two of them were posing for a video the bus driver was shooting of them in front of the planetarium."

"Makes sense," said Rook. "What's a trip to New York without a picture of Uranus?"

Feller couldn't resist joining in, adopting the voice of a tourist. " 'My God, Harry, I can't believe the size of Uranus.' "

"Wanna talk massive?" said Rook. "Feast your eyes on this space junk."

Heat turned to them. "Boys." Then, admonishing Rook, "Definitely a nap next time."

Raley resumed. "The tourist couple volunteered

the video so I could make a digital copy. This part's in slo-mo. Ready?" Rales didn't bother waiting for a reply. Everyone gathered a little closer to the monitor when he rolled the footage.

The screen displayed a barrel-chested senior citizen with silver hair sprayed into a meticulous pompadour embracing a buxom woman of about fifty who wore her jewels proudly and rested her head on the love of her life. Both smiles seemed frozen, but that was due to the video speed, apparent when their eyes blinked in slow motion. "Here comes," said Raley. A few seconds later, a dark form shaped like a bullet descended from the sky at a steep angle and crashed into the roof of the cube. Nobody on the video noticed or reacted, but the video room sure did, resounding with moans, gasps, and a long "Fuuuuck" from Ochoa.

"Can you zoom in?" asked Heat.

"Already done. Now, the more you zoom, the more this stuff pixilates, so it's not real sharp, but there's something interesting. Ready?"

His zoomed version excluded the couple, except for the top of the silver pompadour. Raley had also slowed the video down a step further so, as the body appeared, its movement played somewhat jerkily. A second before impact, he froze the frame.

Rhymer said, "Oh, man, headfirst."

"And check it out." Raley used a pencil to indicate the victim's hands. "Tucked behind his back."

"Who doesn't put his hands out?" asked Rook.

Detective Feller said, "Might be unconscious."

Ochoa shook his head. "If you're unconscious, your arms are all loose." He posed to demonstrate.

They all studied the image. After a few moments, Raley played it out to impact. This time it was met with silence. Which was broken by Rook. "I guess that's what the kids today mean by photo-bomb."

———————

It turned out Nikki Heat's fantasy about a trail of clothes from the door to the bed wasn't so far off—the two main differences being it was Rook's loft, not the Excelsior Hotel, and they never made it as far as the bed. At least not the first time.

Separation had created a hunger and they eagerly flew at each other in a frenzy, the time apart making this reunion feel fresh. Even their familiar ways and places carried a sense of novelty and wild excitement. And abandon. Definitely abandon. Afterward, with her head nestled into his shoulder, Nikki reflected how she had never been with a man who could make her forget everything so completely and lose herself in the instant they were creating. Of course, he could also break the spell.

"Reunion sex," he said. "Nothing like it."

"Hotel sex? Sex on the roof? And what about that time in the back of the squad car?"

"Oh, right. You know I'm very sorry to hear the NYPD is retiring the noble Crown Victoria from its fleet. Fuel economy is one thing. A spacious and, might I say, firm, backseat is another."

"On the topic of firm backseats, how much weight did you lose?"

"Jungle travel is very slimming."

"And what is this here?" Nikki ran her fingertips down from the old indent made by the bullet he took to save her life and traced them over a jagged scar. She slid down his chest to examine it. Even in the dim light she could make out the bas-relief of crude stitchwork, recently healed.

"Later," he said, drawing her face up to his. "Let's enjoy this."

"Oo, man-of-mystery man."

"Yeah?"

Heat rolled on top of him. "Oh, yeah."

They found each other's mouth again. But this time, tenderly. The two held eye contact as she caressed him and took him inside, and then in wordless synchronicity, they spoke with only their most naked, unabashed gazes, each slowly moving, reaching for, and feeling, the depths of one another.

Rook called to order dinner in from Landmarc then stepped into the shower with her. As he soaped her back, he asked, "Now exactly which action figure do I remind you of? G. I. Joe?"

"It was just a wisecrack, let it go."

"Then perhaps one of the others in the ensemble. Storm Shadow? Snake Eyes?"

"Rook, how do you know all these? You're kinda scaring me."

"I ghostwrote a piece on Hasbro for a trade publication once. We all have a past." Then he resumed, "Shipwreck? Snow Job? I know. Firefly. I sort of feel a connection to him. Can't explain it."

Nikki turned and cupped his face in her hands. "This wasn't my favorite sport, you know."

"Don't sell yourself short. I found you downright gymnastic." But he read her, and grew serious. "I know the separation sucks."

"And I don't want to be a whiner, Rook, but two months. . . ." It had started as a mere six-day jaunt to Switzerland to file a quick and dirty glamour piece on the Locarno International Film Festival. But when his editor at *First Press* dangled an investigative

cover story on diamond smugglers in Rwanda funding international terrorists, Rook smelled his third
Pulitzer and hurried his rental Peugeot down the E35
to Milan, dashed through La Rinascente for tropical
clothing, and hopped the next flight via Entebbe to
Kigali.

"Which is why I said no when they asked me to
go to Myanmar next week to cover the human rights
situation."

"I hope you didn't do that because of me. Do
what you have to do. I mean, you know I pride
myself on my independence."

"All too well."

"That's what makes us work. We both cherish
our independence, right?" Then something odd registered on his face, enough for her to study him and
ask, ". . . What?"

But Rook didn't reply. He simply gave her a
knowing smile and drew her close to him. After a
moment, embracing skin-to-skin, under the steam,
Nikki whispered, "Oh. I think a new action figure
just joined us."

"Please," he said in mock indignation. "Must we
cheapen this?"

———

The next morning, Heat brewed herself a scoop of Rook's
stale coffee; and while the water sieved through the
Melitta cone, she watched *Good Morning America*
announce that a tropical depression off the coast of
Nicaragua had now graduated to a tropical storm
with a name: Sandy. Her cell phone rang and Nikki
raced up the hall to the bedroom, hoping to hell it
wouldn't wake him. But Rook slumbered in deep

oblivion as she grabbed it and finger swiped the screen. Heat spoke in a hushed voice as she closed the door behind her. "Hey, Doctor."

"You sound out of breath," said Lauren Parry. "Please tell me I interrupted something wicked."

"He bound me to the bedposts with old type-writer ribbons. I'm lucky I could reach the phone. You still at the planetarium?"

"Oh, hell, no. But I did pull an all-nighter here at OCME with my recovery." It always fascinated Heat how professionals found a vocabulary to cope with the macabre. "I've sent good DNA samples off to Twenty-sixth Street, but that's not why I'm calling. I also came across a significant piece of remains. I'm certain it's a section of upper arm near the left shoulder. Nikki, it has a tattoo. Open your e-mail, I sent you a JPEG."

Nikki thanked her and hung up. Wincing at the outdated French roast, she watched her laptop screen fill with the ME's attachment. Lauren's photo reflected her friend's experience and attention to detail: sharply focused on the pores, lit for clarity, and no flash bounce. The dark brown skin, torn at the edges, had been inked with a slogan in an ornate font: "*L'Union Fait La Force.*"

"Unity Makes Strength," thought Heat. Then, always eager to use her French, she said the words aloud: "*L'Union Fait La Force.*"

"That's on the Haitian coat of arms." Startled, she turned to find Rook standing behind her. "My French is nowhere as good as yours, but I spent some time there after the quake to cover Sean Penn's mission."

"It walks," she said, and stood to kiss him good morning. In his jet lag haze the night before, he'd gamely attempted to unpack from his trip, but mainly just wandered stupidly, making a ludicrous job of it. "Do you even remember me catching you putting your dirty underwear in the bureau drawer instead of the hamper? You fought me all the way to bed."

"Then I must have been out of it."

Nikki offered him her coffee. Surprisingly, he drank it without reaction, while she explained the origin of the tattoo.

When she'd finished, Rook said, "You know what this means, don't you?"

"Of course. There's a possibility I can ID him through the department's tattoo database."

"OK, that. And . . ." He set the mug down and became animated. "Come on, Nikki. This guy might be an alien. Do you know how easy it will be for me to pitch this to the magazine? An alien falling from the sky and crashing into the planetarium? Best. Death. Ever."

———

The NYPD's Real Time Crime Center maintained a computerized catalog of tattoos that proved incredibly useful identifying both suspects and victims. Initially, gang and prison tatts got the focus but, as body art gained mainstream popularity, all sorts of ink from all sorts of people got photographed by detectives and logged into the hard drives on a high floor in police headquarters. If this John Doe from the sky had any recent arrest, however minor, the likelihood that his tattoo would spit out a name and last-known address was very high. So while Rook headed off to get dressed, Heat e-mailed copies of the image to RTCC as well as to Detective Rhymer so he could share it with FBI, Homeland, and Immigration and Customs.

When Nikki went to dump her soggy Melitta grounds, she got a laugh at more hamper confusion. Resting on top of the kitchen garbage was a pair of socks and Rook's prized Comic-Con baseball cap, obvious casualties of his loopy foray into unpacking. As she rescued them, her eye caught something: a shopping bag lying underneath. It was small and of high-quality paper with braided cord handles from a jewelry store in Paris. Nikki hesitated, then, deciding it was none of her business, took her foot off the pedal. The lid dropped and she started for the bedroom with the cap and socks.

Seconds later, her toe hit the pedal again. She wondered—or maybe rationalized—what if something was in it and he had accidentally thrown away, say, cuff links? Or an expensive pen? She set the souvenir hat and socks on the counter and removed the bag, which had been folded flat. She ran her fingers on its glossy surface and felt nothing. After a hitch of minor hesitation, she opened it and peered inside, where she found a receipt for many thousands of euros.

"Nik, you haven't seen my Comic-Con hat anywhere, have you?" he called on his way from the bedroom. She stuffed the receipt in the bag and dropped it back in the trash. But not before she saw what the purchase was.

Bague de fiançailles. She didn't dare give voice to the words this time. But feeling the sudden flush on her face, she listened to her private translation reverbing in her mind: "Engagement ring."

————

On the elevator ride down, Rook surveyed Nikki and asked if she felt all right. She nodded, presenting the most unfazed smile she could muster, which seemed good enough for him. But, of course, she knew why he'd asked. The few minutes it took for them to get out of his loft had played out for her as a sluggish walk through a Coney Island hall of mirrors, only underwater. Her mind swirled with a cyclone of emotions. Guilt at having snooped. Exhilaration at the receipt's meaning. Fear, too. Yes, fear. And more guilt about feeling that feeling. And—fueling the icy center of the vortex—a breath-robbing, knee-jellying numbness. Because she couldn't figure out how to feel.

The sunlight cut sharp to her eyes when they stepped out of his building onto the sidewalk and he took a long inhale of Tribeca, declaring, "God, I've missed this city."

"Subway, not taxi," was all Nikki could think to say, choosing a crowded express train over the intimacy of a cab's rear seat and the conversation opportunity a venue like that threatened to open up.

As they approached Reade Street, Heat lurched into another emotional mode when she made the guy. The long-lens puzzle man from the Hayden stood outside the little park in Bogardus Plaza. Only this time he wasn't holding a camera. He'd gone back to panhandling. "Keep walking," she told Rook. And when he gave her a curious frown, she repeated it, evenly but firmly. He did as he was told for once, and when he reached the corner and looked back, Nikki had vanished.